# THE CAVEMEN
# CHRONICLE

# MIHKEL MUTT

# THE CAVEMEN CHRONICLE

## A NOVEL

### TRANSLATED BY ADAM CULLEN

DALKEY ARCHIVE PRESS

Originally published in Estonian as *Kooparahvas laheb ajalukku* by Fabian in 2012.
©2012 by Mihkel Mutt
Translation copyright ©2015 Adam Cullen
First edition, 2015

LIBRARY OF CONGRESS CATALOGING-IN-PUBLICATION DATA

Mutt, Mihkel.
  [Kooparahvas laheb ajalukku. English]
  The cavemen chronicle : a novel / by Mihkel Mutt ; translated by Adam Cullen.
    pages cm
  "Originally published in Estonian as Kooparahvas laheb ajalukku by Fabian [Tallinn] in 2012" -- Verso title page.
  Summary: "This novel paints a fascinating portrait of bohemian culture in Estonia in the last quarter of the twentieth century. The "cavemen" in question are the regulars at the underground (both literally and figuratively) bar called "The Cave," including artists, musicians, writers, and philosophers, who escape the dreary Soviet reality "above ground" with vodka and high-minded discussion in their secret hideaway. The arrival of national independence upsets the balance of these dissidents' lifestyle, and the narrator recounts how each individual adapts to their newfound freedom. An illuminating and thrilling look into life on the fringes of Soviet culture, both pre- and post-perestroika, as well as a meditation on what it means to be Estonian" -- Provided by publisher.
  ISBN 978-1-56478-708-8 (pbk. : alk. paper)
  1. Dissenters--Fiction. 2. Bohemianism--Fiction. 3. Estonia--History--20th century--Fiction. 4. Estonia--Fiction. 5. Psychological fiction. I. Cullen, Adam (Translator), translator. II. Title.

PH666.23.U8K6613 2015
894'.54533--dc23
                      2015026797

Partially funded by the Illinois Arts Council, a state agency. Supported by the Estonian Ministry of Culture and the Cultural Endowment of Estonia

Dalkey Archive Press publications are, in part, made possible through the support of the University of Houston-Victoria and its program in creative writing, publishing, and translation. www.uhv.edu/asa/

Dalkey Archive Press
Victoria, TX / Dublin / London
www.dalkeyarchive.com

Cover: Typography and layout by Arnold Kotra
Composition by Jeffrey Higgins

Composition: Mikhail Iliatov

Printed on permanent/durable acid-free paper

# THE CAVEMEN CHRONICLE

# THE CAVEMEN
# CHRONICLE

*Brave parishes crumbled*
*Towns flickered*
*An ancient generation buried*
—Fr. R. Kreutzwald

## NARRATOR'S FOREWORD

My identity is not all that important ... at least it will not be at first. Juhan is my name, last name Raudtuvi. That's how my translations and other writings are authored as well (sometimes simply as J.R.). My acquaintances mostly call me Juku. I was born in a town in Southern Estonia. My father was a member of the technical intelligentsia, my mother held a trade-school diploma. My parents moved to Tartu when I finished fourth grade. At university, I was in the economics department and studied accounting. After university, I was funneled into a state institution, where I held a job that was a step up from monotonous paper pushing but not yet a directorial role. I was a normal person.

From the age of twenty, I had been independently studying (out of love, but also as a kind of intellectual refuge) one of the foreign languages that few here speak, and gradually gained a rather good level of fluency. Apart from spiritual gratification, literary translation (from other languages in addition to that rare one) has granted me additional income as well as, of course, admission into intellectual social circles, providing me with the opportunity to communicate with individuals much more developed than I. Without it, I wouldn't have had even the slightest chance to write this work. I have further realized my artistic impulses in amateur theater: first at the Estonian Children's Theatre, then at a student theater (which, in fact, was where I first met Hasso Miller), and later with an independent troupe. I did not even dream of auditioning for the local acting school, however—I knew my limits.

I will, in good time, speak of my acquaintance with my Learned Friend, which began during my final years at university and greatly expanded my intellectual horizon. Just as I will explain the circumstances that led to me becoming a gossip journalist.

Now about what is most important—why am I writing? And why in this form precisely?

I admit that at first, I wanted to write a full-length novel like those of the great masters. The kind where rounded characters and pliable figures unfold before the mise en scène of dramatic events, painted with a vigorous and sensitive brush upon a historically accurate background. Everyone in those novels speaks in their own individual voice, running parallel to the author's witty and wise discourses (or those of the author's mouthpiece). The result? I managed to finish one whole section, sometimes even writing several pages at a time (such as the first chapter about the boys' childhood). There were "granules" in the text—for example, I created an excellent description of one woman's figure, a couple of characters performed highly polished political speeches (I generally do well at those), and I pulled off a few other things. All in all, however, I soon hit a snag. My work covers a long period of time—almost half a century. In order to write about it like the great masters do, I would need to pen dozens of volumes. Who would bother to read such a massive work nowadays? Time changes quickly and it's more than possible that no one would understand me anymore in the future; they would say the writer has dealt with pseudo-problems, got bogged down in his era, was lost in nostalgia.

So, I had to choose between not writing at all and writing in a less comprehensive, less perfect way. I could not go without writing it—my conscience wouldn't allow it. I have waited twenty years (for as long as we've had this new freedom and independence) for one writer or another to handle these things, but it appears no one really plans to do so. Some are dead or infirm from old age, others feeble from youth. The latter have no personal memories of the past, and to try to think themselves back into that time—they probably can't be troubled to make the effort. By all assumptions, they will be interested in completely different things when they are older and more mature.

What came out now is not a molded sculpture or a treatise, but rather some kind of in-between variation. Some episodes are presented literarily; for example, a variety of conversations and dialogues (this skill of mine comes from my time in amateur theater, when I occasionally had to adjust dialogues to make them easier to recite). A large portion of the text speaks for itself, however. And there are a number of things that are not discussed at all, as I presume that the reader is already familiar with the political background (for example). There are too many characters (I am aware of this) and the text is over the top, but what could I do? There were so many figures whose fates I wished to introduce at least cursorily.

Personally, I called my work a chronicle. But then I grasped that this could be misleading, for a reader would approach my text with the same kinds of expectations he or she would have for the Anglo-Saxon Chronicle, Henry of Latvia, Russow, and the other true chroniclers. Wouldn't it be more correct to call it a "gossip chronicle"? I hesitated over whether it might perhaps make my endeavor shallower. It could also prove misleading for a reader, because I do not, of course, write gossip in the ordinary definition of the word; or at least not only in that sense. Eventually, however, I decided that this would be correct. I suppose every chronicle is a gossip chronicle in the eyes of God.

## PROLOGUE

"Is this *really* that famous writer of yours?"

So asked a well-postured, well-fed, middle-aged gentleman with a polished appearance. The question itself was rhetorical, because all signs pointed to the gentleman having recognized the individual in question, and so his reverence was rather feigned, and one could perceive a condescending, inward-turned smirk behind it. The flaps of the gentleman's short dark-green cashmere coat were unbuttoned, allowing his Armani jacket with diamond cuff links glinting on its sleeves to show. His index finger was adorned with a thick, rectangular, and very masculine signet ring set with an emerald. His hair was fashionably ruffled across his tanned forehead, making him look younger than his actual years, and Paco Rabanne afternoon fragrance wafted from his direction with the draft that came from the perpetually swinging café door. The gentleman had dropped his authentic Vuitton briefcase haphazardly onto one of the chairs behind him and appeared not to worry about it, being certain that the café staff would keep an eye on it. This was certainly not part of the staff's duties, but Karl Maiden was a supercustomer—the only one in the crowd here who paid with an American Express Gold Card. Karl was a lawyer who had worked in the state prosecutor's office during the Soviet period, but had become a private attorney upon the new era's arrival. He was popular and in high demand because, among the wealthy, he was regarded as being special ("bohemian, but brilliant!" the ladies sighed longingly; "a sharp guy," the men concurred). In the café, however—or rather in what was left of the once-famous Cave café— he was an ambassador of higher society, of the world of the rich and the beautiful. The fee for one of Karl's court cases exceeded the annual income of a regular guest here. Karl liked going to The Cave, because here was an audience that "understood" him but, at the same time, only looked up to him from below in admiration. Some did so hoping for sponsorship (which Karl sometimes granted), or at least for him to treat them to drinks (which almost always happened); others did so for no reason, out of habit, or "for a change." The line where a creative person's eternally condescending attitude towards individuals involved in finance and economics crosses over into unrestrained brown-nosing is not easy to detect, even for the involved parties themselves.

The individual whom Karl's question concerned was Mati Tõusumägi, who was sprawled over a round café table, the top of his spine hunched, his elbows spread wide, his head in his hands. Mati wore a rustling brownish-grey jacket, dangling from the neck of which was a mottled grey-and-yellow scarf, its fringes nearly brushing the floor. Given the time of year (it was late April), the café floor was relatively filthy from the mud tread into the otherwise respectable pub, even though a waitress dried and mopped it on the hour, as if fighting for the establishment's good name and former glory. Mati's worn and tattered portfolio was on the ground next to his chair, his beige flat cap lay on the table with its brim in a small puddle of beer that had sloshed out of someone's mug. Next to the cap was his own half-drunk screwdriver, which threatened to tip over at the first sudden movement. I nudged the glass to a safe distance and coughed. No reaction. I put my hand on Mati's shoulder—same story. I started feeling sorry for him. If you only recalled who he had once been! And now—in such a state . . . At the same time, I felt disdain along with pity, because how can a person let himself go like that? To tell the truth, I was *angry*. Why had Mati allowed himself to degenerate, why had he made himself easy prey for ridiculers and those with arrogant attitudes towards intellectuals, or—just as bad—for types like that very same Karl, who regarded creative individuals as "infantile"? I knew what Mati's reply would be: it no longer interests him. And that they can all screw off!

Fine, he can go right ahead and think that if he wants, but he could consider the *rest* of us, the ordinary mortals, who are not finished with life yet—*we* are concerned about his condition and fate; *we* have to live on with the fact of his degeneration, justify his actions, and protect him. And the humiliations that he is subjected to inevitably transfer over to us, who feel discomfort and suffer for him. But I was even more enraged by Karl at that moment. Oh, I knew the likes of him extremely well. How couldn't I? I had to associate with them day in, day out due to my profession—*they* are the ones who make up a gossip journalist's livelihood to a great extent. The Guccis and Gabbanas, the Bosses and Rolexes—everything about him stunk of money, behind everything that he said was a sense of self-confidence and self-evidence that is given to those people by money. I regretted not having the strength of Vargamäe Andres[1], because I would have liked to knock Karl and his nasty smirk right onto the muddy floor. How dare he? Who is he *himself*? Here before him was, in fact, a giant of Estonian culture, our former star and flag—so what if he was not exactly in his best state. But I didn't possess that strength; furthermore, I had to consider my position and employment. It's the job of a gossip journalist to report on scandals, not to arrange them. I will definitely still have need for Karl in the future, because titillating adventures always happen in his life; on top of that, it was hard to defend Mati.

Mati suddenly seemed to spring back to life and began mumbling into his arm. But it was hopeless. Not even the most well-intentioned person could have intuited some parable or interpreted any brilliant slivers of observation from the garble, and so my sense of humiliation and aggravation grew.

Then Mati lifted his head. His face was swollen, there was a whitish mark on his flushed cheek left there by his knuckles, and his eyes were puffy, hooded, and gummy. The face was primitive, arrogant, and idiotic.

"What's that'n staring at?" Mati asked in a husky voice, but did not specify which of us he had meant.

"Is this *really* that famous writer of yours?" Karl repeated his question, shook his head with insincere sympathy, and signaled to the waitress: "One bottle of Gorbachev vodka!" Smiling sweetly, the barwoman reached towards the refrigerator.

Mati had revived, however. "Heh heh, writer, heh heh, look, everyone—I'm a writer!" he cackled, imitating a chicken and flapping his pretend wings. "I don't just want vodka for nothiiing, I tell jokes too-ooo!"

"Don't yell—if you have to sit there, at least be quiet," the other barwoman warned him severely.

"What, Elli, you don't know me or what?" Mati asked.

"So what if I do or I don't," the one called Elli replied evasively, and acted as if she was furiously preoccupied with rearranging the sweet buns and puff pastries in the glass display case.

My stomach turned. Why had it all turned out like this? How was it even *possible*? And all that had passed arose before my eyes.

# I

# THE OLD AGE

## THE KREMLIN STAR

New Year's was over for this time around, winter break had ended, and the new academic quarter had begun. Even more snow had fallen sometime around the Epiphany, so the steep mounds piled up by plows and snow shovels tended to obscure the field of view and the large highway on the left-hand side was not visible at all. The tips of fence posts lining the right-hand side of the footpath protruded blackly from the snow, so on his way to school, little Teedu felt as if he were moving along a white trough or the bottom of a ditch. Teedu Tärn stepped jauntily and hummed to himself: *In the morning, when the land is sparkling in the golden dawn, a little rooster wakes me with its crow.* It was a Latvian folk song that they had learned long ago, when he was still in the second grade; but even now, in the fifth grade, Teedu would hum it on occasion. He would have liked to really belt it out, but he couldn't carry a tune. This had become apparent just a few years earlier. During first, and even second grade, he seemed to be able to sing. Their class director led the singing lesson along with all his other duties. Teedu had a lovely, clear voice, and sang very loudly, with passion. The melodies meant for smaller children had also been very simple. It was only in fourth grade, when the melodies became more complex and a conservatory-educated teacher began handling the students' musical upbringing, that it became clear he actually didn't have an ear for it. This was a great shock for Teedu. From then on, he started singing quietly to himself when no one else was around. *Rooster, wake me early, sing ye very loud!*

Drawing nearer to the crossroads, he could see in the distance some dark shape popping up between the snow banks from time to time and then falling with a thud; he also heard someone's voice. Shortly after, the approaching figure emerged from between the heaps of snow. It was Mati, a boy in a parallel class, who was singing loudly while tossing his backpack into the air and catching it: *Heigh-ho, heigh-ho, it's off to work we go. Heigh-ho, heigh-ho!* It was the song from *Snow White and the*

*Seven Dwarfs*, which the children had gone to see at Screen, the local cinema, during the school break. Every once in a while, Mati would interrupt the song by roaring: "I'm a jungle ape! A dreadful, hairy jungle ape!" And he would produce a throaty sound that was supposed to be Tarzan's cry. Mati Tõusumägi was not Teedu's friend, nor was he an enemy. He did not gang up on Teedu as the others sometimes did. Mati lived in the same neighborhood as him, on the other side of the large highway. Once while going to the cemetery with his parents to visit his grandfather's grave, Teedu had seen Mati and his own father stacking firewood in the yard of a single-family house. The boy's father was a mountain of a man wearing tight sweatpants. Mati's mother had been raking leaves by a flowerbed nearby, wearing a light-colored smock or a duster. She was very slender, almost like a young girl. The boys' mothers exchanged hellos, as they remembered each other from a parent meeting at the school. There was a light-blond girl next to Mati's mother — his twin sister, Anu. Teedu had just enrolled in the school that fall, and did not have any friends yet. Earlier, his family had lived in a three-story wooden house on the other side of town. Now, his father's work had given him a two-room apartment in a large apartment block. They possessed an unprecedented luxury in that apartment: a bathroom and hot water. Mati was a new student at the school as well, but he already had friends in droves. His family had come to Tartu from a hamlet in the heart of the country (in northern Viljandi County) and had moved in with relatives, who had a sauna building adjoining the shed in their yard.

Teedu decided to make it look as if he hadn't actually been waiting, but rather that the laces on his felt boots had come untied and that he had been clumsily retying them; when the other boy got closer, it would just make sense to continue on together. The boys greeted each other. They were both the same height, and not short at that. Mati was lighter-skinned with a few freckles on his broad, bold face. Teedu was darker with a less prominent jaw, his expression sadder and more submissive. Anyone would have said that he was a good, well-behaved boy straight away; Mati, however, looked more like a rascal.

"How did your family celebrate Christmas?" Mati asked.

"Christmas?" Teedu asked, perplexed. He had heard his parents mention that word, but didn't pay it much attention. It was something that seemed to have existed a long time ago. "We didn't," he replied. "How's it celebrated, then?"

"Oh, *really?*" Mati's eyes widened. "What're you trying to say—that you guys didn't *celebrate* Christmas?"

"No," Teedu answered hesitantly.

"So Santa Claus didn't *come* to your house?" Mati exclaimed, starting to giggle out of disbelief. "You didn't *get* any presents!"

"He didn't come," Teedu admitted, and added hastily: "But Näärivana did. *He* brought us presents. For Näärid."

"Who's Näärivana?" Mati asked.

"You know—he's the guy with the red coat and white beard," Teedu started to tell him.

"That's the *exact* same thing," Mati cried out in amazement. "How do you celebrate Näärid, then?" he asked after a short pause.

"We brought a pine tree inside. Mom and I decorated it. Glass balls and pinecones, candles and garlands and . . . There was a star at the very top, made out of tin foil. From a chocolate bar. Dad said it was the Kremlin star."

"We hung chocolates on the Christmas tree, too. 'Karakum' and 'Jääkaru' candies," Mati said. "But what did you eat?"

"Sauerkraut and pork and potatoes. My mom made *rosolye*. And there was jellied meat and blood sausage too."

"Exactly the same," Mati said, amazed. "But did you hang thick curtains in front of the window?"

"No."

"We did."

"Why's that?"

"So that they couldn't see."

"Who?"

"Snitches."

They walked some distance in silence. Every once in a while a car would pass by on the other side of the snowbank, hidden from the boys, its tires crunching on the ice.

"But did your family sing, too?" Mati asked.

"N-no. We did listen to the radio. The 'Folk Songs and Traditional Music' program and a comedy shadow too. Liivaku Leena and . . ."

"What—are you trying to tell me you *didn't* sing 'Silent night, holy night,' and 'Come, all ye shepherds, ye children of earth,' and 'A little child is born tonight'?" Mati exclaimed, his curiosity piqued again.

"No, we didn't," Teedu had to admit.

"Well—I guess we sang less this year too," Mati remarked, as if wanting to sympathize with the other boy. "We sang more over where we used to live. Grandma is the main singer now, but she sings quietly, more like singing to herself. After Dad had drunk a lot of vodka he did start belting it out real loud, but Mom told him to shush, it'll sound out onto the street, someone might walk past and hear it, and then he'll be fired from the combine before he knows it."

"Why aren't you allowed to sing, then?" Teedu asked, puzzled.

"You just aren't," Mati asserted. "'Cause of snitches."

"What's a snitch?" Teedu wanted to know.

"Someone who reports you to the *militsiya*," Mati answered knowingly and adjusted his hat importantly.

"Were there no informers where you lived before, so you were allowed to sing there?" Teedu probed.

"No, there were lots of them, but they didn't all understand Estonian there."

"Where was that?"

"In Siberia, of course."

"You were in Siberia?" Teedu asked, flabbergasted.

"Yep. Came back three years ago."

"You sure have traveled a lot," Teedu said enviously.

"Sure have," Mati agreed.

"I've only been to Tallinn. Why'd you come back from Siberia?"

"I went to a Russian school there. We would've come back earlier, but we weren't allowed to."

They walked in silence.

"That's a nice hat you've got," Teedu commented.

"It's made of Siberian furs," Mati said proudly. "We brought it back with us."

The trampled snow grated under their felt boots.

"So when is Näärid?" Mati asked curiously.

"On New Year's Eve, December 31."

Mati counted to himself. "No, Christmas was earlier than that," he stated confidently. "A week earlier." They arrived at school then, and parted ways in the coatroom.

Teedu couldn't shake the thought of Christmas for the whole day. He started to recall that his father and grandmother had seemed to wear slightly different expressions not long before New Year's Eve, and had been tender in a peculiar way, smiling and maybe even sighing more than usual. Teedu hadn't paid it any attention, because who knew what was on those grown-ups' minds; but now he had heard from his schoolmate that some people celebrated Christmas at that time. Had it happened exactly a week before Näärid? Teedu raised the topic at the dinner table:

"Why don't we celebrate Christmas?"

His parents sat in astonished silence. Only his grandmother, who was poor of hearing, smiled to herself as she always did, and said: "Yes, yes, why don't we? He's right, you know."

Teedu's father rose and closed the kitchen door.

"Why are you asking that?"

Teedu realized that his father was very nervous but trying to hide it. "Just because," he replied.

"No, no—tell me," his father ordered. "Where'd you get that? Did someone instruct you to ask? Don't hide anything from us, or else . . ."

Teedu told them about his conversation with Mati. His father looked relieved. He said:

"You're too young to talk about Christmas right now. When you grow up, then you yourself will understand why it's like that. But stay away from that boy, that Mati," he commanded. "You're not allowed to have anything to do with him. Don't tell him that we forbid you to, just don't hang around him." Teedu nodded.

The subject of Christmas came up at Mati's home the same

evening as well. He told his father what he had heard from Tee-du, and wanted an explanation for why some people celebrated Näärid and others Christmas. His father sat at the kitchen table, a glass of spirits in front of him, his face red and worried.

"What was that—the Kremlin star? That's what he said?" Mati's father asked in disbelief.

"That's what he said, yeah," Mati confirmed. "He said there's the Kremlin star on top of the tree, that it's made out of tin foil. They got it from a chocolate bar."

"That's . . . devil knows what . . . How can a young man talk like that? What kind of parents does he have? Don't they want to raise him to be an Estonian? What'll become of all this, huh? You tell me, Mom—huh?"

Mati's mother was frying potatoes on the stove, her hair braided up under a kerchief. She dismissed the question with a wave, humming an old Estonian tune to herself: *It fell so quiet all around . . . And suddenly all that seemed so nice scattered and cracked like ice . . .* His father poured another glass and emptied it. "Damn it, I'm telling you—Estonia is right up shit creek if kids that little have already been turned commie. Mati, my boy, don't you talk to that one anymore. Damn it, he'll go sell you to the Russians, just like that . . . To hell with it, I'm going to the woods, I'm going back into the forest." Mati's mother took the bottle away and hid it in the cupboard: "That's quite enough for now. If you go into the woods or drink yourself to death, then what'll become of us? You could think about that *too*, you know, whether you're an Estonian or a commie." Mati's mother worked as a storekeeper's assistant at the local plastics plant.

Mati's father sighed. "Mati-boy, if you start celebrating Näärid at any point in your life, then know this—you won't be my son any longer." Then he started singing in a rumbling bass: *Oh Christmas tree, oh Christmas tree . . .*

Teedu Tärn could remember another episode involving Mati from that time.

It's late morning on a Saturday in autumn, and the boys are pushing and shoving one another at the bus stop after class, waiting for the boxy green Ikarus bus that will bring some of them into the city center. While scuffling with the other boys,

Mati trips and falls into a puddle that stretches from the un-paved road onto the sidewalk like a great mud lake. His entire side is soaked. He looks angry and is going from one group of boys to the next, pointing to his dripping side and complain-ing: "How'm I going to get out to the country now? How'm I gonna ride on the bus wearing these filthy pants now?" As if it were an enormous injustice and the whole world was to blame for his misfortune. He's intense, that boy. Someone says some-thing to him, and the gang of boys bursts out laughing. But Mati himself laughs the loudest of them all. No, he's not angry, of course — the main thing is for him to have a laugh. But he does indeed go to the country on weekends. Mati's aunt on his mother's side was one of the few in their family that was spared deportation. She lives in the vicinity of Konguta. Mati and his family go there to give her a hand. They get winter potatoes and other foodstuffs from her patch of land.

So as not to appear to be trying to show myself in a better light, I will go ahead and tell of how things were with Christ-mas and Näärid in our family. To tell the truth, things were both ways — that is, we celebrated both one and the other. We did not go to church on Christmas and there was no Christmas tree at home. All the same, however, the children were given candy and told that today was Christmas, and that Christians celebrate it. A candle burned on the table and we sat quietly in one another's company. An evergreen was brought indoors on New Year's Eve, but there certainly wasn't a Kremlin star at its tip. How things were in my other classmates' families — that, I honestly do not know.

## MATI'S YOUTH

During his school years, Mati was a strapping young man and an athlete. He would roar through the streets on his father's side-car motorcycle, prowl the parties in town (where boys would fight, naturally — sometimes with Russians, sometimes among themselves), and despite all his sports practices (he did the pen-tathlon) he wouldn't turn down some dry wine before a school party and even lit up the odd cigarette. His jokes were brisk and buoyant, and he had an infectious sense of humor that came from the heart. He always sang along in groups—he had a nice strong baritone, memorized lyrics almost spontaneously, and when he looked directly at someone while he sang, the latter would involuntarily start to sing along, or at least tap his or her hand or foot. Mati loved to sing in general and would occasionally sing when completely alone—while waiting for someone or something, while working in the yard at home, or just lying on the grass and staring up at the clouds. He knew a great many songs: the ones that everyone knew (meaning folk tunes and those featured on the *American Bandstand*-esque *Horoskoop* show) as well as the ones he had heard from his father's friends, which they would sing when they came to Arnold Tõusumägi's sauna at their aunt's house in the country and "struck up a tune" over beers afterward. (Mati's mother was occasionally worried by these singing sessions, because the men sang so loudly.) It was no wonder that he was a hit with the girls.

In middle school, students had two tracks to choose between: intensive biology/geography studies or automobile maintenance. Mati chose the latter. When the "auto geezer" started explaining engines to them and asked whether anyone knew what a crankshaft was, Mati raised his hand. The "auto geezer" had asked this as a joke, being sure that such whippersnappers would hardly know anything at all about engines. However, while summering in the country, Mati had learned a thing or two about engines from his aunt's husband, who was a mechanic at the *sovkhoz* workshop, and was now able to explain the construction and mechanics of a crankshaft so thoroughly that the astonished instructor said: "You really don't need to come to my lessons at all, but what's to do about it: rules are rules." Why didn't Mati choose the natural studies track, where he would have at least been able to learn something new? I don't know; maybe the reason lay in his schoolboy mentality—better to pass more easily. In any case, he developed a great interest in biology later in life, and for some time even wore a green canvas jacket, grew a scrubby beard, and volunteered in nature preservation.

His enrolling as a history major at university after finishing secondary school was also unexpected. First of all, the competition for getting accepted to the history program was quite stiff, and since his final report card had been quite average, there appeared to be little hope for him. Secondly, he had displayed no such interest in school, and had never even participated in the History Olympiad. Yet this simply showed that those around Mati knew only his outer side. Behind the village-hero and macho-man facade was a pensive and attentive nature. He wanted to go and study history firstly because he wanted to create for himself the most generalized picture of what had taken place in the world before he entered it. He wanted to place himself and his nation somewhere, to situate them on the immense world stage somehow; he wanted just *some* sort of clarity and certainty so as not to live from day to day like an animal with no temporal perception. In this sense, he regarded history as the most general and important of all subjects. His second intention was narrower and more practical. Mati wanted to find out as much as possible about his nation's past in order to make a stand against those who had fabricated that history and planned to fabricate it even further. He had grasped from early on that there was a great gap between what he was told about the past at home— or what he had heard from his father's friends, or come across here or there in some old book or magazine—and everything that was said about it at school and in public overall. He instinctively surmised that his father and his friends were right— that everything in newer books and newspapers had been rewritten, and that people were living more and more in a lie. But already then, he realized that it is difficult to confront a lie unequipped, relying on reason and a sense of justice alone. When one side has print and radio, television and cinema, and the whole country's entire propaganda machine (all of which are underpinned by armed men and prisons, fear, informing, and a baseness instilled into people), and the other side only has an oral tradition passed down from father to son, then the forces are obviously unmatched. That is why you need people who are able to expose the fabricators while drawing upon scientific arguments; people who are familiar with things through their original sources and who know, figuratively speaking, which way the doors of archives and other repositories swing. In order to uncover the truth that is kept hidden from the people, one must occasionally repress oneself and recite the prayers of an alien liturgy. It will all pay off one day—in the event that one does not lose sight of the goal, of course.

I also know that one of Mati's mentors—a wise man brought up in the first Republic—inculcated in him the idea that it is not enough to sacrifice one's own heart's blood, although a person should also be prepared to do so. To overcome a powerful enemy, one needs wisdom in addition to valor. Every man, every last Estonian has blood that can be spilled for a cause; but few possess wisdom. (The name of the man who spoke that way was Medias, and even I had seen him at Café Werner, although I hadn't spoken to him, because he did not talk to just anyone. He had been held in the Gulag for almost twenty years, was ageless, gaunt, and tough. He certainly didn't have teeth any longer. He smoked cheap, unfiltered Priima cigarettes with a holder. He always had a briefcase with him and would sometimes take a book out of it, which he would inspect through a magnifying glass. Medias might have been an underground name, although he was not underground in the classical sense and probably didn't run any kinds of secret societies. He wasn't quite above-ground, either, but rather somewhere in between. One could have called him Mati's "academic father," and they often came into contact over the following years as well.) Mati wanted to become smart now and took the entrance exams to become a history major, scoring nineteen points out of the maximum of twenty (his only four out of five was in German) and getting accepted to the program with no trouble.

At first, Mati maintained a relatively low profile at university, keeping his sentiments under wraps. He did not glue flyers onto fence-planks, nor did he loudly satire the instructors of "red" subjects (although a number of them were so inept that you couldn't help but to laugh out loud), and he even limited the amount of anecdotes he would tell (no more than others, in any case). He took part in all of the absurdities that the curriculum mandated without wrinkling his nose, attending seminars on the history of the CPSU[2] among other events. I have a hard time imagining him keeping a straight face while paraphrasing

Lenin's essays for them. However, he had no problems with the midterms and finals.

In his extracurricular time, Mati formed a group of friends who were very different from the rest of the student body. In truth, it had already begun to form in his secondary-school days. His father had been a Forest Brother,[3] and that opened quite a few doors before him. Mati's circle of acquaintances included several other wise and tough men in addition to Medias—for example those who had graduated from the University of Tartu just before the war or during it, but whom the authorities had never allowed to work in a job corresponding to their area of expertise. There were others who hadn't even gotten to enroll in university because their youth was spent in a deportation settlement in Siberia; when they made it back to Estonia in the early sixties, they saw no point in acquiring any official degree, figuring that most jobs would remain off-limits to them anyway. A few had been kicked out of secondary school and imprisoned for political reasons during the fifties. However, although they lacked any officially recognized education, they were unmistakably adept, had independently become fluent in several languages, and were well read. The majority of those who had gone through the Gulag camps were no longer explicitly afraid of anything, but still kept out of sight. Mati's acquaintances additionally included several pastors who taught at a religious college in addition to working with their congregations. Through them, he had the opportunity to read various educational materials that were mostly typewritten on cheap, semi-transparent paper. These documents did not contain anything explicitly anti-Soviet, but were rather stories and interpretations of the Bible, patristics, the history of philosophy, and other bits of general education. Mati also read the writings of Uku Masing[4]. All in all, he undoubtedly received a more diverse education than the official university program would have offered him. However, his personal interaction with these individuals shaped him even more than reading did. Already, he was acquainted with the majority of those who were later called "freedom fighters." There weren't very many of them, and they mostly earned a living by very modest jobs. The freedom fighters' impact on their surroundings

was not all that great, because they lacked almost any kind of
a public outlet—this was the pre-Internet society, of course.
People were generally sympathetic to them, but were mostly afraid to display it publicly. The representatives of the new
regime had been sitting in their offices for a few decades already, and their power was secure. There were quite a lot of
informers (judging by how much they were discussed), but
when Estonians started to talk about them more specifically,
most people didn't know a single one personally—all were
just convinced of their existence. An informer was a kind of
mythological character, something akin to a "*proletarian*." The
main thing was, of course, that people had started to sense that
the current regime would last from now until eternity—that
they were to live their one and only life under that regime,
and therefore had to try to make the best of the meager conditions. That's the impression I was certainly left with, at least.

Mati also associated with the younger freethinkers, several of whom had been kicked out of university for their political beliefs. Otherwise, it was quite a motley crew—not *all*
of them were nationally-minded, and in their midst could be
found Buddhists, nature-worshiping Taaraists, vegetarians, and
free-verse poets. There were also ufologists, folk healers and
witches, spiritists, abstract painters, pendulum swingers, card
sharks, and who knows who all else. Nevertheless, it was (in
some sense) a unified group, because everyone who belonged to
it did not toe the approved line and dared to oppose the official
norms of living.

In short, although Mati was indeed a heavy drinker, a wom-
anizer, and a convivial fellow from early on, he was *far* from
just that. He was able to control himself "in the interests of the
cause" at first, but not for long. He wasn't willing to compromise his ideals, and this could be seen soon enough.

Mati would fight with the neighborhood Russian boys already in grade school. It had not aroused any wider interest at
the time and was not associated with issues of nationality. Boys
will be boys, and have always locked horns—so his teachers
appeared to believe. And they might have even been right to a
certain extent, because the fights had sprung foremost out of

subconscious rancor and were not directly connected to the occupation. The boys simply got into fights with others who were
different from them.

Mati had even instructed *me*: never walk around in the evening with your hands in your pockets (so as to be able to immediately return a blow), always try to walk in the middle of
the street, and other such pieces of wisdom. I didn't have to
use his advice, however. I was acting in the Children's Theatre
at the town culture center, where we primarily performed contemporary Soviet authors' plays about school life, and when the
rehearsals ended at eight o'clock, I always got right on the bus
leaving from the culture center.

By the time Mati enrolled in university, packs of young people would prowl around town at night, and this was already instilled with more of a political flavor. There was, for example,
the famous Kolpakov gang, which terrorized the Estonians living in the Ülejõe neighborhood (a relatively large number of
Russians have always resided there, both because of the military
airfield and otherwise). The Kure Crew and a few other groups
fought against them. Mati the history student took part in the
brawls. He once showed up at a seminar on dialectical materialism with a black eye and a red pupil. He lied, of course, and
said that he had fallen off his horse and crashed into a barrier
during practice (he was still doing pentathlons). In reality, he
had gotten a good walloping.

All in all, the first years of university were a fun and colorful time for him. Although the regime had begun tightening
the screws elsewhere in society, the university was still very liberal. Young people (those outside the university as well as within) were heavily influenced by the intellectuals, writers, and artists of old who had been silenced and repressed during Stalinist
times, but who were now able to involve themselves in creative
work relatively freely and live normal everyday lives. Several of
their homes and studios were transformed into artists' salons,
where individuals met and conversed. The young guests reverently took Republic-era works from the glass-doored bookcases
and leafed through them with rapturous expressions; they eyed
original Wiiralt graphics and paintings done by members of

the Pallas art society, awestruck. I would come across Mati in a number of these salons from time to time. I also saw him at the Young Authors' Association. He was not 100 percent a "creative person" in the sense of the time, as he "only" crafted articles and essays (a few of his writings, such as those from the student theater, were published in the university newspaper). Back then, this was not regarded as being as important as writing poetry or short stories, which was seen as pure creativity emanating from a "divine inspiration."

The young authors of Tartu and Tallinn actively interacted and paid visits to one another. There is no point in rambling on about these soirées at greater length, because they were probably identical to all other young people's shindigs—with the one difference that drinking and sex was mixed with literary discussion and people reading their works aloud. At one such gathering, I saw a boy (at least he looked very young) who chattered endlessly, jumped and bounced around, and was extremely lively in general. This was my first encounter with Klaus, whom I will speak about later on. I remember especially the time that Klaus climbed onto the roof of the Estonian Writers' Union in the morning half-light.

In those days, the All-Union Leninist Young Communist League (Komsomol) organized camps for creative youth, which I was also invited to on a couple of occasions. One such event was held in Viitna, in North Estonia. About thirty writers, actors, artists, and other young intellects convened there. Quite a lot of alcohol was consumed in our rooms, because each participant had brought a sizeable amount of bottles along with them. It was at that camp that I met Manglus for the first time—back then still a slim young man dressed from head to toe in black, a tiny silver cross around his neck, ambling around without interacting with anyone. Even at that point, he was already much farther ahead of us.

## MR. KULU

Out of all of his teachers, one in particular left an especially deep impression on Teedu. A male instructor named Kulu, who would come to mind frequently even decades later. The most striking thing about Mr. Kulu's appearance was his head: the sincere, somewhat simpleminded expression on his face, shaven so closely that his cheeks appeared to glisten in bright light; the line of auburn hair receding at an early age—Mr. Kulu's head was relatively large compared with the rest of his body, like that of a future human. And this was fitting for him, because Kulu was undoubtedly a future human. He took small steps on his somewhat short legs, but walked with rhythm and confidence. Kulu taught Russian language and gave intermediate shop instruction. He spoke Russian softly and with a noticeable Estonian accent, but on the other hand did so with a sense of mission. The curriculum did indeed include a relatively large amount of Russian language, but on the surface it was a subject just like any other and was not accompanied by anything "ideological" in and of itself. Yet from time to time, it so happened that Mr. Kulu digressed into everyday life during his lessons—especially in the intermediate and later grades. Mr. Kulu did not avoid these digressions, but so much as encouraged such exchanges of ideas, occasionally sacrificing time that should have been dedicated to increasing the students' language proficiency. He was also happy to speak with the students outside of class hours—for example, while harvesting potatoes at the kolkhoz or planting trees in the woods, as well as at school parties when it was his turn to chaperone. He spoke delicately with the students, not forcing his views upon them, but at the same time with a desire to shape them and guide them in the right direction. He felt it necessary to do so, especially at the given time. The situation in society seemed to be growing tenser, and the future depended on whether the students would be able to tell the difference between what was important and what was less so; whether they would see the rightness of the status quo behind its lone shortcomings. At that point in time, from the mid-sixties on, living conditions were no longer improving as they previously had, but rather were gradually returning to what they had been before. Meals worsened year by year, and sometimes even month by month. Fifth-grade students (which is exactly the age at which Teedu encountered

Mr. Kulu for the first time) were exceptionally sharp to notice it. Many foods had disappeared from shop counters over a short period of time. Even Teedu's parents had brought sausages home from the store not all that long ago. *Smoked* sausage was purchased on rare occasion, of course (primarily for some kind of celebration), but they would usually buy the next-cheapest thing (partly-smoked sausage). Now, the meat counters were empty—rolls of black pudding were lying there next to some unpleasant-looking lumps that were possibly intestines. When there happened to be butter, people bought a half-kilo stockpile. Sometimes, Teedu had to run to the street corner to see whether or not there was a line in front of the local shop. Meaning: whether or not there was white bread. Usually, only black bread and a grayish-brown-colored bread were on sale. If people were standing in front of the shop door, Teedu would run home and call out to his mother, then rush back and take a spot in line. His mother or grandmother would come and join him after a little while, then each would purchase one loaf of white bread, just as the ration prescribed.

Once during their Russian lesson, the question arose of why so many foods were no longer available. Since everyone knew Mr. Kulu was not to be feared, the boys felt freer to poke fun. "That's communism for ya!" someone shouted. Wasn't it Mati? In any case, the teacher didn't order him to be silent, but launched into a patient explanation. His pure voice, the sound of which somewhat resembled a trumpet, was clear and strained:

"We have everything we need in our country. There is so much that there should be enough for everyone. We are rich. Therefore—every time that something runs short somewhere, every time that it doesn't reach someone, that means that somewhere, there is someone who hasn't done his job well; someone who has not done his duty. Someone is always to blame. Someone must be held accountable. No other reason can justify it because, I repeat, our country has everything; it has more than anywhere else in the world, and we must do all that we can to ensure that the engine of the state runs without a hitch. We must do our own duty."

Mr. Kulu did not speak angrily, but he was certainly pensive and serious. He was sincere: the children needed to understand things correctly and should not be left to fall under the influence of those jeering and gloating from the sidelines — to be swayed by those who wanted the state to do badly. Mr. Kulu wanted to lay bare the mechanics of society for those who were no longer children but not yet young men or women. They had to be given an explanation for why newspapers wrote that communism was drawing nearer, even though a cursory observation of life seemed to give the impression that it was actually receding.

Of course, Mr. Kulu also had his own moments of weakness, when a dark and irritating doubt descended upon him. *Really — why do the newspapers write that way, inciting hopes in people, all in vain?* he asked himself during those blinks of an eye. Was there also someone who had not done their duty there, in the newspapers' editorial offices and boardrooms? Someone who was spreading untruths, and in doing so lending a hand to the rumors and mockery? Kulu was of the opinion that the public should be spoken to honestly and sternly, without glossing things over. For the one greater Truth, in which Mr. Kulu very much believed, was altogether so powerful and lofty that nothing could disprove it. And this truth was certainly so plentiful that there should be enough of it for everyone. Mr. Kulu even felt that the more he noticed negative details around him (or the more he heard about them), the firmer and more dear that great Truth became to him — the more unwavering his belief became. And why shouldn't it be the same for other people? But no, stop — he was not the right man to say that. He shouldn't think that much, because he did not know everything; he lacked a complete overview of the matter. And most of all: he did not have the mind of a statesman; he knew this with certainty, and would occasionally even tell himself:

"You, Kulu, only have Kulu's mind, so therefore only mind your own Kulu-business."

Yet in spite of this, he knew — or, more precisely, he felt — that he was on the right track. And he genuinely believed in society as a whole, and secretly even believed that before he died, he would see a change: if not true communism itself (he had become wary of that), at least a much brighter life than the one they presently had. He would not live to see *actual* communism, but he would reach the peak of a mountain from which communism would already be visible—from which it would appear as a dark blue line on the sunny horizon. What would be the nature of that life, shimmering there in the distance? Money would disappear, of course—that was general knowledge. But further? Kulu had no definite notion of anything more, and he didn't like to think about specificities. One should not deliberate over communism all on one's own: that ruined the whole charm. It was about the idea, the principle, the new human relationships. At the same time, he grasped that a mortal needs those very details, needs wonders, and therefore, they—the weak believers—should be given an epiphany about communism now. But how could these be given if there were no sausages? Kulu did not need sausages personally. He did like the taste of sausage very much, but he was prepared to wait for it calmly. For one day, there would be so much sausage that people wouldn't even be able to eat it all. Yet this was not *principal*, it was not a goal of its own. What was important was rather that in the future, life as a whole should be plentiful and friendly, full of intellectual and spiritual values. Kulu did like communism primarily because of its new relationships and values. And to be absolutely honest, he liked the progression towards communism itself most of all. (This was certainly wicked to say, his small bit of heresy, but on occasion, he was gripped by the fear that when communism was at hand, then life would no longer be as exciting and romantic as it was at that moment. For Kulu, his life was filled to the brim with excitement and romance at every waking second, and he thanked fate from the bottom of his heart for having been born right then—at a time when he could still be progressing towards communism.) There was a special air to this. Kulu respected idealists, devoted and dedicated individuals in general. He liked when people were bound to something greater than themselves and served what was higher. For this reason, even religious types secretly had an impression on him, although they were on the wrong path. The worst thing in the world was a lack of idealism; to watch from the sidelines, and mock from around a corner. Weren't some of the boys looking at him a little mockingly even now? Take that Mati, for example, whose parents had been in Siberia. Surely they spoke badly of Soviet society at home. Nevertheless, no, the boy probably wasn't mocking him. But he needed to keep an eye on him and have a heart-to-heart talk with his parents. Girls didn't have an interest in these things yet, luckily.

Kulu's mother and father had been relatively old and devoutly religious people who said a prayer before eating, never swore, and went to church. They were simple and ingenuous in their belief, not thinking with their own heads. Kulu remembered having asked his grandmother about paradise after she read an abridged Bible story to him from a thin book. His grandmother wasn't able to give him an answer. Nor was his father. For example, they did not know whether paradise held one big sauna for everyone, like a public sauna, or if each family would have their own bathroom. So, things were vague concerning the details of paradise, just as they were with communism. When Kulu was a little older, he sought an explanation from a religious man who ran a prayer house a couple of streets over. The man answered that we are incapable of imagining paradise in detail because it is something entirely different from our everyday life. Paradise surpasses our power and capacity for imagination, and it is impossible to discuss it in categories of the mundane (meaning saunas and bathrooms)— we simply lack the mental power. Over the course of time, Kulu had started to really like that sort of an explanation, and sometimes felt it applied to communism as well. We do not yet have the necessary degree of intelligence to imagine communism in its particulars. Yet at the same time, he realized that such an explanation was unsuitable for schoolchildren. How do you tell them that we do not have the mind for understanding communism? Although it might even correspond to the truth in terms of substance, there was something wrong about the sentence structure. For the Party had *everything*—even its slogan went: "The Party is the mind, honor, and conscience of our era." Yes—the mind, too.

The man running the prayer house had also told Kulu that there is no absolute clarity on whether paradise is a place or a state, and that the case is the same for hell. Kulu really liked *this* approach as well, and when he later fell in love with communism, it seemed to him that communism was a place just as well as it was a state. When he was older, however, he found that his Kulu-mind had once again reached its limits here, and he stopped racking his brain over the details of communism—just as he had done earlier with paradise.

Kulu sighed and looked at the clock in astonishment. They needed to quickly cover the Russian indefinite case now. It was hard for him to say the grammatical term aloud without the boys starting to snicker: since he pronounced Russian with a deep country twang, the term sounded like the word "pussy" in Estonian. He had been training himself to pronounce it cleanly, and had even tried practicing one-on-one with the school's other Russian teacher—the monolingual Anastasia Petrovna. However, it turned out that the latter actually knew a few words in Estonian, and had begun thinking Kulu had other intentions with her.

One other school lesson stuck in Teedu's mind. It happened a few years later, when he was in eighth grade. They had read a poem in their textbook titled "The Song of the Perturbed Youth." The words were lyrics to a popular song by the composer Pakhmutova. They translated the text verse by verse, and then listened to it on a gramophone that Mr. Kulu had brought along for the occasion. The unaccompanied male baritone sang with passion, extending and emphasizing the words, simultaneously strained and gentle.

Teedu could still remember what the lyrics were, more or less.

*And the wind and the storms and a starflight by night, my heart is restless and the road calls me into the distance.*

Kulu liked the song a lot—the boys could tell. He became downright emotional—staying within the bounds of how emotional a man is allowed to be. It seemed to Teedu that something glinted peculiarly in his eyes as he stared off into the distance beyond the glass window.

Despite his practicing, Kulu's Russian pronunciation became

worse by the year (he had early-onset periodontitis as a consequence of his vitamin-deficient post-war childhood, but his teacher's salary was not enough to acquire a full set of "gold teeth," and Kulu was still saving up for it), and he had recently given up on his efforts to improve it. Nevertheless, he had become even more confident in spirit.

*And just as so often in life, you encounter a genuine love, who walks with you at your side as a friend and a comrade.*

So sang the baritone, and Mr. Kulu felt a sweet pain in his soul because it was all so right. Exactly—a friend and a comrade. Kulu himself was still waiting for his friend and comrade, though, because he had high moral requirements. Walking at his side in the early mornings and the late evenings was a smallish dog with a broad chest and a long tail named Stormbird.

"Those are magnificent lyrics," Kulu said. "That all awaits *you* as well."

Teedu went outside late that same evening. He ordinarily didn't go out anymore at that hour, but on this day his soul was gripped by sublime emotions and was longing for freedom, air, and open space. A chilly, frozen, and soundless night had cast itself over the land. Teedu stopped on his front steps and turned his eyes up towards the boundlessly extending sky filled with small, twinkling stars. The Milky Way was dimly visible from the zenith down to the horizon. *Yeah, that's exactly what needs to happen*, he thought, recalling the lesson from a few years back in which Mr. Kulu told them that their country had everything. *Yeah, we do have everything; it's just that things need to be arranged better*, Teedu pondered, feeling happiness swell in his chest. The fact that they had to use cut-out pieces of newspaper in the lavatory at home meant nothing. That was temporary. Someone was to blame for there being scraps of newspaper and not toilet paper there. He knew that such paper existed. His classmate Uudo's father was a sailor, and they had all kinds of wonders in their home. *It'll come—that paper will come to us, too . . .* Teedu was certain. He looked upwards again and felt as if invisible threads coming from those millions of worlds there behind the stars were joining together in his soul all at once. He could feel clearly and palpably how something majestic, like the impression made by that expanse of sky, was coming down upon his soul. And how something from inside of himself was forcefully pushing its way towards it—was yearning to meet it. He would have liked to hug the whole world and do a good deed for everyone.

In addition to Mr. Kulu's musical machine, something else had helped call forth that instant of emotion. Specifically, Teedu had a crush on Anu, who had light-blond hair, a small, pointed jaw, and a waist the size of an ant's; a girl who studied to get full points and walked back to her seat from the chalkboard with a "clip-clop" (after earning another A). The only trouble was that Anu was Mati's sister, and Mati continued to be a *persona non grata* at Teedu's home. Something resembling the Capulets and the Montagues was budding here. That night, Teedu wrote down his first poem under the confluent influences of Anu's slim waist and Pakhmutova's lyrics. From that time onward, he continued to write poems. He did so in secret, as they already had several recognized poets in their class.

## TEEDU'S MISSTEPS

In the tenth grade, I received an invitation to a pan-ESSR meeting of friends of literature, which was held in Klooga. I was making my first attempts as a translator at that time, and had done an Estonian translation of a children's story by Hans Fallada that was printed in the children's magazine *Täheke*. Teedu was also present at the gathering—I got the impression that he was a lively and good-hearted boy. He talked a lot, generally just innocent childish prattle. At the outdoor party organized that night, in the shrubbery surrounding the wooden dance floor, it turned out that he didn't smoke, nor did he sample the dry wine. He didn't have the courage to dance and would saunter around the dance floor, pretending that dancing didn't interest him. (By the way, playing for the dance was a group of young female guitar players that called themselves The Pea Mice; female musical groups were a rarity back then.)

Teedu's former schoolmates acknowledge that he was a nice, friendly boy in the eleventh grade: somewhat naive, but companionable. Girls liked him because he didn't swear and try to act tough in their company, nor did he always try to cop a feel (back then, people called it "groping"). On the contrary—he was rather polite (for example: when someone dropped something, he would quickly pick it up before the dropper themself could manage to do so). For this reason, a small group of girls (the type of people we called "deepies") started inviting him to late-night gatherings that they held on the closed-glass veranda of one of the girl's houses. Up until that point, only one other young man had been invited: a somewhat shady character nicknamed "Ippe," who was overly developed for his age, somewhat feminine, and swung his lanky limbs as he walked. Now there were two young men in the clique, which gave it a different hue. A few of the girls have claimed in retrospect that Teedu was in love with Ippe. This is hard to believe, however, because Teedu held Anu in his heart. He would sometimes leave with Ippe to go walking together on the city streets; Teedu wanted to discuss matters of the heart with a more intelligent person and the latter graciously allowed himself to be walked home.

Although Teedu did not finish secondary school with a medal (he was unable to penetrate the essence of the laws of physics, but on the other hand excelled at chemistry and especially biology), his final report card was very good and there were only a few lone Bs. He naturally wanted to continue his studies, but for some reason Estonian schools did not suit him—he wanted something grander and loftier. Rumor had it that he wanted to study to become a cosmonaut. The thing was that Teedu wished to unconditionally dedicate his life to the most important thing in the entire universe, and he felt that cosmonautics *was* that most general and important of all fields, because planet Earth was a part of space as well, wasn't it? Sadly, he had no idea where to turn to, or which channels to use. For example, he didn't know how to apply for the so-called SSR-places, which were meant for state subjects of non-Russian ethnicity, and which already existed at that time. He simply traveled to Moscow, asked around here and there, and did things all on his own. He stayed at the apartment of his grandfather's brother-in-arms Ain Gvorkin, who had been a lieutenant colonel in the signal corps. He did not get in, of course—there were at least a hundred applicants for each place. (And was it even the "line" for cosmonautics that he got into in the *first* place?) Nor did he have any doctor-acquaintances whom he could use to get out of the Soviet military, into which he was then conscripted after not getting into college. And even if he had *had* such ties, it is doubtful whether he would have used them. His parents were law-abiding persons—fervent citizens of the state, who believed that no matter what kind of a country one lives in, one must always obey and abide by the laws. Such was life already. Teedu's father feared that if someone found out he had ducked military service, things would get "even worse."

"Everyone's gone to the army," he said to comfort Teedu. "You'll go as well. What's the worst that can happen?"

And so, Teedu went.

No one knows what happened to him in the Soviet army. (Maybe nothing special really happened at all.) Back then, even among friends it wasn't customary for young people to go on at length about their time spent in the military, not to mention when they were in bigger groups. It was as if everyone wanted to silence that period of their life in order to forget it faster. If they spoke about it at all, then they principally spoke about conscription in a superior tone, telling cheerful, obscene, or absurd details. Yet, Teedu did not tell all that much about his two years. Only one circumstance from that period of his life is known to a number of individuals. It was in connection with Mati's sister. Anu was not his official "girlfriend," of course, because for some reason, despite his proper manners, she did not especially like Teedu. Still, Anu was a virtuous girl and allowed him to be her friend. This seemed humane to her as long as the young man was in the military. She hoped that he would forget everything afterwards, anyway. Teedu sent Anu poems from the army. They were in free verse, naturally (most people wrote that way at the time), and about love. Anu, however, had already gotten involved with underground activities in a certain sense. True, this was in the most indirect way possible, and she was not aware that she was doing something subversive. She was simply helping her brother Mati, who had enrolled in university and was putting together samizdat periodicals with a few friends. Anu retyped the texts for the undertaking, because she had free access to a typewriter in an office where she substituted for a regular employee during summer holidays. (She typed out eight copies at a time on thin corn-based paper, so if she repeated the process three or four times, it was almost enough.) She likewise corrected any orthographic mistakes and added commas to the texts before typing them (always the silver-medal graduate). The boys drafting the periodical paid her a little less than what would regularly be paid to a typist, because young poets and nationally-minded students were poor. Anu used the rubles she earned to go watch serious films at the cinema and buy chocolate. One hot afternoon while taking a break from typing, Anu came up with the idea of proposing to Teedu that they publish his poems in their journal. She genuinely wanted to do Teedu a good deed, assuming that publishing his poems would improve the spirits of the young man forced to live in a miserable environment. Teedu did not know what a samizdat was. He thought that a journal was something like the notebooks in which girls write song lyrics. And it was *Anu* asking! She could have asked him practically anything—Teedu would have allowed it. His answer was an overflowing "yes." A few months later, his lovey-dovies were indeed published in the periodical *Entelecheia, No. 1*, right after Mati's own article titled "The Roots of the Estonian Character. An Historical Étude." This happened six months before Teedu's demobilization.

Having arrived home from his long journey, Teedu took a bath, pulled on his clothes for going out, and left. He had written to Anu well before and invited her out on a date. They drank juice cocktails at Tempo Café first, and then went for a stroll in Kassitoome Park. Both of them were in high spirits, and their conversation bounced about cheerfully as they told each other what had happened meanwhile. Both of them laughed a lot. Teedu gradually grew quieter and more serious, sought Anu's eyes, and at one point said: "Let's talk about us now, too." Hearing this, Anu started to prattle even more gaily—about what their former classmates were doing, how Anu's kitten purrs, that the market building had been under repair for a while, and a dozen other things. Teedu remained patiently quiet until Anu drew in a breath, and he repeated his request: "Let's talk about us now, too." Then Anu inquired with great interest about what Teedu was planning—whether he would get a job or try to "get in" to college somewhere, adding that she, Anu, could lend him textbooks or notes. She recommended that he study agriculture, as it "suited his character," and asked whether "there'd be apples" in their garden that year. When Teedu looked tenderly into her eyes a third time and almost pleaded: "Let's talk about us now, too," Anu burst out laughing a little uneasily and emitted a "hmh!" She appeared surprised: "You are an odd one—we talk about us all the *time*. What other 'us' are we talking about, then?" Teedu realized that something was off, and did not push the matter any more. Furthermore, Anu needed to run off to a lecture. Teedu walked with her to the large academic building on Vanemuise Street (Anu was studying economics). At the moment they parted, he thought for a split second of pulling Anu close to him, but grasped that this would be "unjustified."

Traipsing home, Teedu thought wearily that he no longer wanted to live—so unbearable was his unrequited pain of love. He made the decision to wait for Anu; to remain loyal to her, even if it took decades.

While scanning a week-old copy of *The People's Voice* that evening, he came across an article that was harshly critical of young people's samizdat periodicals. Self-printed publications of that sort were a grave ideological mistake. This was not the only piece on the topic. Teedu found a few more pasquinades in *Voice of the Youth*, *Forward*, and *Hammer and Sickle*. He immediately realized it was serious. (Where had he suddenly picked up an instinct for comprehending such things? He had been a naive and innocent young man not all that long ago. Had serving in the Soviet army, even though not a single noteworthy event happened to him there, truly left such a mark on him; had its brutal enormity made him cowardly to such an extent?) He was gripped by horror and started to panic. *His* loveydovies had been published in one such journal. Luckily he was not mentioned in the articles by name! Teedu's first instinct was that he should go somewhere and explain things, should say that he was innocent and had not intended anything "like that." Yet he did not know where to go to do such a thing. He was in anguish for a day and a half. It was summer—otherwise, he might have gone to his old school to ask Mr. Kulu for advice.

Over the course of that day and a half (as he later established with certain remorse), Anu receded to the background of his consciousness, and his romantic agony diminished to nothing in the shadow of a much more powerful sensation (that of fear). Still, Anu was in great danger, too. Teedu wondered whether or not he should also say "there" (when he had located the place in question) that Anu was innocent. Or was that unnecessary, perhaps, since Anu was merely a technical executor in the affair? Still, she should at least be warned; that would be an act of friendship. He was afraid to write, neither of them had a telephone, and inviting Anu to meet solely in order to warn her might come across as overbearing. Teedu's love pangs returned, but in a slightly diluted form.

His longing to see Anu, even if only from afar, gradually lessened after about a month. He started to feel that Anu had been too talkative during their last meeting. If she planned to talk so much her whole life, what then? Yes, and though she was otherwise so lovely, her chin was really quite pointy. How much more pointy might it get over her life? With a heavy heart, Teedu made the decision to break things off with Anu. He realized, of course, that there was actually nothing for him to break off. This put him in a bitter mood, but at the same time he felt relieved, because he would not have to sacrifice himself for Anu after all. He shouldn't butt his head against a wall like this.

As no one came to arrest Teedu immediately, he calmed down about the samizdat journals over time as well, and the whole affair slipped into oblivion.

## TEEDU'S FATE SETTLES INTO PLACE

Everyone who had known Teedu Tärn from before would have alleged that he was a different person upon returning from the military. His interest in cosmonautics had cooled. One can presume that Teedu had stared into the starry sky enough during his night watches, and grasped that while he was searching for a revelation from beyond the stars, cosmonautics was strictly scientific in practice; in order to work in the field, one must be very good at physics and math, which he lacked the mind for. Perhaps he suspected that two years of his life had been wasted, and that he was therefore not allowed to make any more mistakes, and needed to have both feet on solid ground. Solid ground generally meant studying to become a doctor, which Teedu's father also highly recommended, or else some technical field; law would also do. Teedu did not want to become a doctor (as he was afraid of blood), he wouldn't have managed in technical professions (again because of physics and mathematics), and being a lawyer seemed somehow ignoble to him, as he associated it with bending the law. So Teedu went and registered for history, because he very much liked all kinds of stories—he had a lively imagination. He didn't go into philology because it seemed to be a little "much" to him—meaning excessively nebulous and airy, suitable for a hobby but not a profession. His father warned him about history—"A slippery slope, a slippery slope."—but Teedu felt that history was important in its own way, and that if he played things right, it would be possible to establish himself in life *very* successfully by way of it. That was what he told his father, too. The latter just shook his head and sighed: "Let's hope, let's hope it'll all stick some day. That's the most important thing in general—that something sticks. No matter whether it's something bad in and of itself; when everything is changing every couple of decades, a person cannot live." There were no patriotic sentiments guiding Teedu's choice—he simply did not think of such things. He was accepted in the fifth-to-last place, as he had managed to forget a great deal during conscription.

Back then, it was customary to say that the military makes one a man. If by this they meant that a person becomes sluggish and laughs less, then Teedu had indeed become a man over those two years. The twinkle had disappeared from his eyes and was sometimes replaced by the look of a dog that had misbehaved. Teedu had started smoking and would need to clear his throat before he talked. His sense of humor, which was never exuberant, had now pretty much dried up, and he absolutely did not pick up on any irony. He had, however, acquired the habit of telling anecdotes in the army. When doing so, he tended to perform the jokes in a very "lively" manner—getting into them, so to say. For example: when playing a male role, he would speak in a gruff voice, swear, and even scratch himself; in a female role, he would squeak, bat his eyes, and so forth. Yet, he was somewhat short on acting virtuosity, so when he was supposed to speak in a goat's voice for one scene, for example, it would come out more or less the same way as it would when he impersonated Chapayev or Nadezhda Krupskaya. Sometimes he would stamp his feet and roll his eyes as he concluded the anecdote to give greater expressiveness to the performance. For the most part, the stories were not funny, but simply childish, and he repeated them too often. Crowning his repertoire were a number of pieces that featured off-color humor. Occasionally, he would look around seemingly in doubt after his performance, apparently realizing himself that it "wasn't all that great." After that, he usually wouldn't utter a single word more that day. Every once in a while, one classmate or another would catch Teedu staring at him or her with mournful, almost glassed-over eyes. This had an uncomfortable effect, for the most part.

Viewed on the surface, especially in the longer run, Teedu's career might appear to have gone evenly and uniformly. But only on the surface! True, he had prepared himself for an academic career from the very beginning, aiming for a job teaching social and political subjects at Tartu State University, or at some other college, at last resort. Towards these ends, he diligently composed papers for seminars, which were praised by some older and more influential instructors. (For example, I remember his paper on the childhood of the revolutionary Aleksander Repson.) Already for his early coursework, he focused on certain aspects of the workers' movement in Narva. He knew that he would do his next projects on the same topic as well, as he would his final thesis, successfully cultivating the latter into the dissertation for his doctoral candidacy and ultimately his doctoral thesis—all on the Narva workers' movement.

Teedu's classmates saw through this, perceived his cunning intentions, and as a result, their attitude towards him became somewhat disdainful. Their class was generally more European in manner, and even nationalist to some extent—although this nationalism was more in the German or even the French spirit; so, European, all the same. Still, a rigid wing of Päts-like[5] mentality was not lacking, either. The class elite treated Teedu like aristocrats treat someone who holds a lowly job.

However, the ones who believed Teedu to be a bona fide careerist were unaware of one episode, which provoked a spiritual landslide in Teedu during the winter of his first semester and almost brought him to ruin. I was told about this episode by Mati, and I believe him. He was a few years ahead of Teedu in his studies, of course, but students in the same field spoke to one another quite actively and frequently drank together at the dormitories, also in the company of those who did not reside in the dorms. Based on this story, it seems like Teedu really was incredibly naive about political things and believed many things that are hard to even imagine. For example, he only heard about the Molotov-Ribbentrop Pact for the first time in college, from some companions who mentioned it in passing like a piece of common knowledge. Teedu had previously let it slip past, just like the word "Christmas" during his childhood and much more. Now, however, he was starting to suspect that this might be something important. At the same time, he did not want to reveal his ignorance, and attempted to find out about the Molotov-Ribbentrop Pact on his own. Naturally, he used the official Soviet sources in doing so.

It goes without saying that the Pact had been discussed constantly at Mati's home—during his childhood, it had been as familiar a topic as the fairy tale *Thumbelina*. He later heard about it in greater detail from the old men, who still remembered how the unexpected agreement between Hitler's Germany and Stalin's Russia had been received by the Estonian public at the time.

A debate on the topic broke out in a dorm room one day. As always, both the youngest and the oldest students—Mati being among the latter—were present. Teedu spoke up with views that originated from *The History of the Great Patriotic War*. They were struck down so mercilessly by the others (including Mati) that Teedu left the room quite dazed. A couple of attractive nationally-minded girls even called after him: "Go and beat off, commie!" Bumping into Mati by chance at the men's room in the main building the next day, Teedu said: "I'm not going to turn you in to the dean's office, but you don't deserve the title of Soviet college student!"

Mati eyed him for a few moments and asked (quoting *The Good Soldier Švejk* almost verbatim): "Tell me—are you playing an idiot, or are you *really* an idiot?"

"Neither one nor the other!" Teedu declared defiantly. "But I don't believe hearsay. Stalin had to give his country a breather. Show me one place where someone has written about the Molotov-Ribbentrop Pact the way that you talk about it. Otherwise, I'm going to keep saying that's an old wives' tale."

"But what'll you do if I *do* show you? And if it's true?"

"Show me, then we'll see," Teedu said, remaining confident.

And Mati showed him. He acquired through some of his acquaintances a few photo-paper documents in fine type, which had been secretly photographed in the library's restricted collection. The documents were in Estonian, English, and German. Teedu read them. Afterward, he did not attend lectures for several days. When he finally showed up, he walked up to Mati and said: "I'm sorry. You were right." He went through an agonizing internal struggle, and was probably close to suicide. Mati knew that Teedu had even made preparations to defect to Finland through Karelia, but changed his mind at the last second. It appeared he had made his decision, albeit with a heavy heart. He continued researching the workers' movement. From that time onward, Teedu truly was a conscious careerist. Regardless, there had still been a small bump on his seemingly smooth path upwards.

## MATI'S WEDDING

Mati married for the first time in the early fall of his third year at university. The bride's family wanted a church ceremony, and Mati did not have the slightest objection to it, although he was

not religious in the narrower sense, as far as I know. That kind
of a wedding was relatively rare back then, especially in the case
of young people. The Church was generally spurned and held
in disfavor. It would be more correct to say that it had been reduced to nothingness. We did not hear anything about churches being shut down or demolished, of course, nor about religious leaders being pilloried, fined, or deported. But that was
just the thing—we didn't hear anything about it. Whenever I
walked past one church or another, I wondered—*is* there really any activity in there anymore or not? You often couldn't tell
from the outside. There were very few cars in those days, so it
wasn't possible to make any conclusions based on whether any
were parked near the church or not (unlike today, where there
are usually always a couple of vehicles parked outside the par-
sonage). Only once a year, on Christmas Day—that was when
the churches came to life. Everyone knew that on Christmas
Eve, schoolteachers would go to church to check and make sure
no children from *their* educational institution were there. Some
teachers were sent there as part of their official duties; some,
who were in the Party, went there to check unbidden, to demonstrate their loyalty; some probably connected the two with
enjoyable obligation. Even I went to church on a couple of occasions back then (I stood surreptitiously in the back), because I
enjoyed the extraordinary animation that appeared on people's
faces when they crossed the church threshold. But in my opinion, the pastors' sermons were so childish and uninteresting that
for quite some time I did not dare to speak with anyone on the
topic, in the fear that something was wrong with *me*; that the
Word of God simply was not getting through to me.

University students generally enjoyed more freedom than
students in secondary school (they were less dependent on their
homes and faculties), but the upcoming ceremony caused problems for them regardless. A few of Mati's classmates were terrified, wondering whether it would be worth putting their future careers at risk for something as insignificant as attending a
church service. The head of the Komsomol of our class, *Komsorg*
Villu Ebeljalg—a tall boy who had served in the military—
warned that he did not recommend going: not as a member of

the Komsomol, nor personally (he added hastily). *So, what should we do?* people asked one another. The girls were especially indecisive, since a church and a ceremony seemed so beautiful. "Damn it—a friend's getting married, how can you not show up? Damn it!" the boys exclaimed at a loss. *Komsorg* Ebeljalg reckoned it would be appropriate to wait outside, standing in front of or next to the church while the ceremony was being held inside. This immediately begged the question of how far away one should stand from the church door or wall so that on the one hand, the person could still be regarded as having been present at the important event (you can't be hanging out a kilometer away now, can you!), but on the other hand, it would not be interpreted as active participation in the service. Ebeljalg scratched the back of his neck and said that he couldn't take the responsibility for such a decision, and that it would be wiser to ask the university *partorg*. The next day, he announced that six meters would be a completely suitable distance.

Several daring souls entered the church, regardless. There were also older people in attendance, among them old Forest Brothers, pastors, officers and constables of the first Republic of Estonia, and other later-middle-aged men and women. Afterward, a wedding dinner was organized for guests at a tavern on the edge of the city limits; the menu resembled that of a wake, only more booze was offered and the speeches were more upbeat. That evening, a party was held for the younger crowd at Mati's home, where we were able to be completely on our own. The relatives whom Mati's parents had moved in with—thirteen years earlier, after relocating from Northern Viljandi County—had died by that time and left the house to the family. Mati's father—a strong, burly man—had also died unexpectedly of a heart attack after his sixtieth birthday. Mati's mother cooked potato and beet salads the night before her son's wedding, and left to stay with her sister in the country following the dinner. Fall was at hand, and again she needed to go help pick the potatoes for their winter stores and do other chores around the farm—nothing about that had changed. Mati quickly changed out of his wedding suit and into Polish jeans, revved up his father's old sidecar motorcycle, dropped his mother off, and then the party kicked off.

Members of the Young Authors' Association and about a third of Mati's class were invited in addition to other bohemians and shady figures from around town: altogether forty or fifty people. (Teedu was not among the wedding-goers, but—as was only proper—he congratulated Mati the following day.) It turned out to be quite an ordinary, enjoyable shindig; people just ate more. There were not enough chairs, so some sprawled on the floor with looks of relief. The partiers sang a lot—boisterous and vulgar songs at first, then afterward, when everyone had drunk a little more, more mournful and reflective songs; then at the very end, after midnight, they sang songs that were de facto banned, such as "Our Legion Marches On and Our Bearing is Steadfast." Mati, who was a big singer, probably forgot that it was his wedding from time to time. When, for example, the last three-liter flask of wine ran out and someone had to go fetch some taxi-vodka,[6] he rose promptly and announced he would be the one to go. (By the way, I have never seen anyone as skilled at speaking with taxi drivers as Mati was. He didn't say anything special to them, did not hem and haw or butter them up, but they would still put their full trust in him, never thinking he was crazy or an instigator.) However, someone piped up that it wouldn't do at all for the groom himself to go fetch the taxi-vodka—he was supposed to guard his bride so that no one would steal her away; let someone else go. That being said, Mati appeared to become conscious of the situation and grunted: "Ah, right—yeah, of course!" Everyone around him burst into laughter, as he had said it so touchingly. Even the bride smiled weakly, as if out of obligation. A few words about her, also. Piibe was her name—a willowy girl with pale blond hair, probably a year older than Mati. She was absolutely sweet, apparently well-read, and educated in general. Her face was animated, but just a bit elven in my opinion (which could also have been due to the light, of course). Perhaps my overall impression of Piibe derived from the fact that she was dreadfully serious, almost elegiac. I believe, by the way, that this is exactly why Mati liked her. Mati did not need a woman in the usual sense (he could already count several of them per finger, anyway), but rather as a symbol. He subconsciously wanted something tragic for his close surroundings, for his home—someone whose sad disposition would constantly remind him of national tragedy and lost freedom. Naturally, it could have all been much simpler: Mati just wanted to remain a man of honor, and married the girl. Piibe was the granddaughter of a man of the Estonian Republic—her grandfather had been a lieutenant in the Estonian War of Independence. In this sense, the bride and groom had one and the same background, and maybe also a similar code of behavior. Piibe wanted a child from Mati because the boy possessed so much vitality; girls often want a child from such men. Piibe was indeed already pregnant, although it did not show. Perhaps the girl had not actually hoped to marry him, and was now a little confused as a result of her new and unexpected role.

I remember when the clock struck eleven. As usual for the hour, the conversation was about history and politics. I didn't want to take part in it because Aarne Kelberg, who some thought was an informer, was also there. Kelberg nodded all the time, nodded at every rejoinder, but never said anything himself. Of course, he always nodded when he was drunk. And he was drunk more or less all the time.

"Historical justice . . ."

"That doesn't count for a single *kopeck*. There's no such *thing* as justice. Odd that you're spouting that kind of talk when you yourself study history."

"These lands belong to Estonians!"

"That doesn't count for a single *kopeck*. The stronger right is what counts in history."

"Oh-ho! So does that mean what's written in the Declaration on Human Rights—that every nation has an inalienable right to independence—doesn't mean a *thing*?"

"That's for the naive. The Americans themselves have only followed it when it's been to their benefit—take Mexico, take the Philippines."

"But will Russia let us go?"

"Hold on, pour me some more, too . . ."

"Of course it won't. I spoke to a Brit last summer, an acquaintance of my mother. He said that in the West, no one believes that Estonia could peacefully break off from the Union. That's not sound reasoning."

"Take your hand off me . . . please, take it off . . .!"

"You can't jump higher than yourself. That's how history has gone. We have to take our size and capabilities into account. Grenzstein[7] wasn't talking nonsense."

"Grenzstein . . . that traitor!"

A cry suddenly sounded from one of the buzzing groups: "Damn it all! Let's go outside. The first Russian we come across, we'll lynch!" The crier was a young man nicknamed Tuft, who was called that because of his jet-black tuft of hair that stuck up militantly. Tuft had a sickly body, was quite scrawny, and had even been relieved of military training because of his weak lungs, but would get riled up on occasion. Most of the guests snickered at his call to arms. "Ah, what are you on about," someone remarked.

"What—you don't believe me, or what?" Tuft hollered and stood up.

"Listen, don't drink any more," pleaded little Heidi, who was sitting next to him and tugging at his sleeve in dismay. Little Heidi was his girlfriend. Heidi had never had a boyfriend because she was so small (one meter, forty-eight-and-a-half centimeters), and was now scared of losing hers if the frightful Tuft went and started lynching Russians on the street. Tuft shrugged— ah, there'd be time for it later!

"What'll they do to me?" someone piped up at the same time from the opposite corner. "I've been in the army, got *starshina* stripes on me—I'm not afraid. But *you* all of course can fly . . ."

"Not *starshina*, but sergeant major . . ." someone nagged.

They started singing "The Forest Brothers."

I stepped out into the hallway for a moment—it was too smoky inside. I myself have never smoked. At the end of the hallway was a small nook—a wardrobe or a storage space. A girl named Marje—not from Mati's class, but from the town's art school—followed me out. She was tall and very feline. Marje looked around cautiously, and then pushed me into the corner. I thought the darling Marje wanted to kiss me, and I started trembling because I didn't know how to prepare myself for it. So it is when your time to shine catches you off guard. Instead of kissing me, however, the darling Marje took someone's coat off of a peg, laid it over our heads, then pressed her lips close against my ear and whispered: "This working people's state can't last much longer."

*That's a good one*, I thought. *Where'll it go, then—that state?* However, I nodded so that Marje would not leave. She stayed. "I don't want to live here in this working-people's state much longer." Ah-*ha*, I realized. Everywhere is full of microphones—*that's* why she is whispering. The coat draped over my head smelled musty. But then, she kissed me (people still "kissed" back then). Marje's brother had emigrated. Aksel had studied at the Leningrad Theatre Institute and married a Swedish girl (a fraudulent marriage, of course), and now lived in Gothenburg. Marje was waiting for her brother to send a "suitor" to come and get her. Why did she tell me this? Maybe she wanted to do me a service by asking whether I might want a "bride" to be sent to me from there. I was still so foolish back then that I didn't even pick up on it. But thinking back on it now in hindsight, would I really have wanted so very much to be sent a "bride"? Well, I don't know. Probably not, I guess. It's strange now to see those people, the ones who left back then. I always get the feeling that some of them are satisfied, but others aren't at all (although they won't even admit it to themselves, and therefore talk up their own achievements and belittle those who stayed here). The ones who especially stepped on a rake are those who were somewhat older and who left right before Gorbachev came to power. Because now, they have missed their opportunity to step through the door into the new era, and have fallen between two chairs. On the other hand, people who left when they were still young made the right step, since they were able to make a career for themselves in their new country. But who knew that in advance? And in some sense, it is always nicer to be a big frog in a small pond than to be a small frog in a big pond—that's what I think nowadays.

But back then, I was contemplating instead what the darling Marje had meant by "the working-people's state." What is so bad about work, if you look at it that way? *Everyone* worked.

Her own parents worked, the man running the prayer house worked, even the former Forest Brother Arnold Tõusumägi had worked. And in the West, people also had to work; her own brother Aksel worked in Gothenburg. Some loved their work, of course, and some did not. But once again, it was the same on both sides; even in the West, not everyone was crazy about their work. Why else would they be fighting for a shorter work week, then? To me, it seemed that the real working-people's state was actually over in the West. *There* were the strikes and demonstrations, *there* was where workers demanded salaries and rights, where unions held negotiations with factory owners. But could the working people demand anything in the Soviet Union? No one was *that* stupid back then, of course. There was a Party committee to make sure that no one demanded anything. The working people actually got the knout more in the USSR than they did elsewhere. So the darling feline Marje was wrong about that, although it was not her own fault, because the slogan "we have a working-people's state" had simply gotten stuck in her head somehow, and for her, it meant the entirety of the absurdity and slipshoddery that could be found in the Soviet state.

Mati already firmly believed that the Soviet state would vanish from these parts one day. He did not talk about "the working-people's state," but rather just the "Soviet state." Mati didn't waver even once. "That freedom'll come, it will," he said to us, the majority of whom were more skeptical—at least most of the time, as I suppose even *we* had our own moments of enthusiasm. Where was he getting that—was it knowledge or pure belief? I have contemplated the relationship between those two things, belief and knowledge. It was probably Mati's own sort of knowing, which was not based on the actual state of world affairs or on the practical logic of events, but instead on the way in which things are (or would be) right. Freedom is right and lovely in and of itself. And if that is how things are in a state of thoughts or ideas, then reality must inevitably catch up to it, as reality is beneath the state of ideas—it is dependent upon it and clinks and clatters in pursuit. This is how one *must* understand the scriptural expression about "justice should be done in full"—somewhat platonically. That conclusion wasn't all that important to me, of course; at least, I didn't think about it day and night. But nevertheless, I still wanted to make my own standpoint known to Mati one day in order to hear what he thought about it. This would be hard to do, however, because Mati didn't care to listen to a conversation partner for very long — not out of pride or arrogance, but simply as a trait he had been born with. On top of that, Piibe was pregnant again.

## TEEDU'S CAREER

In the spring of his second year at university, the department Party cell issued Teedu a proposal to join the CPSU. Teedu could already feel success drawing near, and said yes. That same night, however, he recalled the free-verse lovey-dovies that had once been published in a manuscript periodical, and the worries that had receded for a time awoke once more. Is a person who has published works in a *samizdat* fit to be a Party candidate? Teedu anguished for a long while about this, but then could not stand it anymore and went to speak with the individual who had written his recommendation for joining the party. *Partorg* Mandri was a pedagogical scholar, calm, mild, and always with a sharp appearance and a gentle voice. He heard Teedu out and nodded understandingly. "It's good that you said this," Mandri said. "We have actually been waiting a long time for you to come and talk about it. At least I have been. Naturally, we knew that you were party to that publication. Could you truly have doubted for a single second that we didn't know?" (To his own shame, Teedu had to admit that he certainly had, although he didn't tell Mandri this.) "Count on us knowing everything. We even know how you spent your time in the army after your studies. We also know the emotions that gripped you when you realized where you had sent your poems, and that you broke off ties with a young woman afterward. Yet that fear is to your credit, because you were overcome with trepidation for your pureness of heart. Or did you think we didn't know about how you did not believe in the Molotov-Ribbentrop Pact? And that you exchanged words on the topic with a third-year student in front of the men's lavatory in the university's main building? There is an idealism about you. By the way, Mr. Kulu recommended you warmly. Kulu was a classmate of mine. We've spoken about you repeatedly." The *partorg* seemed to be unaware that Teedu had planned to defect to Finland through Karelia, and this filled Teedu with an odd sense of relief.

All in all, the class's attitude towards Teedu was not overly standoffish; he was not treated as an outcast, but rather accepted as being an eccentric. For example, there were no rumors going around about him being an informer (which was the case with several other individuals). This was in spite of the fact that Teedu seemed to be easy prey for KGB recruiters. But perhaps he was precisely *too* easy, and that's what saved him. Teedu was not one of the golden youth, was not a witty alcoholic, nor was he an outstanding student. He received a scholarship thanks to careful, consistent work. He had little money—his parents had not been wealthy before and on top of that, his father had now become unexpectedly disabled and was receiving a pension (which was indeed slightly higher than usual because of some kinds of services he had performed), so he could not be supported by them all that much. He lived at home, naturally, and by doing so saved on rent and also on food costs. Still, he wore the very same pair of pants and jacket throughout his first four years at university, did indeed smoke, but drank rarely—primarily when he could not get out of it; meaning when everyone had to contribute equally or when it was free, such as on someone's birthday. Then, he would definitely drink his fair share, although not to the point of being blind drunk. But he did not buy alcohol himself, instead saving his money, without knowing exactly what for.

There was, however, one more reason why Teedu decided to make a career for himself (and this shows his foresightedness). It had to do with love affairs. Girls could have had a real liking for Teedu because he was tall, strong-boned, dark-haired, and had slightly Eastern features. Yet, he was soft and unexciting, lacked a "nature" and initiative, and would also tell his immature anecdotes to young women too often. In any case, he did not officially have a girlfriend. Still, Teedu had been in love the whole time—with one single girl, ever since the opening college ceremony. It hit him like a bolt of lightning or an apparition, and thanks to this, it really wasn't so difficult to give up on Anu, who had turned out to be ideologically unsuitable. At first, no one had any idea of Teedu's fondness for her; it only came out into the open in the spring of his first year. Merle Lootus was the cream of the class-crop. She was light-haired, tall, had a darling face, and boasted a proud womanly figure with breasts that were almost too high. She was incredibly sharp and knew how to perform, at that—her well-constructed speeches, spoken fluently and in a pleasant soprano, were a delight to hear at seminars. The existence of an admirer the likes of Teedu made Merle laugh at first, because many men made eyes at her, including important figures on the Komsomol committee, famous protest singers, and promising young intellectuals. A union between her and Teedu would have been glaringly uneven. This inequality incited sympathy in some observers, while others admitted it "made them sick." Yet Teedu was unrelenting and kept on trying. Things went so far that Merle would cross to the other side of the street whenever she saw Teedu approaching from a distance. And although she was anything but a spiteful girl, she would sometimes make rather cruel jokes about him. However, when she saw that she was actually encouraging some kind of hope in the boy by doing so (picking on me means she loves me!), she gave up having anything to do with him at all. Still, Teedu did not allow himself to be intimidated. He constantly waited for a chance to open doors for Merle. He tried to pay her compliments. He was as insistent as drowsiness. It was truly pitiful to watch at times. When a romance between Merle and someone else came to an end, Teedu would try to talk to her and comfort her. (I myself happened upon this one time, when he and the girl were sitting on a landing on the stairs to the university café. Tears were streaming down Merle's cheeks, and Teedu was trying to wipe them away. I guess a crying woman really doesn't care who consoles her.) At the very least, Merle did not run away from him on these occasions. And all things considered—how long can you manage to keep running away from someone? Especially when said person has decided to become an instructor of Communist Party history, which would suggest that he might possess an immense amount of perseverance and the ability to disavow himself. In any case, Teedu certainly did. And so it went. They gradually became companions to some extent, although definitely more on the level of brother and sister. Merle would not hear of anything more. Teedu wrote old-fashioned letters to the girl (he had given up writing poetry) and promised to wait, even if it were for several decades.

Then came graduation. Teedu was in the Party and was entering a graduate program. Merle was sent to be a schoolteacher in the far provinces, where she had to give up everything that had become dear to her over the five years spent in Estonia's intellectual capital. Suddenly taking their place were small-town tittle-tattle and intrigue, hopelessly boring winter nights, and advances made by local men who thought highly of themselves, but were very limited. Teedu even went to go visit her in the provinces. He brought presents and vividly described the kind of interesting life being lived in the university town; what one or another of their classmates, who had likewise been fortunate enough to stay in Tartu, was up to. It was clear that he spoke about these things with a subconscious ulterior motive. And soon, Merle broke.

The next summer, they were walking around Tartu holding hands. Merle had a happy smile on her face, while Teedu was outright beaming. A "labor achievement," someone called it. The five years of siege had borne fruit. Teedu had stolen the beautiful, pert-breasted Merle away from the witty drunks and brilliant scholars.

## MATI IS KICKED OUT OF UNIVERSITY

Mati Tõusumägi was kicked out of university during his fourth year. He was still involved in underground periodicals, and had published three more issues. While almost all of them were at least partly literary and, if you squinted tightly, could be regarded as simply artistic self-expression by young people, the last one—*Entelecheia No. 4*—was unmistakably critical of the Soviet regime. It was comprised entirely of articles, which in and of themselves were already more dangerous than poems or stories. Mati's own essay titled "The Totalitarian State versus Humanist Society" came immediately after the foreword. This could no longer be tolerated, and state security decided that enough was enough. I myself saw the notice of exmatriculation on the bulletin board across from the dean's office. While for other students, the justification was usually a "lack of progress," in Mati's case, it was "due to behavior unbefitting of a university student."

Mati's expulsion was not reported on very widely in society, of course. But it was, to some extent, an event in university circles. Members of the Young Authors' Association even planned some kind of protest, and only Mati himself was able to quell the hotheads. Why should others be tossed out because of him? Mati didn't seem to feel especially sorry for himself, as he had gotten more or less everything out of university that it had to offer from the standpoint of his personal goals. The main thing for him was that he had figured out his way around history, in the most general definition of the term, had gotten his bearings in the system for cataloguing intellectual assets, knew the archives and repositories, and had studied German, English, and Latin diligently. No less significant was the fact that he had come to know the Soviet university and the people in it, and had gotten an idea of who was swift to go along with whatever the superiors say, and who would do so with a heavy heart—thus, he knew what was possible to expect of someone and what he could hope from them in the future. He no longer felt the need to take the state scientific communism exam or to write a thesis on the subject.

Word had it that the incident made it all the way to the university Party committee. On that note, I will mention one individual—a young brown-haired man with the looks of a movie actor and the height of a basketball player, whom everyone called Hasso. This was the graduate student Miller, who had finished his bachelor's degree *cum laude* as a sociologist two years earlier. This field was not officially taught at the university: Miller had studied in a "special program" led by a famous Leningrad professor, and was holding a sundry of university seminars on

the social sciences at the time. Miller was, in a certain sense, the
leader of the so-called "legal opposition." Belonging to this very
scattered and informal group were a few younger and more dynamic social sciences instructors, members of the Komsomol
committee, as well as creative scholars. For example, Miller got
along very well with the university theater group and was dating the conductor of the women's choir. Miller always looked
directly and inquisitively at passersby, with genuine curiosity,
like an authentic scholar of society or even the natural sciences, in order to see "what phenomenon that passerby really is for
me." Miller had come out in Mati's defense during the meeting of the university Party committee, albeit in an indirect way.
He claimed that Mati's writing contained nothing that in and
of itself might speak against the classics of Marxism and Lenin-
ism. It was demagogy, of course, for—as they answered right
then and there—"our enemies also cite Marx and Lenin." And
every person had to understand that the matter was not solely,
nor perhaps even primarily about *what* had been written, but
rather the fact that it had been published unofficially, outside
of the system, ignoring it, which *was* the greatest sin. Miller's
veiled defense speech earned him a Party punishment without
being put on its warning list, which was not a very harsh move,
but did give him a martyr's halo. Here and there, some people
even started to regard him and Mati as men of the same breed.
Mati scoffed angrily at this, saying that he had no use for the
Reds' patronage.

Rushing ahead somewhat, let it be said: Mati was later allowed to enroll in distance learning, and so he graduated university an entire five or six years later than Teedu.

# II

# THE MIDDLE AGES

## TO TALLINN! "CAVE" LIFE

Eventually, after a few years, about two-thirds of my university acquaintances had landed in the capital. Those who were originally from Tartu or elsewhere in South Estonia, or whose nature fit with the university-town lifestyle, remained behind. Things in Tartu were more peaceful; the wave crested lower. It would have been strange to use the word "monastery" in reference to a town that was home to a Soviet university, and where there were a number of factories (among them the so-called "mailbox" (named for its shape), which was classified because it made apparatuses for military purposes). Still, Tartu had the atmosphere of an intellectual monastery—something hermetic in the best sense of the word.

People naturally remained in Tartu for other reasons, also. For example, Teedu stayed there and started teaching Party history to students. He was made an offer to move to the capital and work in the Party apparatus—at a lower level to start with, of course, as an instructor. However, Teedu decided in favor of the university, because his one dream was to someday see the title of professor in front of his name. His pert-breasted Merle was now an assistant in the Communist Upbringing Laboratory and taking graduate exams, her advisor being the very same mild-mannered Party member who had been Mr. Kulu's classmate and recruited Teedu.

They married and were getting by quite well by all indications. They had two children—Tiina and Margus. A person will get accustomed to anything. Soon, Teedu was a docent. In addition to lectures, he gave presentations at the Marxism-Leninism night college and spoke about the history of the workers' movement not only in Narva, but in all of Estonia. He dutifully visited schools on occasion to tell students about the childhood of the revolutionary Repson, striving to show them the man's human side.

Yet what no one knew about, not even Merle, was Teedu's hobby. Specifically, he researched old house marks.[8] He did this furtively, as he believed it was not "in accordance with the mainstream." He would go to museums and archives (officially on completely different business) and then practice his hobby as if by accident. The marks were relatively old, from the time before the Livonian War. Estonia was already settled by then, and some people were quite well off. They passed the marks down from generation to generation. House marks were the locals' coats of arms, and were sometimes also called "outer" marks. They were not mere decorations on a family's personal property, but primarily carried information pertaining to the object's owner and his genealogical ties to others. Furthermore, they conveyed important knowledge to one's descendants in a simple language. Teedu was not interested so much in why a dish had three scores on it, but was simply amazed by them being there in the first place. It was as if the items bearing house marks possessed a soul, which derived from a home and ancestors being recognizable through them. A mark was a symbol of unity and cohabitation, continuation, the past, present, and future; it valued the core truths of family and life. Teedu could sense the proximity of ancient traditions when he was researching them. His soul sometimes craved it after days of speaking about Party congresses, constitutions, and the classics of Marxism/Leninism. All the while, he didn't at all feel like he was a heretic; not once did it cross his mind that some kind of a deeper dilemma might lie here, that one interest might contrast with the other, that the congresses might rule out house marks or vice versa. They simply belonged to different worlds, to different planes. One was eternal, the other temporal. He resolved to someday also start looking into his own ancestor's house marks. But that, he would do later—when he himself was already firmly "in place." Until then, he just needed to live. And so, he would visit tiny raion[9] museums once or twice over the course of the semester—supposedly in order to research the history of local "Red" figures, but in actuality to inspect artifacts for house marks and count the notches and scores, the dashes and dots, the circles, stars, and numbers.

I will leave Teedu aside for some time now, for although he also "expressed the era," he did this in a relatively unremarkable and stable way—he expressed it inexpressively, so to say.

Mati Tõusumägi was not threatened with military enlistment after being kicked out of university, because he had two small children. He continued living in Tartu and found work as an assistant surveyor. Then, however, his mother found a new partner. Or not exactly a partner—simply a friend from work, I guess. He was an ordinary Estonian man, with trousers and a briefcase, named Olev. He had been in the 8th Estonian Rifle Corps,[10] but this was of no importance to Mati, who was familiar with history and aware of how people had ended up going to war for one side or the other, and carried no animosity towards anyone merely because of it. For example, I cannot imagine Mati demanding that all members of the Communist party be lined up and shot—this despite the fact that he was undoubtedly a radical nationalist deep down. Mati was not narrow-minded in other senses, either. He honored his mother as the Bible taught and as is customary in a proper home, but did so foremost in a civilized way; he and his mother were not all that close. Seven years had passed since his father's death. His mother had dedicated herself solely to raising the children for a long time, anyway. (In addition to his twin sister, Mati had a brother eight years his junior named Vello, who studied medicine and became a distinguished neurosurgeon. Or was he a geologist? No matter—in any case, everyone in our social circle was surprised when they heard that Mati had a brother. And one might guess that Vello's acquaintances rarely associated him with the very famous individual of the same last name.) So, Mati understood his mother—she was already forty-eight by that time, which in some sense was a woman's "last chance" during the Soviet era. Thus, Mati was no "Oedipus" in connection with Olev. Yet apparently the man just did not sit especially well with him, because he seemed too quiet and reasonable. Mati could not wrap his mind around how his mother could switch from the type of firebrand that his father—old Arnold Tõusumägi—had been to such a soft-spoken man. Arnold had had the strength of a bear: he would sometimes lift up a chair with Mati's mother on it and balance it on one leg by some incredible trick. Olev did not do this with a chair, but rather sat on it, raising the knees of his pleated pants politely before doing so. He did not ramble drunkenly when drinking vodka; in fact, he did not *drink* vodka, only beer on rare occasion. Mati himself once told me: "I can't take melancholiacs!" But that would be it—he wouldn't speak any more on the subject. He did not want to hurt his mother, and justified leaving Tartu by saying that the institution had surveyed all of the land in those parts, and his work was now taking him elsewhere. Mati picked up his family and his things and moved to West Estonia—to Risti—with the help of a pastor he knew. He started commuting between Risti and Tallinn daily: one hour on the train there, one hour back. Really, no one was going hungry during Soviet times. Mati worked at the zoo; maybe he did snatch a piece of meat from the lions every now and then. Nevertheless, I believe that things must have been very tight in their home sometimes. Mati was a generous man and wanted to treat others to rounds at the pub. His wife worked at the local preschool, and became ever more religious. Mati rarely brought her out in public. To me, it seemed like Piibe was "somewhere else completely" back then. How they lived together or what they did—that, neither I nor our common acquaintances understood. A jolly, vivacious man in his prime and a being that was fairylike in body and ethereal in spirit— their union seemed like something out of a gothic horror story or an Edgar Allen Poe novella.

As I said, I myself worked in a profession that was not directly connected to cultural affairs. However, I kept in contact with the intelligentsia outside of work, mainly in the evenings. The Young Authors' Association was also active in Tallinn. A great deal of our time was spent at cafés. Soon enough, I started regularly patronizing a place that everyone called "The Cave." It was a semi-exclusive café or restaurant set in the city center and frequented by artists, writers, actors, composers, filmmakers, and other creative individuals. Entry was granted to those with a membership card. A member was allowed to bring guests, but no more than two. This was strictly controlled—the doorkeepers kept track of everyone entering with an inconspicuous but vigilant eye. Regulars were known by face, of course, but new members had to show their card at the door; only later would the doormen remember them as well, and they were treated like old-timers. The Cave was located in a cellar, down two flights of stairs. (It is strange that I've never counted how many steps there were, although I have walked up and down those stairs thousands of times—no exaggeration.) Getting underground was difficult, but once you were down there, the freedom you could enjoy was quite great. Life down there was different from life at ground level in several senses; you descended into it as if into another world. This was due primarily to the fact that The Cave was frequented by a crowd whose thoughts and aspirations were more or less identical to your own. It seemed like you were situated in a different space-time with them. I can honestly say that the Soviet system was relatively indiscernible down there. Which is not to say that nothing but treasonous talk went on from morning to night, nor that any grand schemes were planned down there. No, that was the thing—you lived in The Cave as if the Soviet system didn't exist. Above ground, everything associated with it stuck out much more painfully and incited defiance. You could be more natural below. For us, two and two was always four, to put it in Orwellian terms. The thing that the people here were all fighting against was immeasurably greater than the things that set them apart from one another, and the feeling of a unified front patched those gaps nicely, for the most part. Although differences would erupt from time to time and people would occasionally get into fierce debates and arguments, it was almost always in good nature, and those spats were forgotten as soon as the great common enemy surfaced in their consciousness once again.

Another reason for the relative friendliness and unity was the fact that even "above," at ground-level, where people earned money and lived their regular lives, there were not many opportunities—and I mean this in the very broadest sense. There was little to no chance of accomplishing anything artistic (not in any public forum—the clubs, the galleries, and other places), nor even anything in political and social life in the wider sense. Therefore, the barriers among the artistic crowd (in their professional capacity) were relatively low. Of course, people knew who was especially praiseworthy and who was somewhat less so;

there existed masters, journeymen, and apprentices; but nevertheless—something seemed to unite them all very strongly. And as there wasn't really anyone they had to go and see "above" (I mean, for example, visits to arts patrons, affairs to settle with their sales agents, and other such activities), they were down here in each other's "embrace" as often as not.

I call this "cave life" in retrospect. Many of my acquaintances and I ended up caught in its enchanting clutches. This seemed only natural, and a number of people lived that way for decades, visiting The Cave day in and day out—not necessarily getting drunk or tipsy, but being there for the company. That was where a person's circle of acquaintances could be found, his or her pseudo-family. And—oddly enough—cave life even seemed to come up above ground with you; it began to accompany you and shape your relationships and understandings. Cave life could be found dispersed everywhere, although, yes, The Cave was the center of this life.

As cave life was more enjoyable than normal or "real" life, it also seemed truer. You could say confidently that for certain very senior cave dwellers, their life "below" was genuine and primary, while that "above" was, on the contrary, a place they had to crawl out into from time to time. The latter was simply an unpleasant inevitability, and one needed to slip back into the protective and pleasant den as speedily as possible. In short—it was truly a magic cave.

And only when everything above changed one day did the cave dwellers stand in the bright sunlight, side-by-side with real-life, squinting their eyes. All sorts of unheard-of things suddenly became clear then. For example—that a person whose jovial company you have shared at the same table for ten years, and with whom you have undergone a common experience, has opinions about many things that are completely different from yours; that the person has entirely different convictions, a different sense of honor, a different life-strategy. "It's not possible," the people then said to themselves. "I *know* that person!" But it turned out that it was possible, and even very much so. Some cave dwellers would have liked to slip back into their protective den at that moment, but—alas!—the cave was no more.

In summary, I was lucky to have ended up with such company, because life was spiritually quite tolerable that way. And as for the material side of life—that is *very* relative indeed. It is interesting how we agree now (and also agreed then) that the joy one person gets from a morning walk to the park, for example, can exceed the joy of another, who faces an ocean cruise with ennui. We also acknowledge that the joy we received from one piece of candy during childhood might have been greater than what we feel now when devouring an entire boxful. But to say that, for example, the Soviet-era joy from a piece of good sausage was greater than what we feel now when piling our cart full of the very best the supermarket has to offer—there is almost no good way to speak about that. Although I am not one for absolute relativity, either. Such discussions sometimes make the mistake of considering everything to be relative, of boiling things down to that alone. Because joy is also absolute. A ton of joy is still greater than a kilogram of joy, no matter what angle you look at it, no matter in what terms, if there are terms at all. The person who dreaded the ocean cruise at the outset overcomes his or her aversion in a single evening, starts dancing the tango and drinking champagne, watches a film on TV based on Somerset Maugham's travel stories before dozing off, and may be extremely happy from the second day onward. But after half an hour, a cheerful morning-park walker gets home, where he is awaited by a meager breakfast, bills brought by the mailman or arriving by e-mail—bills the person really doesn't have the money to pay—disobedient children, and a withered, whining wife, who isn't fit for showing anywhere. I mention this in passing, as I plan to pause on life's material side in my chronicle only when it is absolutely necessary.

The spiritual side of life is also relative, of course, and one will have very bizarre encounters there as well. As confirmation, I will briefly tell what Mati said about his aunt. He had yet another aunt in addition to the one he and his parents went to help in the country each fall. But they did not readily speak about the other aunt at home—she was something like the black sheep of the family, for political reasons, naturally. That aunt had once slept with a black man while studying at the Communist

Party's school in Minsk. It gave her a thrill that could never be repeated and had been one of the high points of her life. The man had been a genuine African—the son of a tribal chief and later agricultural minister of a country friendly to the Soviet sphere, and was studying tractor sciences in Belarus. After that experience, the aunt apparently never had an orgasm (she referred to it as her "organum," trying to make it sound more wholesome) with another man again. She talked about it constantly and with everyone, with acquaintances and coworkers. At first, she did so in a regretful tone, afterward with a barb in her voice, but following her fifty-fifth birthday, she spoke triumphantly about how she had not had an "organum" in over thirty years.

There was a political subtext to her story. The aunt realized, of course, that sleeping with a black man may have been possible under some other regime. Buying a plane ticket to the Black Continent would have been enough. But back then, when she was at her sexual peak, this wasn't possible for a Soviet citizen. Thus, it seemed like she would have never been able to sleep with a black man if it hadn't been for the Party school. For it was there in Minsk, on a cot in the Friendship of the Peoples Dormitory, that the deed was done. It was chance; a coincidence, to be precise—and still, it was reality. This was the reason why the aunt was sympathetic towards the former Soviet Union, or at least did not disavow it entirely. She put the occupation, deportations, the Gulag, and Stalin's other crimes on one pan of the balance; on the other, she put the black man's untiring member. It was that simple. Even now, she had an album of grayish-black Minsk panoramas on a shelf. She was aware that the dictator Lukashenko reigns there currently. By the way— she did not disavow Lukashenko entirely, either.

Mati told me this with a smile on his lips, without anger. He also spoke about his great-uncle, who had indeed been deported, but who had also been awarded a certificate of honor by the Presidium of the Supreme Soviet of the ESSR in the early sixties. His great-uncle told it like this:

"I read about it in the raion newspaper. I went and asked the *partorg* whether it was a misprint. The *partorg* called the raion.

The people there said that you don't joke about such things. When I started to leave the room, the *partorg* opened the door for me. He was a shithead otherwise. Maina, our bookkeeper, spent the night at my place again after that; she'd been with Ahto, our veterinarian, before that—he'd studied at the Estonian Agricultural Academy. Then I was given notice to travel to Tallinn to accept the certificate. I asked the school director, Helene Merivälja, how I should behave. I didn't even know what to *wear*. But it wasn't up on Toompea as I'd thought, but rather in Kadriorg. There were a whole lot of people there. Chairman Müürisepp was a fat guy. He looked at everything over the top of his glasses like the pastor's assistant in that film, *Spring* ... Yeah, and then they served cake."

Mati had many stories, and he enjoyed telling them. Of course he would repeat one or another sometimes, but that was no problem—they were also nice when repeated.

### KLAUS

I started associating with many Tallinnites then in addition to old Tartu-acquaintances who had relocated to the capital. Some were completely new to me, while others I had periodically brushed shoulders with at official student functions, literary seminars, creative youth camps, or meetings of young authors' associations—as was the case with Klaus, for example.

There is an old picture in my memory, probably from the very beginning, from the *arche*. We were sitting in The Cave—where else. We had vanished back underground for another night, away from the Soviet regime. The standard carousing was in progress—a thick smoky haze, the loud buzz of conversation, squeals, laughter. Old art-rams were whirling art-nymphs around in oblivious dancing across the narrow strip of floor between the tables, veins bulging at their temples. I was always amazed at how large a crowd could fit into The Cave. And not just in the private booths, where two layers of seated people could be squeezed in, so that some of them were almost sitting on others' laps. But room could also be found for dancing—for dozens of couples, and that cannot be done in two layers, of course, although ... it wasn't unusual for people to jump onto each other's shoulders and trot around as if playing some kind of peculiar polo at around three o'clock in the morning. Everything happened there. And darting nimbly through that wisecracking, quipping, giggling, guffawing, roaring, energetically gesticulating,   patting-each-other-on-the-shoulders-and-knees, vodka-slurping, and cavorting crowd were servers who called out orders over the kitchen door and to the bar, sounding like the signals given by crane operators or aerialists. And I cannot recall any of them ever spilling anything onto my lap or that of another customer. A drop or two might splash off of the table (which resembled an overturned harrow made of empty bottles) and onto your clothes from time to time, and the holes burned into your pants and jacket by cigarette embers gave mending work to fashion designers, of course, but this would happen at the fault of the revelers themselves.

We were sitting—Mati, Manglus, Sõrgats, Maulwurf, Pepe, Kirill, Alja, and Maša were definitely there, among others—and discussing the latest opening-night at the Drama Theatre. Gyrating past our table at that moment was the same chatty young spark whom I remembered from a Tartu orgy, and who had wanted to climb up onto the roof of the Writers' House. He arched his body forward while dancing, his hips remaining artistically stiff, and pumped his elbows back and forth. He was saying something into the ear of his partner—a nymph with long red hair and milky-white skin—at the same time. It must have been something witty, because the nymph kept tossing her head back and laughing gaily, like in an operetta. It's possible that Klaus was reciting one of his dirty poems or variety-show sketches to her, but maybe he was just trying to seduce her. Klaus was very witty, so much so that you really couldn't even hold a conversation with him sometimes. He was like a red-hot pan, from which fat will spray into your face at even the slightest touch. It could be really painful. Occasionally, you simply had to listen to Klaus, not attempt to have a dialogue with him.

Klaus's father was the first independence-era intellectual that the Soviets "tugged along" during the June coup—meaning they took advantage of his authority in order to give the puppet government weight in the eyes of the people. He was even lifted to the status of Academician before being declared an enemy of the people after some time. His primary accomplishment had been the compilation of a large dictionary, which philologists and other cultural figures had long referred to by his name ("I'll check in Puiatu," "What does Puiatu say about it?"). Klaus's mother was a well-known poetess who wrote womanly and nostalgic verses, and whom experts would sometimes call "little Anna Haava."

Klaus's parents had high hopes for their only son, and were rumored to be distressed when he dropped out of secondary school and started taking night classes. Back then, night school was generally regarded as a sign of degeneration: the ones who studied there either couldn't make it in day school, had been in jail, or were losers otherwise. But Klaus simply didn't like regular school — he frequently played hooky, escaping down to a breakwater by the sea for hours at a time. He would sit there on the rocks and daydream, sending the ships sailing off towards the horizon with his gaze. One can guess he would have liked to sail along with them. They were Russian warships, for the most part, but *he* did not know that. He also made "suspicious" acquaintances among the common folk, and even among social outcasts. He loved to wander around the market, where he would socialize with people from the countryside and readily converse with the flower sellers and street cleaners at the end of Viru Street.

It was said that "Little Anna Haava" practically disowned Klaus for not living up to the family name, but this was hard to believe, because his mother had to have recognized that her son was very gifted at an early age and would be able to achieve much in the future. Klaus drew caricatures or comics that were not very graphically advanced, but which always had a sharp point (usually with an unexpected twist). He was decently talented as an actor and was able to do impersonations. Even Klaus's instructors were unable to hold back their laughter when he did an imitation of one or other member of the collective (including the director!) during the 9th-grade school play. He likewise possessed an exceptional rhyming ability, and was able to talk like he was reciting poetry at will. He began writing verse already in grade school, some of which was printed in samizdat periodicals (which had nothing to do with the official school publications). A couple of them were also published in the same issue of *Entelecheia* that included Teedu Tärn's lovey-dovies, retyped onto corn-based paper on an "Optima" typewriter by Mati's sister Anu in the heat of summer. No trouble befell Klaus because of his poems. This was due to a number of reasons: firstly, because he had already left day school by that time; secondly, because his texts were so innocent on the surface that they deceived the watchful security organs; and thirdly, because that publication wasn't the most seditious one around. He later published several books' worth of poems and prose, and that was through the state publishing company. Many of his texts were legendary in certain social circles, becoming passwords for acceptance.

After graduating from night school, Klaus lived as a vagabond or a hippy; I really don't know what he lived off of — perhaps he still visited home to eat sometimes. He then met a few more free souls like him, who were also writers. The pieces they wrote — doggerels and feuilleton material — were published every now and then in the satire corner on the back page of *Hammer and Sickle*, or in the humor magazine *Thunder*. The sharpest things were not let through. There wasn't enough being produced to be published as independent works. The wave of life was cresting lazily. They lounged around at The Sparrow Café in summer, and moved into Café Moscow for the cold season. They drank a good deal of dry wine and smoked profusely, cursed the censors and read their unpublished works to each other, or simply shot the breeze and watched the days turn into nights. There were also a few girls in their crowd. They made plans, most of which were unrealistic. Then the young guys came up with the idea of forming a band (or a "combo," as people said back then) and started performing. There were several practical reasons for this. Firstly, they wanted to gain wider recognition for their creative works. Secondly, they had all run away from home and none of them held a steady job, so they needed to make a living somehow. The combo was named The Hearts. They read their texts and sang. One of the men (Olavi) would strum a banjo, another (Jürka) would squeeze an accordion.

Neither of them were very talented musicians, but it sufficed for accompanying their funny ditties. They made their debut at the Art Institute's student carnival, and their popularity was greater than expected. This was followed by the Youth Summer Days on Lake Võrtsjärv in Trepimäe, as well as the closing concert for the reunion of the university construction *malev*[11] on Lake Kaagjärv. Their myth spread quickly. They took part in a truly rowdy reception at the Tartu University Student Days that same fall. In December, they took the stage (along with several other groups) at a "Literary Wednesday" evening held for talented youth at the Writers' House in Tallinn, which was also broadcast on state television at the time. At first their primary audience were students and intellectuals, but gradually they broadened their target group and started performing all across Estonia.

Their repertoire was on the edge in terms of permissibility. They would blurt out direct criticism of a few less-sensitive issues — such as bureaucracy and everyday nuisances (which were also subject to official criticism, such as in the pan-Soviet newsreel *Fuse*) — while the messages of sketches they did on other topics would reach the audience in a roundabout way, through allegory. When they talked about the ice breaking up, for example, everyone understood what was meant. When they mentioned a solar eclipse that just would not seem to pass, and sang that astronomers were being hung for it, everyone got what was being referenced. Compared to what was allowed in official print, it was a whole different kettle of fish. I don't know if they had to go and get their set approved somewhere; they must have, but Klaus never mentioned it. It certainly wasn't done at the censor's headquarters before every single performance, which would have been practically impossible. It's likely that a post-factum examination was occasionally undergone. When they went to some kolkhoz club or a small village, it wasn't unusual for the local Party ideology official to call them into his office before the show and declare: "Boys, you do understand I don't want any trouble for you or for myself. Sing and do what you're going to do, but don't actually cross the line!" Every now and then, the boys would show him their texts for reassurance. But I suppose they'd still read and sing whatever they thought fit that evening. They were sometimes called back to the office afterward and lectured on morals. And, innocent-faced, they told the official that they had decided to "try out" one or another new song on the audience. *Precisely*— they had not read or sung it for real, but were just "trying it out." What can you do with the likes of them!

On a few occasions they had more serious clashes with the authorities, and once were even slapped with a six-month performance ban. Trouble arose whenever some vigilant individual was present in the auditorium, who felt it was his or her duty to report that the artists "performed in a way contrary to the Soviet regime." This happened only rarely, however. Even local Party members generally observed their performances with sympathy and laughed along— that's a fact, I've seen it with my own eyes. No one's brow was wrinkled. There wasn't the faintest danger of the boys being stuck in jail.

The Hearts became legendary very quickly and remained top celebrities for a long time. People who were young adults or middle-aged back then, and even some who were only school-children, certainly remember them today. The Hearts received more invitations to perform than they were able to accept, because although they had toured around Estonia for three or four years, they were wanted back almost everywhere. By the way— Klaus once said that he had played over three hundred shows in one year.

They were invited by all kinds of venues; for example, the café-clubs that were all the rage at that time. Such establishments often operated in small towns, economic centers, and more peripheral places in general, which were closer for the surrounding folk to go than to a concert or theater in the city. The audience would usually congregate there on a Wednesday or Friday evening, a little better dressed-up than usual. They ate and drank, but wouldn't get hammered. They danced after the show, too. But the main attraction was always the invited guest— a writer, actor, foreign commentator, scientist, or otherwise well-known figure. The Hearts performed in many such clubs.

Offers came from elsewhere as well. Intellectual organizations invited them to their meetings, as did ordinary folk to their weddings, anniversaries, and other significant celebrations. Both city and country folk invited them. It's interesting that a barrier never formed between The Hearts and their audience. An educated crowd would enjoy the artistic/literary nuances of their performances, of course, while simpler people received them more directly, being moved by the melodies, and laughing to the point of tears. The guys performed their comical songs, recited jokes, and for variation would take questions from the audience and just converse on everyday topics. People enjoyed talking with The Hearts because they spoke clearly and coherently, not complicatedly. And even if they didn't say anything new, people still got confirmation that there were *others* who thought just the same way they did.

Though some audiences understood them on their own terms on occasion, everyone got the main message for the most part. And even when some especially narrow-minded Mart or Mikk took almost nothing from it, then they would at least grasp that these were Estonian men who spoke Estonian and sang in Estonian. And although they were personally unable to think, speak, or sing that way, then look at that—there's *someone* who does. This meant that the Estonian race had not gone extinct, its intellectual leaders were alive, and therefore, maybe they themselves and their entire nation might someday have the hopes of living in a spirit of freedom once again. They saw that honest Estonian thought really *hadn't* been forced down into the dirt, but instead was flapping its wings before them, and consequently, they themselves could someday become familiar with the idea of freedom.

I believe they certainly might have felt something like that; and after all, a simple person only requires so much to be happy when there are so many depressing things in life, and when he or she is being squeezed from all sides, intellectually restricted. In any case, when people were on their way home after a performance by The Hearts, they spoke more freely about Estonia's situation than they normally would. This was true even with the *partorgs*, as well as others who had completely driven the subject out of their consciousness. For half an hour, they sat up straight, their pride restored, their spirits light.

Although Klaus was the only member of the trio who did not play an instrument, he was the most famous of the three—or, at least, many of the students who came to their performances did so mostly to hear him. Klaus was only a tad behind the others in his years, but he looked considerably younger than his age. His poet's aura added to this effect, and he certainly had the most artistic nature, suggesting something akin to a child genius. Let it be said that Klaus was a refined man—both in terms of clothing and manners. He wore a bow tie and an unusual half-length blackish-grey felt jacket even on ordinary days. He let his flaxen hair grow down almost to shoulder-length and pressed a dark, wide-brimmed cap down upon it. Altogether, it somehow combined a southwest Estonian Mulgi folk costume with the clothing of a nineteenth-century European dandy. *That* is the sort of appearance he had designed for himself! Klaus had a habit of smacking his lips flamboyantly before answering a question. His fingers were exceptionally slender, like those of a gentleman, while his manners were salon-like, his movements bearing the unmistakable stamp of culture. He weighed no more than fifty kilos, although he was one meter and seventy centimeters tall. He ate very little, at one time surviving off of only wine and cookie crumbs (he loved butter cookies, the little ones that melt in your mouth, saying it was a habit inherited from his mother).

Considering these traits, how could a man like him become close with the village folk as well? It's possible that his overall image or attitude reflected something from the Estonian era, meaning the days of the independent Republic of Estonia between the two world wars, which was increasingly seen by people as a golden age. But at the same time, how did people know anything about that era? Many Estonians had fled to the West or died in Siberia, and those who remained were now old and approaching death. In cities and towns, there weren't many buildings or physical objects that reminded people of that time. The majority of middle-aged individuals had only seen that time in some newsreel clip or on an old postcard. So how could they tell that *Klaus's* nature was "reminiscent of the Estonian era"?

Wasn't that "Estonian era" mythical to begin with? Namely, I am not sure how many of those salons with their dandies and club members actually existed in Estonia between the two wars. Perhaps it is a legend similar to the farms of Mulgimaa,[12] where frocked men were said to have smoked "Havanas" during the thirties (I have heard such tales told). But that might mean that there's no real difference between myth and reality, because otherwise it wouldn't have been possible for such a genteel person to be able to bring a highly non-genteel crowd to ecstasy by reading them such refined texts. People knew many of Klaus's doggerels by heart. I might also mention that Klaus's voice was loud and expressive, as piercing as a foghorn.

As The Hearts were so famous, "getting them to yourself" became a question of prestige. Venues contended for them. This sometimes amused The Hearts themselves, but it mostly caused them discomfort and even embarrassment, because it was hard for them to turn people down. The richer kolkhozes would reserve them at the beginning of the year already—for harvest festivals, St. John's Day celebrations, as well as for Fishermen's Day. A hefty amount of vodka was drunk on such occasions, of course, and they wouldn't perform very complicated repertoire because the crowd wouldn't take anything from it.

Sometimes they were driven to the concert by whomever invited them, sometimes they drove in Jürka's car.

"It's strange that we didn't become alcoholics," Jürka recently said to me. "Our tab was *always* covered, and our tables would be littered with bottles. We were even given a bottle for the road on occasion."

"But you had to be at the wheel, didn't you?" I asked, astonished.

"Sure did, but we'd be able to keep drinking when we got back to the city. All of the doormen knew us, and as soon as we got ourselves in line for some bar, they'd beckon us with their finger right away and say, 'You guys, there—right this way, please!' And it's not as if we were short on cash. Most of the time, they'd hand us money in an envelope after a show. And it was quite a nice little amount for that time."

Their personal age of "goldenness" began in the second half of the seventies and lasted until the beginning of the nineties—thus, almost fifteen years total.

I first realized that Klaus was truly famous when we went with a group of people to a small island off the coast. We had two side-car motorcycles for getting around, the second of these being Mati's. While driving to the island's only store, we passed the college's local *malev* group lounging on the roadside after having lunch. Klaus barely stuck out of the sidecar, but was recognized regardless. When we exited the store with our purchases and were about to start driving, two young men wearing *malev* uniforms approached us and asked politely whether we might come and visit their group that evening, because there was apparently going to be an initiation ceremony. Specifically, they would be greatly honored if Klaus would conduct it. (Klaus himself, by the way, had never attended an institution of higher education.) And so we went. The students had come up with an impromptu program that centered around Klaus (as well as us, the rest of the group, for appearances), whom they parodied in a friendly way.

It's strange to think that this sort of "celebrity following" took place even before there was any kind of star culture or media carousel; before gossip journalism and exhibitionist television programs. Klaus hadn't even appeared on TV yet (apart from that one event at the Writers' House) and still, just flashing by in the sidecar of a motorcycle was enough for him to be recognized (to tell the truth, it did happen at a curve where we had to slow down). In short, it was all very moving: the young people really wanted to interact with an intellectual.

Wait a second—did that really happen on an island? The more I think about it, the more I feel that it was actually in South Estonia. Yes—because Mati, who had graduated university by distance learning, had quit his job at the zoo by then and gone to work at a regional museum in Setomaa.[13] That's whom we probably went to go visit that time. The store was the not-yet-famous Ruusamäe shop. Although it must have happened several years later, then, because Mati was writing his book at the time. That was exactly why he wanted to go be a museum-rat in Setomaa—so he could find peace away from the bohemian lifestyle and the clamor of the capital. And his novel came out in 1985. Three years before that, Klaus had already long been a national celebrity, so him being recognized should not have surprised us especially. But at the same time, where was Mati's new wife, then, if it really happened in Setomaa? His wife definitely *was* around by that time, although she wasn't his actual wife yet, but rather his girlfriend. I can't seem to remember his wife being there. Maybe it did happen earlier, then.

I'll get back to Klaus at some point.

Before that, I still have to introduce many individuals who also "expressed the era" in one manner or another (I have some kind of an *idée fixe* with that expression—expressed, didn't express, expressed all the same, etc.).


## THE ENDLESS ROUND DANCE

All of the people in that new world where I found myself appeared to know one another, and social life was bustling. Several young poets and artists lived in cellars or attics, which they had talked housing administrations into giving them, and for which they paid only symbolic rents. These spaces were grandly called "ateliers" and were officially designated for working alone—no one was permitted to live or sleep there. No one checked up on this, however, and things with no direct connection to artistic creation would often take place at the ateliers. The years went quickly by, and suddenly the young poets and artists *weren't* so very young anymore, but had become acclaimed figures. Some of them moved into nicer ateliers. Still, social life remained basically the same.

It might have been 1979 . . .

I don't know how many days the party had already been underway by the time I arrived at the atelier of the monumentalist Elgar Tuudleja. One might guess that it was only the second or third day at the very most, because the attendees' trains of thought were still chugging along briskly, and there was no lack of conversation matter; nor was anyone quite cockeyed, either.

Yet this might not have meant anything in and of itself, and the party could have begun much earlier, too. Those long parties (or, not really "party"—that's just a nice, innocent word made up to refer to debauched benders!) had one distinctive feature. Although there was nothing unusual or shameful about taking part in them (one could also encounter men in ties and ladies in sharp-cut dresses there), it was rare for any one person to take part in a long party from beginning to end. No—the composition was in a state of constant fluctuation; the party or drinking binge was a continuous project (someone even compared it to the journey of the Olympic torch). People stopped by, some came, some went, someone took a break meanwhile so as to carry on at full force afterward. Someone did a little week's worth of work in the meantime, and then joined in again. Thus, it could easily be the case that when a party ended, no one who had been there at the start was present. Even the host could disappear for a while—in order to travel to an international festival, for example (just as the monumentalist Tuudleja had done then; no one there when I arrived had seen him), handing the keys and authority over to their partner or someone else they trusted for the duration. Ending the party before its natural extinguishment or throwing the guests out was, for the most part, out of the question, because it would have created a bad vibe. A party *was* more important than some international festival.

Although the crowd would fluctuate, the atmosphere of a party would remain exceptionally coherent. In addition to the fact that a large number of those present knew each other from dozens of similar kinds of gatherings, everyone was also kept up to speed with what had happened over the course of the previous days: what and how much had been drunk, which topics had been discussed, and what conclusions had been drawn. Those who had been there for longer summed up the wittiest jokes and the gayest moments for the new arrivals, who did so for the next ones in turn, until everyone started to feel as if they had personally been present for the birth of those jokes and happenings.

How did one end up at these gatherings? There was no Internet and no cell phones, not to mention Facebook or Twitter; many even had to make calls from a telephone booth. Still (in town, by way of The Cave), people mostly knew where the biggest party was going on at the moment, and whoever was in the given mood for it simply *went* there. No one asked incredulously, "How did *you* know about this?" or "What are *you* doing here?" In most cases, a newcomer would arrive carrying a bottle inside his or her jacket to share, but if someone needed a little hair of the dog and didn't have enough money for it, then they weren't turned away, of course. They *were* all Estonian men and women alike; all of them were fighting the occupation. A party resembled a living organism, like an anthill or a beehive. At the same time, it was like traditional bread making, where old leaven was taken for baking a new batch, and thus the bread never ran out. Or else it was like a fire that was perpetually kept going. Sometimes, however, the comparison was more readily made with a forest- or bog-fire, which could take ages to extinguish.

About a dozen people had settled into the expansive skylit space—it had been built specifically into an atelier, since the occupant was a monumentalist who would not have fit into an ordinary cellar or attic. The guests sat on sofas and armchairs made of old, creaking leather; others made do with stools. A young flaxen-haired man wearing a suit had sat or slipped down onto the floor with one arm extended over an armrest, as if he wanted to heave himself up using it as support, and would mumble something to himself from time to time, his eyes closed. A frizzy-haired young woman wearing gigantic earrings was tapping with stoic determination on a cassette player that apparently did not want to play. The rest were conversing lazily. It felt just like a sort of work in progress, in its morning stage; not everyone knew one another yet, but they didn't let that stop them from spending time together amiably because of it. In addition to Mati, I knew Arvi and Tobi, who were writers; the critic Endel; the graphic designer Toomas; and also, marginally, the singer Klarion—a young, patriotic, barrel-chested man. Sitting in the corner was Poindexter, a puppet actor and master of the absurd. It was my first time seeing the three remaining men. The women there included Alja, Maša, Lipsik, and Anks.

Alja's name was actually Alvi and Maša's Mare, but at the given time, it was socially fashionable to call one another by the Russian equivalents of their proper names. I wasn't entirely clear on this fashion's backstory. I figured it out intuitively: a Russian was not an agreeable phenomenon in the Soviet context, of course—more like an opponent or an enemy—so this renaming was a way to turn something on its head. It's also possible that it had something to do with repellant magic: the opponent was turned into an everyday thing, domesticated, even made banal, so that there was no need to fear it. Perhaps that is how some demonstrated their fearlessness, their audacity to play with fire. Perhaps they did it to imply that they were such tough nationalists and had achieved such a high level of sanctity that they could allow themselves to play around with Russification. But there were others who were simply liberals who saw the use of Slavic names as a colorful democratic splotch that contrasted with a worldview that tended to be black-and-white. They were emphasizing that they were above narrow-mindedness and ignorance. One way or another, this kind of ostentatiousness had to show the social group's high standard.

In connection to this, I recall that some of the high-ranking local members of the Communist Party had an opposite custom—they Westernized the names of the intelligentsia. (This is a little-known fact, as you could count such functionaries on one hand; party leaders interacted very rarely with the intellectuals, overall.) The phenomenon seems that much stranger because several top-level, ethnically Estonian Party leaders addressed one another Slavically by their first name and patronymic, which could solely be explained by an enormous lust for adulation (a number of comrades wanted to rush ahead of the times with Russification). Even so, Mati himself once said that a member of the Central Committee called him "Matthew" (!), and even with the correct pronunciation. Andres was called André, Mihkel was Michel, and so forth. I, Juku, who was sometimes Ivan, Vanja, or even Ivanushka to friends, was once called John (with bizarre consistency) by a party member, but was Jacques to his deputy. What was behind these Party men's strange habit? I suppose some were doing it ironically, demonstrating their superiority, and even mocking us. Some, however, apparently thought that they would give an impression of being less like a traditional geezer by doing so, and thus wanted to show themselves in a better light.

Alja was an attractive young lady by general opinion: slim and coolly graceful. She had a round face and the shape of her eyes resembled those of a Kazakh or a Tatar. The unusually wide space between her eyes gave her a somewhat lion-like appearance (some teasingly called her the "Tatar lioness"). She carried her long, slender arms slightly forward from her body, her palms facing outward, as if she were about to take something into her arms. Alja was the most famous young poetess of her generation. The lovers that she chose for herself were those that were chosen by no one else. By doing so, she implied that she was free and above everything, and that she did not care about anyone's opinion. She had a habit of speaking in a whisper—whoever wanted to hear her had to prick up their ears. And if the person didn't listen, she couldn't have cared less. Her friend Maša (aka Mare) was not a creative type per se, but simply an intellectual snob—a hetaera who worked at a library. She was loyal to Alja to the very end and always fought on her side, no matter what the issue. Whereas Alja would whisper, Maša had the habit of stretching words out derisively. Her most dreaded insult was, "You're *so* monochromatic . . ." The last word was pronounced "mo-no-chro-maaatic." She would say this to almost everyone at one time or another. There was no sin more dreadful than shallowness in Maša's eyes. Maša, meaning Mare, was not a beauty, and was even a little on the ugly side, but had a warm, agreeable, and sexy effect on people. She would reap suitors for herself from Alja's wake—those pleasant, talented men, who actually wanted to hit on the latter, but were left empty-handed since they weren't puny enough. They hoped to get closer to Maša's girlfriend through her. And so, Maša had her advantages. Toomas, who had a degree in biology (he was a self-taught graphic designer), once said that Alja and Maša's relationship was symbiotic like that of a crocodile and the tiny bird that cleans its teeth. We just couldn't understand which was which.

I remember how Doctor Muld—a psychiatrist who consorted with the artist community and was a very cynical gentleman—once claimed that Alja was actually "the queen of the losers," and gave a cold-blooded reasoning for the statement: he alleged that Alja feared having a relationship with a normal, talented man, because she wanted to be dominant and was apprehensive of the man using her in his own creative works — of putting her intimate details on display. Upon hearing this, Alja's face turned red, she spluttered, and disappeared from the room so quickly that everyone was left astonished. Maša went after her, but not before shooting a "God, how *mo-no-chro-maaatic* you are . . ." into Doctor Muld's face with exceptional scorn. Everything was soon forgotten, though, because Alja and Maša were permanent members of our group, whereas the psychiatrist was a chance visitor. And Maša lived with him for an entire year (a very long time) after that.

I had arrived at around one in the afternoon, when everyone had mended their hangovers with "Saku" lagers. Two empty green plastic crates lay in the corner, and the coffee table was stacked with two half-finished and five or six unopened bottles of beer. The partiers were gradually shifting towards the stronger stuff. On a plate next to a large bottle of "Long Play" (aka Moskva Vodka) were slices of pickles, sausage, cheese, and bread. There was also a bottle of sweet wine, but probably more for appearances — no one appeared to be sampling it.

I sat down on a stool and started listening.

"Oh, boys; oh, boys — if you only knew," Arvi moaned, grinding his teeth. "If you only knew."

When Arvi started grinding his teeth, it usually signaled a dark depression that was soon to descend. His friends were accustomed to it. As if he wanted to console Arvi, Endel said:

"You're a great guy, Arvi. You're a great guy too." The second was meant for Toomas, who was sitting next to him. "We're all great guys, actually."

Silence followed. Everyone was touched; no one was planning to joke about what had been said.

"I'd like to *do*," Toomas said after a while.

"Yeah, I'd like to *do*, too," Endel agreed, and the others nodded.

"But we can't, we're not allowed to," Arvi said, gripping his head in his hands.

"Those assholes!" Tobi hissed, pressing the words through his teeth.

The door slammed. Sass, who had apparently gone to get vodka, entered the room, smiling victoriously and swinging paper bags in both of his hands. "Guess what, guess what . . ." Seeing that everyone had the air of an undertaker, he was taken aback and asked, "Guys, what's wrong?"

"Ah, it's nothing," Toomas said with a dismissive wave. "We'd like to *do*, but they don't let us."

"It's hard, it's hard," Arvi sighed.

"W-w-well," Sass started up more cheerfully again, "it certainly *shouldn't* be for you. *You're* our guy in . . . the corporation." We called the Party "the corporation" among ourselves. It was a dose of friendly irony—Sass himself emitted a "heh heh," winked at the others, and patted Arvi on the shoulder. "Just teasing you . . ."

"Cut it out," Ms. Elfriede Liidel said, nudging him. Liidel, whom everyone called Lipsik, was Elgar Tuudleja's long-term partner and comrade in arms. The ageless and respected Lipsik was an interior designer, and was also known to be a serious reveler. "Do you think that things aren't hard for Party members? It's *very* hard for an Estonian man to be in the Party." Lipsik had hair dyed a reddish brown, fat cheeks, and soft, small hands like dinner rolls.

Arvi's expression was that of a great martyr. "Oh, boys, if you only knew," he repeated.

Arvi was born in Siberia. His parents were wealthy industrialists during the first period of independence. Occasionally, when Arvi was nicely boozed up, he would scoop up some companions and go to a factory, located just outside of the city center, where the machinery had been acquired by his grandfather from Germany before World War I. The factory director did not obstruct them, just urged him to be as silent as possible when passing through the workshops. "Men, you do understand—this is no joke," said Ülo, who was an upstanding Estonian man and a great admirer of the arts. Arvi would sometimes heed this, but would sometimes nudge others during their walk, cough, and announce at an emphatic volume: "You see how well my grandfather's machines are working!" The aproned woman who was busy at one of these "machines" naturally did not understand, only smiling deferentially, since a number of faces in the group were of national renown. They usually stopped by Ülo's office afterward. Ülo wanted to discuss matters of worldview, while the others couldn't especially be bothered. Ülo always had fine liquors in his cupboard—these were put to use, of course, and the men's expressions became kinder. At the end, Arvi would always say: "Well, fine—you can keep on using my grandfather's machines for a little while longer, as long as you do it for the good of the Estonian people. You've got my verbal consent as their legal inheritor." This took place during the second half of the seventies, and sounded like a very bold statement.

Another thing I will add about Arvi is that he studied astrophysics in Moscow during the 1960s, and remained there for his postgraduate degree. That's precisely why he joined the Party back then. However, the events in Prague shook him awake. At around the same time, he discovered in himself a penchant for writing. Back then his Party membership felt like a loathsome burden, although he did not say so explicitly. He worked on the Cinema Committee in a position of high responsibility, which he wouldn't have gotten under any condition if he hadn't belonged to the Party.

Time spun calmly onward. People raised their glasses, but in moderation, with a sense of prospect, and everyone was in a fantastic mood. Bit by bit, I began to realize that of the three figures I didn't know, one was a freedom fighter, the second a foreign Estonian, and the third a nationally-minded communist. Although I didn't know how the three of them had ended up at the atelier that day, their presence at Tuudleja's was nothing odd in and of itself. They didn't seem to be acquaintances—or at least the nationalist didn't appear to know the other two. However, one got the impression that he believed he had happened upon the headquarters of the resistance movement, because he wore a stiffly reverent expression, listened to everyone with the utmost attention, and strove to behave in an exemplary manner. The freedom fighter had apparently come with Mati—he looked familiar to me from Café Werner in Tartu. The foreign

Estonian turned out to be Arvi's guest—a documentary film-maker from an American TV channel who was doing a film on the Baltic States. Artists and freedom fighters generally felt a mutual sympathy, and many of them socialized with one another at the time—but not all of them. In retrospect, it seems like "freedom fighter" meant something similar to "artist" or "intellectual" back then; in any case, there was a shared component. All endeavored to achieve freedom in their own way: whether a social and national freedom or an intellectual one. The creative crowd also thought highly of foreign Estonians and foreigners in general, because they were in communion with freedom—it was as if they had mastered freedom and now represented it. As a result, foreigners and foreign Estonians were always admitted into artists' dens and to their gatherings. I suspect that people from abroad might have gone through a culture shock from that. The majority of them were entrepreneurs, businessmen, or otherwise busy, who hadn't especially come into contact with artists or intellectuals before and often didn't know how to react to what they did. Indeed, some of them might not have especially *respected* artists. Even those foreign Estonians who held cultural types in high regard were blown away when they ended up at The Cave, as they had never seen artists together in such numbers before. It was like some kind of a massed cluster or colony. They also might have been surprised to hear people openly speaking against the system there. It didn't correspond to their conceptions of a police-state. All the same, a guest never stayed alienated for long. When spirits were already a little high, the local artist would daringly look straight at the foreign entrepreneur (or whomever it happened to be at the moment), grunt, raise his glass, and declare: "Long live free Estonia!" The foreigner would soften instantly upon hearing this, and concord had thus been struck. Why waste more words? In retrospect, back then it really felt like it was enough to say "Long live free Estonia" and everything would be just fine.

As for the relationship between nationally-minded communists and artists, freedom was a unifier for them to a certain extent as well. The former were fighting dogmatic manners of thought and desired greater autonomy from Moscow. The artists first and foremost wanted freedom of expression. However, they were often of differing standpoints in interpreting the past (Estonia's in particular), and therefore mainly avoided the topic, in order to avoid starting an argument that neither side really wanted. Artists and nationally-minded communists were both living in the moment—endeavors of the present drew them together. Although both also dreamed of a better future, these futures were not quite identical. The commies were more rational, planning more for the long term, and more systematic, representing the "paternal element" in this intellectual union, so to say; the artists, on the other hand, were feminine and childish. It is worth noting that while artists regarded the freedom fighters as highly as they did the nationally-minded commies and got along with both, the latter two groups were generally incompatible.

On occasion, even shady characters or outright criminals would end up at such a gathering. People might hit it off with the person at first, because even a criminal was outside of the system; was "anti and free." Yet, when they started to probe each others' views and discuss the overall situation in greater detail, no friendship would develop. Their backgrounds were too different and the criminal lacked any broad, positive plan of action. An impoverished aristocrat might have fit in with our social group, for having been used to all kinds of privileges for a long time, they would also have difficulties adapting to universally-applied standards of behavior. Alas, Estonia had no true aristocrats.

## PEKKA

The atelier door swung open, and Pekka peered in. I first met him at The Cave about a year earlier, when the second global gathering of Estophiles took place in Tallinn. The Writers' Union had fought in the Estonian Communist Party's Central Committee to secure permission for organizing those kinds of events. Anyone in the whole world who had an interest in Estonian culture received an invitation. It turned out that the number of such people surpassed all expectations, coming in at nearly twenty. It was a motley contingent in terms of education, age, and background, and even included one Tierra del Fuegan (a man of Croatian descent who came from the part of the island belonging to Argentina). After the official part of the gathering, I ended up in a small group that headed to The Cave for a smidgen of relaxation before bidding each other adieu. Our cohort's central figure was the legendary builder of the Finnish-Estonian bridge—Auntie Ruosu, who was of Livonian descent. I remember that it was at five o'clock, still daytime. Most of the booths were empty, and the waitstaff were sitting at the bar swinging their legs and chatting with the bartender, Ingvar. It was dim and the air felt like it usually does in a ventilated bunker, meaning fresh, even cool, but still of questionable purity. The only noteworthy customer was a toothless old man hunched over in the corner—a former lead dancer in the national ballet, who was jabbering to himself:

"Yeah yeah, 'ts how it was, yup, one boy 'v his was'n the Party, a commie, had another'n, too, an' they was liv'n together all nice, notta problem 'n the least. *Understand?*" He said the last word in English. It was his mantra, which he repeated every five minutes. He was nicknamed "Understand."

We took a seat. The others struck up a lively conversation; I, as the youngest and least significant member of the group, was silent. I heard about what was going on at the Tuglas Seura cultural bridge in Helsinki, what polemics were running in the *Hesari*[14] columns, what kinds of intriguing books had been translated into Finnish, and other news from our northern neighbor. I heard that their cultural magazine *Apollo* had just gotten a new editor, and that the man was currently in our midst! Lasse-Martti was barely twenty-seven years old, light-haired, bespectacled, and had a hairdo that looked like he had been wallowing around somewhere. Ants, who was the editor-in-chief of our literary magazine and also sitting at the table, expressed somewhat impolitely his amazement that such a young person could be "put" in such an important position. Yet Nikodemus Orgussaar, a translator of epics and co-organizer of the Estophiles' sabbath, who was sitting next to him, smiled clemently. He had spent time in Finland twice already and knew how things went elsewhere. He exchanged glances with Auntie Ruosu and explained:

"But Ants, that's how it *is* abroad! Young people *are* in manag-
ing positions there. It's only here that everything is run by geri-
atrics. Over there, twenty-five is just the right time to head a
company or become an editor-in-chief, Ants!" Ants opened
and closed his mouth silently at this and guiltily refrained from
speaking for the rest of the evening. *I* had also been amazed, to
tell the truth, and was glad that I had not shown it. I ordered
my usual small juice-and-vodka in order to continue maintaining my nerve. It was apricot juice. But that's how I could drink
vodka. I myself was also twenty-seven at the time. I suddenly
felt how that age compelled me to feel.

Pekka was also at the table with us then. He was young as
well—probably younger than I was, but who knows. We used
to say that you couldn't guess a foreigner's age, because they ate
different food than we did. People also alleged that all of them—
even the poor ones—were "stuffed full" of vitamins, so neither
the cold nor illnesses daunted them. Where they acquired those
vitamins (especially the poor), and who "stuffed them full" and
in what way wasn't especially clear. In any case, the people who
spoke that way would also smugly inform us that everything
in the West was much more advanced than in Soviet Estonia.
This was not 100 percent true, in my opinion (I had seen with
my own eyes a woman at the Kopli taxi stand who spoke Finnish but wiped her nose on the back of her hand and had a generally disheveled appearance). There were young just as well
as there were old and middle-aged people in the ranks of foreigners, too. In general, it seemed to me that the people "from
that side" were relatively similar to us in spite of everything,
even though differences could still be found, of course. For example, they did not possess a particular quality that, for lack
of a better alternative, I am only able to call "sinewy sodden-
ness." This does not only imply a toughness (not the so-called
Finnish "*sisu*," or "stamina"), but rather the ability to tolerate
absurd and unpleasant situations without even bothering to
crack an ironic joke. You simply *are*, you bear it, and you carry
on with your life again afterward. Like a dog that just shakes itself
off after taking a beating.

Pekka had studied Estonian at the University of Helsinki
and spoke it quite fluently. He hadn't finished his studies yet,

as he was making a living as a travel guide for Finnish tourists alongside his classes. This tourism (just like the whole "Finnish thing") had started to develop about fifteen years earlier, when a ferry connection was put in place between Helsinki and Tallinn, and the country's tallest building at the time—the Viru Hotel—was built in the middle of the city a few years later. Groups of Finns started to visit Tallinn, each with its own *matkanjohtaja*, tour guide. These guides all spoke a little bit of Estonian, of course, which didn't mean each and every one of them loved Estonia dearly. A job is a job, and that's also how they saw it. However, some of them held a greater interest in Estonians and Estonian culture. Pekka was one such person.

He had translated a short story by Mati Unt for his seminar project. The story included a certain subcultural expression that he didn't understand, so he turned to the author directly by mail. Mati explained it to him and added, "Stop by if you can," just as he said to everyone. (Rushing ahead of myself, I can add here that Pekka later translated more Estonian literature.) Pekka came to Estonia every month, sometimes even more frequently. Someone would always bring him to The Cave, where he met many people, and so things progressed from there. Everyone in our circle became familiar with him before long, so when he now peered in through the monumentalist Tuudleja's door, he was greeted with cheerful shouts.

Pekka was a tall young man with somewhat coarse, light-colored hair, was neither fat nor thin, rosy-cheeked, and had an amiable disposition and an innocent look in his eyes. He wasn't exactly handsome, but was clean, polite, and pleasant. (Yes, back then, it immediately stuck out to me that their bohemians did not take things as "full-on" as ours did; meaning they weren't thoroughly filthy, but rather designed to look filthy.) Pekka would wear a beige wool sweater that he had purchased here (in order to support Estonian handicrafts, according to him) and jeans, and carried a bag or a satchel over his shoulder. It was out of this that he now fished out two 330 gram bottles of Koskenkorva Vodka, doing so with a very natural movement and not at all ostentatiously. This was met with approving murmurs and squeals.

Pekka was calm and reserved, like many Finns. He took a seat, smiled, and listened for a while to what the others were saying before opening his own mouth. In terms of personality, he embodied modesty. For example, I don't think any of us were aware that he wrote poetry. This fact came out in the open now, because Mati, who was sitting next to him, announced at one point:

"Pekka just gave me a copy of his poetry collection!" All eyes turned towards them. Mati continued dramatically: "He tried to do it so that no one would see, and I guess he got away with it, too. We should accept that kind of modesty on the one hand, but on the other, it shouldn't discourage us from bringing attention to a fresh literary event." Mati raised a blue notebook above his head, waved it around, and then handed it to Tobi, who (being from North Estonia) could read Finnish fluently. Everyone wanted to see and touch the notebook, and so Tobi passed it around. I checked it out, too. The collection was light, maybe about twenty or so poems. The paper and the print quality were on the poorer side, much poorer than with the poetry collections of our own guys and gals. At the same time, though, it was still an actual print—not like the self-published journals, the *Entelecheias* and others of our time.

"When did you write them?" asked Endel, who had worked in publishing.

"This summer. I took them to the printer three weeks ago," Pekka replied. The others oohed and aahed, since our books were printed at the very earliest a year after giving them to a publisher.

"What'd they pay you?" Endel inquired.

"They didn't pay me anything," Pekka said, and laughed. He answered everyone's questions very obligingly, visibly glad to have the chance to speak Estonian.

"I don't understand," the essayist Maulwurf mumbled, rocking his head from side to side. He was the soberest of us and an otherwise rational person. "You're not paid anything?"

"No."

Someone coughed, the rest were silent. Pekka himself did not appear to grasp that his words might contain anything out of the ordinary. "More Koskenkorva for anyone?" he asked, lifting the bottle. Tobi decided to delicately change the topic, turning the conversation back to the Drama Theatre's latest debut performance. Had their *Hamlet* been a depiction of the current totalitarianism or not? Pekka listened attentively, only taking a few brief sips from his glass. After about an hour, he stood, picked up his satchel, and said he had to go.

"Go? Where?" Mati asked in surprise.

"To work," Pekka explained.

"What work?" the others asked, not comprehending.

"Yeah, take a look at us—we don't have to go anywhere," Tobi said.

"I have a tour group, forty tourists—their lunch and free time are over now. I have to take them around."

"Say, Pekka—why do you have to work?" Tobi asked insistently, unable to wrap his mind around it. "You're an *artist*. An artist doesn't work. Or if he does, then only in the event that he himself wants to."

Pekka laughed. "One doesn't disrupt the other, you know."

"No, but seriously. Why do you work?" Alja whispered tragically.

"To earn money."

"For what? What do you need money for?" Lipsik asked in a motherly tone. "My child, believe me—there's no happiness in money."

"Yeah, do you have several families to provide for, or something, and that's why you have to scrape money together?" Alja whispered, making everyone laugh.

"Admit it—you've got a lover, don't you," Maša said in Alja's support, starting to pick up momentum. She liked that clean, orderly boy, and felt that she had to take him under her wing, especially because he was a foreigner—no matter that he was poor and didn't even receive honoraria for his writing.

Pekka burst out laughing. "I don't have a lover or several families. I wouldn't even be able to provide for *one* family right now. I'm a poor college student, and an even poorer poet. I need to earn money so that I can pay my tuition, buy food for myself, and pay the bills for my one-room Helsinki apartment."

"Isn't your honorarium enough?" Sass had been in the bathroom and missed that part.

"I don't get an honorarium," Pekka explained patiently. "I'm glad that I don't have to pay to be published."

"But how are *we* paid?" Sass exclaimed.

"That, I don't know," Pekka said. "I don't know why you're paid. No one pays me."

"You do live in the Free World, don't you?" Sass reckoned.

"I do," Pekka agreed.

"Then why don't you demand an honorarium?"

"From whom?"

"I don't know. From the state."

"Why should the state pay me for those poems when the state hasn't ordered them from me?" Pekka asked in response.

"Who ordered them, then?" Poindexter asked maliciously. Maša snapped at him: "Oh, don't be so *mo-no-chro-maaatic . . .*" But Pekka apparently sensed that Poindexter was the only one who grasped the point of the conversation.

"*No one* ordered them. That's why I can't *demand* that anyone pay me an honorarium."

Sass furrowed his brow. "But who handles those cultural things for you guys, then? In your country, I mean."

"Oh, many do. There are all sorts of groups, and there are libraries and reading clubs and other institutions. But they don't pay honoraria. If a poet goes somewhere and reads his poems to an audience, then he'll be paid a performance fee sometimes. But he has to be a really well-known poet for that to happen. Otherwise, you normally don't get paid for publishing."

A strange silence took hold in the atelier. There was a tough nut to crack here, especially given the present mood. On the one hand, what Pekka was saying seemed right, and why should he be lying? On the other, though, it was incomprehensible. Pekka probably guessed that a cultural barrier had cropped up, and—revealing delayed signs of impatience—asked:

"Can you order a taxi from here?"

"What taxi? Order a taxi? We ain't in Helsinki, here." The singer Klarion always became aggressive when drinking.

"Of course you can," Pekka retorted confidently. "I was told that you can. It just takes a long time. That's what I meant. Is there a telephone here? There is? Great, I'll give it a try."

He tried. The number was busy, as usual.

"Listen, Arvi—can't you get a taxi through your Party systems?" Sass asked.

"My God, how *mo-no-chro-maaatic . . .*" Maša wailed.

"Why don't you ask through Intourist. They have their own lines," Arvi huffed. He did not enjoy being reminded of his membership in the Party. He said the number.

"Hello, I'd like ... Thanks!" Pekka hung up the receiver. "They promised one within forty-five minutes."

"What are you going to do with your wards?" Toomas asked.

"I'm taking them to the Rocca al Mare Open Air Museum, and then to the Song Festival Grounds," Pekka answered.

"What for? Better to invite them over here," Toomas proposed. "I don't know if I'm more interesting than a peasant museum, but Tobi's definitely more interesting than a festival stage."

"I don't think that'd be a good idea," Pekka said cautiously.

"It's a *very* good idea," Maulwurf interjected forcefully. "You can show your tourists our intellectual elite—the likes of which they couldn't see under any condition otherwise."

"Yes, you may be right about that," Pekka agreed hesitantly. "It's just that ... I'm not sure if they'd be able to appreciate it. Or if it would interest them at all. They're ordinary people, you see. Maybe next time, though. I'll talk to my bosses about it. But that's the kind of work contract I have right now, and I have to stick to it. Thanks for having me. See you next time!"

It was impossible to keep hold of him.

When he was leaving, Pekka stopped from shutting the door at the last moment because someone was mounting the stairs. The newcomer entered a moment later. It was a very noteworthy figure, who—just as with Pekka—will come under discussion more later, and therefore, I must pause on him at greater length.


## MANGLUS

Most people's lives have some kind of a happy period—their time to shine, which they think back upon nostalgically all their remaining years. Some were child prodigies, others became the head of their gang of friends, a third group's glory days were in college (where he or she turned out to be the "soul of the class"), and a fourth became a Don Juan, rich, or the parent of gifted children after graduation. And there is one final hope—of being a "nice, clean elderly person," or even a grand old man or a

wonderful old dame. Needless to say, there are all kinds of combinations and variations. Some lucky souls may even experience
multiple happy stages. For example, it might happen that one
wonder-child is overshadowed during his or her puberty, but
"breaks" into the foreground again in middle-age. It is extremely rare for someone to stay at the top for their whole life, but it
appeared that Manglus was one such "chosen person," who had
been appointed by fate to always succeed in everything. Admittedly, I do not know about his childhood in greater detail. He
apparently wasn't exactly a wonder child (at least I haven't heard
of him being one); but as he possessed remarkable physical
strength and an average appearance (in the best sense, meaning
he had no physical defects such as saggy ears or a lazy eye, which
children ridicule so cruelly), one might guess that Manglus's
childhood was adequately pleasant. As a child, and even slightly
later, he was able to subconsciously enjoy his similarity to others; the sense of "fitting in" that came from it and the ecstasy of
dissolving in a mass, which is probably a necessary part of any
happy childhood. (In reality, childhood *is* a happy time in and
of itself, by definition, which can only be ruined when someone is thoroughly different from his or her peers — no matter
in what sense.) Manglus didn't become aware of his uniqueness
too early on, so it did not split his soul in half or give his identity a tragic undertone that would haunt him throughout his
life. He was already a prominent figure in middle school — an
informal leader. He had a vast social circle that wasn't limited
to his school or his home street. For example, he went to take
drawing lessons from a renowned artist, who in turn introduced
Manglus to his other students and adult colleagues. Manglus was
also said to have been particularly skilled with women — people
even talked about some kind of an affair with a female college
student who had been doing student teaching at the school. After that it was art college, long hair and avant-gardism, group
performances and his first solo exhibition, high-level jobs and
state recognitions. It was all smooth sailing. Now, at the age of
thirty, he was a famous and worldly man, who had even been able
to travel around the world (regardless of the fact that he was not
in the Party). He was a good communicator, accommodating

and eager to help, and gave the impression that his goal really was to find commonality with other people. His conciliatory and diplomatic manner charmed almost everyone he crossed paths with. Even now, he left a relatively ordinary impression in terms of appearance: a little taller than average, more broad-shouldered than lanky, his hair slightly but not very curly, his eyes grayish-blue but not like those of a film star, his voice more soft than loud, and so forth—in no way did his features make him stick out in your mind. However, all Manglus had to do was to start talking, and he would have his conversation partner listening to him and fully under his control over the course of five minutes. What did he do to achieve this? He emanated force and self-confidence; he seemed to govern everything around him—living beings just as well as (which is absolutely remarkable) the material world. For example, his movements were very clean. They were not elegant in a feminine way or powerful and unwieldy in a masculine way, but rather well-regulated and measured—not too long or too short; not jerky, but at the same time not lethargic, either. When he reached for some object, even if it was just a lighter, one was involuntarily amazed by how he did so with such a precise, correct, and heaven-blessed motion. He didn't fumble around, didn't knock anything over, didn't rummage, drop, or rifle through things—his hand arrived at it with millimetric precision. It was all very beautiful, harmonic, and suggestive; as if it were done by a lion relishing in the act—if we might imagine a lion lighting a cigarette.

The way Manglus picked up a lighter was the way he did everything else in life, and things simply flourished in his hands. He undoubtedly took personal enjoyment in being able to do so much and get everything in order. Manglus loved to say about the rest of us, "you're little one-regime guys." By this, he did not mean the political regime, but rather our living and labor regime. We protested, of course, but had to admit to ourselves that he was right to a certain extent. Specifically, we—some more, some less—were either a, b, or c. Manglus, however, was just as much a as he was b and c together (and x and y to boot). We were the so-called cultural or intellectual types (although we weren't little runts or runtesses, naturally; that was an overstatement by Manglus). In addition to us, there were people of action somewhere (in the very best sense): those who built stations and executed transactions, who bent over open ribcages on operating tables, who steered ships and did all the other things that were necessary for keeping things in motion. And then there were the Party politicians, although they were not respected. (People of action were also in the Party sometimes, but it wasn't definitive in their case, because — for example — a ship and an ocean or a person's open ribcage had nothing to do with the Party.) Then there were the scoundrels, the derelicts, and the criminals, who certainly did not stick out much but could be encountered in dive bars, near dumpsters, in shantytowns on the outskirts of the city, and elsewhere. Finally, there were the masses or ordinary citizens. Every person belonged to one group or another, adopting its behavioral patterns and spiritual posture. Yet Manglus wanted to transcend these boundaries — one group was not enough for him. He wanted to be both an artist and an official, a buddy and a boss, a man of action and an observer, flesh and spirit (his enemies added that Manglus wanted to be underground and in the Presidium simultaneously), and mainly, of course — to always be the winner.

It is true that Manglus did business "above" and associated with the authorities. This was done both officially (which was understandable in his case, being a high-level functionary) and as a private individual (he was, for example, an expected guest at the birthday parties of high-ranking officials' wives), which some regarded as bizarre. He socialized with bohemian artists "their way" (speaking "their language," as he himself would say with a chuckle), and they regarded him as one of their own. He interacted with the authorities in a completely different way, giving the impression of a young and effective character who had a "realistic sense of life" and "knew how to behave." As for the other individuals and organizations that Manglus had ties to — I don't know much for certain about that, although all sorts of rumors circulated, such as that he was extorting someone, or that someone was extorting him. People alleged that he had a love child with a general's daughter, and much else.

It is likewise true that Manglus socialized "below," associating with the lowest of scoundrels (I will return to that further on). When he was asked or warned about it, Manglus would nod approvingly and state pensively: "*You* shouldn't associate with them, for sure. Nothing good will come of it."

"But you?"

"I'm a different matter," he would say very straightforwardly. Manglus had a dreadful love of risk—of almost any kind. I'll always remember how he once drove from Kose-Risti to Tallinn steering the car only with his legs—meaning he held the wheel between his knees. Manglus himself was smoking cigarettes and humming "La Cucaracha" (not taking it seriously, of course). The ladies in the back seat were screeching. It was only at the roundabout between Järvevana and Leningrad roads that he wasn't able to make the turn and had to use his hands at the last second.

As for his artistic work, Manglus had gone far (and no doubt deservedly), although I'm no expert. While he was outwardly jovial and carefree for the most part, he could, during a period of intense work (prior to the coming of some exhibition), be very diligent, ascetically severe, demanding, and on his guard. He only "practiced the spirit" at certain times in his life, although he did so then at a level just as high as that of the highest-level practicers (although there were likely a few exceptions). It occasionally felt like Manglus wanted to show that if he were to ignite, then he would be an even greater artist than those who "grind out" their art one day after another and practice the spirit from morning to night—as if they were practicing some kind of a profession. Those who knew him only by his impressive side were unaware of this—observing how he directed "games" in his formal office garb or received foreign delegations. Some also said that he was a person of cool or even cold sense, who was merely standing in a polite relationship with the muses, and from time to time, one could hear scathing condemnations of him among the younger artists. Although he wasn't known for treating vast and thought-provoking subjects, his works were brilliantly executed in a technical sense, were unsurpassable from a formal angle, and showed the experts how at home he felt in the secretive problems of the art world.

Additionally, Manglus wrote completely tolerable articles on art, and even composed poetry on occasion.

What did he practice when he wasn't practicing the spirit and not toying with power or associating with scum? He practiced the flesh. Manglus was as lustful as an angry bug. He had a beautiful wife who adored him, and an exemplary family with two talented and obedient children who adored him, likewise. This type of exemplary family was as much a part of Manglus's image of perfection as a button is to a jacket (fine, a little more — we'll say like a lapel to a jacket). Then he had a mistress, who was even prettier than his wife and adored him even more. On top of that, he had female acquaintances of every standing and age, who were out of their minds about him, and with whom he just "was." One might guess the profusion of women also had a high symbolic value for him. *He* was the man who could, in everything. I was amazed at the self-confident way he used women. Manglus simply satisfied himself with them, but they were highly flattered to be the subjects of his gracious satisfaction. And Manglus would just give a little smirk.

The simultaneous lives he led and women he had would sometimes annoy some of us, and we would poke fun at him. This primarily concerned his doings "above." Imagine: everyone is sitting in a friendly drinking session, the hour is relatively late, and all of a sudden Manglus shows up wearing a vested suit. From where? From a reception organized by the Party and the government for the ESSR's leading laborers!

"How can you *go* to such places?" Tobi once asked critically.

"*I* can," Manglus replied very simply, but in a way that radiated terrible arrogance. "It doesn't affect me." And when Tobi had no instantaneous comeback, Manglus added with feigned care and concern:

"But *you* shouldn't go, certainly not . . . *if* you should ever be invited. It could ruin *you*, most certainly. Could go to your head. You're an *artist*. Maybe you would fall in love with the dogma, and soon you'd start running around and preaching it to everyone like some Bible-thumping old hag."

The others laughed, but Tobi would not recognize his defeat:

"You said 'artist.' So, am I to understand that you place yourself outside of that? You're *not* an artist — is that it?" This piqued people's attention—things appeared to be moving towards issues of principle.

"I'm an intellectual," Manglus said. "There's a considerable difference. There are artists, and there are intellectuals." This was followed by a pause, which Manglus carried like a good actor. "Think about it when you get home," he added. And as a sign that the topic had been exhausted, he turned towards the barrel-chested singer Klarion sitting next to him, who lost his ability to think as a result of this unexpected show of attention and merely stared back at Manglus, opening and closing his mouth repeatedly.

Yet I agree with Manglus's claim. And the more time has passed, the more prophetic his words have turned out to be. A large number of artists *truly* are not intellectuals. The opposite is also true, of course: intellectuals may not necessarily be artists.

So, what did Manglus do when he was not practicing the spirit or the flesh? Well, he partied. He enjoyed eating and drinking and had an enormous capacity for both. There *were* forty eight hours in his day, after all.

Manglus's social circle included people who did not belong to either "below" or "above," and with whom the rest of us mainly did not associate. One of them was the aforementioned Hasso Miller—the somewhat younger Tartu sociologist or social psychologist (he was involved in both fields), who once defended samizdat periodicals at the university Party committee meeting. After that, he directed (covertly—it was officially headed by another individual) the operations of a research laboratory, which, however, the authorities shut down at the end of the seventies, as they suspected the influences of Western theories in it. Miller was nevertheless allowed to continue working at the university (there were some very well-known communist revolutionaries among his relatives, and thanks to them, he had influential patrons). Miller gave lectures at several colleges in the capital at the same time. He even taught a course on psychodrama at the theater institute. The future actors were enthralled by him. Miller was not a national celebrity—his name would certainly flash here or there, but mainly in specialty publications. On the other hand, his opinions were well respected by many. Some disdained him, while others practically idolized him, saying that Miller could shake the foundations of sociology around the entire world with his work if he only willed it. The thing was that, for some reason, Miller didn't especially want to do any such thing (his supporters would say that he was keeping a low profile on purpose, as he did not want to expose himself to the fury of the powers that be, which might have been true). Instead, he wrote enchanting and high-flying ponderings (columns in today's speak), exactly two typewritten pages long, which were printed in one newspaper's weekly cultural section. In these, he would construct abstract hypotheses, illustrating them with specific details that often contained innocent and mischievous sexual references. Miller had an extremely logical way of thinking and loved when things were expressed clearly. Even his short columns were easy to understand and written in a clear language, always offering readers a pleasant experience.

I am unable to say whether or not Miller expressed the age. Still, he was interesting in other respects. The formerly unnoticeable Semitic lines on his face had deepened by his thirtieth birthday. From then on, he was a slim, frizzle-haired gentleman from the Levant with a handsome mocha beard and a small mouth. Miller smoked long, thin menthol cigarettes and wore a polka-dot bow tie. I heard that while speaking about Manglus one time, he said: "Although we are diametrically opposed on most issues, I can at least understand what he is thinking. But as for 'those others' (he meant the "cavemen" and artistic people in general)—they are impossible to understand, because they are unable to think systematically."

Coming back to Manglus (because he is much more important)—why was he the sort of man that he was? His high intelligence and rare alcohol tolerance were usually the reasons given. The first quality encourages a person to give all opportunities a try, to test out their options, while the second quality assists any such endeavor, for one is able to stoke one's fantasy without toppling over halfway through. Nevertheless, these two qualities do not explain everything. I knew plenty of other highly-intelligent individuals who could down two bottles of vodka over the course of an evening and walk home upright, and from time to time *they* would organize parties so rowdy that you really had to watch yourself. However, they didn't practice the kind of trans-categorical simultaneity of life that Manglus did; rather, they kept nicely to their categories—meaning they were either a, b, or c. Occasionally, Manglus himself would mention that he was inspired by the classical humanist idea; something like Leonardo. And that he really *was* today's last Renaissance man. But I don't believe that self-myth. It was actually much simpler: it all came out of extreme arrogance—"I am capable of it because that is what I have decided." Manglus had an iron will, and he always kept complete control of himself. The most straightforward example is this: having been a smoker since middle school, and not an ordinary one, but a passionate smoker (smoking two packs a day and enjoying it), he quit at the drop of a hat and never smoked again. Why did he do this? At that time, smoking was seen as a masculine habit, and over half of the art community smoked. Wasting yourself through nicotine was just as firmly part of being bohemian as all other kinds of hard-and-fast living. Manglus certainly did not give up smoking for health reasons. (Although a focus on health awareness could already be found in the USSR, and some circles saw it as the regime's official propaganda. Smoking carried a certain air of social protest during the occupation.) He was only twenty-eight then—an age at which most people don't consider quitting, because they aren't yet hacking up a lung in the morning. He simply quit because he had decided to do so.

Manglus never appeared to feel any kind of blind rage that would make him lose his sense of reason. He exacted revenge clearly and effectively. This was sometimes done in a passive or boring manner, but he never did fail to take revenge. There was malice within him, but it was a cold, calm, and rational malice. To top it all off, Manglus always had a lot of money—a suspiciously large amount.

"How do you do it?" a simple-minded newcomer would occasionally ask him, without specifying what was meant by "it"—that was already obvious.

"You've got to get along well with him," Manglus said, pointing his thumb over his left shoulder.

"What?" the first asked, not understanding. "With whom? With Olaf Utt, the Communist Party Cultural Department Director?"

Manglus shook his head. "With *this*." And then he would press two straight fingers from each hand against his temples, making the sign for horns. He would additionally wave his open palm around under his tailbone, as if there were a tail there. Manglus did so in an almost blasé manner, as if he was bored of having to explain something so elementary. People laughed at it, but I'm not sure that everyone—especially the ladies— took it as a joke. I fear that some felt an icy breath upon them for a quarter of a second. And as everyone knows, such things only boost ladies' interest; the person's attractiveness grows in their eyes. Blood on someone's hands does the very same thing.

Understandably, Manglus had his opponents and people who were jealous of him. Some regarded him as a bastard. In an enraged outburst one time, someone said that he "impregnated kitchen maids." Another whispered that Manglus received his entire artistic education by leafing through foreign magazines in the waiting room of the Hiiu Venereal Disease Clinic. (Which is certainly bullshit, because how could there have been foreign magazines there during the Soviet era?) I also heard it alleged that he "stole" other artists' projects and realized them himself. Likewise that he prostituted himself to elderly ladies in order to receive his first high-level positions.

Sometimes, after some successful activity, Manglus loved to say while rubbing his hands: "Men do business, idiots just romanticize." He would occasionally modify this, saying simply: "There are men, and there are little runts."

Once when he had drunk quite a bit, he asked me teasingly: "And who the hell are *you*?" This put me into a funk, because it was one of the few times that Manglus addressed me. He didn't actually expect an answer. Naturally, I knew what "sort" I was, and he knew that I knew that he knew. Namely, I *am* a little runt. Or, better put—not a little runt, but a little worm. I was afraid of public life back then. He was not.

And so, Manglus now stepped into the atelier of the monumentalist Tuudleja and smiled simply, so simply. He was dressed elegantly, wearing a soft brownish-grey checkered suit and a tie (meaning he was coming from somewhere or going somewhere). He spoke little, as was usual when he was sober. Regardless, his entrance had an immediate effect on the group. The energy level seemed to rise; everyone wanted to show their good side. Even Arvi turned friendly all of a sudden. The conversation continued from where it had left off, discussing Pekka.

"He's a great guy, otherwise," Toomas said.

"Yeah, I think so, too. But a little simpleminded," Endel agreed.

"Simpleminded like a Finn," someone added. "They're great, but simpleminded."

"Yeah, we really are more clever," Sass said. "We've become much more savvy by living at the crossroads of history. We're savvy mongrels, we are." Sass was a big dog-lover.

"Finns are monochromatic," Maša reckoned, not dragging the word out that time.

"It's not only the Finns. It's the same story with most Westerners," Tobi said. "All of them can only fit one thought in their head at a time. It comes from the fact that they're able to live a natural life. There's no double morality in their society, they don't have to think twice all the time."

"Is that really a very great achievement? Thinking twice about everything all the time?" Endel asked doubtfully.

"It might not be a great achievement on the Richter scale, but it's a fact that it refines one's personality and makes favorable conditions for the creation of good works of art," said the essayist Maulwurf, who was an authority in the field of intellectual refinement, to set things straight.

Everyone was satisfied with this conclusion. They had been repressed and trampled down, but on the other hand, they were refined and interesting! And the fact that *they*—the refined and the interesting—had to live in the sort of outhouse that the country currently was, filled them with self-pity on the one hand, and with pride and a sense of martyrdom on the other.

"I wonder if Pekka's poetry is any good," said Tobi, who

wrote poetry himself. He continued without waiting for a response: "To tell the truth, I don't believe it is. If he still has to work ... I'd understand if he went to work because he's crazy about working. Or if he visits Estonia to practice the language. But the fact that he has to make a living by it ... probably means he isn't exactly the best of the best, then."

"Yeah, who can really see inside another person, anyway," the nationalist communist chimed in diplomatically. This would remain his only remark over the course of the entire evening.

"What do you mean, 'see inside'?" Tobi retorted. "Listen — when he still isn't paid for it? Don't come telling me that there isn't a *single* poet who is paid an honorarium in all of Finland. Some surely are."

"Ah, let's just say cheers to Finland and the Finns," the freedom fighter proposed. "Let's drink to the memory of the Estonian armed volunteers in Finland."

No one argued against this, and each took a sip with a certain kind look on their face.

"But why are *we* paid, anyway?" Endel asked, as if it was the first time he had come upon something so important.

"We're paid because we're just that good," Sass asserted resolutely. No one wanted to disagree. Everyone — except Mati, who was otherwise gentle-natured and enjoyed pleasant company — appeared to be busy silently investigating the contents of their glasses, but secretly peeked over to see how Manglus would treat this. Manglus paid the comment no heed.

"Have you ever imagined us under capitalism?" Sass asked Tobi.

"Of course I have," the latter replied. "Every now and then, I can't get to sleep at night, and that's when I think about capitalism."

"How we'd live then! Oh, how we'd live!" Sass drifted off into a daydream and Toomas picked up the conversation:

"Man, think about it — you could write about anything then. Absolutely anything. You could criticize everything. I dunno how good we'd still be, then!" Toomas's face took on a dreamy expression. "Oh, freedom!"

Tobi, who could read Finnish fluently, was more skeptical.

"You can find all kinds of literature in the Free World too. You can't say that everything's top-notch. Take for example . . ." And Tobi listed off a number of authors whose books were unfamiliar to us, but who he said were very popular in the West, even though they weren't especially worth reading. "We've got some things better here," he reasoned.

"What does that have to do with us?" Sass snapped back, not letting himself be unnerved. "We wouldn't lower the bar, nor would we start churning out yellow press. We only want to make art. And when there's capitalism, then those who want to can and *do* make art."

"Hold on," Endel said, at odds. "We can make art and write about almost everything right now, too, if we're just clever about it. That's not the question."

"What *is* the question, then, if you will?" Sass asked with emphatic politeness.

"I suppose the question is whether you'd get by as a writer in the Free World. I haven't heard of there being very many freelancers in Finland. Most of them still hold some other kinds of jobs."

"You mean Pekka?"

"No, I mean in general."

"You need to be a good writer—I'm sure you'd break through then," Sass said confidently. "Money isn't the goal for the creator—it comes along with everything else on its own. Why shouldn't I break through in capitalism?"

"Sure, why not? I just raised the question," Endel remarked diplomatically.

"How do they pay over there in Finland?" asked Toomas, who was not familiar with the Free World.

Tobi explained: "Let's suppose that a book costs 105 marks at a store. The author will get about 10 percent of the cover price."

Sass made the calculations in his head and exclaimed: "Then I would've made three hundred thousand marks with *The Hottentots' Waltz*!" That had been his latest novel, fifty thousand copies of which had been printed. "That's a good amount of money. And it wouldn't be in measly kopeks, but in foreign currency. Damn, what I'd do with that money!"

"But what if only five thousand were bought?" Toomas asked doubtfully.

"Our books would be bought every single time," Sass remained confident. "We'd break through no matter where." Toomas was also a popular writer.

"If only our guys would be allowed abroad. We'd clinch it," someone sighed.

"Absolutely," Sass agreed, pouring vodka for himself. "There's nothing to even talk about here. We'd clinch it in every field."

"Think about it—you *yourself* can publish your own book if you've got dollars," Toomas dreamed out loud. "You're your own boss."

Everyone fell silent and added up in their heads how much they might earn living abroad. Then, abruptly, Manglus shifted and all eyes turned towards him. It was as if everyone was expecting something. Manglus took a small sip with a decorous flourish, placed his glass on the table, and rose: "Excuse me."

"Where are you off to now, you just got here?" the others exclaimed, making a fuss and almost clinging onto him.

"I have to stop by one other place," Manglus answered indistinctly.

"Bullshit you do," Tobi said. Manglus emitted a friendly snicker.

"Maybe we'll see each other tonight?" someone asked hopefully.

Manglus chuckled and made no promises.

"Hey listen, tell us first—what do *you* think about it?" Tobi demanded.

"About what?" Manglus asked innocently.

"About what we were talking about here just now. About that money, of course. How much would we earn in the Free World?"

"Yeah, why didn't *you* say anything?" Alja whispered. "You have to say something, too, if you want to be a man."

"What's there to say?" Manglus said and laughed, then suddenly became serious. "You're talkers. Simple talkers."

Silence took hold after he spoke. What did he mean by "talkers"?

"No," Manglus said, looking at his watch, "I really do have to go now."

"Go, go, complicated man," Mati said almost to himself. Manglus looked back attentively for a moment at hearing this. He and Mati generally seemed to get along on neutral lines otherwise. That was the impression I had been left with. Manglus would occasionally attempt to tease him subtly, but Mati would pretend not to understand. There was some kind of a tension between them—that was noticeable. Why? Manglus was an alpha male, and already by his nature could not tolerate another alpha male next to him. Mati, however, could tolerate one—even very well, because he was friendlier and not a jealous man at all. And the more he was able to tolerate, the less Manglus could.

As for Manglus and Klaus: I truly cannot recall them ever having spoken with each other, although it would have been natural in a circle as small as ours. Manglus probably avoided him. Klaus's reactions came at superhuman speed; furthermore, he had a much louder voice, and was thus able to "make a clean job" of it. Manglus was deeper and disdained him somewhat. In any case, there was probably a rivalry between them. Yet just as a tiger and a lion never come into contact with each other in nature, Manglus and Klaus did not socialize, although they certainly knew each other. Klaus was happy to sit with us in The Cave, although not so frequently, due to his busy performance schedule.

## POINDEXTER

Everyone sat staring after Manglus in exaltation.

"You'd all be Pekkas in a capitalist age," Poindexter said in the silence that had ensued. At first no one appeared to realize where the voice had come from or what had been meant by the word it said. A few words about Poindexter now, and his connection to the era and its expression, as always.

Poindexter, who was a puppeteer, was an unusual character in many senses. You can find people who are tight-lipped when sober, but when they drink the smallest drop or get high, then the conversation just runs on and on. This can get tiresome, not only because their script is vapid and jumps from place to place, but because we're not used to such a "change in gears." Poindexter spoke little when he was sober, but not to any extreme—he simply left the impression of being a taciturn individual. But when he drank, it was like he extinguished altogether, becoming quieter and quieter. He would look out at his companions from his corner of the room as if he had gone mute, wearing an expression as if he dreadfully wanted to say something— straining so hard that his facial muscles cramped, although not a single word would escape across his lips. And then suddenly, at the most unexpected moment, when everyone had gotten used to his silence, Poindexter opens his mouth and utters something odd, irrelevant, and blunt, which upends everyone's moods for a few blinks of an eye ("as if a teaspoonful of cold sewage-water has been poured down your collar," as someone put it). The same "quips" might have come across as humorous coming from some other person's mouth, but with Poindexter they never seemed to make you laugh. For example, he once asked out of the blue: "Can you tell me why a sea lion has seven legs?" Or: "Who was Kalevipoeg on his mother's side?"[15]

Or imagine the following situation. It is midday and company is gradually starting to gather. People are recalling the previous evening and night, repeating the wittier things that were said, recreating the events, going through the sharper moments, and laughing—everyone is taking things very casually. Someone is already stroking someone else's hair, someone is singing raucously, someone's new buzz is starting to merrily take shape— the usual. Poindexter has sunk as deep into the corner of the couch as possible, resting there like a stuffed animal forgotten by a child at the cabin last August. He has abandoned the group, and it pays him no attention. Yet suddenly, Poindexter awakens. He is moving his mouth, but no words come out. Everyone is taken aback—the dead man is awake! Then this corpse looks attentively at those around him, directly, one by one, and asks: "What is most important?" Naturally, no one is able to produce anything intelligent in reply. I cannot say the general mood is

ruined, or that anyone starts feeling ashamed, sensing the frivolous state of their consciousness in comparison with the intense brain activity of this fellow creature. Everyone *knows* that
it is just Poindexter (meaning Pets, which was his actual name).
But it makes you feel weird all the same. Maša once told him
crossly: "You *sure* know how to do it! You probably ask 'what
is most important?' when you're in bed with someone too."

Was Poindexter truly interested in what he asked, or did he
simply have that kind of questioning style? In my opinion, he
was a special little runt who did not go along with the general
"praying," but rather lived some kind of life of his own (although
unknowingly). He rarely laughed at the others' jokes. Not that
he disliked them—it was as if he let them breeze past his ears
instead. Sometimes he started to laugh when no one else was
laughing. And while some other people's laughs are infectious
(like Mati's) and tug you along with them, even when there's really nothing to laugh at, everyone felt uncomfortable at hearing
Poindexter's laugh, even when the joke was absolutely hilarious.
When this happened, people laughed along hesitantly and with
a certain sense of regret, because "something wasn't right about
all of it." (Doctor Muld had called it a "rapee's orgasm"). Still,
everyone was used to Poindexter, and when he was in the group,
everyone felt that it was a "full set."

Poindexter is important from my chronicle's point of view
foremost because of one question, which he posited frequently.
The question was: "Will Estonia ever become free?" Back then,
it seemed like almost the same mad ravings as his thing about
"Kalevipoeg's mother's side." The difference was that while one
could ignore talk of a sea lion's seven legs, or even "what is most
important," one couldn't do the same with Estonia's freedom.
Some said they believed in it, but most people generally replied
negatively or dodged the question. I don't think that everyone
answered honestly and straight from the heart, of course. Although people were no longer afraid of informers, for the most
part (we couldn't be bothered to think about them), some reckoned that it was better not to open up in any case. Sometimes,
they ducked behind a wisecrack. "Ah, better to just drink up,"
they would say in annoyance. Friendlier people would guide

Poindexter to the side and say: "OK, calm down, Pets." Brainy types who were encountering Poindexter for the first time would occasionally start to seriously make their case for why the question was not fit for an intellectual. Specifically, they would say a person can feel intellectually free anywhere, and then quote the classic saying that one can love and write poetry everywhere, and will make a living on it nowhere. (I remember someone commenting on this thoughtfully, saying that although the observation is correct in and of itself, there *is* still a difference between "not making a living" on it here, in the john (meaning in a totalitarian society), or there, in the Free World.)

Poindexter himself did not react to people's responses in any particular way, seeming to let them breeze past him. He also never posed his question to the same person twice. He had some kind of personal bookkeeping system to track this.

So now, Poindexter had broached a sacred topic by doubting whether Estonian writers could become millionaires in a free society and "clinch it" on a grander scale. No one tried to argue with him, and just looked at each other, at a loss. What do you say to something like that? Everyone was having a friendly time together, experiencing a sense of collectivity, and all of a sudden—a whiny wrong note like that.

"You've got to think on your *own*, not like us," someone spoke up heatedly.

"You must have had a bad day yesterday," Lipsik said with a motherly laugh. She had a sunny disposition and never took things too complicatedly. "*That's* why you're grouchy."

But Poindexter moved his jaw back and forth, rolled his eyes, and continued stubbornly: "Why do you think the Estonian public will start buying your books?"

"Well, why shouldn't they? Explain *that* to us," the attack sounded from several mouths.

"But why don't people buy them in Finland, then?" Poindexter asked.

"The Estonian people are a special people," Mati said.

"The public never buys worthy art or worthy literature. Art is supported by patrons," someone spoke doubtfully.

"Yeah, well—who's our patron right now, then? And check

this out—my last novel sold forty thousand copies without any kind of a patron."

"But aren't the Party and the government our patrons?" that same doubting voice asked.

"Are you crazy?! The Party and the government actually *hate* us."

"Yeah, but they gild us up, too."

The debate was going at full speed, but already without Poindexter, who had once again sunk into the corner of the couch and was thinking his own thoughts. Suddenly he reawakened:

"You say 'we' this and 'we' that all the time. Who's this 'we'?" Namely, Sass had been talking about "our generation." Poindexter was now even putting *that* notion in doubt!

"Aren't *we* 'we,' then?" Sass asked, boggled.

"Yeah, but who *are* those 'we'?" Poindexter repeated his question.

Endel came to Sass's aid: "We, well, the we who are sitting here—*us*, you know? Our generation. We have our taste, our convictions. We've got common ideals."

"How do you know what my ideals are? I might not like your ideals at all."

"What—you *don't*, then?" the rest of the group asked in bewilderment.

"No, I'm not saying that either . . . I'm simply theorizing. We haven't *spoken* about those ideals."

"Spoken about them? What for? Isn't it clear already, then?" Sass asked, his puzzlement growing even further.

"Why do you think that if we drink vodka together here, then we have to like the same things?" Poindexter came back resolutely.

Vodka drinking? What? So was that all they were doing here? If not, what was it, then?

Sass was unable to say what it was on the fly, but it wasn't your run-of-the-mill vodka drinking, in any case. Poindexter, that jokester. They were much more *refined* than that; the brilliant representatives of their generation. The front line of the age ran through them. They carried the weight of being upon their shoulders.

"How is it possible for some people to get out on the wrong side of the bed their whole lives?" whispered Alja.

"And why doesn't he move the bed?" the singer Klarion asked, and burst out laughing. He wanted to say something more, but a clumping noise came from the stairs and the door was thrown open. Two men marched in—one immensely large, the other small and nimble. They were famous athletes: a weightlifter and a sailor. Their arrival was quite out of the ordinary, because athletes and creative intellectuals rarely came into contact at the time. However, the elite are the elite, no matter in what field, so if you look at it that way, it made perfect sense. Athletes and bohemians lived very different lifestyles, of course, so they could not spend much time together, even if they dearly yearned for each other's company. Athletes constantly had to attend camps, from which they weren't even allowed to go home to see their wives, since not a single ounce of their athletic form was allowed to go to waste. Artists, on the other hand, spent a huge amount of time with women—they *searched* for their own form (i.e. inspiration) in the company of females. That was how things were with women, artists, and athletes. But these two men here were no longer very active—their big athletic achievements had been made years and years before, when they were members of the USSR national team. Now, they were coasting through their final seasons at the local club level just for kicks, living civilian lives and enjoying the attention that their arrival elicited. Who they knew at the party and who had directed them to the atelier of the monumentalist Tuudleja—that, I do not know. Maybe they actually weren't anyone's friends and had come just the same; had "followed the scent." I repeat: that sort of randomness and unpredictability *was* one of the charms of those get-togethers.

"May we take a load off?" the large man thundered. The group murmured their good-natured assent. No one looked surprised, although at least half of them recognized the men. Maša emitted an "eep" and pressed her hand over her mouth.

"What'll you have?" Endel asked politely. "The clear stuff? There's still beer, too."

"Good ol' clear stuff for us, as always," the large man rumbled, and tossed the offered shot back with great pleasure. A spirited discussion began not long after, borne out of a desire to talk about the problems of one's own and hear about those of others'. Everyone was mutually attentive and kind. The general consensus was that things would be better in every way if Estonia were independent. Then, Estonia could submit its own Olympic team. There could be a number of competitors in every area. At the present moment, athletes could only get into the Olympics as a part of the USSR team. However, it took a tremendous amount of effort to be selected for it.

"You've no idea how fucked over we were in the pan-Soviet camps," the little man said. "When the coach had to choose between me and a Russki, he always picked the Russki. I had to be twice as good—then he simply couldn't overlook me. And the Latvians and Lithuanians were fucked over the same way. But if we were free, damn it—how we'd get it done *then*! Then, the world would *really* hear about Estonian sportsmen. And here we are now, stuck in a rut." He sighed and drained a shot.

"Absolutely," Sass reckoned, opening a new bottle. "And you know how hard it is for an Estonian writer to get translated into a foreign language? Only by way of Russian first, by way of Moscow. Just imagine that—you can't do it directly, gotta go through Moscow."

Soon enough, the large man—a world champion in weightlifting—turned emotional and embraced Sass. "It's hard for all of us, but we won't give up, goddamn it—we'll keep at it. You're a great guy, you know that? Are all writers as great as you guys are? I never met a single writer up until now."

They wrapped their arms around each other's necks like brothers. It was an identically tragic fate that they shared—both had been flung into an awful time and place. If only the conditions had been otherwise, then they *sure* would have shown them!

"Hey sugar," the small man said after a while, addressing Maša. "Where's the phone here?" When he was shown where it was, he made a call:

"Elvi, you know what? I'm here with some writers . . ."

Suddenly Arvi, who had been silent for quite some time, probably even napping, burst out in song:

"*Out, out, out of the Republic . . . !*"

No one attempted to sing along, not that it had really been *meant* as a sing-along song. Most of those present did not know the words, and even Arvi always sang only the first line of the first verse. With that, he reached total blackout stage.

Things carried on as they usually did. Taxis were called to take us to The Cave. While we were waiting for them, Poindexter awoke from his lethargy once again and addressed the freedom fighter:

"Tell me, please: do you think that Estonia will become free?" He apparently did not know who the man was. However, the freedom fighter didn't take offense, didn't start to laugh, but rather took the question seriously:

"Yes, I believe it!" he replied simply.

We took Arvi home and pushed him through the door into the arms of his wife, who tried to smile at us. At The Cave, we socialized with witty drunks of every suit and color, as well as with otherwise-congenial people, among them the *Stammkunden* Doctor Koobalt and Mr. "Devil." The latter worked in retail and would say every five minutes, "*Those're* the kind of Estonian guys I like!" and order a new bottle.

At midnight, everyone started to hop around doing the presently-fashionable "Chicken Dance," flapping out their elbows and stooping from side to side while snapping their fingers at their temples. This did not directly express the era, but was simply a sign of it.


I feel that I have put too many things in one boat. Memory brings together years and events, people and textual excerpts that actually stood detached in time and space. All of it most definitely could not have happened during a single gathering, whether solely because when Arvi got drunk, he would roar his "Out of the Republic" after half an hour, but that which is written on the preceding pages would not have fit into such a short period of time even under the best of intentions. Nevertheless, this is of no major importance. Whether it happened on that occasion or some other time, it still happened *sometime*. The more years that pass, the more that entire era melts together in my memory into a single, unbroken gathering, which in my case lasted for seven years or even longer.

## TIME AND MONEY

Nevertheless, Pekka did not invite his Finnish tourists to join the company of our artists and bohemians the following times either, but instead continued taking them to Rocca al Mare and the Song Festival Grounds and walked with them in the Old Town. Sometimes they would take an early morning bus ride to Tartu, where he would acquaint them with the university and the church ruins on Toome Hill. They drove back the same evening—foreigners were not permitted to stay in Tartu overnight, because there was a Russian military airfield located next to the city.

The Finns' tours were usually three days long, and on the first night, sometimes also the second, Pekka would come to The Cave. Before and after that, he would hang out at someone's atelier or home. This was how he came to know quite a large part of Estonia's cultural individuals over a relatively short period of time, as his interest in them was methodical. Furthermore, he drank very little and had a good memory.

Pekka's Estonian, which had already been good at the start, very soon became so good that no one could tell anymore whether he was an Estonian or a Finn.

Pekka would take literature back with him from Estonia, and helped our cultural figures organize appearances across the bay. He also helped to publish books about Estonian culture. A small circle had developed in Finland, including locals and a few students from Germany and elsewhere, who had come to study in Helsinki and took lectures on the Estonian language. They were called "Estophiles," and they would visit Tallinn for official events (such as the one I spoke about before) and other happenings. They would often come with Pekka their first time, but they soon made acquaintances on their own and started making the rounds without him. After a couple of years, they began putting out a magazine in Finland that published materials related to Estonia. Pekka was appointed its editor-in-chief.

The years went by. Pekka was still in a hurry because of his tourists, and he still had to call taxis and leave in the middle of a gathering.

"Where are you rushing off to—you're the editor-in-chief, aren't you?" Tobi asked one time. "Look at me: I'm only a deputy editor-in-chief, but I've got time galore. I might not have to go anywhere at all tomorrow or the day after. I'll call and tell them that I'm simply not coming."

Everyone laughed. It was the truth.

"Others should be busy, not you!" Maša instructed.

"Ah—in reality, no one should be busy," Pepe interjected. "A gentleman is never busy."

"What kind of an editor-in-chief am I, now—it's not like it is with you here," Pekka said, laughing along good-naturedly. "I'm the entire editorial staff, all on my own. It's not as if I get a salary. Look—I'm so stingy that I can't even bear to pay *myself*!" Pekka would make somewhat simpleminded jokes every once in a while.

"So how come the Finnish state is so poor that it doesn't have the means to employ more people? *That's* what I don't understand, you see," the film critic Sõrgats said, shaking his head.

Pekka dismissed the comment with a wave. "Things are different with us." No one tried to contradict this. Pekka was one of us. That was the main thing.

Several more of Pekka's own poetry collections were published in Finland. One day, he even graduated from the university. Still, the tourist groups remained—he would dock in Estonia with them at least once a month. It was only a dozen years later, immediately before Estonia became free (although there is no direct connection), that he came a few times on his own, without groups, saying that he could finally allow himself some minuscule expenses then.

There are a few more stories about Pekka that I can remember.

The conversation turned (I don't remember how) to work and private life. Pekka said in a modest, yet dignified manner:

"We aren't in the habit of calling each other about work matters on the weekends."

"Ah, what do you mean—you can call all the time," Endel reasoned.

"*Again* some kinds of prejudices," Alja whispered.

"You've got to practice the spirit all of the time," the film critic Sõrgats reckoned.

Pekka stayed diplomatically yet bullheadedly silent.

"I gotta say, I gotta say in any case that you guys up there in Finland have become a bit official. A bit ... bureaucratized. And not just externally, but also internally; in your attitudes," Tobi observed patronizingly.

"Well, y'know, our bohemians do everything, too, of course," Pekka acknowledged. "Some might break into your home at four o'clock in the morning and want to sleep with your wife."

"Hee-hee"—Angelina (aka Anks) started laughing. (She did not express the era.)

"I'm sorry—do I understand correctly that your artists *aren't* all bohemians? That yours are like two separate groups?" Sõrgats asked inquisitively.

"I don't know everyone," Pekka replied, "but I suppose they're probably not."

"Whereas *we* even have bohemians who aren't artists at all," Sõrgats stated proudly.

One evening, we were sitting at Üllar's apartment in the Mustamäe district. The room was filled with people. Üllar had published something in Finland, and had asked Pekka to withdraw the money with the publisher's authorization and bring it across the border. After lunch, they went to the Intourist store on Tartu Road. Pekka had to come along, because the store was only permitted to sell items to foreigners. We were now waiting for them. Üllar's wife Epp entertained us as well as she could; the guests strove to show that they *were* having a good time. In reality, everyone was slightly tense. Then there was the sound of footsteps and sputters of laughter coming from the stairway, and soon Üllar appeared at the doorway, having bought three pairs of shoes. He had, of course, celebrated the occasion with some imported Finnish beer at the store bar: his face was now glowing and he was in an exuberant mood. Before entering the living room, he tossed the shoes down right there in front of us: the first to plop onto the blue carpeted floor was a pair made from black patent leather, followed by some reddish-brown sneakers with enormously thick soles (which were probably expensive), and finally a pair of summer shoes with ventilation holes in them. A middle-aged woman unknown to me picked the shoes up and placed them neatly in front of the bed. It later turned out that she was a Swede. We watched her sympathetically— they're not all that aloof over there, after all! The lady apparently realized that she had done something wrong, gathered the shoes up again, looked at them, and then shoved them into the lap of the man sitting next to her, who passed them on in turn, until the shoes fell to the ground once again. No one picked them up anymore, although several people managed to trip over them throughout the course of the evening. This was how Üllar indicated that he was above the material world, and the others participated in his holy desecration of material with reverence and gusto. "We may be poor, but we have our dignity"—that's probably close to what they wanted to say. It was an impressive spectacle, and I peeked around to see whether or not the foreigners in our company were able to appreciate it. But it seemed to me they weren't. A foreigner stays a foreigner, no matter whether he is a bohemian or an artist—that's what we thought.

And one more episode, likely from The Cave (where else?). We were supposed to go to someone's birthday party and were discussing what food or drink to bring. The conversation turned towards visiting culture in general.

"My *god*, the way they count money there abroad," Lipsik said with a sigh (she visited her female colleagues frequently). "When they go to visit someone, they bring their own food and drinks along with them. And afterward, they tally up their totals with the hosts to see who has paid how much. I've been told that's the custom in some parts of Germany."

"They do it that way in Belgium, too; at least in the part that borders with Germany and where the Germans live," someone said, expanding on her claim.

"Yeah, they really do things differently there," we all sighed together. Those poor souls over in Germany and Belgium!

"Generally, nothing's done without money over there. You have to pay for every move you make," Tobi asserted.

"Then I suppose you *yourself* are paid for every move you make too," Toomas reckoned.

"That's degrading," said Endel. "You can't take money for every little thing you do. An intellectual doesn't take it for everything. It's an intellectual's characteristic trait to do some things without money, too."

"I wonder how it is in Finland?"

"We should ask Pekka when he comes."

"I wonder if he'll even see the point of the question."

"Boys, why are you talking so uglily?" Maša whined disapprovingly.

"But it's the truth," Manglus spoke softly. That was the decisive argument.

Tobi then told the group about how he had once gone to a nightclub in London. Not the most expensive one, of course, but not quite a bunker, either. "I met one dude there—educated, but an alcoholic. I had a hundred pounds in my pocket that Moscow gave me for pocket money, so I wouldn't end up getting embarrassed in front of the other countries' delegates at the congress."

"So, you really *were* all given money by Moscow to take along, too—impressive, guys," Endel said, laughing.

Tobi continued: "I told the dude that in Estonia we have a different attitude towards money than they do. I said, look: I've got a hundred pounds here—I can set it on fire or throw it away with total peace of mind; I won't even blink an eye at it. He says, 'I don't believe you.' I said I could also buy him a beer, too. 'Two!' he says all honey-tongued. 'Buy me two beers! Please!' Then I say, 'Ask me the same thing in Estonian, and I will.' I told him how it sounds. That guy, the bastard, had a really good flair for languages, *repeated* it exactly, and got his two pints."

We listened to Tobi's recollection like it were a beautiful folk tale. We felt immeasurably superior to that unknown foreign alcoholic; to that unfortunate clubgoer. Even Manglus, who had seen a lot in life, chuckled and then declared: "I'll buy you guys a bottle of Grem." Grem was a brand-name cognac that cost twenty-five rubles, which was quite a lot.

"Two, buy us two!" cawed Maulwurf. "I'll say it to you in clear Estonian."

## THE KISS OF A BELLE

I have mentioned Mati Tõusumägi relatively little in my descriptions. This is firstly because I wanted to record the background; to convey a picture of the world in which he moved. Secondly, although he was often the life of the party just as he was in the earlier days, he was nevertheless not an individual who always and consciously wished to dominate—to be the groom at every wedding and the deceased at every funeral, as they say. No—he was also able to sit calmly in a corner, smile mellowly, and enjoy the others. He observed people with a positive gaze. That's exactly it: I felt that he loved people. Thirdly, this was because Mati was not anyone back then, officially. Many of those surrounding him had higher statuses and had gone farther in their fields. Mati's past accompanied him like a shadow. In his free time, he translated from Russian, which he was very fluent in because he had attended a Russian preschool in Siberia. He translated children's literature as well as a number of works of history, such as a book on Papua New Guineans and their researcher, Miklouho-Maclay. The publishers generally didn't allow him to take on historical texts, but the Papuans seemed to be at a safe distance both in terms of time and space. No one had heard of there being a fight for national freedom there; ergo, not even a politically disloyal translator could endanger the Communist Party's main agenda through them. In addition, Mati translated a short monograph about a little-known pre-Incan empire, and another on a certain period in Greenland's history when people didn't live there yet, only seals. In addition to translating, Mati churned out articles on all kinds of topics. Naturally, he wasn't allowed anywhere near the "issue" here, either; however, he did write about cultural things that seemed ideologically unimportant to the authorities: a stop-motion animation film, an exhibition by amateur photographers, museum conferences. In the field of literature, he was limited to shedding light on the activities of poetry clubs. He only had this journalistic work thanks to the fact that he had friends and advocates in editorial positions, who with the tacit approval of their superiors (as long as nothing crazy happened) permitted him to contribute and earn a little extra money. He was no specialist in the areas that he wrote about, of course (the newer trends of handmade knitted items, for example); he mostly wrote general overviews, but he certainly didn't write any worse than most others. Whereas Mati's name was printed on the title page as a book's translator, he had to use a pseudonym at the foot of his articles for a long time. He used several of these, including "Settler" (this made it through the Glavlit censor due to the fact that he put the first name as "Account," so the Glavlit took it as humor). It was only after Gorbachev-era liberalization that Mati was able to use his real name for his articles.

I do not know whether or not he wrote anything else during that time. But he certainly read a lot. Although his official status was modest (a malicious person might have said that he was a literary jack-of-all-trades), he was known, appreciated, and loved in certain circles. Yes, Mati was loved (so his love for others was a requited love, which is moving and occurs rarely). On the one hand, this was because he possessed that easy and mischievous nature that is often found among the so-called "simple folk," but which is rare to find among the upper echelons of the intellectual pyramid. It would always happen that when he started singing and looked straight at someone else, the latter would also start to sing along (although not everyone—not Manglus, for example). On the other hand, this was also because everyone knew that he was smart, a freethinker, and a nationalist, despite the fact that he was unable to disclose his opinions and aspirations in print or broadcast media. It was as if he was a manifestation of the preliminary phase of a real freedom fighter. "Freedom fighter" was a very strong word. I noticed that whenever a real freedom fighter happened to sit down at a table in The Cave (this happened rarely, because some of them had emigrated and the rest lived in reclusion, so those moving around in public could be counted on both hands), the group became more serious. The men would drop their batty antics or their cynical jesting and the women would stop their frivolous chatter for a while. Everyone strove to behave more intelligently, to have a more disciplined attitude, and even to physically sit up straighter. It felt as if an altar or an icon had been carried in procession across the room; as if a tabernacle had materialized in everyone's field of vision, and the people awoke for a moment under its spell, and the recollection or the knowledge from somewhere in the past reached them: "Yes, we are *we*—we really are!" Of course, this kind of state did not last for long, and when the given person had left the table, some of those still sitting there sighed with involuntary relief; before long, the revelry turned even wilder than it had been before.

The following memory might seem foolish or trivial; still, it is typical. We were sitting in The Cave. Gathered around the table was a motley group, as usual: Mati, Endel, Maulwurf, Poindexter, the film critic Sõrgats, Pekka, and a whole flock of ladies. It might have been around nine o'clock; thus, the best time. We had been wisecracking with one another for quite a while. Mati was especially on a roll. One of the ladies was the rock painter Astrid Ulp—a belle in her indeterminable thirties; a woman in full vitality with powerful curves, large blue eyes, and a sensual mouth. Astrid had a scandalous past. She had been a competitive gymnast in her youth, and danced in the variety show when she was a high-school senior. (Students probably weren't banned by law from kicking up their heels in a variety show, but it was certainly disapproved of, because I am unaware of any other such instances. Astrid's father was a colonel in the *militsiya*—maybe that explains things.) She then enrolled in the Art Institute to study stone painting and became quite renowned in her field. At the same time, she had gained even greater fame as a party animal. I had gotten the impression of her as a woman who backed down from nothing, and who, when she started lusting for something, had to get it. I noticed now that this belle was peering at Mati with glassy eyes. They were sitting almost across from each other at first, but every time that someone stood to go to the bathroom, Astrid maneuvered herself one spot closer to Mati, and soon they were sitting side-by-side. I more sensed than saw that she was stroking Mati's thigh underneath the table. Then an exchange of views regarding Michelangelo Antonioni developed between myself and Sõrgats, who was sitting next to me, and I didn't look in their direction for some time. When I looked again, however, neither of them were there any longer. *Got it*, I mused, *the belle has snatched Mati up*. I rose slowly and went to walk around the room, casting sidelong glances at all the tables. Namely, in The Cave, it was common to go and exchange a few words with an acquaintance, to stand there holding your glass, and then have the short conversation turn into a longer one, to take a seat "for just a minute," and end up just staying at the new table. But Mati and Astrid were absent from the main room. I peered into the coatroom—same story. They hadn't *left* together, had they? No, the doorman was not aware of them going. Next to the bathroom was one more room, where tinier banquets were sometimes held, and into which broken chairs had been shoved. Something told me that they were in there, and I had the impulse to play an innocent prank. I opened the door to the nook with one swift thrust. The room was dark. I could hear kind of movement for a second, followed by silence. I fumbled at the wall and found the light switch. At the other end of the room, two people had pulled apart from each other just moments before. It was indeed Mati and the belle. Both looked disheveled and had odd expressions on their faces. They had probably been kissing in the darkness. No, they most definitely had been kissing. "Godspeed, friends!" I announced, and exited delicately. Mati returned to the table a few minutes later, an indifferent look conjured onto his face. The belle arrived after a while, too. "Such a long line at the toilets, huh?" Maša asked. The belle nodded with the look of a martyr. Later that night, when Astrid had had more to drink, she openly had her hands all over Mati; but everyone was already blind-drunk by then, anyway.

That episode seems completely unbelievable now. Today's Astrid would first call three paparazzi onto the scene when she crawled into the nook, and would give them a signal for when to enter and photograph.

In short: Mati was loved for his easy and fun nature, and for his love for the truth. Manglus was loved for his power and superiority. Klaus was loved for his talent. Pekka was loved (partially) because he was a Finn. Girls loved men for what they were.

"That's basically the wrong classification," Manglus said when I dared to present my observations to him years later. "The soul still needs material support. Women aren't divided into those who want love and those who want money. All of them want everything." Manglus was an expert, of course. And he always provided something material as well. He himself once told me about how one morning, he stuck a twenty-five-ruble note into the palm of a young woman (who, by the way, was completely decent) and said: "Take it—you've got none, anyway." The girl certainly blushed, but was very glad at the same time.

## RUI

I started running into Rui at that time, also. I remembered him from my first year of college, from the dormitory, where he loved to wander around at night with a sage look plastered on his face. He studied there for a year before he was kicked out. He himself claimed that it was for political reasons, but I didn't believe it. It wasn't necessarily because he wasn't bright, either. Rather, it had to do with the more general orientation of his personality. Rui was somewhat childish and emotional; he would get going on one thing and then forget about everything else. For example, it would have been possible for him to be invited to Central Asia to herd livestock, and only when he was thousands of kilometers away from home, before falling asleep staring at a velvet-black expanse of sky, would he remember that he actually needed to be studying for his exams.

After being kicked out, Rui was something between a hippy and a punk—as much as the Soviet period enabled it. Later, when I met him in Tallinn, he looked exactly the same as he had a decade before: long, loose hair, small wire-framed glasses, frayed skin-tight jeans, and a satchel. Rui was situated somewhere on the periphery of intellectual society: he wasn't quite *in*, but he wasn't *out*, either. Many people knew him. Rui would occasionally end up at The Cave, and it was then that I was able to study him more closely. He was a figure who left a funny impression at first, but one that was soon a little less funny. Every once in a while, he would say something absurd, at which everyone broke out laughing, especially when they were enjoying a little post-bender hair of the dog. Of course, he would repeat his successful joke. People laughed the second time, sometimes also the third, but then later would only yawn. Rui would then realize that enough was enough, and would try to come up with a new bit of absurdity. It was like his main attraction; he seemed to think that he always had to clown around. In reality, Rui wasn't tolerated so much for his originality, but because he appeared to get others' jokes; at least he would laugh in the right place. He had read a thing or two, and could remember things retold by others. In any case, he reacted to cultural keywords (when the title of some work or a writer's name was mentioned to him, for example) and did not just stare back dumbly. By the way, Mati also knew Rui and seemed to even be fond of him—for some reason, he saw Rui as a "poor little guy."

Rui always greeted me laconically, but with a slightly repulsive overfamiliarity, saying his "Hey, there" as if he were whispering a rather racy secret into your ear. We had exchanged casual rejoinders before, but always in the presence of some third person. On that day, I was walking back from Pikk Street, where the publisher's honorarium office was located. I had received several hundred rubles for a longer translated text, which for me was a considerable amount, and was mulling pleasant thoughts of how I would spend it. Suddenly, I see Rui approaching from a distance with his then-inseparable companion, the fat Umbu. Umbu never spoke, only laughed incessantly. I nodded politely but icily, and meant to continue on my way. Rui, however, stepped out in front of me.

"I'm not very closely acquainted with you, my good sir," I said as decorously as I could manage. Occasionally, that kind of tone helps.

"Nor I with you, but who cares," Rui replied, shaking his head. Umbu burst out laughing. "I've got a *foul* headache," Rui announced. "I'd like to do something about it—gimme a little loan, would you? Of course, we could also stop in somewhere *together*, too, in order to celebrate the publication of your immortal translation. That way, you can drink off of your own money, too." This was Rui's typical shamelessness. I weighed the options in my head. There was only one that I did not want—to "stop in" somewhere and converse at length with him. Maybe

I could buy my way free? Rui seemed to read my mind.

"Gimme a fiver," he said compellingly. "You've got to give it to *me*—it's like a sacrifice to the holy altar. It'll make both of us happy. You know, it's always pleasant speaking with a wise man like you."

I coughed at the compliment and remarked that five rubles was quite a lot of money. Mightn't a "threer" be enough for a few mugs of beer at a bar?

"A threer?" Rui shouted so loudly that passersby turned and watched us curiously. I felt embarrassed, but that was exactly what Rui was trying for. "A *threer!*" he screeched even louder. "Where'll I go with a *threer!*" Then, however, he returned to his original posture, becoming chummy and patronizing once again.

"Don't fight it, man. It was fate that brought us together now. It happens, right? Bam, today wasn't your day. Listen— a lot's demanded of him who's given a lot. You get my drift, of course, don't you? Not talent, but money." I chuckled involuntarily: how did he know about my honorarium? Nevertheless, he announced the amount that I had been paid almost to the ruble. *There is a type of guy*, I mused, *who's able to count others' money*. Even so, I gave him a fiver.

Later, I realized that he says his "a lot's demanded of him" bit to everyone he filches money from. There's always someone who hears it for the first time, and who laughs at it like it was an impromptu witticism.

Rui was occasionally quite sharp, or at least very imaginative. For example: he once claimed that Communist Party members have the might of twelve men, and can materialize anywhere in the world at will—as rain, fog, or rats. However, they have to be able to visit the basement of their Party headquarters from time to time in order to sit at the oval conference table there. If they haven't been in that room for a while, then they lose their strength.

## A CLASSIC'S BIRTHDAY

Thinking back on those years, we in The Cave felt that nothing was happening in society on a political plane—that everything was like stagnant pond water. All the same, some currents were probably still moving somewhere—but we were unfamiliar with the youth. We were *unable* to know them, because time passed quickly in The Cave, and we believed that *we ourselves* were still the youth—that no other youth even existed.

It was the mid-eighties: perestroika had not yet begun, and on the surface, nothing really forecasted its arrival. The public was celebrating the birthday of our most famous writer. Already close to a decade earlier, the man had become a hit in Estonia and a symbol of national culture with his poems and novels.

"If *I* had that kind of talent . . ." young writers would whisper, their eyes burning with admiration.

"We do, we *do* have a few grand old men left," dignified elderly intellects would remark with pride and life-tempered wisdom. As the literary great was bought, read, and loved so widely, there was also a need to celebrate his birthday on several levels and in multiple stages. A gala was organized in the most prominent state performance hall, the Estonia Theatre, where the cream of society—including government and Party figures—gathered. The second-most-important event took place in Tartu, where the writer had attended school. Additionally, literary soirées were held across the entire country: in libraries, schools, and elsewhere—even in preschools, because the literary star had also written a children's book. A memorial stone was unveiled at the writer's birth-house in a small village, and a fishing trawler was named after him. A postage stamp was issued in his honor in Moscow. His birthday was also marked in several locations abroad, where the maestro was invited to appear on the occasion of new published translations of his works. Yet the most intimate, spiritual, and patriotic gathering took place at the Writers' House. (This event was purely for his colleagues from the literary sphere; none of my actor, singer, or artist friends were present. This was good, in its own right. I admit that I had slightly concealed from them the fact that I am a nationalist by heart.)

Just as was custom at such events, speeches were given at the beginning of the evening; but on this occasion, they were a degree more open-minded and stimulating than the ones that

had been given in the Estonia Theatre or elsewhere. His colleagues were glowing, one trumped the next with his or her es-
prit, and everyone had something funny or deep to recall about
the maestro. Among the other attendees was a small delegation
of schoolboys. They were actually the first to show up at the
Writers' House—an hour before the event began, when Leo
Vims from the literary propaganda office (a pleasant old booz-
er) was still setting up chairs in the auditorium. (This was his
duty, as was checking to make sure that the water in the pitcher next to the podium was fresh. To do this, Old Vims usually
sipped straight from the mouth of the pitcher, smacked his lips,
and said: "Ah, worse's been drunk!") The boys seemed to be almost children, although they were probably fifteen or sixteen-
year-olds. They claimed to be members of the Mother Tongue
Society's youth section, and said they had come to congratulate
the maestro in the name of the younger generation. They asked
Vims where they could get undressed. Vims did not understand
the question at first, and replied that they could leave their coats
in the coatroom. However, it turned out that the boys wanted
to take off more than that. Vims then led them into the small
space behind the stage, where a sound system meant for playing
the national anthem on state holidays was stored.

When it was the boys' turn to take the stage, they exited
the backstage nook in single file, wearing white sleeveless shirts
and short black shorts, as children did during gym class back
then. They looked a little awkward, but determined. The boys
had prepared an entire program of living literary dioramas, by
which they illustrated the stages of Estonian literary history.
They took a seat on the floor around the edge of the "stage" and
started forming compositions one by one. (One of the boys—
apparently their ideologist or artistic director, who was wearing a suit—sat in the corner and issued quiet orders, snapping
his fingers.) First, the tallest of the boys was the only one left
on stage: he stood with his side facing the audience, one leg in
front of the other as a sign of wandering. He had a bindle over
his shoulder and a floppy hat on his head, with hair from a peasant wig spilling down onto his shoulders. It was Kristjan Jaak
Peterson, who walked from Tartu to Riga! This was followed

by the "Viru Vow" of Kreutzwald, Faehlmann, and Nocks on Rakvere's Castle Hill followed. The birth of *Kalevipoeg* and the "Young Estonia" and "Siuru" literary groups were not left undepicted. When they reached the year 1944, one of the boys made rowing movements in a "boat's stern" while two others mournfully watched the fading shores of their homeland, singing a beautiful lament. After that, a portion of the troupe stood with their backs to the audience and formed a "barbed-wire" fence by holding their fingers spread wide over their heads! Walking in front of it on their hands were writers who had remained in their homeland, with *partorgs* holding their legs. At the very end, a "worker" and a "kolkhoz woman" climbed onto their backs, and the whole thing collapsed. It was done cleverly, so one might get the impression that the collapse was accidental. The boys even apologized and repeated the performance, but it fell down again. Things didn't go better the third time, either. The audience understood, and chuckled.

The young men were not very athletic—their faces were flushed after the exertion of the performance, and some even had little belly rolls (the type of people we called "deepies"). The one snapping his fingers in the corner, who could be regarded as their spokesperson or informal leader, was downright chubby. Still, the audience was enthralled, because it had been something truly fresh. The older female writers sighed tenderly as they watched the boys.

Whether or not someone had authorized them to perform—that, I do not know. For some reason, I think that the Mother Tongue Society's youth section did not even *exist* at that time.

During the wining and dining (even this part was unusually warm and intimate) that followed the program, the boys huddled shyly in a corner, sampling the potato salad and savory appetizers; they did not touch the alcohol. They wore school uniforms and had light peach fuzz on their jaws (the boys apparently had not shaved for a month before their performance, in order to have a more "considerable" impact). We struck up a conversation with them on the topic of literature. They were surprisingly up-to-date with everything, having even read Mati Tõusumägi's essays in the samizdat journals. Mati himself was there, also. He seemed to smile a little condescendingly at them at first, but became very friendly when he saw that the boys were erudite.

When I peeked into The Cave late that night, just checking to see if anyone was there, Mati was sitting at a table alone with the boys' spokesperson. The former was already quite sauced, while the boy had a tortured look on his face that he was trying to hide with all his might. It was absolutely frigid outside that day, by the way; the virtuosic writer had been born in a cold month. However, the boys had come to his birthday celebration without winter coats—they had marched from the Victory Square trolley stop to the Writers' House wearing only light jackets. When we inquired about this, they said with straight faces that they were practicing for Siberia "if it should be necessary." I hope that Mati took the spokesboy home by taxi—scuttling around in the dead of night without a coat would be overdoing it, all the same.

In short, the boys left the impression of being deferential, decent, and educated. At least three of the members of that group became a part of the new government after the restoration of the Republic of Estonia.

The government truly does include three men whom I remember from times long ago. And the event honoring the maestro, which I described above, really did take place—how couldn't it have? But are these things really connected to each other? I sometimes suspect that I might have actually made it up; might have constructed it in order to adjust the course of some individual's life to my own goals, to show how he got things done back *then* already. I'm not quite sure of whether I met the boys there at the legendary author's birthday celebration (the writer himself, by the way, was not present). The more that I think back to it now, the more it seems that in reality, it all took place on a ferry sailing to Saaremaa. And they were not members of the youth section of the Mother Tongue Society, but rather of the Nature Protection Society (because that really did exist), who were on their way to Viidumäe in order to plant some kind of very important and patriotic plants that had started to die out elsewhere in Estonia. Because stripping yourself down in the auditorium of the Writers' House—that seems a bit much. On the other hand, many people are naked on the ferry in summer. Yes—*that's* probably how it really was, by all assumptions. Especially since environmental protection was one of the main substitutes and secret outlets for the resistance movement back then. But was the literary maestro on board the ferry, too? It's completely possible that he was, because he had a summer home near the Sangla windmills, as Estonians generally know. So, everything fits. But where does that leave "practicing for Siberia," then? No doubt it stuck in my mind from some other situation. It wasn't unknown for someone to charge out of The Cave, storm drunkenly head first into a snow drift, and start shouting anti-Russian slogans. But where did the pyramids come from? Was it really from the Discovery Channel?

Such were the surroundings in which Mati Tõusumägi moved. I could recall a great deal more—the events rise from my memory ad infinitum, like the earth on the fields of Vargamäe,[16] lifting up stones from its bosom.

It is strange that there existed another world contemporaneous with the world of The Cave, somewhere a few hundred kilometers away, inhabited by Teedu and his pert-breasted Merle. Forming one part or sub-section of this world was the university's Department of Communist Party History, where they taught things that no one directly believed any longer (with the exception of a few retired individuals).

Over the years, Teedu had of course begun to realize that some saw him and his colleagues as very naive people who were removed from the public, living in their shells and taking their own imaginings as reality. However, things were even more complicated in Teedu's mind. The fact that he didn't protest and was prepared to close his eyes to the truth was not primarily due to his own career interests, but rather due to higher considerations. It appeared to be the same case with several of his colleagues. People never spoke about dogmas in their private conversations. They did, however, voice all kinds of opinions on

the organization of society; even abstractly and philosophically. What is a purposeful society, and for whom?—that was the
question. *Cui bono?* When young Teedu heard this "cuibono"
for the first time (probably out of the mouth of Hasso Miller—
that savvy guy sitting between two chairs), he could not make
heads or tails of it. Even so, he looked into it and studied it,
thought about it. Everything went at a gradual pace with him.
Teedu knew that some of what he said during lectures was not
the truth, strictly speaking. Yet is strict truth at all possible in
questions that concern something as vague as human life? Or
even if it *was*, then would have been of the highest importance?
Wasn't, for example, the fact that it would soon be forty years
without war in Estonia significant? If one were to leave out the
deportations, then people had lived a peaceful life where steady
rules had applied for a quarter of a century already.

Even if the truth existed, then how many people knew how to
handle it—knew how to deal with it in a balanced way, and not
solely according to their personal interests? No, the truth alone
could not be a goal in and of itself. Nor could one ask whether
religion was truth. Still, religion had come in handy a number of
times in history. Teedu saw more and more similarities between
religion and communism, but he kept these to himself. Truth
and wisdom were not as important as friendship, solidarity, and
love for one's neighbor. What was important was being human.
Being a good father, being a good husband. Being a good kolkhoz head, brigade chief—even a good *partorg*. Everything else
was trivial compared with that. Refraining from doing others
harm as much as is possible. A factory director who loved his
subordinates like a family was more in favor with God (in the
event that one existed, of course) than a freedom fighter, who
solely wanted to prove to people that they had certain rights.

Teedu had started to feel that even though he had become
an instructor of Party history (although Party history *was* still
social studies in the wider sense) for much more mundane considerations (being in darkness and unknowingly, to tell the
truth), it had been a good and proper choice all the same, because his job accomplished work that was important for the
public good—he was standing watch over the order of people's

lives. So, all in all, everything had still gone well. For living, only living was necessary. Human life was all there was. Having excessive sympathy for people was unnecessary. Teedu had come to realize that people love rulers. Belief was needed to organize people's lives correctly. The Soviet regime was needed for people to be at peace. Leaving the national aspect aside, it was a fully functional society. (One time, Teedu came up with the idea of starting to translate the Party vocabulary that had been adopted as loan words into a more organic Estonian. For example, the clumsy phrase "the dictatorship of the proletariat" was unappealing and unnatural to people, and could be said some other way, maybe even dialectically reinterpreted. Teedu had quite a lot of these notions. He tiptoed around the subject with the department director. The director was enthralled by the idea at first, but not so much later. Ultimately, he recommended Teedu to give it up. It appeared that someone had set him straight in the meantime.)

Teedu gave ten lectures per week on average, and held eight seminars. The lectures were to his liking. He spoke effortlessly and in a lively manner, often having to restrain himself because he tended to get emotional and open himself up in front of the students. But he also drew energy from the auditorium and often felt fresher after a lecture than he had before.

The instructor's world was not composed merely of lessons and teaching, either. Teedu frequently worked in the library. He had developed yet another hobby in addition to house marks: Chinese culture, or the Ming dynasty to be exact, which had been the longest stable and peaceful era in Chinese history. Millions of people had lived a secure, orderly, and comfortable life for several centuries. Teedu himself undoubtedly had a life like that at the time. He sometimes felt that he was happy, and lived that way for seven years or even more.

At that same time, Mr. Kulu, who had finally saved up enough money for his gold teeth, was still giving Russian language lessons somewhere. His Russian pronunciation improved thanks to the dental upgrade, but not to the extent that he had hoped. He still played Pakhmutova's "The Song of the Perturbed

Youth" for students, although no longer from a vinyl record, but rather a cassette player. He still stared out the window into the distance while it played, his eyes glinting. His message for the children had altered slightly. Instead of repeating that we have everything, but there are guilty people somewhere who are not fulfilling their duty, and therefore it does not reach others—instead of that, he had started saying that we *could* have everything. Mr. Kulu had definitely switched to the conditional in his manner of speech: that grammatical nuance spoke worlds in terms of global history, and this was how he continued to express his era.

Kulu had gotten married to one of his former students meanwhile, but the woman had left him after a couple of years because, in her opinion, he was "stupidly honest." His short, broad-chested dog Stormbird was dead.

## LEARNED FRIEND

Social life whisked me along and threatened to devour me like a vortex. Luckily, sober thought had not left me for good, and I admitted to myself that I was not 100 percent a creative individual. When the wave started lapping too high and the ecstasy I felt from my own life was on the verge of swelling to overlarge proportions, I always said to myself: "Let the creative types live the way they want to—you aren't meant for it and have to get by another way! You shouldn't burn out like that, but should instead occupy your time steadily and smartly. You're not a crack shooter of big ammunition, but rather a steadfast and hard-working slogger; a vigorous military trench-specialist of culture!" One unusual connection also helped me to maintain my mental balance throughout these times.

When I brought my next subsequent submission (a translation, as always) to the editorial office of the magazine *Soviet Youth* one late morning of January 1984, the secretary Lhea handed me a letter. I opened it quite indifferently, even grudgingly, because the people who sent letters to the office usually did not have an especially deep connection to the cultural world, and were occasionally outright imbeciles. Years earlier, I had kept a few letters containing words of praise (I stuck them in a box that had previously contained assorted candies), but soon realized that this was not much wiser than holding onto tram tickets, clothing price tags, receipts from fines, and other scraps that record the flow of life as paper bearers. Still, though, I would read through the letters sent to me before tossing them into the wastebasket (there weren't many), and would reply to a couple of the more intelligent ones. The given letter was addressed to "Honorable Chronicler!" and written at the end (I checked this immediately) was "Learned Friend." The formula seemed familiar, but from where? From what time? I had to rummage around my memory for a few good moments before I remembered. Yes, of course! It had been long ago, ten years earlier ...

My parents had divorced and started new lives after I graduated from secondary school, and since I didn't want to be a burden on them, especially since they had both generously agreed to support me in my studies, I lived in a dormitory during my time at university (only in the fall of my fifth year did I rent a room in the Supilinn district so as to write my thesis in peace). I met many people there, including a semi-eccentric (eccentrics can be found everywhere). To this day, I do not know what Illimar Robinson studied—whether it was Russian philology or psychology; in any case, it had to be something in the humanities, because we lived in the dorm for students of the History and Linguistics departments. Illimar looked nothing like an intellectual: he was tall and lanky with big feet and hands (it would have been more correct to refer to the latter as "mitts," because you could hold a soccer ball with one of them, flippers aren't needed when swimming). His face was rustic and rounded with high cheekbones, sharp chin, his hair coarse, and his eyes small, narrow, and sly, as if they wanted to say: "*We* already know, don't even come near us with your yammering." His arms and legs swung unusually, meaning they did not move synchronically as with normal people. We others walk with our right leg and left arm forward, and vice-versa. But Robinson's left arm and left leg would go at the same time, then his right leg and right arm in turn, and he would do this all the time. It was not noticeable in everyday life, because he had a furtive stride and kept his hands in place—at his side, in his pockets, or behind his back. Yet things were hard for him in line drills during military training, because there, one's arms had to move like threshing flails. The Russian officers would gather along the side of the training grounds to watch Illimar like some freakish animal, and would shake their heads, muttering: "*Nu i chudovishche!*"[17] I heard that at first they even wanted to send him to the medical committee for tests to see if he was possibly faking it. But then they just decided to relieve Illimar from collective marching, because someone like that would have ruined the whole beautiful row with his waddling. So, while the rest of the men beat their soles tempestuously against the asphalt and roared out salutes, he had to practice alone on the edge of the grounds. What he accomplished there resembled a dance instructor who had gone quietly insane.

This half-eccentric lived on the same floor as I did. He wasn't sociable, wouldn't even greet others, and carried himself like an autistic person in general. That is just it—he was not arrogant, but simply lived "elsewhere and beyond"; greeting others was not even a thought that crossed his mind. At the end of the dormitory corridor was a small nook—a couple of armchairs and a tiny table—that was called the "break corner." Illimar enjoyed standing there and looking out the window. This is why the doe-eyed couples in love, who wanted to make out and feel each other up in the corner, couldn't stand him. Illimar would stand in the break corner at all times of day, from which one could deduce that he slept irregularly. In any case, when I sometimes got back late from a gathering in the city, the first thought that struck me in the morning twilight was that pranksters had dragged some kind of a sculpture over to the dormitory window, and it was eying passersby with its stony face. In reality, it was Illimar observing the world. I once went and stood next to him for giggles. I do not know what drove me to do so—certainly not a desire to tease him. And what did I find out? If you stood next to him for ten minutes and started talking about something apropos of nothing, then he would unnoticeably start to speak along with you, and not on any trivial topic. Quite the opposite: if, for example, you

remarked that "the sensibility of trees is undoubtedly uncondi-
tional," then it was possible for a long and substantial conversation to evolve out of it. But we usually just stood there without
exchanging a single word. I realized then that it is very interesting to be silent together with someone — in the event that you
know the other person is like you in certain ways; that they feel
and think a little like you yourself do. We once stood that way
for forty-five minutes before each going our separate way, having first rotated towards each other politely and given a soft nod,
as if in gratitude. It was after this that I had the idea of sending
him a letter — officially, postmarked. He replied — amiably and
with finely-tuned phrasing, not at all tersely, but rather in ful-
ly-formed thoughts, using polite expressions, just as in a work
of literature. And so, our correspondence began. One time, I
decided not to post the letter, but instead physically placed it
in the alphabetized mail slots next to an information board
in the dorm's foyer. However, I was given a concealed rebuke
in the next reply that Illimar sent me — it seemed important
to him that a letter be sent in the proper manner. And that is
how it stayed. Such correspondence may seem strange, but if
you think about how even married couples sometimes speak
to each other in written form or call on their cell phones to the
next room over, then it isn't all that odd.

What did we write about? We discussed things (in truth,
each presented his own positions about them) that have always
seemed important to young humanities students only just discovering the world. The topics were intellectual and abstract
almost without exception (for example: the subjectivity of
happiness and unhappiness, the immortality of the soul, the
purposefulness of the world, love as deception). I admit that
for me, it was a little bit of a game, a ritual; I cannot say what it
was for Illimar. A friendship did not manifest between us in any
other form, and we knew nothing of each other's personal lives.
Upon graduating from university, things turned out such that we
did not exchange our new possible coordinates. Our internships
took place in different towns, and we rarely crossed each other
in the dorm at that time (although even when I was living in the
Supilinn apartment, I had my mail sent to the dormitory so I

might have a reason to stroll to that good old familiar place.) Thus, we indeed disappeared from each other's radars, and our written correspondence came to a lull for almost eight years.

I *had* occasionally called Illimar Robinson "Learned Friend" at the beginning of my letters. I addressed him like that casually and a little teasingly, but at the same time still justifiably, because Illimar was carrying a book beneath his arm most of the time and was learned, too — in quite a different way than the rest of us were. I soon began adding "The Chronicler" (which turned out to be foretelling) to the end of the letters in place of my real name. Still, though, I had written my proper name in the beginning. It is possible that Illimar had indeed seen it somewhere in print now — for the first time in eight years. He read Estonian-language literature (and journalism) very rarely.

Standing next to the secretary's desk from which the bored Lhea peered at me with unconcealed curiosity, and realizing who the author of the letter was, a warm feeling flooded my heart — my dear Learned Friend! Illimar was undoubtedly a special case. By this, I do not mean his behavioral or his psychological eccentricities, not to mention his appearance, but rather what can be called the dominant of his inner world, his particular sound, or his fixed figure. Illimar had been interested in all kinds of romantic phenomena since a very early age. This was not simply an interest, but, to put it more precisely, a fondness; an affinity of spirit and blood. His entire being was tugged towards them — he was perpetually encountering them, he identified with them. Romanticism may be too broad of a notion. Illimar was fascinated by the intellectual current that carries life forward; by the spiritual blaze that bears people upon its breaker. People start behaving differently than they normally do in the situations inspired by such blazes, and no longer act under the compulsion of mere everyday needs. Instead of being spurred along by reproduction, feeding, and survival, as well as, for example, entertainment or a competitive spirit, they are instead driven by visions and inspirations. People sprout wings and their eyes spark.

In some respects, it is surprising that Illimar never took an active interest in the actual practice of art. I think that the visionary spirituality that accompanied art was too self-evident in his mind. Art *had* to be a sphere of life designated for visionary spirituality alone. This is what comprised both art's strength and its weakness. When the influence of art on society was great and tightly interwoven with other parts of life, such as in German Romanticism or during Estonia's period of national awakening, then it generated powerful visions that were able to influence the masses. However, when art secluded itself from life, turning into a domain of specialists, so to say—into a workshop of thrill-craftsmen—then it could easily acquire the image of being technical knackery. By way of the boastful levity by which art brought attention to itself, it could even ridicule another "endeavor's" format. One way or another, art was put outside of parentheses in Illimar's mental accounting.

He was captivated by romanticism and the basic intellectual particles in life in the broadest sense, especially in the sphere of "historical creation," using politics as its tool. This concerned both the "particular," meaning individuals and events, and the "general," such as epochs or the intellectual structures spanning different eras. In order to give just the slightest idea of his admirations, I will mention that his personal pantheon included, for example, Pericles, Leonidas and Marcus Aurelius, Meister Eckhart and William Blake, the "Founding Fathers" of America, Garibaldi, the polar explorers Scott and Amundsen, the astronaut Neil Armstrong and Mother Teresa, Martin Luther King and Mary Baker Eddy, the Seventh-day Adventist prophet Ellen White, Albert Schweitzer, *batko* Makhno, and who all else. Yet, he also admired the rise of Spartacus and the Crusades, the American colonists' westward drive, and the eastern one of Russian colonists. He was fond of druids, samurais, and the Red Latvian Riflemen, the self-sacrificing workers of Estonia's rural libraries and the wandering actors of every era, animal rights activists and Chekhov's *Three Sisters*. In this, he was not disturbed by the fact that it might have been an antithetical or outright adverse phenomenon in practice. He held the same level of respect for Grand Inquisitor Torquemada as he did for Jan Hus and Joan of Arc, Wallenstein, and also Charles XII, Napoleon, and Metternich, the Jesuits, and the Free Masons. I remember how his eyes shone when he saw a nun who had ended up in Tartu by chance, and how he shed a tear hearing "La Marseillaise" in French. He had a weakness for national anthems, church music, and revolutionary songs in general. To elaborate further: although several religious figures numbered among Illimar's favorites, this was not due foremost to religion. He once wrote:

*It is not important what you believe. It is important to believe in general. To believe that there is something else apart from our mundane life and the material world. To believe that our existence does not conclude with our presence in this circle. To believe—that means to resist, to refuse to admit that we are a tiny bubble on the surface of a puddle. Oh why oh why is it regarded as the utmost dignity to stand up straight and thunder out such hollow prattle as: "I am human and proud of it, because I know that I am the center of everything and that all ends with me; I will take the battle upon myself; I will go into the storm"? Why is it more dignified than, on the contrary, saying: "Yes, I know that there is something greater than me; I want to belong to it and be a soldier in its service, to put myself at its disposal"? Matter, or the things we perceive, are first-given; they come to us of their own accord, so to say—so what kind of an art recognizes that? It is a feat for me, too! The true sublime is exactly the opposite—it is a revolt against spontaneity and* force majeure. *Romanticism is the inability and unwillingness to reconcile oneself to the featureless first-given to the sad original state, to the debasing reality.*

So he wrote after his third year at university, and it sounded somewhat childish. He later partially renounced his phrasing, claiming that he had "developed." And he specified (or repeated, rather) that he was not interested in religion per se— in eternal bliss and life beyond the grave—but instead in the overlapping part that connects a religious individual to others whose lives are likewise guided by a spiritual dominant. I stress that for Illimar, the main thing was always the elation and the stimulation that is sparked when one progresses towards a dream; when one endeavors towards something, whatever the goal may be. Paradise or soulful bliss were fitting objectives to have, of course, but Illimar was not intrigued by paradise in and of itself. I realized that paradise was boring to him, because it was the final station and therefore static. "Where can you progress to from bliss?" he asked while staring out the dormitory window, down onto the street, where a young man and a young woman stood pressed against each other, the first snowflakes falling around them, the city water tower their backdrop.

Officially, Illimar's college thesis was on the American writer Saul Bellow. In reality, it should have been titled "Romanticism and Christianity." You might remember that the main character in *Herzog* once began writing a study of same name. However, Bellow did not reveal what the study addressed in greater detail. "Romanticism and Christianity" was simply a literary sign for him — an image depicting the main character's spiritual level. I was left with the impression that my Learned Friend wanted to revive that treatise now, while pretending that it had to do purely with literature. In reality, he was being clever about it: for he was not interested in Bellow, but in romanticism and Christianity *specifically*. His main thesis was that Christianity is history's absolute greatest romantic phenomenon overall. Over the course of one-and-a-half thousand years, it had dominated people's minds to the extent that it made them reside in a spiritual world — if one treats the spirit as the opposite of mortal, i.e. "normal" life. Throughout all of those centuries, the most crucial thing for people had been something that could not be touched or perceived, which no one had ever seen. The fact that this "something" enveloped all of society, all of its aspects and degrees, was thus the triumph of the imagination. The primary thing — once again — was that man was spurred on by the elementary spiritual element.

Naturally, Illimar was not able to write about this word for word in a Soviet college thesis. Although Bellow was not banned, because he was intellectually critical of American society, nor was romanticism (some extensions of it were even highly honored, such as the revolutionary romanticism of Maxim Gorky), Christianity was "out" in any case. (Let us recall that at that time, it was only possible to address many things in critical form alone. For example, one did not write a dissertation on Western philosophy, but rather "a critique of Western philosophy." We, the twenty-year-olds, already knew this customary truth of Soviet humanities studies well.) And so, Illimar wrote the central section of his thesis as if it were Moses Herzog's monologue, putting it into quotation marks, from start to finish! At the end, however, he personally disproved it in two sentences as being a "utopia of the bourgeois intelligentsia of Western society." He "welded" the obligatory Lenin quotes to the start and finish. All of it was so transparent that it was hard to believe he had deceived his advisor. The latter was more likely in silent collaboration with him. In any case, Illimar successfully defended his thesis. A few years later, a modified and condensed article version of it was published in the literary monthly *Looming*, and that was already without Lenin or any sort of refutation. Still, the piece failed to receive wider attention, because it was regarded merely as a literary study, or as the written confession of a man of faith who had renounced his beliefs.

Although Illimar was not religious, he had a sense of sympathy *for* religion; to him, Christianity was "romanticism squared." Monks were the greatest romantics and had Illimar's admiration—hermits, as well as monastery and mendicant monks. Monks were professionals; they had "gotten ahead" of others. He viewed monkhood as mankind's greatest achievement. He was unable to pass by a monk without first walking over and speaking a few words in Latin (which he had studied independently), after which the monk would make the sign of the cross above him (if it was indeed a Christian monk). He likewise loved everyone who lived like monks, although he himself did not officially belong to any order. He had considered the possibility of entering a monastery as a lay brother, but had come to realize that this "would not improve him any more."

Despite his love for monks, Illimar was not a lunatic or a monomaniac in that sense: he understood the inevitability of carrying on the human race and earning one's daily bread. Women were definitely necessary, too. He generally spoke and wrote very little about females—probably for the same reason as with art. He regarded them as romantic beings already by their nature, and as sharing a common element with idealism. *They* were also outside of parentheses, and in that sense did not need to be handled separately. The parallel with art was that much greater because women could give spiritual movements a second pair of wings, but they could also reduce them to narrow, earthly personal dramas. Illimar himself (at least this is how it appeared to me) was not especially close to any women, but he didn't ignore them when they happened to cross his path. He was not averse to socializing with women, but it wasn't what was "most important."

I had gotten the impression that Illimar planned to continue his work after university. In this, he might not even have been thinking about publishing books and defending dissertations, because he was motivated by a global vision. I know, for example, that his longer-term wish was to compose a sort of registry or encyclopedia of everything in the history of humanity that had been borne of a "spiritual flame" (the compendium was going to be titled *Vaimu vakuraamat*, referring to a historic record of feudal holdings and taxes in Livonia, which would now consist of spiritual entries). He admitted to himself that such a task was beyond one person's means. For this reason, he mulled ideas of establishing some kind of a center or an office. His models for this center were (and to an equal extent) the sociology laboratory that was run at the university back then (which was soon shut down by the authorities) and the Communist Upbringing Office (which operated until perestroika). He sometimes even dreamed of building a global network of collaborators. Experts from every land and culture would record the epochs of spiritual inspiration in their own cultures' histories, outline the general character of these, the more outstanding representatives of the eras, significant events, their spiritual and material infrastructure and attributes, and so forth. When my Learned Friend spoke of this, his eyes would be focused towards the sky ("where the clouds disappear") and his narrow, clever eyes glinted. A couple dozen seconds later, he would sigh happily, clench his fists, and beat his forehead and chest with them. "Work," he would proclaim, "I must work!"

Nothing came of his grandiose plans initially. Namely, the KGB interfered. Out of young naiveté, Illimar had started seriously recruiting collaborators for his center. Naturally, his letters to foreign research centers and persons (including to the Carnegie

Institute, the recently opened Pompidou Center, the Dalai Lama, and Bob Dylan) were intercepted and read, and Illimar was summoned to speak with security officers. There, in the Tartu security headquarters located on Vanemuise Street, they came to the conclusion fairly quickly that the case did not concern an active opponent, but rather an "eccentric." In spite of this fact, Captain Ivar Sidorov of the Third Administration (which took care of academics), who handled Illimar's case personally, told him with exceptional emphasis that Soviet power is the most romantic thing in the world, and if Illimar did not "cut the crap," then he could not hope for mercy.

"You know, romanticism can be found in Vorkuta[18] as well—*other* visionaries are sitting there waiting for you already," Captain Sidorov said with a chuckle. He saw himself as an intellectual, and in his mind, the word "visionary" was a foul insult similar to "faggot."

The center and the encyclopedia were thus crossed out for the time being, but man is free in his thoughts. No one could forbid a low-profile village schoolteacher (which Illimar very soon became, holding the job for almost ten years) from practicing something for his own use at home, be it distilling or dreams about turning the world towards the light of romanticism. Illimar was involved in the latter of these two activities— the years that had passed meanwhile had not shaken his belief. He continued to hope that humankind would become spiritual once again, and believed that "great things were to be expected." However, he kept this belief to himself, because "the time was not yet ripe." He was similarly unsure of where the "thing would launch from." He never mentioned the prospect of something happening in Estonia. Thus, if Poindexter had posed his question to Illimar, the response would probably have been "no." Illimar didn't believe that Estonia would become independent. In truth, it wasn't important to him—just like everything else that did not concern the red-hot axis of his mental world.

Why did he write to me now? Doubtless a person, no matter how hermitic and introverted, occasionally has the desire to share his or her thoughts with someone. Perhaps Illimar corresponded with others as well—I did not ask. Just as I did not

know whether anyone opened and read our letters in the meantime.

When KGB Captain Sidorov told Illimar that Soviet power was
the most romantic thing in this world, he had wanted to make
fun of Illimar. Yet, unknowingly, he had nearly hit the nail on
the head, because Illimar believed more or less the same! Fine,
maybe not the *most* romantic — Illimar ranked neither eras nor
situations — and definitely not for the entirety of its duration,
but it was romantic for sure. Illimar had great admiration for
the Russian revolution and the years immediately preceding
and following it. (By the way, his nightstand held a tattered
copy of Nikolai Ostrovsky's *How the Steel Was Tempered*.) By
his understanding, there was an immense amount of enthusiasm in society back then. During the twenties and thirties, people genuinely believed that they were building a city of the sun.
The fact that its name happened to be "communism" was of
no great consequence. They were living for the future. In spite
of Stalin's repressions gradually gaining momentum, life as a
whole was not alienated or degenerated; "red tape" was not yet
ubiquitous. A lofty and romantic sense of living could allegedly
be found even during the Khrushchev Thaw.

Illimar additionally had an interest in Russians as a nation,
and had ruminated on them at length in his letters. He found
that the Russian psyche possessed ideas very much alien to
him as a European, and thus as a representative of Enlightenment ideals. At the same time, he was fond of the Russian nation's noble religiosity and general support for spiritual values.
He believed that religion is an integral part of their psyche, is
uniquely interwoven with it, and that this sets them apart from
Westerners. The Soviet regime did not root out the Orthodox
religion, but instead replaced it with a different kind of belief.
Another bulb had simply been screwed into the same socket. I
must say in all honesy, of course, that Illimar himself had never been to Russia — his knowledge stemmed from authors who
dated back to the turn of the century (Solovyov, Rozanov, Flo-
rensky, Berdyaev) or even earlier (Katkov), and who were more
or less Slavophiles. He regarded the Orthodox faith as deeper

and more developed than Roman Catholic beliefs in every sense (*theosis*, meaning a lifelong approach to God, was especially admirable). He found almost nothing for himself in Protestantism. In his opinion it was, on the one hand, abstract — a discursive trick that takes place on the level of consciousness; and on the other hand it was horribly demanding — a process of pulling oneself up by the hair, which a person is incapable of doing (or if he thinks he is, then he is deceiving himself). Even Kierkegaard, whom he had once tackled with zeal, was ultimately a disappointment. "He rattles on and on," Illimar sighed, shaking his head, "dryly rattles on. Although he writes like a young god." He had even considered converting to Orthodoxy, but realized that this would be dishonest, because mere admiration for romanticism is not a sufficient cause for such a step. However, he enjoyed walking in the vicinity of small wooden onion-domed churches, leaning against the wooden pillars next to their entrances, and shutting his small, sly eyes in bliss. From mid-June through mid-August, when schoolteachers were on vacation, Illimar could be encountered from Mustvee to Varnja on the shores of Lake Peipus, where he would hike through Old Believer villages — speaking to no one, pestering no one.

Why did the security forces not take advantage of him? A young Estonian scholar who respects the revolution and the Russian psyche — wouldn't that have been a welcome propaganda tool? At first glance, the state "organs" could be accused of having low-flying fantasies and acting inside of the box; yet if one considers the matter more thoroughly, it becomes clear that the "organs" behaved wisely from their own point of view. Illimar's belief and love merely *appeared* correct, because they were in tune with the slogans' glossy truth. In reality — according to the quintessential point of a totalitarian regime — they were false to the very core and more dangerous than any kind of moderate opposition or indifference. This is primarily due to the fact that totalitarianism is rigid and constant, not a storm or a drive — stasis is its most general feature, not dynamism. One must not aspire to reach totalitarianism's glorious peaks (if such things should exist) with gusto and in a heightened state of mind. One must gnaw through oneself, carving out mountains of corpse flesh with a scalpel while moving in the summits' general direction. Every inquisitor knew that an overly eager believer is suspicious. An earnest communist would have made the same impression during the last quarter of the twentieth century.

Illimar lived a hermit's life during college and even later, and this was to his own benefit, because if he had floated his positions more widely, he probably would have fallen upon the daggers of Estonia's Finno-Ugric advocates. This, however, would have been unjust, because even though he was not an active nationalist, he was *far* from taking issue with Estonianism. He simply treated Estonianism as a researcher would—critically, recognizing that which was worthy of recognition to the fullest extent. And such things *weren't* so scarce in Estonianism. In his treatment, the romantic periods of Estonian history included eighteenth-century Moravianism (although what he appreciated most about Moravianism was not its religious content, but the social aspect of the Unity of the Brethren movement, the revived spirituality among the peasant folk, and the rapture of self-doing), the period of national awakening (with which a few other initiatives were affiliated, such as the national collection for building the Estonia Theatre), as well as the Estonian War of Independence and the Forest Brothers. Also worthy of his attention were the zeal for sports and the sobriety movement triggered by the feats of Lurich, Aberg, and other Estonian heavyweights. Noteworthy points from Estonia's later period were, in his opinion, the country's theater revival and the samizdat periodicals (which started in the second half of the 1960s, and with which Mati Tõusumägi was also associated in its later stage). As a whole, he praised Estonianism's lasting nature, although living in the same spot and cultivating rye for five thousand years was not very attractive in his eyes. "Moss is older than we are," as he tended to say.

And so, we started exchanging letters. Once a month on average. I do not know why this was the case; why it was not more frequent or infrequent. Such an interval somehow lent a sublime, old-fashioned, and stable effect. You were left with the feeling that each letter was the fruit of a month's worth of mental labor; was considered, careful, and cleansed of excess.

I did not analyze my attitude towards Illimar more profoundly or compare us in terms of type during university. It was simply nice and interesting for me to be acquainted with a person like him. It probably fed my vanity as a young person, because for a student of the humanities, every strange acquaintance is like an extra star on a general. (I will admit honestly that the existence of this acquaintanceship tickled my personal sense of pride for a long time even later on, and I did not speak about my Learned Friend to my companions on purpose, jealously keeping him to myself. Mati remembered Illimar, of course, but foremost as an eccentric. He did not laugh at him, but rather chuckled good-naturedly, although he even did that rarely.) In any case, now — being significantly more experienced — I mused about Illimar more meticulously, dissecting and classifying him. I also dug up a few of our old letters, which I had luckily kept. In short, what developed was a picture that astounded me and could also be admired, even though his view of the world was not the same as my own. I found that it needed to be complemented with a different, somewhat opposite way of thinking. As for my own position in connection with this, I can say that back in the day, I was fascinated by the so-called "little-acts theory." We had been taught at school that this characterized the "people of mixed ranks" (*raznochintsy*) of Russian society during the second half of the nineteenth century. I don't want to limit it to a Slavic context, however, because it is general for humanity. According to that worldview, one must act steadfastly and work ceaselessly — day in, day out; step-by-step; without glamour; gritting one's teeth. Not at the very top with the conductor, but down among the choir singers — in your own section. Not expecting praise, not receiving medals, and not earning fortunes, with your only fee being the knowledge that you are carrying out something necessary and acting in the name of society and mankind. Although you are a little person, you are necessary, because all in all, *thousands* of people like you push life onward. Truly, truly — even *more* can change as a result of these little people's efforts than it can from the Atlantean efforts of a handful of outstanding souls. In any case, the outcomes of "little acts" (I don't know why I put those words into quotation marks just now) are more lasting than the temporary bubbles of change churned into foam by the visionaries.

I don't want to be misunderstood: I also like the dynamic intellectual epochs, to which Illimar was partial. Who wouldn't! However, that was the very thing about it: loving them and being partial to them is as easy as pie. What is much more difficult is to love a "man of little acts," an untiring moiler-mole of the gray everyday.

So, in some senses, Illimar and I were opposites. And that was fantastic, in my opinion. Where *else* would freedom of thought have gone to! On top of that, it had to do foremost with aesthetic taste, because neither of us lived entirely according to our own views. It was actually Illimar himself—the man who thirsted for the "high and lofty"—who toiled away in the little backwater of Vana-Põgioja like a *zemstvo* character of times long gone, even lower than grass in terms of appearances. And this at the same time that I, who supported the little acts theory . . . well, yes, I suppose I was also grinding out work, little by little—hauling tiny stones to the Great Wall of Culture with my translations. But I was also a "caveman" in the meantime, and there, people certainly soared at lofty heights.

What Illimar thought of me, or whether he thought anything about me at all—that, I do not know. We wrote only on the conceptual level. A few topics that he rested upon during the following years were: "Does fiction exist anymore?," "Is it possible to die from the nobleness of one's soul alone?," and "Original sin: myth or reality?" Since he had a fondness for the natural philosophers of olden days (he loved to repeat that "all possibilities have been played out in antiquity"), in one of his letters, he debated whether it is possible to imagine a strawberry so big that a snail would be taken aback before it, and would not set itself to eating said berry, because it no longer regards it as a strawberry.

You will hear much more about my Learned Friend on these pages. Now, however, we return for a moment to the main character, who would otherwise slip out of our sight.

### MATI'S NEW MARRIAGE

The majority of Mati's friends could sense that his family life had not been in the best state for some time. Many who hadn't known him in the earlier days were surprised to hear that he was married, because "he did not look the type." He attended social events with his wife very rarely, and Piibe had probably never been seen in The Cave. And when a man is incessantly sitting alone in a pub, drinking and singing, then it is no wonder when some nymph draws her words out in exclamation: "Wh*aaaat*? You've got a *wife*?" In the interests of truth, I must say that at the beginning of their marriage, Mati had invited his wife to come everywhere with him; had wanted to integrate her into his group of friends. Yet, he had abandoned this, coming to understand that sitting in that kind of company conflicted with the woman's outlook on life—even if the company happened to be good. This had to do with their individual worldviews as well, and the cynical claims that the "sweater" (Mati often wore a sweater) and the "knit skirt" (Piibe knit a large portion of her own clothes) had simply grown tired of each other, and furthermore that there had never even *been* love in the relationship (alleging that it was a union based upon a nationalist idea) may not be correct, or at least not completely true. The main reason probably lay in the fact that Piibe, who had been religious before they were married, had grown in her faith, becoming ever more rooted in it and turning away from the world more and more. Mati, on the other hand, whose sympathetic relationship with the Church had been foremost a protest against Russian authority, felt his actual belief (which had been negligible even prior to then) weakening over the years. I suppose he was probably puzzled as to why someone would deepen their faith at the very same time that pressure—political and other—was being relaxed. So I am unable to say what part either of them played in estranging the other, or from which side the initiative came. They divorced, in any case. I passed Piibe on the street by chance after the divorce. She was walking slow and erect, almost without moving her arms, and staring fixedly ahead, her gaze melancholic and severe. It felt as if she were wearing a veil, although there was none. To say in advance—Piibe also remarried after some time, to a missionary who was passing through town, and soon moved to join the Copts in Egypt. Thus, the regular dilemma that crops up for a married couple's mutual friends—who stays on whose "side," and whom will they associate with from then on—did not come up in their case. We did not even *see* Piibe anymore. Their children returned to Estonia afterward (one translates from Arabic, the other is involved in business), but their mother apparently joined a convent.

At the same time, it is completely logical that Mati's new relationship quickened their separation. Piibe was religious, and the faithful are usually not as swift to dissolve a union as nonbelievers are. A strong prod was needed.

Agnes Aadler was a pretty and talented woman, who was seen as having high prospects in her field (a few years later, she defended her doctoral dissertation proposal at the age of twenty-seven, which was early for that time) and was also a freedom fighter to some extent—this resulting from her area of study (ethnography falls under the so-called "nation-sciences"). She was close to ten years younger than Mati, although the age gap was not very noticeable. Incidentally, it did not even cross anyone's mind that Mati could one day grow old. He was so awfully *vital*, and appeared to be becoming even *more* vital next to his young, pretty wife.

Why did Agnes marry him in particular? She did have a number of other suitors on the horizon at the same time, among them one very upstanding and smart person named Timmu, who was partly in our social group (he withdrew and buried himself in work after Agnes and Mati wed, and is now entering his twilight years as a bachelor). Timmu was heavily infatuated with Agnes—one might say that it was the sole true love of his life. Timmu was also a bit of a freedom fighter: he studied Vepsian loan words in Estonian, using it as a cover to promote the Ingrian-Finnic agenda. He did not stand on the barricades, because it did not fit with his nature. (Yet, who of us stood there at all? Some merely shouted slightly louder than the rest.) Timmu was well-meaning, tolerant, and always took others into account. When, for example, someone reached a checkout line at the same time as him, he would step aside, saying: "Go ahead!" He did not try to barge his way ahead. He put money away for the future by honest means, did not smoke, and drank in moderation. He was almost Mati's antithesis in many respects. Not that Mati was *rude*, of course, but he was less delicate all the same. On the other hand, Mati possessed a great deal of "funk," i.e. vitality. Timmu did not possess "funk," and this was indeed the deciding factor. In the interests of truth, I must say that Timmu surpassed himself on this occasion and did not step aside voluntarily; he did not say "Go ahead!" to Mati when they reached the door to Agnes's heart simultaneously. It is always up to the woman. *She* is the one who looks to see who possesses "funk"—who could provide her with the most vital offspring. Sometimes it even happens that if the husband himself does not especially care to make an effort (meaning he does not care about marriage), then the wife makes do with a child. The main thing is that life and the human race carry on powerfully. Therefore, the claims that Mati won over a "poor man's ewe" might not have been entirely true. No doubt the ewe herself was also looking to see "who" and "how."

Agnes's relationship with faith was similar to that of most young to middle-aged intellects, meaning well-intentioned but not very deep. She had come into contact with Estonian Church history to some extent thanks to her ethnographic work, but the idea of having a religious wedding ceremony did not come up between them even once—they simply registered their marriage at the Family Status Board on Pärnu Road. Where to hold the party? At the institute where Agnes worked, or Mati's place at the zoo (he had gone back)? They decided that the institute would be a safer bet. The table was set up in a room where two other researchers worked during the daytime in addition to Agnes—one a Selkup,[19] and the other a specialist in the Kamassian language. Attendance was high— the hallways and windowsills were teeming with partiers holding glasses and puffing on cigarettes. Poindexter asked Agnes at the most unsuitable moment: "Excuse me, do you believe that Estonia will become free?" (Agnes only smiled charmingly in reply.) Manglus also strutted through the institute wearing the kind of expression that said it would merely take him a wag of the finger for Agnes to abandon Mati and follow him instead, although he would mercifully forego this wag. (The next day at The Cave, he alleged, seemingly offhandedly and to a tighter circle, that Agnes was not his type, and that Mati's eyes were too round.) Klaus was in extremely high spirits, could not keep himself under control, and scaled the roof of the institute (a good number of people hoped, or feared, I should say, that he would hoist a blue-black-and-white flag there). He and his band would have gladly performed (for free, naturally), but the space was a bit too small for it—the amplified sound would have been deafening in the hallway. It was probably the most uplifting wedding that I have ever attended. The guests were, for the most part, still relatively young but already wise people, who were united by common value assessments and also fond of one another. The bride and groom were easy on the eyes and worthy of each other.

Mati and Agnes did not have their own home yet, so they slept right there on an L-shaped sofa in the corner of the room. There was no way to make a wide wedding bed out of the sofa parts: each had to sleep on a separate branch of the couch. I think they slept with their heads touching. That's youth for you: they still had something to talk about. Old people would perhaps sleep with their feet together, although it is depressing to imagine people so poor that even in their advanced years, they have not been able to acquire any bedstead other than an L-shaped corner sofa. But what do I know—maybe they actually sleep on the floor after the wedding, if their love is very great. The cleaning lady, grumbling, woke Mati and Agnes early the next morning—she did not know what to make of such a thing, as they had forgotten to invite her to the wedding. A couple of months later, Mati and Agnes managed to rent a room in Keila. I went to their housewarming party. We brought them a space-heater, a Latvian-made coffee percolator that sputtered and sprayed from the spout, and other household items. Someone gave them several-year-old volumes of the "*Looming* Libraries" literature extras. To this day, I am amazed at how people had the heart to give them away. What is most important, however, is that the director of Agnes's institute brought them a written-off but still useable typewriter so that Mati could do his side work at home (he had been typing it up at night in the zoo's office before then).

## "THAT IS ROMANTICISM"

I received my next letter from Illimar at about that time (February 18, 1986). It was, in reality, an essay in itself, and one of the most controversial that he had ever sent at that. As it is connected to his "main topic," I reprint it here in its entirety.

### HITLER AND STALIN

*(As it is seen by Illimar Robinson, a teacher of general subjects at the 4-class Vana-Põgioja School)*

*The two dictators have been compared to each other in innumerable written works. Many researchers have overwhelmingly emphasized their similarity in doing so. Selected concurrences of events and of the courses of their individual psychological lives have been presented towards these ends. The origins of these concurrences have led to speculations, which have in turn generated the discovery of new concurrences. Without rejecting such a method entirely, one must acknowledge that researchers have largely proceeded from the deductive method in doing so; they almost follow some kind of universal pattern of dictatorship. It seems to us that although a number of concurrences undoubtedly exist (for example: both were almost completely devoid of empathy; and for both of them, state subjects and fellow citizens served as material for executing their ideas), one must not let oneself be deceived by them, nor must one single out superficial similarities in places where extremely substantive differences lie beneath the surface.*

*It suffices to look back and take a wider view of history for us to see the differences in the greater picture. Stalin was like some kind of a bug or a rodent, a tarantula or a mystical giant rat; in Hitler's case, the first comparisons that come to mind are an evil witch or a hysterical devil. Stalin is characterized by pale monotony. Although his behavior featured a great deal of unpredictability, its manifestations were earthly and relatively limited. He made no moves on the so-to-speak "wider scale" that could have been called gestures. He lacked visions of national greatness, with the exception of the most general of these—that Russia must be feared. Stalin's favorite area of activity was cadre or personnel issues; more simply put, the world of intrigues. People have spoken of paranoia in his case, as a consequence of which he apparently believed traitors were lurking everywhere. He was right to suspect this at the beginning, as the Bolsheviks' power had not yet been secured and discord sounded even among their own ranks. Stalin removed one opponent after another. Every opponent was identified as an enemy at that time. However, Stalin's later repressions did not derive from even the slightest realistic danger. He sat in power as securely as possible, given the lack of an opposition. Yet the repressions deepened. It was not paranoia, but rather the indulgence of a maniac; an enjoyment borne of extreme voluntarism — I do what I want, and because I have decided to want it that way! Stalin's absolute peak was the demonstration of his subjective will, so he behaved in direct contradiction to any kind of logic that the mortals surrounding him naively expected to be shown (and this absence indeed caused them to search for all kinds of fantastic interpretations for their "master's" behavior). One essential aspect of an absolute autocrat is that he is not tied to anything; not hobbled. He cannot tear himself free of everything (for example, every being is dependent upon material and the laws of nature), but everything that can possibly be abandoned should be. And the logic of ordinary behavior can undoubtedly be abandoned. It is replaced by: "I want . . ." This is why Stalin eradicated his better military officers, for example. There is absolutely no proof that the officers would have been disloyal to him. True, personal revenge was not out of the question in some cases. So, for example, this or that commander had covered up substandard military actions that Stalin had taken during the days of the Russian Civil War, and now had to pay for it with their lives, because Stalin liquidated the witnesses to his moments of weakness. It was for this reason that the so-called "Old Bolsheviks," who remembered Stalin as he had been prior to his rise, were also subject to obliteration. Yet, this cannot justify the obliteration of thousands of cadre officers. Might not a parallel be seen here with how Hitler did not tolerate his own cadre soldiers, the old-school officers? No, because the similarity is superficial. Hitler's attitude towards the upper strata of the Wehrmacht was undoubtedly shaped, among other factors, by the commoner's inferiority to the aristocrat and the autodidact's complex before the trained specialist. Yet even so, this was not primary. Specifically, Hitler genuinely believed that the military's higher command was short on high-flying thought; ergo, they were incapable of standing at the height of his plans. This feeling transformed into intoxication when his unconventional tactics met with success during the initial phase of the war. And let us not forget that Hitler certainly removed a large number of (higher) officers over the course of the war, but more often than not, they were not imprisoned or executed.*

*Conjectures to the effect that Stalin liquidated someone because he feared a conspiracy targeted against him are, in the best case, incomplete truths. One must also observe Stalin's behavior towards lone individuals in order to comprehend his nature. We are aware of how Stalin loved to summon people and assure them that nothing would happen to them. The given individual sighed in relief— if the "master" himself had said so . . . The next day, Stalin would have them arrested. That is the most authentic sadism there is. Or was anyone truly able to believe that Stalin had Molotov's wife sent to the Gulag because he believed the beautiful Polina to be an enemy? It is equally out of question that he suspected this of Molotov and thus wanted to hold him hostage, because the latter was loyal to him through and through anyway. No—this was the behavior of a psychopath. At the same time, we know of instances where Stalin turned a blind eye to a person's "missteps," because that was the way he "wanted" it. In that sense, one seemingly classic example is when he would not approve a death sentence brought to him for signing, as the name of the given person (whose existence he had not even heard of before) seemed "interesting" to him in some way. (That is already a bona fide "aesthetic" argument!) In short, his behavior lacked logic, and not by chance, but intentionally.*

*Hitler also bred intrigue, deceived, and broke agreements— both at home and interacting with the outer world. He did so methodically and, altogether, more than most statesmen have done; yet his infamy is not based in this. Hitler was a great bluffer, whose bluffs succeeded until September 1939. And perhaps they would have continued to succeed, had he left Russia alone at that time. History is the history of the victors. What is important in the given case, however, is that Hitler generally rewarded the loyal individuals around him for their services, and vice versa. His behavior was,* as a whole, more expectable, predictable, and logical than that of Stalin.

One of the great differences between Hitler and Stalin was the attitude each had towards his respective land. The claim that both figures came from the margins of their nations has often been emphasized. In the one case, an Austrian made it to the head of the German Empire; in the second, a Georgian managed to command the Russians. This kind of a claim is extremely superficial. The Austrians and the Prussians were pure Germans through and through in terms of race, language, as well as everything else. Hitler's dream was to realize that which had been forbidden by the Treaty of Versailles—meaning a union of Prussia and Austria, so that all Germans could be united.

Stalin was, however, truly marginal. Georgians are not closely related to Russians in terms of genetics, culture, language, or any other quality. (Although both are Christians, they belong to separate churches.) Stalin despised Russians for the most part. Yet he did not love Georgians, either, because he had a sense of distaste for his childhood and his youth. Nothing was dear to him.

Thus, while the one dictator was uniting the people and acting on a sense of patriotic pride, the other was taking revenge. Proceeding from this, we rarely encounter an expression of pride for one's homeland in Stalin's case (the reason for which is indeed partially a dearth of emotion in general). He personally lacked a burning enthusiasm; the latter was fabricated by Stalin's retinue, who designed the Stalin "myth."

Stalin was like a manorial taskmaster or a gardener who finds himself on the emperor's throne. What is such a man capable of doing? By and large, something low or banal. The idea and execution of five-year plans was a high-flying idea, but this was not Stalin's merit. You could say that the era was extremely romantic, but it was not thanks to Stalin; rather, it was in spite of him. Stalin was, by the most well-meaning assessment, an enabler—like a teacher or a coach who swings open the door to the storage closet and hands out a few balls, which the boys can play with in the gym or on the sports field.

Hitler made a racket in the name of a glorious future for his country and his people. This future was, of course, abominable, *because it envisioned the trampling down of many other peoples. However, he could not be criticized for a lack of patriotism until the final months of the war, when the Führer "let his people down."*

*For us, the romanticism of the Jewish people's path of destiny is beyond a doubt. Hitler also recognized this in his own strange way (at least during a certain period): according to the dictator, there were only two ancient, "unmixed," and strong races left in the world—the German and the Jewish peoples, "one of which had to die." If there had been no anti-Semitism or Holocaust, how would the future world have regarded Hitler? No worse than Peter the Great or Napoleon, I believe. If even Genghis Khan is honored; if Attila, Chief of the Huns, is no longer depicted as some kind of monstrous butcher, then why make an exception for Hitler?*

*People have attempted to draw parallels between both dictators' attitudes towards the fine arts; alas, these have likewise been superficial. Hitler's own was much deeper and more serious. He had wanted to enroll in an art academy, and had the committee been of a different composition and mindset, it is not impossible that he could have gotten in. (And he might have even learned how to draw people!) He had some degree of talent, all the same—he even sold some of his little pictures at pubs (true, at trashy ones). Stalin's interest in art, however, was limited to writing poetry—just like many young people, and at about the same talent level. This cannot be classified as an artistic tendency, but rather an idiosyncrasy of age.*

*Hitler's education was spotty overall, but his relationship with history became fateful from a statesman's perspective. He was fascinated by history and regarded himself as its tool, although he only knew a tiny, distorted bit of it. Worst of all—he set out to study history already knowing in advance what he wanted to find from it, seeking confirmation for his prejudices. Such a person will always find it. Adolf Schicklgruber's socio-historical visions were eschatological, yet were those of an artist—they had the power of imagination and a grand aspect to them. What are Ioseb Jughashvili's visions next to those? Stalin may have altered millions of lives, but neither vision nor imagination were behind the acts; there was merely derision, the suspicion of a sick mind, and scorn.*

*If we view the two dictators side by side, we see on one side a torch that is smoldering and burning out of control, and on the other an enormous, rotted, dimly glimmering log. On one side there is a dragon, and on the other a giant spider or an immense medusa lurking in the darkness. Hitler was an uneducated bumpkin, but in certain ways he also possessed a fineness of the soul. Stalin's fineness of the soul manifested itself in his ability to play people off of one another, in the twisting socio-psychological passageways of which he was a true master. Hitler was inspired by Nietzsche. I do not know who Stalin's favorite philosopher was, or whether he had ever read any philosophers at all. One became emotional listening to Wagner; the other was moved by the ditty "The Firefly."* Mein Kampf *is nonsense, but what does Stalin have? The brochure "Marxism and Problems of Linguistics," which was written by other people. Did Stalin author any articles at all? Or could he boast of any other kinds of intellectual accomplishments?*

*Both were supposedly beaten harshly by their fathers as children. Stalin probably even more so. However, is this fact very determinate? Many have taken a beating—such as Chekhov, for example; but this did not make him into a dictator.*

*Stalin was not a completely "self-made man." Although even he had to break through by his own means, he was almost immediately able to start leaning upon a party that had existed before him and took him unto its fold. He moved up the career ladder on the Party's shoulders, and also cultivated intrigue within its ranks. Hitler lacked that kind of a structure: his reinforcements and entourage developed much later on. He had to create everything on the grassroots level and all on his own. Although Stalin also had to eke out a living at one point, the trough in Hitler's life was significantly more miserable.*

*Let us return to the question of vision. For Stalin, power was a goal in itself. He no longer had any great aspirations after the 1930s, as the Soviet Union had officially ceased preparations for the world revolution. For Hitler, on the other hand, power and control of the State were a means for executing his global vision. To sum things up: even when speaking of a criminal, one can tell whether he commits his crimes to a greater or a lesser effect; I prefer Hitler to Stalin in this sense. Although his visions are close to hallucinations, they (please forgive me for such an aesthetic perspective) are nevertheless somehow more exciting. Stalin is as boring as a corvée peasant's dream, or standing next to a conveyor belt and filling tin cans from morning to night. Listen to the two dictators speaking, and all becomes clear. Hitler had the power of mesmerism. It takes some searching through history to find that kind of an ability to mobilize people. It is a shame that this was used for the wrong thing. Stalin, on the other hand, lacked mesmerism. As a result, his rise to the top was also quite unexpected—his competitors (foremost Trotsky and Bukharin) were fantastic orators and dazzling personalities. Yet this is the very reason why I believe all of the recent dictators around the world have admired Stalin more than Hitler. The source of inspiration for Orwell's Big Brother was not the Third Reich, but Soviet Russia. Chairman Mao was certainly more a student of Stalin than he was of Hitler. Hitler can never become the rule of thumb due only to his personality; rather, he will remain an exception until the end of time. There is little to learn from him; one is unable to orient towards him or copy him. But Stalin—that is a whole system, a handbook, and a paradigm.*

*P. S. There are great contradictions and great irony here. Stalin was the symbol of an era, and people acted, fought, and died with his name upon their lips. Stalin himself did not possess the slightest shred of idealism, although it was abundant in society at the time. People did not know what we know now—that it would all flop one day. Because of this, many people were also relatively happy back then.*

I must tip my hat to Illimar, because he was exceptionally well informed about both dictators' lives, especially given the conditions of that time. This confirms yet again that even behind the Iron Curtain, it was possible to educate oneself and catch up with global thought. It all depended on motivation and perseverance. Illimar, for example, listened to the Russian-language Radio Liberty and the BBC, which were not scrambled in Estonia (Anatol Goldberg was its beloved radio voice), as well as the Estonian-language Voice of America. He read in German and Polish, not to mention ancient languages.

I believe I understand what troubled Illimar and why he dispatched that essay to me. He was disappointed that Hitler's vision and momentum had been spent on the wrong thing. And he detested the German smugness, which is sometimes summarized with the saying *"Bier, Bratwurst und Bumsmachen."* Germany weighed upon Illimar's soul, and when he returned to it in a later letter, he claimed that if he had been able to speak to Hitler in private, he would have been capable of changing the latter's mind and channeling his energy elsewhere. I attempted to picture Illimar Robinson as Adolf Hitler's advisor. Though I strained my powers of fantasy to their limits, it was ultimately completely impossible to imagine this.

What's more, Illimar's most ardent admirations were reserved for the Jews and the Israeli state. He was fascinated by the Jews' strong identity, which had enabled them to remain who they were and avoid dissolution over the course of three thousand years. How many larger and more powerful nations had assimilated and disappeared from history during that length of time! The fact that Jews ate, married, and did everything from birth to death according to the old precepts was a sign of the immense importance of the fundamental spiritual element in their lives. Without this, it would never have been possible for them to maintain their faith and the purity of their race, especially seeing as how they had not had a common homeland or language for two thousand years.

Illimar respected the way that Jewish fathers strove to give at least one of their sons a high level of education so that he might become a rabbi, as well as the fact that such a son—even one poor in property—was regarded as a welcome suitor.

Or take how the new Israeli state was created! It had been born out of a flash of genius. Someone coming up with that kind of idea is nothing new for us in cultural history; however, all of those cities of the sun, phalansteries, and other utopias have remained curious fool's errands or, in extreme cases, test-tube runts. Nevertheless, the Jews accomplished the task—the country that they created began to function. They brought the Hebrew language back to life there: over the course of merely a single generation, it turned from a museum language to a common spoken tongue for all citizens—was this not an unbelievable feat, further emphasizing the nation's extraordinariness?

(Illimar knew, for example, how much less the Scottish and other Celtic nationalists had managed to accomplish in reviving their own native languages on the British Isles.)

The Jews' devotion to defending their country was exceptional. Illimar knew the courses of the wars of 1948, 1968, and 1973 down to the particular details. He admired Haganah as much as he did the Irgun, the Mossad, and the Shabak.

Illimar, who was an individualist by nature and solitary by lifestyle, nevertheless had a deep fondness for kibbutzim. There were also all kinds of camps in the Soviet Union—Pioneer, Komsomol, as well as others—where officials strove to promote communal living and develop a collective mindset. And no doubt a genuine spark had once been found in these undertakings (definitely before World War II). Perhaps they still had it during the second half of the fifties—such as when people traveled to the "Virgin Lands" of Kazakhstan. Maybe some builders of the BAM[20] even still believed in something. Yet it all belonged to the past by now, and the modern-day forms of communal living in the Soviet Union seemed like parodies; they could not be taken seriously. The kibbutzim were not, however, an alienated Slavic thing, nor were they the communes of simple-minded hippies or fanatics awaiting the end of the world somewhere on the edge of an American desert; rather, they were voluntary associations of developed individuals, expressing their descendants' desire, the desire of an entire root nation of Western culture, to live according to a higher code of ethics. Gathered in a kibbutz were not pinheads or herd-followers, but young people who had attended college and spoke foreign languages. It was not an anachronism or *archaica*, nor had it been born in the blaze that follows wars and revolutions, when emotions run high. True—Israel was under constant siege by Arabs; the country was in danger. All the same, the kibbutzim's existence had not developed as a direct consequence of this. The kibbutzim would also have developed without an international conflict, because the basis for them was the decision of each participant that living in such a way was the right thing to do. A kibbutz *was* a little like heaven on earth. People lived in harmony, caring for one another and subjecting their egos to the rules of communal living. Illimar was fascinated by how everyone in a kibbutz was equal—they worked, raised children, and did other chores together. And in doing so, things did not go downhill for them like with erstwhile lackeys who become noblemen after a revolution; they did not start shirking their responsibilities and shrugging their burdens off onto one another's shoulders, but instead did their duties, understanding them as a reflection of humility and reverence for their people's tradition of perpetuation. Even if they were not very religious, they felt at all times that there was something greater and more important than them. *This* is precisely what enchanted Illimar.

The kibbutz thing was still going strong to that very day (although at a somewhat diminishing tempo). "But the Jews are bigger communists than the *Russians*! Why don't they get along with each other?" Illimar had written in surprise when he heard about the kibbutzim for the first time. And it's true—the kibbutzim were not spoken of in the Soviet Union at all. This was partly due to Israel's overall image. But even if the official propaganda had not stamped Israel as a Zionist and imperialist country, one of the "greatest enemies of the peace-loving world," there still might not have been mention of them. Moscow was simply jealous that the Israelis had accomplished with ease what the Kremlin had wanted to create, in the name of which it had gone to extremes, and eventually failed.

Illimar acquired tapes of the kibbutzniks' rousing songs and would occasionally play them in the dead of night, holding his head between his hands, humming along joyfully (he had no singing talent). He wanted to become a Jew himself for a while, but then abandoned the idea, just as he had given up on joining the Russian Orthodox Church. He had no opportunity for becoming a National Socialist, of course; nor did he want to. Nevertheless, he liked (parallel to the kibbutzim) the *Wandervogel* movement, which formed in Germany towards the end of the nineteenth century. Children and youth went camping out in the great outdoors and sang around a campfire. Illimar enjoyed the German people's enthusiasm for the mystical "German forest" and he also liked the way they marched with torches, along with many other things that happened in Germany during the thirties.

He watched Leni Riefensthal's *Triumph of the Will* multiple times (the first part was stronger, in his opinion). This did not impede him from admiring the heroic resistance of the defenders of the Masada fortress to the Romans' year-and-a-half-long siege; nor did it obstruct him from having respect for Theodor Herzl, Ze'ev Jabotinsky, Ben-Gurion, or Golda Meir. He probably wished that Riefenstahl had made her film about the feats of the Jews. And, of course, he would have especially liked it if Hitler had loved the Jews, and discriminated in their favor (as Hitler's advisor, he would have liked to convince his superior of the necessity for this). For in Illimar's mind, there was a certain intersection of that time period and the Jews, which was expressed in the strength of their fundamental spiritual element. They were all deeply spiritual figures — they all possessed spirit, force, and power of imagination. In Illimar's mind, Hitler should have been the King of the Jews. A mistake had happened somewhere, but where?

I wrote to Illimar saying that he should destroy his writings. But he probably forgot.

## MATI'S FIRST NOVEL

A gossip-stoking event took place right at the beginning of the Gorbachev era: an unknown individual published the novel *The Springs of Life*, which received the award for Best Prose Work of the Year. Soon enough, rumors started to circulate that hidden behind the name "Merlin August" was no other than Mati Tõusumägi. The first to come to this conclusion were those who were familiar with the course of Mati's life. There were an eye-catchingly large number of coincidences. The book revolved around the main character's childhood in Siberia, his return to Estonia, and his adaption to a new environment. Right at the beginning of the work, the little boy meets a classmate on the way to school and is surprised upon hearing that Christmas was not actually celebrated in the other boy's family. The circumstances were recorded with photographic precision, including the furs of the sables shot by a neighbor woman and the hat sewn out of them for the boy—a hat that his new schoolmates (and especially their mothers) were jealous of. Many of the details were colorful—for example, the deported child learns what a flush toilet and toilet paper are for the first time at the home of his wealthier classmate. Although everything was seen through the eyes of a minor, the work was not a children's book; the narrator's attitude was not explicitly the wisdom of an old man, but was certainly derived from a more general historical perspective. The book ended with the death of the main character's father; the boy himself was still attending secondary school at the time.

How could such a book receive an award? There were still a couple of years left until the social "thaw." However, the book's orientation was not openly political. It was only by reading between the lines that one could surmise why and how the family had ended up in Siberia—it was not mentioned that the boy's father was a Forest Brother.

Almost everyone was delighted by the book. How fresh, how rich, how straight to the heart it pierced! The few conservative-minded people who regarded the work negatively or, in any case, suspiciously, were somewhat assuaged by the text's added linguistic value: Russian-language concepts also found in the jargon of Estonian deportees were used originally.

Mati did not deny his authorship, but he did not thrust his way into the spotlight either. The book was translated almost immediately, and the author was already credited by his real name in the published translations. In any case, Mati became a famous writer and an officially-accomplished man overnight.

## ILLIMAR AT THE CAVE

When perestroika began and society livened up, and when the Citizens' Committees and the Popular Front of Estonia formed a few years later, then Illimar also perked up. He did not become involved in politics, of course, nor was he even a local activist, but rather he stayed true to his habitual observer's attitude. He still lived as a semi-hermit in one wing of the Vana-Põgioja schoolhouse, which was a century-old building where the snow would drift into the stairway in winter. Yet from his

letters, I grasped that he was emotionally very engaged in the
overall processes.

## ILLIMAR'S LETTER FROM JULY 21, 1987

(N.B.— Here and henceforth, I will not reproduce Illimar's letters in full so as to conserve space.)

*Honorable Chronicler!*
*I have developed a new habit. The entire time that I have lived*
*here, I have gone to the store in the closest town once a week. I*
*still do this now, only that whereas I used to immediately hop onto*
*my bike and pedal back after acquiring my goods, I now stay by*
*the shop a little bit longer. I stand there and watch people; some-*
*times, I even chat with them a little. However, as doing so would*
*be strange otherwise, I grab a bottle of beer like the other men do,*
*and sip on it just for fun. I do not like beer, I have not gotten used*
*to it, but it is good to stand in such a way. I enjoy hearing how peo-*
*ple discuss things. They have changed! You can sense greater excite-*
*ment in them. They speak on topics that were completely absent*
*from their discussions earlier, such as freedom, independence, and*
*nationhood. I find this to be very invigorating. The people are on*
*the right path. Perhaps I am mistaken, but I can hear the incredi-*
*ble music of history. Just as little rivulets flow in Vivaldi's "Spring,"*
*so do tiny brooks of zeal, passion, and belief flow there by the store*
*now. Could it really be that an age of spirituality, ideas, and grand*
*notions is starting to arrive? It seems so. That which must come will*
*be achieved.*

The first of the two times that I met with Illimar Robinson after
college occurred during this period. He had come to the capital to attend a seminar of USSR educators that was being held
at the Sakala Center. It is hard to say why the raion's education
department had decided to send *him*. Illimar was certainly not
in their high favor—he was tolerated and kept in his job solely due to the fact that there was a shortage of teachers in the
countryside. It could have been, of course, that some bigwigs
with keen intuition sensed something was changing in society;

that new processes were underway, and therefore, it would be wise to send that "Põgioja eccentric" specifically—let them see in the capital that original types, maybe even ones that were "in the spirit of a completely new age," could be found in the periphery as well.

What motivated me to get together with him? Illimar's most recent letter, which was borne of lofty states of mind, and the fact that he had agreed to emerge from his den at all gave me reason to believe that he had "opened up." I decided to bring him into our social group at The Cave. I thought it might be interesting for him to be there—he would see new people, hear what was being talked about, and have an opportunity to exchange thoughts with someone. Overall, more and more non-artistic people were being invited down into The Cave towards the end of the Soviet period. Ever more often, someone would arrive with a troop of foreign Estonians or other foreigners trailing behind them. Upon entering, this person would, without fail, look around worriedly and self-importantly to show that, *look—I'm coming in with foreign Estonians; consequently, I'm also "with it."* Why not take Illimar there—a man who *was* a rare example; much rarer than most of those foreign Estonians.

As Illimar and I had not seen each other for nearly a dozen years (and it was not as if we had been that close *before*) the distance we felt between us when we met in front of Café Moscow was understandable. I asked how he was with time. He shrugged vaguely and replied like Goethe that "time is his field." When we were walking, I noticed that Illimar's limbs still moved asynchronously as they always had—his right leg and right hand still swung forward together, and then vice-versa. This peculiarity seemed to have even intensified, and it moved me strangely.

At The Cave, Illimar looked around carefully at first, as if he was recording everything to memory. (Doing this, he somewhat resembled a zoogoer inspecting the little goldfish, pythons, turtles, and other creatures in a terrarium.) Illimar asked the doorman for the time, and when he was told what it was, he jotted something down in his notebook. Luckily, quite a lot of our own crowd was there. We took a seat. Illimar remained silent, his eyes slightly squinted and his mouth pinched haughtily.

He drank little, and did not laugh at even the best jokes or give the slightest reaction to even the most voluptuous nymphs' charms. He did not even honor them with his polite attention. My acquaintances initially made an amiable attempt to strike up a conversation with him (several of them were also capable of speaking on philosophical topics to a considerable extent), but gave up upon receiving Illimar's gruff, one-word responses to their prompts. This was truly a shame, because the evening turned out to be one of the most spirited ones that I could remember of late. After closing time at The Cave, we went to the artist Muis's atelier in the same building to finish out the evening. As always, the group included old and young, men and some women. Things turned quite hellish at the atelier. The seventy-year-old (but ageless, outright childish) poet Vanasaba climbed onto the back of the critic Sõrgats, and wanted to fly off into the May night through an open window with him. One KGB man, who was mid-ranking and moderately dangerous, had come along with us—apparently out of an intoxicated person's inability to desert a group. The rest would tease him for the sake of variety, although not too aggressively (in the manner of: *look at us playing with fire—we're fearless, but at the same time talented and jovial fellows*). The KGB man allowed himself to be teased, but from time to time would insinuate that he could bare his teeth, too: all it would take was him wanting it, and he could make the shit hit the fan for everyone in a terrible way by the very next day. And he might, perhaps, refrain from doing so merely because he could appreciate the group's spirited nature, as he himself also had some spirit in him. There was a tension, in any case, and that spiced things up. I peeked over at Illimar every now and then to see whether he was actually able to appreciate the beauty of the game, but he did not appear to be too impressed by it. When he went to the bathroom, Maša asked where I had dredged up such a hatchet-faced man, and the poetess Alja whispered: "Tell us— what quarry does he mine in?"

Illimar boarded a bus early the next morning, discontented. He only mentioned our meeting briefly in his next letter, saying that at The Cave and the atelier, he had seen nothing but a handful of cocks and hens in heat, who "thought who-knows-what about themselves," but were actually only the "playthings of fate."

## TEEDU AND THE WAFFLES

Teedu Tärn finished his lecture—the last of that academic year. He had held it in one of the university's two large circular auditoriums, located in the chemistry building. These were used for lectures that were mandatory for all students, such as social and political subjects. Teedu rubbed the chalk off of his fingers (he had just finished drawing a diagram illustrating the increase of Party democracy during the period between the previous congresses on the blackboard), holding his hand cautiously away from his body in order to keep the blackish-grey suit that he usually wore in the auditorium (even now, in spring/summer) clean. It was already a little too hot to wear the suit, which was made of 60 percent cotton and 40 percent synthetic polyester; however, this counted for nothing, since good customs are worth something, too. A professor should dress appropriately—meaning correctly, academically, inciting respect. Teedu was indeed only a docent (he could hope to become a professor after about ten years at the very earliest, when a number of his older colleagues had successively retired), but he was already preparing for professorship now, getting himself accustomed to good practice.

He placed his syllabus papers in a thin black attaché case. Many of the faculty owned that kind of a small briefcase, except for the most ancient of them, who generally preferred a traditional pigskin portfolio. Teedu bid farewell decorously, nodding his head in a dignified manner (once again a trait of a proper professor), although hardly anyone noticed it in the buzzing auditorium. A few moments later, and Teedu exited the chemistry building and stepped outside.

It was a lovely day in late May—final exams would soon begin, but glimmering after them were two months full of fishing and other summer joys. For some time already, he and Merle had been visiting their cabin property in Rannahänna on the weekends, trimming the trees and brush, raking and sowing.

Teedu strolled towards the Emajõe River with measured paces. He lived in the Annelinn district. Four years earlier, they had gotten a very comfortable four-room apartment in a custom-designed building pleasantly close to the city center—he didn't even need to take the car out of the underground parking garage to go to work. Teedu enjoyed walking home.

The warm, fresh air caressed Teedu's face, and his heart became so light that he closed his eyes in delight. How he loved that single square kilometer around the university's main building! For ten months of the year, it teemed with energetic boys and girls, and one could cross acquaintances at every step. On the narrow streets and the little squares, next to the fountain in front of the Town Hall, in front of the theater, even in the vicinity of the market and the bus station—unexpected and fleeting, yet heartfelt and informative conversations with colleagues from a range of fields of study could take place anywhere. In this way, a person constantly experienced being a particle of something bigger—he or she belonged to the common *alma mater* bloodstream. Even the most minuscule detail from that daily path was worn into Teedu's brain and gave him a feeling of *home*. The buildings surrounding the Town Hall Square were the same as they had been even during his childhood, although a number of changes had taken place in the lower-level shops. Yet the café where he had eaten donuts with his mother was still there, for example; so was the stamp and sheet-music store located to the left of it. Even the tableware outlet on the right-hand side had preserved its original function. Diagonal to the university across the square, on the corner of Oktoobri Boulevard, was an ice-cream stand, where he used to wait in line together with his grandmother. Next to it was an improvised counter that had sprung up at the end of the sixties, and where on New Year's, Victory Day, and the holiday marking the October Revolution there were sold tangerines, jarred peas, or red peppers, as well as—occasionally—fresh cucumbers (in spring). The counter stood unused at other times, so in truth, it was not even noticeable. Right now, however, a small crowd of people swarmed around it. Teedu felt his good mood rapidly fading. He walked closer to it across the square, and established that his hunch had been correct: beneath a shade drawn over the counter were two young men busily selling waffles. Teedu had tried them himself, too. (Teedu had a sweet tooth. He had started consuming alcohol less year by year, but when he ended up at a restaurant, on the other hand, he would often begin reading the menu from the dessert section, and he always had a few "Kalev" chocolates stashed in his jacket pocket.) He had enjoyed the waffles. Nevertheless, those crunchy pastries topped with custard were making Teedu inexplicably disturbed at the moment. This feeling had nothing to do with the waffles as a baked good, naturally, but rather with what they symbolized. The waffles were a sign of something greater, and within this "greater" was something suspicious, dangerous—almost apocalyptic. The waffles did not originate from the state retail network: so-called "cooperatives," meaning private entrepreneurs, were involved. One might think—*So what?* Commission shops *had* existed for ages; there was one located on that very same corner, fifty meters from the ice-cream stand in the direction of the Town Hall. And market vendors were selling sauerkraut that was made at home, not in a combine. They sold berries and mushrooms, flowers and tomatoes, and sometimes even puppies and pigs. The introduction of private retail did not yet pose a danger, and was even recommended by the regime. Looking at it from one perspective, the waffles were an extension of this. The cooperatives had been brought to life and approved by the Party itself the previous year—Teedu knew this for certain, as he had spoken about them in his lectures. But all the same, his heart knew that from another perspective, the waffles were not at all the same as the mushrooms and the pigs, as the market and the commission shops. The latter had been nicely integrated into the state system—were "contained" by it and peacefully in place. Yet within the new was something hidden or sprouting; something that Teedu would have liked to speak up about, to open people's eyes to—yes, he wanted to warn the Party. His suspicion was already aroused by the fact that while market vendors were old women, the young men in the waffle business were the same age as those who sat in his lectures. The old women busied themselves at the market because they had done their life's share of work elsewhere, and were now realizing the strength-surplus of their retirement age. But these young men here—did they plan to dedicate their entire lives to retail instead of labor unlike everyone else? Teedu was a supporter of gender equality and did not divide professions into "masculine" and "feminine" ones; still, selling goods at a counter was not an activity worthy of a man—male salesmen and clerks were more suitable over there in the West. And most importantly: under no circumstances would the old crones take the next step—they *stayed* by their cabbage barrels and their milk cans filled with chanterelles. They were simply so *old* already. But if those youth form a cooperative today, won't they already be doing something else five years from now? (Teedu was unable to express what that "else" was more specifically, nor did he even want to think about it.) Where would they end it one day? Would they even be able to stop?

Taken from one perspective, Teedu supported the waffles because he was not blind to the fact that many things were unavailable in stores. The belief held by his former Russian-language teacher, Mr. Kulu, that we have (or could have) everything, and that if there *isn't* something, then someone is to blame—that belief had weakened for Teedu over the years. No, we certainly did not have everything. And Teedu did not believe at all that the constant waffle deficit was some individual person's fault. Nor did he especially believe that making production planning more effective might have any effect in terms of the waffles. From that angle, private entrepreneurship was a welcome sight. On the other hand, Teedu was a very peace-loving person and greatly appreciated stability on all levels. He was, by nature, cautious about any kind of change. It was because of this that he wondered: all in all, would stability without waffles perhaps be better than a period of unrest that included waffles and the very best there was to offer? *We've gotten by without waffles up to now, maybe we could just continue that way*, Teedu pondered, shaking his head. Did everyone *always* require waffles, then? Perhaps only the brightest could be allowed to have waffles, so they might serve as an incentive? These were serious questions, and Teedu would have really liked to debate them with someone. However, there was no one to do this with. Teedu sighed, discovered that he had come to a full stop in the meantime, and continued on his way.

*Ah, it's nothing—maybe it will all pass*, he attempted to reassure himself while strolling across the arch bridge over the Emajõgi. Still, out of intellectual honesty, he had to admit to himself (although reluctantly) that the waffles were—yes, they were!—a sign of *revolt*.

He arrived home, quietly opened the door, and stood there staring: at the end of the spacious entryway was a smaller nook that they used as a coatroom. The folding door to it was open, and Merle was presently ironing there. She had the day off. The radio was playing, the woman was engrossed in her work and did not hear his arrival. A strange thought flashed through Teedu's mind: if a revolution were truly to unfold and turn everything upside down, would Merle leave him then? Because she would not have to *get* anything from Teedu any longer. He wouldn't visit their privilege specialty-goods shop twice a month any more, or bring home chunks of meat, bananas, and other shortage goods anymore. In their new life, Teedu would no longer be given a large, comfortable apartment or be paid a high salary. He would be an overdriven workhorse; a spent booster rocket. Merle, however, was only thirty-six—a woman in her prime, as they say. Teedu was aware that quite a few men envied him because of Merle, believing that Teedu had gotten a better wife than he deserved. This was not true, though! Those who made such claims didn't know the pains he had gone to in order to win Merle's heart. But what was certain was that the woman would be capable of starting a new life without him. With whom? With some waffle seller? Teedu felt an ache sting his soul. Wasn't *he*, Teedu, despite giving lectures about something he didn't totally believe (for who *could* believe all of it?)—wasn't he nevertheless just a hair better than those waffle sellers? For his lectures had some kind of an intellectual aspect to them, regardless. Did a waffle have an intellectual aspect? No, it only had custard.

He had never discussed matters of worldview with his wife, although both were social scientists (Merle worked at the Party Archive). Neither one had ever asked the other whether or not he or she actually believed in something personally. Work was work, and if you did it well, then you were better off. But if you earned more with waffles? Teedu was unsure whether he himself would be capable of starting a new life without Merle. They had been married for twelve years by that time. Eleven-year-old Margus and ten-year-old Tiina were watching TV in the living room and snacking on something. They were good children (almost old-fashionedly good in Teedu's opinion) who studied properly and didn't quarrel excessively. Strange—they even possessed a sort of childish (!) tender-mindedness. A warm feeling flooded Teedu's heart. Merle raised her eyes, saw him, and smiled cozily.

"Merle, if something were to happen to me, then what would you do?" Teedu wanted to ask. However, he refrained. Perhaps Merle would have asked in reply: "Do you mean that if Estonia breaks away from Moscow and you are thrown into a cell, will I come and bring you care packages?" No, Teedu knew that his gentle wife would never have asked so bluntly. *Maybe nothing bad will happen anyhow*, Teedu thought, leaning his attaché case against the coat rack. An appetizing smell wafted from the kitchen.

### ILLIMAR'S LETTER FROM SEPTEMBER 1989

*Honorable Chronicler!*
(. . .)
*I sense in the air the same winds that blew on St. George's Night*[21] *and during the era of national awakening; in the days of Koidula, Hurt, and Jakobson. It seems that intellectual activity is arising, and Estonia is arriving at a new heroic age, which will take a dignified place next to Moravianism and the Forest Brotherhood in terms of its romanticism and idealism. Estonia, you are standing on the threshold of great shifts and a miraculous beginning; your springs of life have opened up.* (. . .) *Signs of new life can be seen everywhere. Last weekend, I went on my great pilgrimage for this year.* (Let it be known that Illimar never visited Tartu more than once per year, and some years, he even forgot to do that. He had not gone to the capital even once since gradu-

ating from university, not counting the teacher's seminar that I already mentioned.) *I saw a new phenomenon at the bus station and in a couple of other places: street vending. Waffles were being sold. I bought a few. They sure tasted good! However, the main thing is not their culinary value, but rather their symbolic significance. Waffles are the Estonian nation's manna, which should be eaten on the journey across the desert of transition so as to gain strength for reaching the promised land of independence. Cotton candy also serves the same purposes, although it is a little too sweet for my taste.*

*The closest Citizens' Committee is located ten kilometers from here, but the people of our village are going there to register in hordes. Several men have consented to join the Defense League or the Home Defense Guard. The main question is: where can weapons be acquired? You wouldn't be able to show us the way, would you? Weapons are needed in case the Russian tanks come. A number of the older men have dug up Suomi KP rifles from their flower beds that date to the German occupation. I am sorry that I treated military instruction cursorily during my time at university and now cannot be of any aid for the locals with advice or force (I am indeed reading a treatise on warfare by an ancient Chinese theoretician — Sun Tzu; you have certainly read him). Chapel-Peeter came to the rescue and is starting to organize marching and firing drills for the men (he was in the landing forces in Afghanistan before becoming religious).*

*People are joining our mixed choir en masse; all of the vocal sections are complete. Overall idealism is high. Only the schoolteacher, ol' Red-Kustas, warned people, asking them: what paradise are you expecting? You will just end up with a new ruler who will take the very last from you, and so forth. But he was shut up at the meeting. Blacksmith-Jass killed a hog and shared it with the whole village. He said: this is how we'll start sharing everything in the era of freedom!*

*A fact that heralds the arrival of a new era is that lately, you have not heard of anyone having an abortion (such things become common knowledge here, in Vana-Põgioja, almost immediately). On the contrary — a full three men's wives are apparently expecting, which has not happened in a long time. In every respect, holy elation is better than a nice, peaceful little life.*

*Yours,*

*Learned Friend*

## MATI'S SECOND BOOK

Three and a half years after his debut, Mati Tõusumägi published his second book, which differed from the first in several
aspects. It didn't speak of childhood, but instead about the present day and the future; about the fate of the world, to be more
precise. The gaze of the narrator-protagonist was no longer innocent or fresh, and it was augmented, seemingly incidentally,
by a higher wisdom and an inverse temporal perspective similar
to that in *The Springs of Life*. The main character of *The Assistant
Teacher of the Sign of Aldebaran* was a frowning, mature man;
a ponderer/observer (there was little traditional activity in the
new novel) who leafed through albums that contained photos
of antique ruins to pass the time, and went on a trip in present-
day Europe, describing what he saw and deliberating on the
fate of the Old World. This main character was, by the way, a
former college instructor of Party history, who had thrown his
hands up at his own career because he was "disappointed." He
had genuinely believed what the state leaders said at one time,
and had been in love with the idea of building a new society (a
city of the sun) and the romanticism that came with the formation of the "new man"; he had also been involved in Eurocom-
munism, and had set up a hippie camp near the town of Nõo.
Now, he was walking through all of the most important sites
in Europe, from Stonehenge to St. Paul's Cathedral, nodding
and saying: "Mmhmm." The main character would occasionally emit a demonic, spasmodic laugh, but one could sense that
a refined and suffering soul lay behind that laugh. Although
it was not explicitly stated that he had emigrated, it was clear
that this was the case. The financer of his long voyage around
the continent remained unclear—whether it was some publisher or the Voice of America. The book's polished style was
dynamic and filled with pathos, downright Old-Testamentish
in some passages. When the author dropped his aphorizing and
described what his character was seeing or hearing in any given
moment, then one could instantly recognize the poetic vision,
the keen sense for detail, and the graceful style of *The Springs
of Life*; however, there were not very many of these pages.

As for the author's real-life experience, Mati had only visited Europe once while writing the work—on a bus tour to Poland. Given that Poland is a very Catholic country, this may have inspired the Old-Testament style of the new novel. Furthermore, after the protagonist returns to his homeland (it wasn't explained how the Soviet regime tolerated this), he converts to the Christian faith (he did not specify which confession), completes the necessary classes, and takes a job as a deacon at a small-town church. The work ended with the character entering the rectory, where his young wife is serving the local townspeople her homemade buns and coffee one Sunday morning, after having performed his new job's duties for the first time. That evening, however, he looks up at the sky, seeing the constellation of Aldebaran there.

The book's reception was not as unanimous as that of Mati's first. A number of readers were still enthralled—some even liked it more than *The Springs of Life*, although they were in the minority. Freedom fighters criticized the book for not being linked to the present moment in time, at which Estonia was standing on the border between two ages and the threshold of a great future. They also complained that the job of a nationally-minded writer should be to give sense to this moment and prepare people for what was to come. Truly, the book didn't offer all that much in this regard; it didn't call people to the barricades, but instead ruminated more generally. In some places, the work gave the impression of being a resignation to the Prague Spring of late; alternately, one could interpret the activity as happening in the distant future, when half a century had passed from the present day. Estonia was spoken about in veiled terms, sometimes being called the "blue, black, and white Land of Canaan."

Some thought that this was not Mati's fault, but rather that of the Soviet printing process, which always worked incredibly slowly. Society had changed a great deal over the course of the year and a half it took for the book to reach shelves after the manuscript had been delivered to the publisher. Some assumed that even Mati himself had not foreseen that things would so quickly be put "out in the open," and instead applied self-censorship while writing it. I personally doubt this, however, because

Mati was confident that the Estonian state would come one day and wrote as freely as he deemed necessary—meaning he wrote for a free people. Perhaps the problem was simply that he wanted to make "art" too much, had yearned to write even better than he had the first time, and thus overdid it a little. In spite of all this, his book was significantly better than most other authors' best books. It was just that the audience's expectations were so high after Mati's first work that they all expected a miracle now. This is the typical "second-book syndrome" as it has been explained to me.

Most of us "cavemen," the experts that we were, regarded the book with heartfelt neutrality, because we all liked Mati as a person and were glad that he was doing well and didn't turn out to be a one-book wonder. People got down to busily translating that novel as well. Now, Mati was finally "recorded" as a writer, so to speak, and as likely as not was already making his way into school textbooks.

Initially, Mati himself probably believed his new book would be a miracle, too. Yet when it started to become clear that the work was not *quite* a miracle all the same, he wasn't especially downcast, nor did he hit the bottle any harder. I don't know what he felt in his heart, but we even overheard him poking fun at some of the critics that had read who-knows-what into his work. And he really didn't have time for wallowing, because society had started to transform ever faster, and the things that were happening were more important to Mati than literature. He didn't even *write* all that much over the following years, as I recall. I lost sight of him entirely for some time. He came to The Cave more and more infrequently, and finally stopped coming at all. Mati's long-term acquaintanceships with the freedom fighter circles had remained active in the meantime, and he now integrated into a new social movement by way of these contacts. In reality, there were many such movements, and they generally happened away from The Cave. My own "cave life," on the contrary, deepened at that time. I cannot say why. As I am not a very political creature, I had no noteworthy interaction with the new movements, although I naturally kept up on what was happening and crossed my fingers for them.

I guess that I was afraid it was all too good to be true. But maybe I wasn't really thinking anything at all; maybe I was trying to think less.

I imagine that during those years, Mati dedicated himself to the restoration of Estonia's continuity on a constitutional basis. I say this without any kind of pathos. Since Mati did not elbow his way into the foreground and was not seeking personal success or brilliance, he wasn't a very prominent participant. However, I do not doubt that his contribution was much greater than it appeared. He didn't do anything substandardly, but rather always dedicated himself fully, even though this was often on the level of "little acts." Why not big ones? Once again, I cannot say. He had all the makings for this (although he was not a public speaker). I was cleaning out my drawers recently and discovered a simple white sheet of paper, fifteen-by-eight centimeters. Typed on it in blue ink was "Estonian Citizens' Committees. Document no. 0438-16. June 30, 1989. Tallinn." The signature is somewhat sloppy, but if you use a magnifying glass, it definitely reads "M. Tõusumägi." With this document, I was registered as a citizen of the Republic of Estonia on the basis of continuity, and was counted among the body of the future Republic of Estonia. I remember going to pick up the document. It was in a building on Harju Street. The room contained three or four desks staffed by office workers. I was handed the document by a taller, thin, middle-aged woman with short, curly blond hair and glasses. She shook my hand ceremoniously and congratulated me on registering to be a citizen of the Republic of Estonia. The woman was not Mati in disguise—that I can tell you for sure. No doubt he had signed it at the end of a long workday. I wonder whether or not he realized when he signed it that the Juhan Raudtuvi, whose name was printed on the document, was me—one of the "cavemen." I imagine that in those years, he would only sleep once every three days, and even then in a military overcoat (no—not an overcoat, of course, but a sweater), just like in the days of the civil war. And that Agnes brought him soup (no—not soup, of course, but French fries, or even waffles) in the Citizen's Committee Office in a mess tin (meaning a thermos). But I have gotten a little ahead of myself.

# III

# THE NEW ERA

## LOAFERS IN THE SINGING REVOLUTION

It was an August afternoon in 1988. We had been loafing around at Ott's place in the Kalamaja district for the second day in a row. The Cave had been closed for five weeks as it usually was in summer, and there was still a week left until its reopening. All of the usual characters, whose ateliers and cellars we normally went to party at, had gone out of town as if by common agreement. They were holed up in their summer homes, soaking their legs in the sea, catching crayfish in a river, plugging away at a haystack, or mimicking bird and animal sounds in a forest, collecting plus-points with their wives. We who had stayed loyal to the city and were stubbornly holding our positions had nowhere to go on to from there—but no one had even the slightest desire to simply leave; to shuffle off to his or her own home. On top of that, many were just getting into drinking-shape and it would have been a shame to let that go to waste. Therefore, we decided to endure the coming week, for there wasn't much longer to suffer through any more—normal life was already glimmering on the horizon. We drank cocktails mixed from Polish spirits that were sold in one-liter bottles and a cheap Finnish juice concentrate, which we called *"Mehuka."* A splash of tap water was also added to the concoction. Almost everyone drank this beverage—commoners as well as the more affluent, the doers of both mental and physical labor, men and women, the informers and those being informed upon, Estonian and Russian speakers; it might have even been drunk by schoolteachers and *militsiya* officers, because it was cheap, did not have a nasty taste to it, and got you pretty drunk. Furthermore, vodka-juice cocktails were pretty much all we had been drinking for the past decades, with the exception of brandy (when we had the money for it), beer (when it was available), and, on special occasions, whiskey (when someone came visiting from abroad), Soviet sparkling wine (on New Year's, when one bottle was provided per household), and everything else we could get our hands on. People were not fussy back then. People also drank dry wine some time long ago, but this was too far in the past for me.

We spent some time indoors at first, reclining on mattresses laid out on the floor, which we called a "*levälä*" and which resembled a fenced-in child's "paddock." We decided to move outside, though, seeing how the weather was nice. Ott lived in a two-story wooden house, with the ground floor and stairway made of stone, that had been renovated recently. Seen from the street, the building had a generally civilized air to it, and so the large, old-fashioned yard accessed by the back door felt like it was from another world. The yard left the impression of being overgrown, in spite of the fact that someone's little garden tracts with onions and carrots poking out of the soil could be seen here and there, and golden chain and gladiolas grew next to the path. The rainwater barrel in front of the old washhouse barely stuck out of the tall ferns. Beneath the trees was a table that smelled of rotting wood and some simple benches, which had been worn smooth over time and made you think that cards or dominos were played there in the evenings. The tall old lindens and oaks were still thick and green and offered pleasant shade. The gate to the neighboring yard was open, and at one point a middle-aged Russian man who had neither money nor vodka appeared from behind the neighbors' shed. We could see that the man was having a rough time, and we amicably motioned him to rest his legs in our company. This cheered him, and he brought us a hunk of sausage and a scrap of bread as *zakuski*.[22] Everyone was taking things very leisurely, and the mood was mellow and carefree. Poindexter, who had done acrobatics as a child, climbed up a tree and hung there like a sloth for a minute before heaving himself up onto the thick branch, remaining there motionless for about half an hour.

Ott did not have a TV and did not subscribe to newspapers. The building's only radio (a loudspeaker, to be precise) was located on the bathroom wall, and could not be switched off in any way other than by unplugging it. However, as it was a bother to plug back in again, the device played quietly all the time. As a result, anyone having longer business to conduct in the bathroom would usually bring back news from the greater world for the others as well. So it was now.

"We should probably go to the Song Festival Grounds," announced Endel, returning from the bathroom.

"What's there?" someone asked doubtfully. "I was just over there. The Blue Pavilion's under construction, you know."

"No, there's some kind of a thing going on over there right now," Endel said. "Crowds have gathered."

"What crowds?"

"Yea-ah, are they making a revolution there or something?" the poetess Alja whispered.

"Sure seems like it," Endel reckoned. "They're supposed to be waving blue-black-and-whites there, even."

"Brave men!" someone declared. "Let's drink to that."

"Let's check it out," Endel pressed on. "Think about it—maybe later, it'll turn out that something *historic* has happened. They'll ask: where were you at the time?"

"But it doesn't really *mean* that," someone reasoned. "We can always *say* we were there. Who'll check?"

"Course you can, but you'll *feel* crappy about it," Endel stung back.

"Maybe someone's filming it . . ." the film-critic Sõrgats speculated.

"Great—then we'll *watch* the film and afterward, we'll tell our children how we were at the Song Festival Grounds and overthrew the regime. But we just weren't in focus, didn't luck out, right? Or even better—we'll just say that *we* were the ones filming. Our hand was holding the camera. We'll go to Pioneer meetings and say that." And with that, Ott emitted his famous Homeric laugh.

"Maybe there won't *be* Pioneers then," someone conjectured.

"Don't worry—I'm sure there'll still be something," Ott said, dismissing the question with a wave. "There's always some little bugs running around. The blue-black-and-white pioneers! Yea-ah—not as if those things'll change," he sighed sagely, and rolled himself a cigarette with a rolling machine acquired from Sweden.

"It's not worth being so primitively realistic, either, thinking we ourselves should have to go there," Andrus stated. "What've we been given a mind's eye for?"

"I see that the Stanislavsky school of thought speaks within you," Sõrgats said. "You're an *actor*. You have to imagine something for yourself every evening. One night, you feign being in love with some old hag; another time, you're agonizing over the fate of the kingdom. For you, it's easy to imagine a revolution happening on the Song Festival Grounds. But we're different than you. *I'd* sure like to see what's going on there with my naked eye."

"What do you need that for?" Andrus asked. "What're you going to do with it? Does it somehow further your self-realization?"

"Doesn't matter what for. I'm a documentalist. I'm the eye of Dziga Vertov. I have to see everything."

"And I might want to paint it," Pepe backed him up. "The painting will be named 'The Execution of Mixed-Choir Singers on the Song Festival Grounds.' Singers dressed in folk costumes and thick wool socks are tied to the mouths of cannons, *Dyadya* Valdur from the KGB is standing next to them, his hand raised to give the order. All kinds of other executions are happening in the distance. Folk dancers are being tugged into quarters between Tori horses. Yeah—and the directors of the Head Song Festival Committee and chief conductors are hanging from the arch of the shell."

"That's getting to be a bit much," someone mumbled. "You can't fit that all in one painting."

"Sure I can," Pepe confirmed. "It'll be in the style of Pieter Bruegel—a wide picture with tons of figures and concentric circles of action, without perspective."

"You boys sure are cynical," Maša interrupted. "You talk as if one should be earning something from everything all the time; like everything should be made into a sellable good. What about your soul? Think about what you might be missing out on. Maybe history really *is* being made there. Think about it—your *nation* is out there! That really has *feeling*."

Ott considered this for a moment. "Of course we need to go," he finally said. "You think I don't see that?! It's just that . . . nothing'll *come* of all of it. And then things'll be even worse than they are now. Morally, I mean. So long as there isn't anything,

I can at least dream that something'll be *done* about it someday. But if it's all been botched, then it's not even possible for me to dream anymore. Dammit—I'll be so down in the dumps then that I'll descend into third-stage depression."

Regardless of this, he stood up, brushed his pants clean, and said: "Boys, let's go check it out. This way won't do, either. We're drinking it in here, but maybe a war's really broken out there."

"Probably no hope of getting a cab," someone reckoned.

"What cab ... The cabbies are all at the Song Festival Grounds flashing their top lights. We're the only ones loafing around here."

We had one more for the road before leaving, and since we were afraid that there wouldn't be a single place for us to quench our thirsts on the way to the festival grounds, we mixed ourselves some drinks to go in soda bottles. We emerged from the pleasantly cool and shady backyard into the bright sunshine of the street, and commenced our long journey through the stifling heat towards Kadriorg. The neighborhood seemed terrifyingly devoid of people—we didn't cross a single soul on the next couple of streets, either. Crowds were even sparse downtown. This also could have been because it was a sunny Sunday in early August, and people were taking advantage of the opportunity to be at their country homes, of course. We marched down Narva Road—infrequent buses and trams whirred past us, but there were still very few people. It was only near the Russalka monument that groups of people appeared. Most of them were walking in the same direction we were. Soon enough, some kind of booming could be heard coming from the Song Festival Grounds. There was a huge throng near the front entrance, so we decided to circle around and go in the back way. Climbing up the slope of Lasnamäe, we could hear snippets of amplified speeches and the roars of the audience. We still could not see anything yet, however. People were bustling about with blissful looks on their faces. As we reached the crest of the hill, the view that unfolded was astounding. The entire enormous expanse of space was chock full of people—they were even standing in the aisles between the benches and on the edges of the grounds. Never in my life had I seen so many people at once.

Someone was giving a speech on the stage in front, and when he finished, the crowd shouted something. I could not work out what it was, but it certainly was not "hurrah!" This already felt strange, because by my recollection, whenever a crowd had shouted something in unison, it had always been "hurrah!"

I looked around, and soon spotted a familiar face. It was my colleague Sven—a respected and educated translator—in his wheelchair. We walked over to chat with him.

"Boys, how does it feel?" he asked excitedly. "It isn't a little too early, is it? Or is now right when we should be lighting a fire under its ass?" Sven spoke about his hopes and his doubts. He was afraid that one could find both provokers, who had burrowed their way into the ranks of the national movement and were purposefully forcing the events, and simple-minded hotheads, who would blow a hole in the bagpipes. Everything could collapse in either case. Right now, he claimed, it would be a mistake to drive away the sections of the SSR leadership and the Communist party who had gone along with the new developments, but who wanted to act with caution and take things step-by-step. Their plan was to prepare Moscow for the idea of Estonian independence to become a reality. Banging one's fists on the desk would not be sensible. "Otherwise, Moscow will have no choice but to come at us with tanks, even if just to save face," Sven reasoned. "Therefore, we have to stand side-by-side in formation right now. If there's a fracture among us, it could be fateful for Estonia," he asserted confidently. "Our nation is so small that we cannot allow ourselves a Russian-style civil war. No doubt the time will come when every person's weighed separately, but right now, it has be together."

Poindexter, who was the only one who had stayed with me to listen to Sven (the others had moved on), asked: "Do you believe that the Estonian Republic will come?"

Sven was a very honest person and did not answer right away. He thought for quite a while before he answered softly: "It *should* come." Poindexter and I went to find the others.

One speaker was replaced for another on stage, but the speeches' content remained more or less the same. The points were relatively generic and mostly grandiose, nationalist, and romantic. The audience was in an exceptional state of mind, absolutely electrified; each and every individual was greeted with an enthusiasm that caused the air to vibrate — no matter whether it was a freedom fighter or a nationalist-minded communist, an artistic person or a countryman. "I don't recognize the Estonian people," Tobi murmured in astonishment.

"Look, there's Mati," Ott suddenly said, and pointed. "And Klaus, too!" Sõrgats added. Yes, they were on stage. This filled me with a positive, proud feeling. There were certainly other artistic folk standing on the stage as well, very important ones among them, but check it out: we, the "cavemen," were represented two-men-strong, and thus it was as if we ourselves were standing at the focal point of the events. Klaus wasn't actually alone, but was there with the full lineup of The Hearts. They had apparently been invited for entertainment purposes, because *some* kind of a band must be at such an event, even if only for the audience to be able to take a break from the smart speeches. A moment of pause had indeed just arrived, and The Hearts stepped up. The audience greeted them with cheers. Klaus was in the center, and walked up to the microphone. I thought that he would perhaps say something from their usual concert program, but no — he simply congratulated everyone. Then, they performed a few of their most popular satirical songs and one new one, too, which certainly was not the funniest, but had been written just for that event and was very well received. A few audience members even started prancing around on the grass in front of the stage — as much as the space there allowed.

Then a chubby, middle-aged man — a popular leader nicknamed Fatty, who had recently gained renown — approached The Hearts. Speaking into the microphone, he said that the entire nation now stood as one, that their endeavor was progressing, and that victory would come no matter what. And he added: "What's most important is that now we are free *in our souls*. We are no longer afraid. We no longer need to hide our thoughts, for freedom is dawning. Now, my friend Klaus here next to me has the freedom to write and sing just as he pleases!" And he wrapped his arm around Klaus's neck. Klaus froze. We all knew how dreadfully Klaus detested physical contact. I had personally seen how he yelled when someone tapped him on the shoulder from behind unexpectedly. Yet, it goes without saying that he could not let this show and duck out of the chubby man's embrace right now. The crowd could have interpreted it as a lack of consonance among the freedom forces. And so, the wiry Klaus allowed himself to be hugged by the chubby popular leader, who was three times larger than him. The crowd roared with enthusiasm. (Afterward, Klaus said that he blacked out for a moment. "But I decided to ride it out for the Estonian people," he added proudly.)

One speech after another was given on stage — by the way, it felt as if each new speaker was trying to out-pathos the one before him in order to impress the audience, whose level of attention would likely have started to drop otherwise. As a result, their phrases became ever more grandiose, nationalism rocketed sky-high, and the future seemed like a fairy-tale land.

Then Mati took the stage. I don't know whether it was planned or improvised. People were on cloud nine, and the atmosphere was so full of electricity that it is completely possible that everyone wanted to say something to their nation at that very moment. (Perhaps the people on stage also started to feel that they each had some kind of a "personal" and especially precious nation, to which they needed to speak personally.) I was a little wary, because Mati had a great love for conversing but, as far as I knew, was not a good speaker. Mati indeed did not say anything clear into the microphone for a while. He stood there, and then blurted: "What's more to say!" He uttered this in a such way that, bit by bit, the audience started to giggle, then did so ever more loudly, and finally even started to applaud. The audience understood this as him saying that speeches are speeches, calls to action are calls to action — that's quite enough of them, because everything important to say has been said; now, they needed to start doing. Mati walked over to Klaus, and they returned to the microphone together. I suppose some expected them to talk about something-or-other then. But instead, Mati started to sing in a voice trembling slightly from excitement. That, he knew how to do. *"My Fatherland dear, where I was born ..."*—but his singing voice was good, just like a pro! Klaus joined him immediately. They sang in harmony like Simon and Garfunkel, everyone's favorites, with the smaller man singing the lower part. I am always amazed by how powerful an effect the simplest of songs can have on people. I guess we all possess certain deep layers of feeling, which are touched by those tunes and those words. I had not heard that kind of singing before, nor have I since. The song elevated people's moods as high as they could go, and the crowd released deafening shouts of joy.

And with that, the event ended. Maybe the organizers had something else planned, but these things would have seemed superfluous in the wake of such moments, and they realized this.

Mati spotted us and motioned that we should come backstage. Quite a lot of people were moving to and fro there in the auditorium. Someone said hello to us—we did not recognize Agnes right away. She was wearing a Muhu folk dress and had a blue-black-and-white scarf around her neck. She was looking unusually attractive—how proud she must have been of Mati! Maybe it was just an illusion, but for a moment, I thought I saw Manglus's face flash among the important figures on the other side of the room, too. Mati introduced us to the chubby popular leader who had hugged Klaus, telling him our names one by one. "We've heard of you, how could we not," the man said very contentedly at every name, and shook our hands. When it came to be Poindexter's turn, the latter asked: "Do you believe that the Estonian state will come?"

"I do," the chubby popular leader replied sonorously. "I believe."

"My *God*—and we almost didn't *go*," Maša sighed on the way back to the city.

"Dammit, yeah—sure was something," Endel remarked with a lump in his throat, and lit up a cigarette. I noticed that his hand trembled a little when he struck the match.

We sat down at Ott's place once again, but the drinking just wouldn't seem to get going anymore. No matter what we started to discuss, the topic always seemed trivial and out of place, so we soon went our separate ways and did not meet up for an entire week, until The Cave reopened.

## TEEDU'S ABYSS

Teedu was also standing on the slope of Lasnamäe that Sunday. Alone, without speaking to anyone (still, even complete strangers *will* start to converse with one another in such an atmosphere), and without exchanging elated glances with those standing next to him. He had not bounced around, hooted and hollered, or pumped his fist, but instead quietly shrouded himself under a tree next to the footpath, trying to attract as little attention to himself as possible. He had driven to the capital half-secretly. Even Merle did not know he was there. He had told his wife that he was going to the suburb of Nõmme to visit a former schoolmate and discuss "Tallinn affairs." It was one of the only times he had lied to his wife. Why he did this, he was unable to say even to himself, and he had even less of an idea what problem he had in going to the Song Festival Grounds anyway. Yet he couldn't have done anything else, because he felt something drawing him there unrelentingly, with almost supernatural force. This pulling contained both the disturbing enjoyment of staring into an abyss as well as curiosity—the temptation to find out *how things really are*, in what direction and how far they had progressed. Teedu also wanted to know whether the executioner's axe hung above his head; how far along they had gotten with drafting his death sentence. He simultaneously wanted to know this and and was scared to find out. Teedu was also worried about what might happen to him at the Song Festival Grounds, even though he had admitted to himself that it was a childish fear. He was too small of a figure for anyone to recognize him among the crowd and try to lynch him. And even if he *had* been a bigger cheese—all the same, today was not that day. No, certainly not today . . .

The impressions Teedu was left with that evening shook him to the very base of his soul. Such a unified national expression of sentiment moved him to the point of tears (the emotional person that he was) as a phenomenon in and of itself; as a result, he had

nearly forgotten the reason why that mass of people was demonstrating, not to mention the nature of his own position against
the background of the changes yearned for by the nation. However, when he had wiped a tear from the corner of his eye and
his levelheaded sense returned, he was troubled by the scene he
had just observed. And not solely out of a sense of personal safe-
ty. Teedu didn't believe that anything would happen on the political plane. If it were to happen at all, then certainly not at this
moment. It didn't pay to even *dream* about full national independence—flirting with that idea was irresponsible tomfoolery by
the Estonian people, in his opinion. National cultural autonomy, greater economic independence—*these* were realistic goals,
and they *sufficed*, more or less. That for which the flames were
being fanned and momentum being given here, on the other
hand, could be followed by severe consequences. The empire
had not gone anywhere (Teedu realized, appalled, that he had
used (although only in his mind) the expression "empire," which
was certainly taboo); it was indeed rusty, but it was strong and
ironclad. It wasn't worth waiting for a white horse. But nevertheless—the scene Teedu had viewed had an inexplicable effect
upon him, and for a few moments he was almost jealous of all
the people whom fate had not ordained to be a college instructor of Party history.

Casually, the image of a boy with a dripping side, standing
at a bus stop near their old school thirty years earlier arose out
of his memory and before his eyes.

On his way home, Teedu was distracted and very nearly ran
over a cat on the road to Lustivere.


## 1989

With each passing week, Teedu felt more and more as if a great ed-
ifice were crumbling. Certainly not collapsing yet, for the structure appeared monolithic from the outside, just as it had before.
Yet somewhere, something had visibly sagged, and various tensions increased, causing something else to give way elsewhere,
and all in all, it threatened the stability of the entire structure.
The line separating the room's ceiling tiles had sharpened

all of a sudden, as if someone had drawn a bumpy line across the space with a pencil, and a whitish-gray dust and even small fragments would drop from the gap from time to time. Beneath the wallpaper were cracks, which in some places even ripped it apart. Visible wind corridors had formed between the cinder blocks, and as a result, one would occasionally feel as if there was a draft in the room, even though the doors and windows were all shut. And if you were to inspect the building more closely from the outside, you would indeed discover with surprise certain oddly-shaped fissures, dating back to who-knows-when, that had burst open in the foundations and the walls.

Fall arrived and a new semester began at the university. For the first time since marriage, Teedu had not felt the utter joy of the summer. His mind would continually turn back to his worries about the future, and this only worsened. The atmosphere at his *alma mater* was peaceful on the outside but strained within, and this also extended into their faculty. There was nothing more to be guided by, and no one to obey. The newspapers no longer provided clarity. Occasionally, the writing in them would be as it always had been—the CPSU, ECP, and City Committee still existed; there were plenums and decisions, the Komsomol and leading laborers; the titles of People's Artist of the ESSR and even that of the USSR were still awarded to creative intellects, and the recipients certainly did not refuse them. The publications themselves remained the mouthpieces of the local organs of power, judging by the print information beneath the newspaper titles. Yet when you started to read them, you would come across such heretical and brazen stories on every other page that—by golly! The articles teemed with the kinds of expressions that, just two years earlier, would have doubtlessly cost an editor-in-chief his job.

One got the impression that no one knew what was permitted and what was not. Everyone was trying to push in a certain direction—some urged others to be bolder, while at the same time the latter were urging the former not to blow a hole in the bagpipes. All in all, something indeterminate was taking shape around the newspapers—something that resembled the dimness of wisps of fog and marshes. One section of people trudging sluggishly through that marsh seemed to be waiting to pounce in the right direction and take up favorable positions at just the right moment. Until then, they would assert fuzzily but resolutely to anyone inquiring: "*It's boiling, it's boiling, how can it not be!*" Another section of them, whom Teedu had been in the department with for ten years or gotten to know in nearby institutions, were pretending that everything was just as it had been before, and that if something *were* to change, then it would be in accordance with the main agenda.

Nevertheless, Teedu noted that several of his colleagues—especially those who were in higher positions and had, until then, been highly *inaccessible*—were suddenly very available, were outright nationally-minded, and wanted to talk with everyone. They wore cheerful expressions when doing so, sometimes even loveable ones, but as soon as they believed themselves to be alone, then an anxiously pensive or outright leaden look would fall across their face.

Students were being taught, but no one was controlling what was spoken at lectures and seminars; in what kind of a light the history, the present, and the future were being served. It was every person's own business now—everyone had to know personally what he or she was speaking about and what was being risked in doing so; what bridges were being burned behind them or what roads were being paved.

Teedu was gripped by an existential fear—much greater than what he had felt when his poems were published in the samizdat journal, or his constant fear that his secret hobby—the study of house marks (not to even mention his handling of the Ming dynasty)—would be revealed. One could receive a Party reprimand for these things, but it would eventually be retracted—if, in the given instances, the authorities were convinced that you really were "one of their own guys" and agreed to play according to the rules. Now, however, Teedu's right to exist at *all* was being put in doubt somewhere. He could tell that some of his younger colleagues felt the same way. They didn't speak about it candidly, but it was squirming on the tips of their tongues. Time was passing, and it seemed to not be working to their benefit. And then at some point, almost casually, the decision was made

in the hallway of the social sciences building to spend the weekend at the university's resort in Kääriku. The excuse was: "Let's
relax." There was nothing unusual about it—the faculty had
certainly been to Kääriku before. There was a sort of group that
would occasionally go to discuss "guy stuff." It included people
from several departments, and a few were from outside of the
university. Teedu's Kääriku peers on that occasion were Aivar,
Rein, Andrus, Gunnar, Kaupo, and Vladimir; older colleagues
included Peek and Norman, in addition to the laboratory
worker Joobel, who secured the beer and took care of the basic-
needs side of the event.

Miller, however, did not come. Everyone was secretly disappointed by this, because Hasso was savvy and could have explained things to them. Of course, one could have guessed that
Miller would not come. Now, just as always, he was moving
around in different spheres. Miller had always treated his colleagues with deliberate politeness, but it was evident that he
was rather trying to erect walls between himself and them by
doing so. Indeed—he probably despised them. Miller was not
a Eurocommunist, but something more refined. Back in the
day, a number of Miller's older colleagues would say semi-open-
ly that he was a wolf in sheep's clothing. Still, he was not booted
out of the university—the backbiters claimed it was all thanks
to his ancestry. (This could *hardly* have been the only reason.
Some alleged that Miller privately advised the very highest ech-
elon of the ESSR's Party elite, but that was more of a rumor.)
One got the impression that Miller was not placing an emphasis on an official career, and was not elbowing his way into administrative jobs. He had not even defended a thesis for doctoral candidacy. Oddly, *this* was the very aspect that especially
offended some of his colleagues, because by failing to do so,
Miller seemed to be showing how little respect he had for the
popularly recognized hierarchies and values, and consequently
also for the people who aligned themselves according to them.

Teedu could only remember one time that he had conversed
one-on-one with Miller. They had met by complete chance at
Stockholm Arlanda Airport when a thunderstorm was raging
outside and all of the flights had been delayed. They drank coffee

and cognac at the bar. Teedu would not have ordered alcohol, but he felt that it was the right thing to do at the present moment. He wanted to speak with Miller because he admired him. Indeed — Miller shared a wealth of information quite nonchalantly. It was entirely different from what Teedu encountered on a daily basis. Miller's points were not dissident, but rather left the impression of being scientific and unbiased. Teedu felt himself getting smarter with each passing minute that he listened to Miller. He was extremely disappointed when his flight was called out. Their conversation had, among other things, even briefly turned towards Teedu's department. Speaking about one individual in particular, Miller had told Teedu: "Don't have too much to do with him." He did not comment more on the matter. Years later, it turned out that the person in question was someone who supplied the KGB with information on their department.

At Kääriku, the men went skiing and then went to the sauna. In between bouts of soaking in the steam, they spoke about the world and the weather — drifting from the new student café to the Kalev basketball team, to the latest trivia tournament, to women. "Why aren't we talking about what *matters*?," Teedu wondered fretfully. "Are we just going to keep beating around the bush? Are we *really* just going to disperse without addressing what's important?" But no, luckily not. When they were drinking beer in front of the fireplace in the anteroom after sauna, Kaupo spoke up on what was weighing upon everyone's hearts. What will happen if Estonia *does* break away from Moscow? Would guys like them be lined up against a wall? The group determined that things could not go that badly. *One hundred thousand people* would have to be lined up against a wall in Estonia were that to happen; almost every eighth or tenth adult. Sure, maybe the Party's foot soldiers could be excluded (it was hardly likely that anyone would touch them), but a good ten thousand would definitely need to be "neutralized." Yet this was unrealistic, and would merely remain the wishful thinking of a few extreme nationalists. In reality, not very many would be "neutralized," because such a tiny nation would not survive even a small bloodletting. And here in Estonia, there was nowhere to deport people other than Ruhnu or Värska. Maybe there wouldn't even be any repressions, although someone's baggage might certainly be used as a trump card in the settlings of scores that was sure to come. One must be prepared for that, but such things are normal, because isn't there always a battle underway already? *Let's not be naive,* someone said, *we've always been one another's competitors, too.* The form of life would change, but the content would remain the same. In that regards, no out-of-the-ordinary tragedy was to be expected. The only people with a true axe hanging above their heads were the ones who had connections to the KGB. Everyone in the room chuckled at that comment, but somewhat nervously, and started to drink their beers more quickly.

### THE WRITERS' SPEAKING CHOIR

The above-ground moods also extended down into The Cave, of course. By the end, it was not only frequented by bohemi-ans: serious types could be found there, maybe even in greater number. Many of these were now socially active and associated with the "cause." But we, who regarded ourselves as the nucleus or the think tank of The Cave, also became more active. We lis-tened with excitement and deference to those who knew some-thing about "the cause"; we did not interrupt them (as we had sometimes done before then) or make ironic quips. Even *we* felt an indistinct shudder of exhilaration when they asserted: "It'll all let loose, how can it not!" And when the smarter ones— those who were privy to "the cause"—had left the table, we would hold longer discussions among ourselves about culture, the Estonian society and state, and the connections between them. In the interests of saving space, I have composed a small "montage" or "collage" of all of this. The following thoughts were certainly never put forth all at once or by the same peo-ple; it's also possible they were not exactly worded as such. As far as I know, no one wrote them down or presented them like some kind of a manifesto. (I have also made it more literary and "striking." In doing so, I have perhaps been influenced by the slogans once intended for official demonstrations, which appeared in the publications *Noored* and *Rahva Hääl* prior to the Soviet holidays in November and May. The erstwhile grade-school spoken choral tradition likewise resonates within them, as does—naturally, as always—my own participation in community theater, where I had to adapt dialogues.) This kind of a crystallization is, perhaps, necessary to characterize the era.

And so:

*"We are standing on the threshold of a glorious future."*

*"All people will love the arts and poetry in the future; books and newspapers will be published in myriads; theater, concert, and exhibition halls will be brimming with people; TV and radio stations will endlessly gush programs onto the airwaves—programs whose deep moral transfiguration will cause people to radiate goodness, and whose scope will entertainingly broaden their horizons."*

*"The widespread practice of reading in Soviet Russia—on subway escalators as well as in line for toilet paper—did not derive from true interest, but rather from the lack of freedom of choice. People had nothing else to do. In Estonia, however, people read out of a true love for culture. Therefore, we will also continue to read when we have our own country. Things in Estonia will not go like they have abroad, where interest in reading vanishes under the influence of consumer mentality. Our books' print runs will not decrease; our good prose writers and poets will be read just as much in the future as they are now. Under the conditions of freedom of choice, our nation will choose intellectuality."*

*"It won't go for us as it has for others. We will not repeat others' mistakes. Don't even hope for it—we won't, no matter what! We will learn from their mistakes, instead. We'll construct a welfare state founded on solidarity. We'll go forth in unison, extending a helping hand to the weak."*

*"We'll create strong ties with foreign Estonians who want to contribute towards Estonia's development. Their enthusiasm, knowledge, and skills for how to live in the Free World cannot be allowed to go to waste."*

*"Minorities and foreigners will be honored in our nation state—they too will be working for the good of Estonian society; their contribution cannot be allowed to go to waste, either."*

*"In Estonia, everyone will study and will receive a scholarship.*

*A small nation cannot allow a single gifted child to be deprived of the opportunity to thoroughly develop his or her talents, and thus be unable to contribute to the general good, as a consequence of material reasons. We will care for the elderly. However, the elderly will also study and make their own contribution, within reason."*

*"Overall—no one's strength may go to waste in leading Estonia's economy to blossom."*

*"That is how our state will rise—driven by spirituality, borne from idealism, once inhibited but now unleashed rapidly into never-before-seen heights, bolstered by gusto, becoming a shining city on a hill."*

*"We will boost our population. Every family will have four children. The Estonian woman will become the most beautiful in the world."*

*"We will put new arable lands to use. We will fill the countryside with life. Cheerful clamor and singing voices must sound in every corner of Estonia."*

*"We will create the best climate for entrepreneurship."*

*"We will preserve Estonia's ancient and pure nature, establishing new environmental preserves. Birdsong will echo everywhere. Frogs will return to the ponds and marshes. The birds and the frogs will be our friends. People will come here from polluted Europe to vacation, and it will be like paradise to them."*

*"Everyone will be very dignified."*

Here at the end, I further assembled a brief dialogue (so that it might be clearer).

*"Who will start arranging all of that?"* asks Doubting Toomas when he has read through the preceding text. He has an intelligent nature, wears a dull herring-shaped tie, and resembles an archivist.

*"I suppose we ourselves will,"* chuckles a man under the age of thirty, who is wearing a folk-patterned sweater. *"We Estonians."*

*"But then why, so far, has no one—not a single nation in the world that has liberated itself from a foreign power—accomplished anything like that to this very day?"* asks Doubting Toomas with persistence. *"Why has their idealism and sense of principle fizzled out before long, to be replaced by a cult of objects and the pursuit of life's most ordinary pleasures? Why do*

*they no longer read, think, or focus; no longer care for one anoth-
er or want to go forth in unison? Why has harsh individualism
taken the place of solidarity?"*

*"Estonians are a special people. It's already been set that way by
destiny and can be seen from history," Sweater says, smiling confidently.*

*"What—so an Estonian is not like all other people, then?"
Doubting Toomas asks especially disbelievingly.*

*"He isn't," Convinced Sweater replies, sounding especially, espe-
cially convinced.*

Nationality became very important in The Cave. This was
shown even just by the fact that when two people were arguing
about something back then and were already butting skulls, all
it took was for a third person to say:

"Are we or aren't we all Estonian men?" And the arguers
calmed down in an instant.

KGB men were now a very rare sight in The Cave. It could
be that they were busy preventing the oncoming events.

When night fell, people in The Cave danced the lambada—
a new, fashionable dance with a yearningly groaning, wearying
rhythm, and wantonly stamping movements.

## FYODOR VLADIMIROVICH.
## IVAN IVANOVICH. VASSILI

Another year went by—a hazy, apprehensive one full of growing
tensions both with Moscow and within the country. If someone
would have discussed the topic with Teedu then, he would have
solemnly claimed to have already been an Estonian nationalist during the Soviet era. For example, had he not always been
irritated when Ivan Ivanovich pinched him? Ivan Ivanovich was
the nearly fifty-year-old iron-toothed secretary of the Party City
Committee, who handled ideological issues. Pinching was a
habit of his. He would pinch everyone, even women (although
certainly not high-ranking superiors). He would pinch his fellow Estonian Party members with exceptional pleasure—those
whom he called "little brothers pecking at big brother's table."

He didn't trust them. "There's always some kind of a worm hiding in you guys," he would say threateningly to Estonians, facetiously wagging his finger at them. He always called them by their first name and patronymic, which wasn't customary in Estonian culture. Teedu's father had been Voldemar, and thus Teedu himself was Fyodor Vladimirovich. Ivan Ivanovich made jeering remarks about Teedu's Russian. Thanks to military conscription, Teedu spoke his "second mother tongue" (as it was semi-officially called) quite fluently, but very softly and with an accent (which should partly be ascribed to Mr. Kulu). Ivan Ivanovich was, for all intents and purposes, monolingual, and all he knew how to say in Estonian was "hey-hey" and "vana munn," meaning "old prick." He had heard Estonians saying, "Lend me your zither, Vanemuine!" and singing about the mythical Vanemuine, who went to go play a zither.[23] A certain combination of sounds had stuck in Ivan Ivanovich's head, although not accurately. He had noticed that whenever he used that combination, those around him would start to snicker, and so he continued doing so—even in the company of ladies. For Teedu, however, that song was part of the Estonian nation's past—it had been sung by his mother and father; had been sung by all of his ancestors, who had fought against the German manor lords in the time of the Estonian national movement. And therefore, he was obviously offended, even in his best of moods, when the irreverent Ivan Ivanovich lampooned the lovely song like some kind of savages' "bar-bar." Why did such an imbecile have to be on their city's Party Committee? He was a disgrace to the Soviet regime. Teedu would have, in any case, preferred to do business with Estonian members of the Party. How had he not been a nationalist, then?

Or take Vassili, with whom Teedu had been recently discussing political developments each time they met. Vassili was his "hometown Russian," who had lived a couple of houses down from his old residence. Vassili spoke Estonian fluently, as his parents had immigrated to the country even before the Russian revolution. Vassili was a pensioner who used to work in the state prosecutor's office, and his wife had been a friend of Teedu's mother. Teedu did not exactly *like* him, of course, but he felt that it was useful for a person to have Russian friends. Attention would certainly be paid to the fact somewhere, and this could only be advantageous for him. Therefore, he visited Vassili quite frequently, and had even introduced Merle to him once (when things had progressed to that point), as if expecting the Russian's approval.

"What's all this about, then?" Vassili had asked with outstretched arms during the Singing Revolution. "We've been living together as friends this whole time, living side by side — nothing was wrong, no one complained about there being any kind of national repression. But now, all of a sudden, Estonians and the Estonian language have been *oppressed?*"—"No, they haven't," Teedu replied automatically. Why get into an argument? And he thought to himself: *How the hell do* you *know whether or not we were living as friends? Maybe only you thought we were, while in reality, we weren't at all—we were just keeping our mouths shut.* He didn't want to be unjust, because Vassili was an honest person nonetheless—a simple and frank Russian soul. Yet Estonians had obviously been oppressed: that much was clear. Even Vassili was oppressing him, completely unknowingly, solely by his lack of imagination—he was unable to *understand* how he and people like him had oppressed Teedu and the entire Estonian people purely through their presence as a large nation.

When Teedu found himself unable to sleep at around four o'clock in the morning (this happened frequently now), he would find himself arguing with nationalists in his mind. Don't they even *start* believing that only they ... As if being an Estonian man in the Russian Communist Party had been easy. That goddamn "old prick" ... Mocking our beautiful song ... And there were a lot of those kinds of "pricks"—the higher you went, the more there were. Teedu wished that men like Ivan Ivanovich didn't exist. He actually wished that men like Vassili didn't exist either, although he didn't dare admit this to himself. He wanted socialist nationalism. Estonia should have been an independent socialist republic, in which people had jobs and bread and there was peace in the land. That would have been the best. Would he have liked to step into Ivan Ivanovich's shoes personally? He held himself back from thinking that far. Mill-

er would definitely have been better suited for that position if
. . . if he were a little friendlier. Had he descended from his lofty
pedestal; had he abandoned the pastor-like flippancy of a man
who possessed higher wisdom. That goddamn Miller . . . Teedu
would doze off to such thoughts after an hour or so, and would
sleep soundly until seven thirty.

Teedu's angsts would usually abate in the daytime, but came
right back in the evening. Even though he had been a nationalist, he had only been so inside. On the surface, he had still
been an honest lecturer of CPSU history. He was honest both
ways. (However, one of these honesties could now turn out to
have been a mistake. How dreadful—why did this choice have
to come to a head during *his* own lifetime!) He thought, on the
one hand, with tenderness and sadness about his own mother
and father, who had been forced to bury their hopes and had
not had the courage to celebrate Christmas through the end of
their lives. And all that was currently happening was wonderful just as well, of course; for who didn't desire to be the master of his own house? This opportunity appeared to be materi-
alizing now.

On the other hand, he also had his own little life to live,
and he knew both from history (based on Chinese society in
the time of the Ming dynasty) and from personal experience
that it is possible to live pleasantly, orderly, and safely under any
regime. It is possible to be beneficial to society and work just
enough that it does not become unpleasant, and to take pleasure
in your activities the rest of the time. It is possible to do good
deeds for people, which is of utmost importance. Teedu had
been able to do that prior to then, but was uncertain of whether it would continue that way. Probability said he still had the
greater portion of his life ahead of him. *Did I make the wrong
choice, all the same?* he asked himself, in agony. (Again—would
he have been prepared to take Ivan Ivanovich's job? Not the old
Ivan, but the "new one"? If the Estonian people were to demand
it? No—in the light of day, Teedu said to himself decisively:
*You, Teedu, only have the Teedu-level; don't go reaching higher
than your wings can carry you!*)

Teedu decided to keep a low profile. Who knew how far

those new nationalists might go. He certainly did not have any outright enemies, as far as he knew. The dissident Kribalds—a former colleague who taught Party history; Teedu had attended the meeting where it was decided to throw him out of the party—was not the enemy type, but primarily a theoretician; a warrior for truth and justice. He had wanted to cleanse and improve communism back in the day, believing that communism meant spiritual uplifting and the freedom of choice. This had been seen as a mortal sin higher up, of course. Kribalds had made it known to the college Party Committee that he wouldn't be averse to going to work in Paris for a year to acquaint himself with the French version of communism. He had been completely sincere in doing so. This request was the reason he was kicked out. Afterward, he leaned towards the nationalist camp in his quests for spiritual freedom, and was currently regarded as a dissident and a martyr. People had forgotten about his once genuine belief in communism by now. If you took it that way, then Teedu had helped to neutralize the very *greatest* communist, which could be tallied up as a positive act in and of itself. However, Teedu felt that such logic was outdated, and his signature on the meeting's minutes was a stain upon his conscience. (He would not have kicked Kribalds out, but there was naturally no point in resisting the majority. Kribalds would have been booted anyway, because that was what had been decided higher up. It would only make Teedu a marked man. Yes—now, it would have been very beneficial for him, but back then, it would have been comparable to suicide.) No, Kribalds would not start attacking him . . . Teedu was unable to suspect anyone else. But you never know. For example—even now, a number of men might be jealous that his wife was the pert-breasted beauty Merle. ("Too good for his kind. A worn-down, dried-up lab worker would have been good enough for him!") Teedu's most serious competitor on the path to Merle's heart had been a member of the college Komsomol committee back in the day. A man of the same name had started giving public speeches recently. Just the other day, Teedu had seen his name at the bottom of a collective appeal. An unpleasant shudder passed through him, and he thought: *Oh, that would be quite the coincidence.* But something told him it was one and the same—an intellectual who had been brushed aside in the meantime. There weren't that many people named Aaberkukk. Might Aaberkukk start throwing wrenches in the gears for him?

## ILLIMAR'S LETTER FROM AUGUST 1991

*Honorable Chronicler!*
*Although we live in the provinces and are deplorable by nature already because of that, even we are up to speed on what is happening in the republic. We have heard that Russian special-forces units are surrounding the Tallinn TV Tower and that anything can be expected from Moscow right now. The men and I spoke about it by the store. They are of the same mind as you all are in the capital. Endure, and once more—endure! Death here or in Siberia, but we'll do it! We made plans for how to come to Tallinn's aid.*

*The local* partorg, *Jõgever Klaasmets, publicly announced that he is discontinuing his Communist Party membership. After that, he was also allowed to drink beer with the others outside the store. Little Kusti, a funny guy, asked: "How'd you do it, how'd you get out?" Jõgever thought for a moment, then saw that there was some kind of a power cord plugged into the wall, went over, and pulled it out—ka-chunk! "Just like that," he said. Everyone got it. Jõgever forgot to plug the cord back in, and all of the scant butter, milk, and sausage that Mai the grocer had stocked up on for the next few days went bad. Kusti said—once a* partorg, *always a* partorg, *no matter if he's in or out. But the others denied this, saying—what're you picking on him for, he wanted to do good; you've always got to give a person the chance to mend his ways.*

# IV

# THE NEWEST AGE

## AN IMPORTANT DAY

When the independent Republic of Estonia was declared, Teedu was sitting in the department office. There were fewer than two weeks left until the start of teaching. The radio was on. Teedu started to sweat upon hearing the results of the Supreme Soviet's vote, and realized that he had not been ready for such news yet, all the same; that he had still just been thinking: *who knows what will happen?* Occupying the room in addition to him was the laboratory worker Joobel, who was Russian-Estonian—a small, scrupulous, skinny, bald man of sixty. They rose as if it had been agreed upon beforehand, stood at attention, and shook each other's hand. "Congratulations, comra— . . . Mr. Tärn," Joobel said, catching himself. "Congratulations, Mr. Joobel," Teedu said.

That evening, Teedu walked home as if through a fog, seeing nothing and no one on his way. A joyful, blissful, and slightly vacuous expression was on his face, like that of some female saint in ecstasy. Every little while, he would shout out: "Oh, how good I feel! Oh, how happy I am!" He did not shout it all that loudly, of course, but not completely to himself, either. He whinnied with glee inwardly, striving to remain politically expressionless at the same time. Teedu was dreadfully afraid that someone might think he did not like what was happening.

Having arrived home, he turned both locks on their outer door and hooked the chain on top of that, not considering how the other family members would get in. He stormed into his office, bolting it shut as well, slumped down onto the couch, and sat there motionless for five minutes, waiting for his ability to think to be restored. He wanted a shot of cognac for the first time in several years; alas, they had no alcohol at home. His first thought was to resign from the university right then and there. He had a prepared letter of resignation, just in case. One night some time before, when Merle and the children were sleeping, he had crafted a secret pocket out of plastic and cloth in his attaché case, and had been carrying the letter around with him at all times so that it could be put into play posthaste if necessary. It could come in necessary if things came to "reckoning," and heads started to roll. There were two copies of the letter. One's date was left open, the other was dated two years earlier. He had even had them validated at a notary's office. Teedu imagined that if it was necessary, he could perhaps use it to show that he had already changed his mind and wanted to leave the lectern of false teaching earlier—not just when everyone was doing so to save their own skins. He had grasped from a number of clues that a few of his colleagues had similar letters set aside. One colleague stored his letters in a luggage locker at the train station; the other had buried them on his cabin property.

Now, it certainly appeared that the time to put the letter into play was at hand. For about five minutes, Teedu felt that he was capable of doing so. Then, however, he was reminded of Merle and the kids. How would he support them? Teedu hadn't done any other kind of work, nor would he have known how to. What was more—he didn't *want* to do anything else. History fascinated him; he couldn't just drop it. Party history was certainly not actual history (he naturally understood this fact), but it was better than nothing at all. And he had house marks and the Ming dynasty for his spiritual needs. Having considered all arguments for and against, Teedu decided that he had to wait to see how others would act. He should not take hasty steps on his own. He unchained the front door and flipped open the other locks.

When the children came back from tennis practice, Teedu stealthily observed them to see whether they would look at him disdainfully, or peculiarly in any other way. However, he did not notice anything. Before going to bed at night, Merle said to him casually: "You're not to blame for *anything*." This filled Teedu's heart with gratitude. *How good and wise a wife I have*, he mused happily.

He did not appear to interest anyone over the course of the next few days. Teedu brought it up with his colleagues in a roundabout way. "Let's wait and see" was the general opinion.

Teedu calmed down a little, but not entirely. When Saturday came, he headed for Raadi Cemetery in Tartu's Ülejõe district to check on any opportunities that undertaker's offices might offer. He couldn't come up with any better ideas at first, but he didn't want to just sit with his hands folded in his lap, either. Perhaps it would be possible to get some kind of a job at an undertaker's office? Not an actual researcher's position, of course, but something akin to a local historian? He could inspect the most important graves in the cemetery, collect oral histories, compare them to those at other burial sites, and other similar things. He *was* a diploma-holding historian, and the deceased belonged fully and utterly to history; their time was irreversibly past. In that respect, there was a connection between the history of the deceased and that of the Party. Teedu's longtime involvement in one should have favored his involvement in the other, also. *Oh, the parallels that are popping into my head!* Teedu thought in wonder. It was good that no one could hear what he was thinking. *But no*, the thought rushed into his head the next moment: just the opposite—it was a *shame* that no one could hear them. For now, they were the *correct* thoughts. Teedu would have liked everyone to hear how correctly he was thinking. But at the same time, he pondered, the way he was thinking probably wasn't especially interesting to anyone. This thought filled him with peace.

*But why not dedicate myself to pure knowledge?* he debated while strolling towards Raadi. The world held all kinds of theories. They had been outlawed in their system until now, but everything *was* supposed to change henceforth. Perhaps he could master some new theory and start applying that to the dead? *How might it be according to Foucault?* he wondered. Or Baudrillard, for example? Teedu had read articles in Russian that were critical of both. He was already envisioning having a small, cozy office in the one-story building located in the yard of the undertaker's office, where he would start working all safe and secure. As long as the pounding coming from the adjacent coffin workshop wasn't too much of a bother ... That kind of an inconspicuous job wouldn't be a bad option at all. It would be much better than collecting scrap and recyclable paper. He knew that in the early fifties a number of intellectuals who had been labeled enemies of the state had been forced to do this to stay alive. No one else would hire them. Yet Teedu would not be able to bear that now. He would have to go around knocking on strangers' doors, where people would toss into his face *A Brief Course on the History of the CPSU, Scientific Communism*, or the small brochure that he himself had published on the university's Rotaprint printer to be used as teaching material ("Methodological Guidelines for Mastering the History of the CPSU"), and would scoff: "Goddamn commie—eat your own shit now!" But no, that would be impossible—old recyclable paper isn't collected that way anymore these days. But how is it collected, then? *I must find out, whatever it may cost me*, Teedu resolved, unable to say how that knowledge could be useful to him. The peace that had come to him had meanwhile been swept away, and he felt almost feverish. What had the dissidents done when they were fired during the eighties? Some had probably become gravediggers. Now, they were supposedly coming into power—consequently, their cemetery jobs would be freeing up. Perhaps he should try finding work there? Someone doing physical work is always more trustworthy than a mental laborer in the eyes of a regime, because he thinks less. But did Teedu personally have the bones for a gravedigger's job? He had never done sports, and had quit doing morning exercises already years ago. *I should start working on it again*, he promptly decided. *You cannot withstand the storm of the ages without physique. Muscles are needed in a forced-labor camp, too*, he reasoned. *Push-ups . . . weights . . . splits . . . No, splits are an excessive luxury; they won't be necessary behind the barbed wire. But you've got to be capable of throwing a punch if someone comes to rip your bread ration out of your hands.* Teedu's thoughts were truly muddled and scattered.

He made his visit to Raadi, and it began quite humorously. He asked at the undertaker's office if they had any spots, and the older lady, who wore an old-fashioned suit and had elaborately coiffed hair, thought he wanted to purchase a gravesite. When Teedu politely clarified the error, the woman shook her head but promised to look into it. "Right now is the sort of time when no one knows what tomorrow will bring. Maybe those kinds of jobs will come, too. My personal opinion is that there certainly *should* be such an individual—a biographer or a historiographer—at a cemetery. Ultimately, it *is* all of our common past." Teedu perceived that the older woman was educated and felt similarly uncertain in the whirlwind of the ages, and that drew her closer to him. He nearly handed the woman his business card so that she might contact him if a "corresponding position" were to arise, but at the last minute he decided not to. Who knows who was in contact with whom, and where such stories might end up.

Stepping out of the little office, Teedu was very satisfied with himself for not having behaved imprudently, and decided to look around the cemetery a little. He viewed the epitaphs on famous graves with an expert's gaze, touched a number of the more outstanding monuments carefully, and straightened a tilting candle in front of a fresh cross. He walked around for a little while longer, and left the cemetery in quite an exuberant state of mind. Even before then, he had noticed that strolling around a cemetery lifted his spirits.

One month passed after another. Not a single one of the instructors in their department quit, nor did anyone in the former Department of Historical Materialism or even the Department of Scientific Communism (a few did indeed retire, but they probably would have done so anyway). Leaving did not come into question at all: not in private or in public. They pretended among themselves as if everything was going as normal, and that the public had other and more pressing problems. It gradually started to become clear that a "reckoning" was unlikely, and that heads really would not start to roll. One after another, Teedu's colleagues withdrew from the CPSU. Teedu did so as well—without any great fuss. Afterward, he was overcome for a period by a peculiar feeling that was a mixture of irresponsibility and absurdity, growing self-confidence (from getting away with a dirty trick) and impunity, and a schoolboy's springtime let-it-all-slide mood when it has become clear that he will have to repeat the class, anyway. *Is this all really, truly happening, and to me?* he asked himself at such moments. He generally tried not to focus too deeply on making sense of his surroundings,

or to ruminate over what good was coming of what was going on, or whether it was just. *Live, one must live*, he repeated to himself time and again, *even if only a day at a time, one
must live*. The others were continuing to teach at the university, and so was he. *There have been much, much greater pigs than
I*, he assured himself. One must atone for his sins through diligent work, although in Teedu's mind, he basically *had* no sins.
But this was of no consequence. History had taken a different
path, and if he had to atone, then he was prepared to do so in
order to escape "the people's just revenge." And why shouldn't
the Republic of Estonia have use for an individual with lecturing abilities, too?

Subjects were switched out in the college curriculum, research centers became institutes, and many other things received new names. Another new development was that an instructor's job was no longer guaranteed for life. A competition
was organized for every position, and a fixed-term contract was
signed by the winner. The instructor had to try again after five
years. Yet there was no worry about this at first, because the
committees making the respective decisions were mostly staffed
by old acquaintances. Teedu was confirmed without a hitch. He
became an instructor of twentieth-century history. He didn't
lose a significant amount in terms of salary. The inflation level
affected him too, of course. An ebb could be felt in the economy overall, because the supply lines of the so-called *Nomenklatura* (to which he belonged in a roundabout way) had been
broken. Ordinary stores were empty. Still, he continued to be
employed by the state, and that gave him certainty. Teedu liked
being employed by the state. He was feeling better and better, and was sleeping more soundly again. This new Estonian
age was not at all as bad as he had feared. Especially since now
there was no Ivan Ivanovich pinching him with his boney fingers — rumor had it he had relocated to Moscow. Vassili, however, had simply moved on to another world. Teedu suspected
he had become embittered over the last couple years of his life.
He had not spoken to Vassili since the restoration of independence, and felt a little guilty because of it. Yet, he also felt relief,
and so he said to himself: *The fact that I am relieved shows once*

*more that I am a proper Estonian. But the fact that I also feel guilt means that I am still human, too.* In short, he was put into such a good mood that he retrieved the 250 Swedish kronor he had saved from pocket money once given to him for a conference in Gothenburg (the entirety of his foreign-currency reserves), which he had stowed away in the bottom of a drawer, bought a handsome, colorful tie from a store owned by an American-Estonian joint enterprise, and became even younger by way of it.

### ILLIMAR'S LETTER FROM OCTOBER 1992

*Honorable Chronicler!*
*(. . .) A record! It turns out that as many as five women are expecting in these parts!*

*I am currently in an extraordinary spiritual state. Bright vivacity, vision, fortitude. We live in an outstanding era. Now that freedom is also officially at hand, we are just getting things going. Our nation and our state are small—what mobility/advantage that gives us! How easy it is to turn the state in the direction we wish, to change everything, to execute even the most grandiose reforms. And all of it is in our own hands. What else—if we put new systems in place, then we will catch up with the rest of the world and even surpass them. Let all nations observe and envy us—this small miracle nation; how they succeed at everything! This topic also came up in front of the store. The men agreed unanimously that they are prepared to tighten their belts; the main thing is that now we have our own state and freedom. Tõiv promised to make soup out of old boots. This victim's mentality speaks of a higher, romantic mindset. People are acting in the name of something greater than them.*

*The beer ran out before the store closed. Peedu, Lall, and Volli shared a bottle of vodka between the three of them.*
*I am reading the Fifth Book of Moses.*

### ILLIMAR'S LETTER FROM MARCH 1993

*Honorable Chronicler!*
*(. . .) There were not many men to talk with at the village store. There was no beer either, by the way.*

*Peedu and Meos are busy getting property returned to them.
Peedu has a farm to receive, but a zootechnician lives on the property and wants to keep the better part of it. He built himself a new
stable in the heart of the plot during the Soviet era—that's why.
Peedu is taking him to court. Meos want to be compensated for his
grandfather's windmill.*

*Everyone is getting privatization vouchers. I am also planning
to make my one-room apartment my very own.*

*What will become of the kolkhoz? It was, but is no more. People
reckon that agriculture should stay nonetheless.*

*Tractors have popped up at a few men's homes.*

*I am reading Lermontov.* A White Sail Gleams *is a good poem.*

## MATI STARTS PUTTING UP A FIGHT

Mati came to The Cave the same evening that the independent
republic was declared. We had not seen him in some time. He
appeared on the stairs wearing blue pleated pants and a white
V-neck sweater, beneath which he wore a white dress shirt and
a dark-blue tie. He was not carrying a briefcase on that occasion, but his pockets were bulging a little. Round, merry eyes
peered out from his broad, daring face. He stopped, scanned
the room, and chuckled to himself, as if wanting to say: "Everyone's here. As always!" We waved him over and made space.

"Good friends—cheers to freedom," Mati declared, raising his glass. Everyone lifted their shots; some in silence, others murmuring approvingly. "We did it. Actually, we really are
a bunch of lucky ducks," Mati said when he had taken a sip.

"Are we really?" Manglus asked, looking around as if he did
not understand what was being talked about. No one paid him
any heed, though; everyone was gripped by the new moods.
That night, we sang euphorically at The Cave until it turned
light outside. Probably all of the proper Estonian songs were
sung through. We pranced the *Kaerajaan*[24] on the grass in front
of a nearby church in the morning twilight.

That night, partying and song could be heard all around,
and random passersby greeted each other enthusiastically.

Life started to progress at an insane tempo. New and completely free art exhibitions were already being organized, new and completely free publications were being made; even the authors of operas and film soundtracks were enjoying every inch of the new freedom of creation.

"We have a telephone at home now," Maša said one day. "We'll be able to talk more."

"They talk a whole lot on the telephone in Finland, too," said Pekka (who was naturally present and keenly following the changes) with a well-meaning nod.

"We'll start getting better food soon," someone said dreamily. The others did not comment, as if the person had said something improper.

Months passed. People joyfully ascertained that their secret fears of possible vengeance from Moscow or the breakout of internal chaos had been for naught. Estonians started returning from "the front" and adjusting to life in peace-time. Mati took a job as the editor-in-chief of a magazine. It was a literary/current-affairs publication that focused on materials in the field of history, with a special emphasis on national problems. The editorial office was located in a historicist villa near the Old Town that looked straight out of a fairy tale. Altogether there were seventeen rooms on its two floors, all with parquet or mosaic-tile flooring, white porcelain heating ovens, fireplaces, and other luxuries. True, the villa was no longer in the best shape — signs of dilapidation could be seen here and there. Its former owners were to blame. It had been occupied by editorial offices even way back when (meaning up until the early seventies). I myself had been to the villa a few times, and remembered everything still being nice and intact then. However, the KGB had begun to turn its eyes towards that pretty place at about the same time, and naturally got its wish. The offices had to relocate elsewhere. It appeared that the new owners had not renovated the building over the course of the intervening quarter century.

Two more editorial offices and one umbrella organization were sheltered there in addition to Mati's magazine. Mati liked his new position, because issues of history and nationality had always been dear to him. Being the editor-in-chief of a monthly magazine also did not break his back, leaving him enough time to handle his own creative work as well as for social life. Mati did not draw up any immediate plans for a longer written work, however, deciding to take a rest after that tiring period of his life, and only later think about tackling a grandiose, epic work. In this work, he intended to immortalize the transitional period with a single pre- and post-shift narrative in order to show the shift in people's psyches in the eddy of the ages. He was intrigued by the way different social groups had lived through what had taken place; by the people who had been inspired by the new age and those who had been traumatized by it; by the question of who were the winners and who the losers. In a broader sense—how much justice and how much injustice had there been, and can the concept of justice be applied in relation to such processes at all? Mati had gained a little weight by that time, but it "spread" evenly over him, and so he still appeared to be in good shape. He acted very benevolently towards everyone once again and smiled just like Buddha. When he occasionally ended up at the pub late at night, he sang like he had done long before, with the one difference being that the beautiful Agnes was sitting beside him (as often as her ethnographic work allowed it), staring lovingly at her husband. Why *shouldn't* Mati look blissful? A great job had been done, and goals had been achieved both in wider society and in his creative work. It felt as if things would move forward almost on their own and ever upwards. *Heigh-ho, heigh-ho, it's off to work we go!*—that is what Mati could have sung.

Nevertheless, he was not destined to enjoy this cloudless cheer for long. The first thing that furrowed his brow under the new regime was when someone surfaced to demand that the villa be returned to their possession—the representative of a foreign Estonian living in Botswana. Luckily, it soon turned out that the claim was fraudulent—made by a two-bit lawyer, who hoped to hook a big fish in the murky waters. For a short while, Mati could breath with relief. However, financing worries arose before long. The rent per square meter for the villa was certainly not astronomical, but those meters were quite numerous; the bills for electricity, water, and other utilities were also rising quickly. The magazine's print run, which at first had been exceptionally large, soon began to decrease. While before, almost half of the money needed for getting by was accrued from sales revenue, it now came to barely a quarter of it. They managed to make ends meet by using this together with the sum given to them by the Ministry of Culture for "operational support"; however, the employees' wages were paltry and weren't keeping up with the rise in living costs, and authors' honoraria were symbolic. Mati went to Toompea to speak with the Minister, who was an old acquaintance.

"We've actually been thinking of you for a long time," the Minister said when he had heard out Mati's worries, nodding his head sympathetically. "We have a plan. We'll simply give you that building. Take it—it's *your* house now. You won't need to pay anyone rent anymore. You'll have absolute freedom."

"Oh, *really?*" Mati exclaimed, beaming.

"Yes, really," the Minister said, enjoying Mati's surprise. "You wouldn't have believed it if I myself hadn't said it just now, huh? What can I say, Mati,"—(the Minister always called people in the arts by their first names)—"culture is very important to our governing coalition as a whole, and especially to our party. Our little republic *perseveres* on culture. We must become great through spirit!"

Mati was happy for a little while, but not for long. Prices rose, and people were spending almost their entire income on food and other basic needs. Since life was hard, people mostly wanted to read easier stuff that might relax them and offer oblivion. The print runs of magazines that published serious content fell even further. Mati no longer earned more than about 12 percent of what was needed by way of subscriptions and sales. Advertising revenue also dried up. Six months after it turned out that paying rent was no longer necessary, the other expenses had grown to be so much that Mati could no longer afford to pay his ten employees' salaries. It was not even worth dreaming about renovating the lovely villa, the costs of which would have become more expensive by several-fold after a few years.

Mati set off on the road to Toompea once again. The Minister was not present or was unable to receive Mati. (Mati arrived without giving advance notice, as he was used to doing from old times.) However, this did not stop him. Having already climbed up the hill to the Castle, he had to get his wish, too. He had a plethora of acquaintances higher up, because many of those with whom he had restored Estonia's independence now held important jobs. He went further and further down the halls of the Castle and was finally received kindly by almost the very highest superior there himself, who was just finishing up with a meeting. The Minister, whom Mati had actually come to confer with, was sitting in the room, too. Mati spoke about his worry with emotion and heartache in front of the entire Cabinet. He was listened to attentively, and some even took notes.

"Mm, yes," someone acknowledged when Mati had finished. "It's a complicated situation. But where are we to get the funds?"

"From the state treasury, naturally," Mati reasoned. "We *made* this state. Well, properly speaking, we restored an old state, but in essence, we still created a new one. Therefore, it goes without saying that we will get money. We don't want it for *ourselves* — it's in the public's interests."

They nodded at him understandingly. Culture is naturally of the utmost importance for a nation-state. Still, although no one denied him outright, money was not placed straight into the palm of Mati's hand. They said — we'll take a look at it, see how tax accrual is in the spring, what the budget turns out to be like, and how things are on the whole — and told him to come back after a couple of months, when the budget was being drafted.

A couple of months later, it turned out that there was very little money in the state treasury; on the other hand, there was an immense amount of people who needed it. Pensioners were living in poverty, children's interest groups were floundering, infants were not getting milk, doctors were threatening to leave the country, teachers were only giving lessons out of a sense of duty, and business had to be stimulated so that the economy could get back onto its feet and companies could start producing goods in order to increase exports and boost salaries.

"What should we do, then?" Mati asked helplessly.

"Rent out a part of your building," he was advised. "You have seventeen rooms there, but only three editorial offices and an umbrella organization's headquarters—what if you were to squeeze in a little? And do you really need to keep so many people on the payroll?"

Mati was so offended that he stayed tight-lipped. Especially given that, as it coincidentally turned out, there were already rental candidates! Norwegians (or, to be precise, Laplanders) wanted to rent out a part of the building (or, to be precise, the entire second floor) in order to set up the Lapland Cultural Institute. The contract would be long-term and the rent extremely favorable. Still, the thought of it made Mati see red. Why should they have to give away a part of the building? It was nice and comfortable for them currently—there were two toilets located on every floor, and some rooms even came with a private restroom. The editors all had their own offices (for the most part) which, among other things, even included a couch that could be used for speaking with guests, but which could also serve as a bed for a quick nap, or to spend the night if needed. Why should they have to move two or three to one room now? One could not practice their creative work properly that way, nor could they stay the night.

Mati went around in a very irritated mood those days. "They want to make their own institute in our rooms! They're being taken away from us and given to some *foreigners. We're* supposed to squeeze in. But I won't let it happen like that!"

This time, he went and called upon the very highest superior there was, but again returned empty-handed. He was advised to accept the Laplanders' offer. In truth it had already been accepted, since the building was occupied by other chief editors in addition to Mati, and they had agreed to the deal.

"This is *moral bankruptcy.* This is demeaning. This is the shame of the Estonian state," Mati fumed loudly in The Cave.

Pekka tried to argue with him: "Have you really properly considered whether or not you need so much space for your own use?"

"What do you mean, 'do we need it'? There have always been editorial offices in that building, they were there already during the first Estonian Republic. It's *our* building, period."

"Yeah, but it's not as if the building will be taken away from you. I mean — you *could* use the rest of it to bring in some money. There's nothing demeaning about that," Pekka said to placate him.

"What does *that* have to do with it?!" Mati exclaimed, not seeming to comprehend. "That's the kind of moral you guys have over there — always earning and earning. But not everything has to earn something with culture. You get me? It's a question of principle. Damn it — the commies were able to stretch out during the Soviet times, just kept on taking one thing after another from us. The KGB made itself a nest in that building, the *Okhranka* stripped culture of it. Was that not them mocking us? And now foreigners are taking it. Is that normal? Is that the country we made, or is it not?"

"What are you accusing foreigners of?" Pekka asked, surprised. "This fear of foreigners that you seem to be feeling — isn't that an aftereffect of the Soviet regime? Is Estonia a free country, or isn't it? If there's a building for selling or renting out, then that's what it is. Why don't Laplanders have the same kind of a right as others do? They're a solid group, through and through. Would it be better if they put a brothel or some other unsavory thing in there?" Mati smirked for a moment at the mention of a brothel, but immediately grew dour again. "On top of that, the Institute will start paying you good rent money, and will be directly supporting your culture by doing so. You'll be able to pay wages, hand out honoraria, and even renovate the building with it."

"I agree," Mati acknowledged. "And I thank them for their help, without any sarcasm. I just don't understand why our own country can't support us? What did we make it for?"

"Maybe the country has no money."

"How does it not? Where *is* that money? It's all *ours* now; there has to be money."

"Money's needed for everything. Look at how your people are living. Most of them are deep in poverty. You need to come back down to earth already."

"Don't come here lecturing us, boy! All you foreigners can

get lost!" Mati shouted, starting to get riled up.

"But they're *our* foreigners, aren't they?" someone murmured. "The good foreigners."

"They are, yeah," Mati agreed after thinking for a moment. "But I still don't like it." This was not said angrily, and those sitting at the table chuckled good-naturedly.

"Moreover, you really *might* not need so many employees," Pekka reckoned cautiously, but only poured more fuel on the fire by doing so.

"Oh, yeah—we're supposed to let a number of employees go, too. But why?" Mati said, seizing on Pekka's statement.

"You can surely get by with fewer. Look at how I published a magazine *alone* back in the day," Pekka reminded him.

"Don't go comparing those things! *Khui s pal'tsem sravnil.*" This was a filthy Russian expression that referred to things that were completely incomparable to each other. Mati was partly right, because Pekka's magazine had been more like a tiny booklet.

"I'm not denying that," said Pekka. "But still—you don't need that many employees, either. I made my booklets alongside other work. I'd say that three employees would be enough for you guys if they worked full-time. Then they could be paid a decent salary, too. Right now, your editorial jobs are practically sinecures."

"And why *not*? Why shouldn't intellectuals have sinecures in a national republic, so that they can get smarter and study the meaning of existence?"

"Of course they may, if there's money for it. But you don't *have* money."

"Ah, but there'll be more soon . . . Who says there's no money? Of course there is. It's just being given to the wrong place," Mati snapped.

"You're starting back from the beginning, like a little child."

"Goddamn capitalists," Mati sighed. "They don't understand a thing." Everyone laughed.

"What? Can you repeat that? Did I really hear you right?" Pekka even cupped his hand around his ear theatrically.

"Goddamn capitalists!" Mati roared. It wasn't actually clear whether it was said playfully or seriously.

Pekka dismissed him with a wave: "I can't talk any sense into you." And he added: "You all really *have* been spoiled this last half-a-century."

"Prick!" Mati retorted. "Finnish prick."

The others at the table started to protest then:

"Why is he a prick?" the poetess Alja whispered.

"A prick is so *mo-no-chro-maaatic*," the forever-loyal Maša supported her.

And that is how the evening went. Speaking of which, Mati began to exhibit a habit of lambasting others. It was not uncommon for him to speak first and think later.

The Laplanders did set their institute up in the villa. I had not been in the building for two years and did not even recognize the interior at first. Everything had been renovated and upgraded, from the new front door, which featured a buzzer intercom system, to the electric shoe-cleaner in the entrance hall. Three editorial offices were now situated along one hallway on the first floor, requiring four people to work in the main room. The Institute was located on the second floor. There, the workers bustled about briskly, but not overexerting themselves—Nordic-style. Not a single one of the employees was a Laplander, of course, but there was a stone mosaic on the wall of the main room (a few of the partition walls had been removed): reindeer pulling a sledge carrying small figures clothed in furs.

In reality, Mati had nothing against making a little space in the house. Pekka had been right—his employees did not actually work eight hours a day, but rather showed their faces every other day, for the most part. And so, two people could comfortably share a single room—under the condition that they came in according to a sliding schedule. They could even spend the night there. However, in his mind's eye, Mati had envisioned a Center for the Fine Arts, an Institute for Memory, and several other associations or organizations associated with "Estonian causes" also coming to occupy the villa, and would have liked to keep space available for them. As for who would have financed these new institutions—that, he did not consider. His principle was that necessary things must first be established, and no doubt the source of the money will later become clear. This was the daring and idealist approach of the revolutionary-era, and

Mati could not comprehend why it appeared to be lessening among his former brothers-in-arms, and why it was almost absent in new figures. Everyone seemed to have turned into cautious calculators; into people rolling coins in palms. Mati felt betrayed and cursed them, especially the new ones, and did so in somewhat strange company every now and then.

## ILLIMAR'S LETTER FROM MAY 1993

*Honorable Chronicler!*
*The men are confused. Jõgever Klaasimets, the former Party secretary, founded a joint enterprise with the Germans. It is operating in the former sawmill, which was shut down. Why did* he *get to it first? How did he know? Why weren't the others invited? Utu asked Jass if he would have had money to put in. Utu says—where would he get that money? But Jõgever had money and put it in. Where did Jõgever get the money? From the bank, he said. Some said it was probably the salary money that was unpaid by the sawmill, but others said that the wages were ultimately paid out. But it made people even angrier to think that* Jõgever *was given a loan in the first* place. *The men are indignant—how can a bank of the Republic of Estonia lend to a former partorg? The men said they'll tear Jõgever to pieces and won't put any more money in the bank.*

*The joint enterprise manufactures all kinds of knobs—for furniture, doors, even for little boxes and other containers, including for the hatches on outhouses. The knobs are attached using an especially strong glue. The whole output is going for export—not a single Estonian man or woman may buy those knobs.*

*The schoolteacher, ol' Red-Kustas, is getting people wound up, saying it's an historic injustice and that the Germans are oppressing us again. I don't think that concerns the men especially. They can't take the fact that Jõgever is involved. Not as if they themselves would've cared to mess around with that knob shop. But Jõgever shouldn't, regardless. Who should, then? Someone should come from somewhere—someone completely pure and sinless—on a white horse and in a white suit, and should start directing the Vana-Põgioja Knob Shop. That would be very romantic, of course.*

*There were a total of two kinds of beer in the store, but there were even fewer men than last time.*

## A MEETING WITH KLAUS. MONEY

For some time already, I had been noticing that Klaus had changed. No, he wasn't glaringly in any funk. He continued to participate in everything, went to The Cave and even traveled, and appeared on the surface to be completely content. He would still make witty quips, and whoever started up a conversation with him would soon be blown over and out of breath from the returning barrage of fine, cutting remarks. Klaus also dressed distinctively, just as he had before—a mix of dandy, bohemian, and South Estonian peasant. He was not about to start wearing sweaters or a revolutionary's khaki-colored shirts, which had become a popular trend at the time. (In doing this, his attitude was always that he understood the exceptional nature of his dress and was enjoying it!)

Still, it appeared that the joyful glint sparkled in Klaus's eyes more rarely, and he would sometimes clench his jaws tightly—he did not have that habit before. At first, I thought it was just physical fatigue. He and his band had been touring across the country for several years and had performed at uncountable seditious meetings when the liberation movement was picking up steam during the transition period. These events were held by both the Estonian National Front and the Citizens' Committees—Klaus wished to help both (often without charging for the performance) while maintaining his independence and not allowing himself to be recruited to either camp.

Klaus and I were good acquaintances, but not close enough for me to be unsurprised when he came to visit me out of the blue one day. It happened at the editorial office at the end of a work day. (Afterward, I figured that he wanted to unburden his heart and spill his soul to someone like me, who was not too good of a friend but still familiar with his situation.) Despite my surprise, I was genuinely happy to see him. I saw immediately that he seemed very distracted, as if bothered by some kind of distressing mental strain. He took the first book he came across off of a shelf and eyed it, not appearing to see what he was looking at. At the same time, he became unnecessarily and too pushily anxious, probably without really even knowing why. Then he looked down, ashamed, and flashed an odd, pointless smile. I intuited that he wanted to make known something irrefutable and extraordinary—something that seemed impossible to him. He seemed to be blocking it internally. He looked as if he intended to get up and leave, because what he intended to say was not dignified enough in his mind.

Yet suddenly, he lifted his eyes and stared at me so confidently, so full of intent, and at the same time so unexpectedly and with such a cryptic look on his face that it startled me. Judging by his expression, it appeared that he was certain that I already knew the reason for his coming, even though he had told no one of it. However, you could also read that he was waiting in the hopes that I would take mercy upon him, saving him the humiliation of being the first to say it. But then, abruptly, he slipped back into a hazy thoughtful state. A new nervous twitch that I had not noticed during the Soviet era distorted his face (he had large eyes, a broad forehead, a relatively long nose, and a wide mouth).

"I really don't know why I came here," he then uttered apologetically and disdainfully, as if waking from a trance, and stood up. But after a couple of steps, he turned around, came back, and broke down. The corners of his mouth were trembling violently as he whispered with passion, his head dropping even lower:

"I have no . . ." He became choked up and broke off. It was obvious how hard it was for him to continue. Even so, he finished, almost in a whisper: ". . . money. I have no more money!" He got the words over his lips and seemed to collapse upon himself.

I was completely flummoxed: money? Was he delirious, or what? I had expected some kind of a grand bloodguilty confession, or an admission of his disappointment in the Estonian Republic, or I don't know what—a murder of passion or at least being a KGB informer.

In order to say something and break the silence, which was becoming embarrassing, I asked: "Don't you get side-gigs like you used to?"

He waved the question away. "Who'll invite us to play? It

doesn't interest anyone anymore," he said. I couldn't believe it. The man was probably in a state of depression. But when I started to think back, I realized that I really had not heard of them performing for quite a while. But that was just it: I had to specially remind myself of it. The thought had not stuck out to me on its own (nor had it to others, no doubt). This was partly because my personal time had started to disappear, as if borne away on the wings of a bird, and the arc of my life was curving upward. I had no time for thinking about what Klaus and his companions were doing or how they were making a living. Everyone was living *somehow*; everyone had designed some sort of "structure" for themselves.

I asked him to take a seat again and set about trying to give him some advice. He calmed down, started to talk, and I eventually got a clearer picture of the situation. It astounded me. I repeat: there are things that are hard to imagine. First of all: Klaus's fame in the corridors of power continued to be great. Back in the day, every last person had wanted to be his friend or acquaintance (or at least say that they had been in the same group of people as him), and so it was now as well, basically. Under no circumstances should he have complained that his audience had abandoned him (Klaus was vain and thirsty for love, as are most artists). To that day, Klaus performing at the Song Festival Grounds five years earlier was still fresh in my mind. Had he not then become a true champion of the people, and was he not pampered? And now, he had freedom on top of that. I emphasize the latter because in my circle of acquaintances, Klaus was one of the most earnest and vocal proponents of freedom. His soul simply *needed* it—in some old-fashioned or timeless sense, almost in the spirit of early nineteenth-century German romantics—and he had rejoiced over its arrival from the bottom of his heart; not out of fashion, like some did.

When independence was restored and the Republic had been declared, things went as they always had for Klaus for a little while. Parties were thrown and people congratulated one another. But the honeymoon breezed by and life was quickly rearranged. Everyone got busy working on something; each and every person began avidly occupying themselves with something that might interest them. The spiritual elation subsided over time and gave way to grounded, practical activity. The Hearts were extended less and less invitations to perform — just as it was with other groups, incidentally. Not that Klaus would have had the will or even the strength to continue at the old pace. It was also necessary to rest in order to relax and enjoy life. However, the months had passed, he was very well rested, and was able to make more of an effort again. But there still weren't many invitations to perform coming in. There were many reasons for this. A free media, where everything could be spoken about directly, had formed with the disappearance of censorship. There was no longer a need for the euphemizing satirical ditties with which The Hearts had traveled around and made people laugh. (There were also no longer *partorgs*, who would have called them into their office for a friendly scold prior to the performance!) The audiences would certainly still chuckle at criticism of the old regime and laugh at reminders of old nuisances, since they were still fresh in people's minds, but they wouldn't do so as whole-heartedly as they had before. So what about the old order?—Now, one needed to figure out how to get a leg in through the door to the new life and not be left high and dry. And since the state and the regime belonged to Estonia alone, and everything seemed dear to people, critique was no longer popular — not in newspapers, nor in lyrics. People still had use for entertainment, of course, but new groups were appearing by the dozens, and The Hearts had to start competing with them. And, by the way, what was most important was no longer sharpness of wit, but rather how well you could dance to the tunes.

The nation was going through a problematic economic chapter. When The Hearts were actually invited to play somewhere now, they were paid less; sometimes the organizers even apologized for it. The recently circulated Estonian kroon was expensive — one didn't give it away as readily as the occupation-ruble. You could do anything with money now — it was just as good as the dollar or the pound. Only that, yes, there was so little of it. The older and middle-aged people were especially parsimonious, and they were the ones who had remained loyal to The Hearts to some extent. Klaus said that it seemed to him as if in some places, it was looked down upon for performers to ask for money. This was probably because they had given completely free performances earlier, and the people knew it.

"Do I truly . . . have to get a job?" Klaus asked as if conferring with himself.

What could I answer? Was I to propose that he start writing for our publication? He would surely have laughed me out of the room—*he*, a gossip journalist?! He had never tried that profession, and even if he were to get the hang of it, he would still have been one of many; not a star like before. On top of that, I didn't have the authority to hire him. How could I help him, then? For a moment, the thought of offering to lend him a hundred kroons flashed through my mind. Perhaps he had gone several days without eating? But I buried the thought instantly, because it could have offended him to the bottom of his soul. Instead, I started to say (by the way, I was not fibbing in the very least, because I remembered well what I had once said to the darling Marje, who had pressed me into a corner) that there is nothing demeaning about work, and that artistic intellectuals have a false sense of shame about earning money. The notion of labor is very broad—one just needs to find work that suits him, and so forth.

"You're just saying that . . . out of compassion for my situation and to say something," Klaus sighed. I acknowledged that it is harder for the likes of him to find work than it is for others, because he is so famous and wouldn't be fit for just any old job.

"Like a weather girl fired from TV," Klaus said, and burst out laughing. "Overqualified!" I laughed with him. We talked more, his depression appeared to gradually give way, and he became how he always had been, making ironic cracks about himself and others. Klaus left the office in an almost peaceful state of mind, having first implored me not to breathe a word about our conversation to anyone.

That visit made me think. Something would not leave me at peace. I repeat: it was very difficult to believe that someone would have wanted to ostracize Klaus or to "defeat" him. More likely, it was just that no one gave a thought to what was going on in his life. For if they had, there definitely would have been some kind of a national collection for yesterday's heroes, which—even in that monetarily scant time—would have made Klaus and a few others like him wealthy persons. However, Klaus would have rather died before allowing something like that to transpire. The collection would have replaced pauperdom in his own eyes. He was unable to demean himself. "I can't bear laughter," he once said (*he*, the greatest ironist there was!). It had been exceptionally uncomfortable, outright embarrassing for him to talk about money, even with me. He would have to be given money somehow incidentally or in secret, so that he would only find out about it later. For example, someone could have placed an unmarked envelope containing five-hundred-kroon bills somewhere he would find it (certainly in a place devoid of people—best if in a desert or on the tundra, in an abandoned zoo or a disused cosmodrome).

Perhaps we are to blame for not being able to arrange that. But as I said—the possibility of the likes of him not having money seemed not to cross anyone's mind. Maybe they imagined that he was like some head of state who does not have an official income, but who does not *need* it, because for him, everything is free: restaurant owners regard it as an honor when he dines at their establishment, taxi drivers give him a ride for nothing, grocers gesture for him to pick out whatever he wants for himself, and so on. However, it turned out that nothing was free for Klaus—everything was the same as it was for his fellow mortals. The prices of things that had been available before the restoration of independence rose, and there were more and more things to spend money on. This came in the form of new taxes and bills just as well as temptations. Just one detail: Klaus was an ardent smoker, and especially liked little brown menthol cigarettes. ("More" brand cigarettes, the same that Hasso Miller smoked—although they were actually meant for ladies.) Whenever he acquired foreign currency from somewhere during the Soviet era, he always spent it on them. Now, "More" and dozens of other brands were freely available, but they weren't cheap.

Klaus had earned a great deal of money in the intervening

years, but had apparently not put anything aside; saving was not
in his nature. Money didn't interest him in and of itself. It had
come to him relatively easily, and had gone even more easily.
Klaus liked to throw money around—many could remember
how he occasionally bought drinks for the whole Cave, sending a bottle of cognac and sparkling wine to every table, lovably
giving the order: "I simply ask that everyone bring themselves
to a happy state in an hour!"

I could likewise recall how Klaus disparaged foreigners for
their attitude towards money. "It's undignified groveling," he
claimed. I'm also reminded of a cozy get-together one August,
when a small group of us were sprawled out on Stroomi Beach,
which was one of our favorite spots back then (there was no
swimming area, it was reedy and untidy, drunkards made a
racket, and random passersby had sex in the clumps of grass).
We made a fire. (No, that seems unbelievable—we were probably actually attending a yard party at Svjatoslav's place in Mähe,
because why would we have had a bonfire on the beach? Lighting bonfires was not one of our habits. But Svjatoslav's wife Veronika was a fire-worshiper and lit fires everywhere. Or maybe
Veronika was with us at Stroomi that time? No, why would she
have been . . .) In any case, I can still see Klaus bending over to
light his slim little "More" cigarette from a half-burned stick.
While doing so, a fifty-ruble note fell out of his breast pocket
and landed at the edge of the fire. Klaus had already sprawled
back, and could not be bothered to push himself up again. The
green bill was already lightly smoldering, but it could have been
exchanged at a bank. Someone directed Klaus's attention to
what was happening, but he only nudged the bank note away
disdainfully with his shoe. To this very day, I can still envision
the toe of his Pomarfin shoe and the singed money. Fifty rubles was a very large amount to me back then—almost half a
month's salary. I had only held such a big bill in my own hands
on a couple of occasions.

As an aside: what all haven't I heard said about artists and money in the newer age! For example, a work trip took me to N.
village, where well-known variety artists were supposed to per-

form that same evening. I dined at a local pub and happened to overhear what was being talked about around me.

"Poets shouldn't be *given* money—it offends them," someone reckoned.

"They don't even *eat*," another added. "They just sit in a library for a while, and miraculously recharge themselves again there." His wife (probably a medical worker) informed him that one poet had gone without eating for twenty days, but showed no signs of weakness or worsening health. On the contrary—he apparently became even better-looking! And while it is generally true that the bad breath of a person on a long diet worsens because the body is ridding itself of toxins, the aroma of Chanel No. 19 came from the mouth of this poet. And when he died one day, his corpse apparently smelled exceptionally well, because it was saturated with Poesy.

What is "definite" public knowledge next to such pieces of wisdom? Knowledge that I have heard in innumerable variations—for example, that artists are on the state's payroll, that they receive a regular income from the Ministry of Culture, that they are exempt from paying income tax, and so on—and that therefore, it isn't even worth *offering* them money. This is especially true because for a poet, going to meet the public is not work or an obligation at all, but rather an immensely satisfying undertaking; something like a bride meeting her groom.

Klaus tried his hand at this and that. Friends contrived various opportunities for him. His voice could be recognized on a few dog food commercials (which made us laugh, because Klaus's love for cats and phobia of dogs were legendary), and he recited Lydia Koidula's poem "Do You Know a Mother's Heart?" in an oratorio performed by the Academic Men's Choir at the national Mother's Day function. He also tried being the master of ceremony for a wedding, but fainted because of the banality of the situation. Luckily, the best man poured a spoonful of brandy into his mouth under the table, so Klaus revived, made some especially brilliant quip, and everyone thought the scene had been staged. From then on, Klaus only emceed under the influence.

As if Klaus didn't have enough worries already, his life was complicated by the following circumstance. In the days of the National Front (or was it at the time of the Citizens' Committees?), he had developed a relationship with a nationalist-minded young woman from the "revolutionary brigades." Over the course of revolutions, it is common for relationships to be formed with ladies (often idealistic aristocrats) who, thanks to the magnanimity of their soul, have felt the urge to "help out" in the whirlwind of change. Klaus's young woman was something between Celia Sanchez, Tania Bunke, and the main character of Aleksey Tolstoy's story "The Viper." She wasn't exactly endlessly beautiful, but pleasant and with a deep psyche—the type who is clearly prepared to sacrifice the blood of her heart. In short, it was a very moving phenomenon. She and Klaus were involved for a full four years, and she accompanied him around the country. She did not get married, did not create a family, but sacrificed everything in the name of The Idea.

Klaus had long since been married, of course. His wife, Tiia, and he had been childhood friends. Their son Gustav was already old enough to be "forming a band." Klaus had reached the age at which most people divorce (if they do so at all), so it was as if the last chance to start a new life was ticking for him. This even more so because Tiia was a few years older than him, and wasn't extremely enthusiastic about nationalism (she worked at an Estonian-Swedish joint enterprise, often spending time abroad).

Klaus's double life had not especially bothered him as long as he was "speeding around on a *tachanka*."[25] Yet when peacetime arrived, it was inevitably going to present him with a problem. The young woman did not force marriage upon him, nor does one *have* to marry groupies. The groupie-culture in Estonia was generally not developed enough yet. Groupies "surround" an artist, of course, and a few of the more outstanding ones assist him in a fundamental manner in practical life, serving as full-on managers. But, yes—it's not as if the groupie will do all of that for nothing; a groupie wants money and pretty things. Klaus had no money. The young woman was not a groupie, to tell the truth, but something more than that. Still, though.

Klaus's wife Tiia descended from the upper strata of Soviet-era researchers, and they lived in the so-called Academics' House in the city center. It was a pseudo-classicist building with pillars and other "excesses." (In Soviet times, there had even been a *militsioner* stationed in a vestibule in front of the door.) The groupie, on the other hand, was not of refined lineage, but rather the child of simple parents from the South Estonian town of Abja-Paluoja who now lived in an apartment block in the Mustamäe district. Klaus was unable to desert her because it might have given the impression of standing on the side of the rich (Klaus was very egalitarian despite his outward aristocratic disposition). The groupie had graduated from the Department of Medicine and started a career as a radiologist just a short time before the Singing Revolution. She had now taken a job in this field, and was making a relatively good living. She worked with peaceful self-evidence and lived optimistically; she had no inner struggles. Klaus could have even asked her for money—they would have been able to live off of the young woman's salary temporarily. I know that she even delicately alluded to that possibility. However, Klaus was of the opinion that he would have had to marry the groupie in order to do so. Still, it is doubtful whether that would have changed anything, because Klaus was very old-fashioned in some respects, and the idea that a man is the head of a family, whose duty it is to provide for his wife, was lodged deep down in his soul. He had already been forced to swallow his pride in a similar type of situation earlier in life. It was when he was courting Tiia. Klaus had been a broke bohemian (he was in a row with his mother and father), and his future wife secretly fed him in their kitchen when her parents were not at home. At that time, they had been young and in love up to their ears, and on top of that, it was in a different kind of society, so maybe Klaus really didn't have to feel so demeaned. The guilt sprung up in retrospect when, twenty years later, he was speeding across the country from one speech-ridden meeting to another with a groupie, not daring to admit to himself that he had betrayed his wife, who had literally fed him the finest morsels from the palm of her hand. Klaus could give up neither Tiia nor the groupie.

Klaus and I happened to speak on that topic once. "You have to break up when it's the right time," he said, adding that the right time is when the woman is still fresh enough to catch someone else's eye. He was apparently afraid that this time had passed for Tiia. He was convinced that if he were to leave his wife, then she would no longer find a new partner, would have to spend the rest of her life alone, and that naturally weighed upon Klaus's conscience. At the same time, he knew that if he did not tear himself away right now, then there was a high likelihood he would never do it and would live in Tiia's company to the end of his days. He was likewise dismayed by the idea of an old age shared by people who are mutually growing apart from each other. It would have been a small relief for him had he been able to buy his way free of his wife (although monetarily, Tiia—who was employed at the joint enterprise—did not need that in the slightest).

What is worse is that Klaus probably didn't even care for the groupie anymore, in all honesty. For if he had, then no doubt he would have allowed himself to be fed a little with the radiologist's salary—if it's love, then there's really no reason to be ashamed, is there? Yet it seemed the love *was* running out. An artist's soul is restless; it flits from flower to flower. The groupie's calmness and resoluteness, which had seemed so admirable to Klaus during the transitional period, had an insipid and monotone effect on him in ordinary life, and started to become annoying. How could he possibly live the rest of his life in such a key?

It's possible that Klaus had already taken a liking to someone else. In any case, there were whisperings about a socialite chick who allegedly wanted to take advantage of the "old" man. I had seen that girl: she was pretty, but extremely high-maintenance—the type that knows the price of everything. Then it turned out that the radiologist was pregnant by Klaus. Klaus wanted to ensure the future of the mother of his child, wanted to buy his way free from his wife, wanted to be a man of honor in every respect. He also wanted to dash off onto a new adventure with the socialite chick. He would have needed three times as much money as he used to, but in reality he had several times less than before.

Mahvalda, our editor-in-chief, wanted to invite Klaus to be a guest of honor at our "The Handsome and the Sexy" party (we throw such an party once a year). She asked me whether Klaus would come: "He would only have to say a couple of words into the mic in front of the crowd . . ."

I replied that it would not, in any case, be best to engage Klaus straightforwardly, but instead in a somehow roundabout way.

"But he'll get *paid*. You yourself said he's got difficulties right now, didn't you?" A note of perplexity rang in Mahvalda's voice. She had begun her journalistic career during the Soviet era, and something of that erstwhile respect for the artist apparently still lived within her. But seeming to be ashamed of it, she went on more stubbornly: "What's so special about him, anyway?" Yes, what was there . . . I promised to extend the invitation personally and add in the necessary words.

Klaus read through the invitation and stared directly at me with a look of stupefaction: "So they want to make a fool out of me, I'm guessing?!" I tried to explain, but to no avail. He would not stoop to play the fool. However, it turned out that from then on, that was primarily what people *agreed* to pay him for.

Soon enough, the story went around that the socialite chick was leaving Klaus. And so, the case became ever more complicated, and Klaus's nerves, which had always been brittle, were probably starting to wear thin. It was rumored that he started using cocaine, or—as they said—"snorting lines." (What did he *buy* it with? Did he borrow?)

I spoke with Mati about Klaus. Mati proposed that we go to see Fatty (that former popular leader, who in all truth was not very fat anymore, because he had lost a great deal of weight during the stressful transition period). Fatty now held a very important position in government. We asked him whether or not it might be possible to support Klaus from the reserve fund, which we called the "revolution till" among ourselves, and which, according to my data, included a department of national culture. Couldn't he be allotted some kind of a minimal stipend, or be hired at a small salary for appearance's sake—as an artistic advisor, for example?

Fatty remembered Klaus from the Song Festival Grounds, of course, and was well aware of his musical activity during the transition period. He asked us to take a seat and started to talk about the overall situation: "Let's be honest: there's hunger in the countryside. We need to build narrow-gauge railroads to Järva-Jaani and Virtsu. Several groups hostile to the Estonian Republic have popped up." Fatty's words were decisive, and his tone even threatening.

When he had finished, I worked up the courage to remind him about what we had come for: "So, then . . . with Klaus . . . how'll it be?"

Fatty placed a hand on my shoulder: "I'll say it to you honestly, like one Estonian to another. Artistic people have specific problems. They do have crises on occasion. I know just as well as you do that he will not die of starvation. He'll go from one admirer to the next, he'll be given food to eat, and not *only* that." Fatty laughed ambiguously. "That's how he'll get by. We, however, have to figure out how to support the average Estonian family right now. Elections *are* coming up soon. Propaganda has to be organized for them. The majority is indeed on our side, but there are only so many seats up on Toompea."

Klaus did not receive any aid from higher-up. Mati appeared to have a very bad feeling about things after that visit. There was a nasty aftertaste in my own soul from it, and from that time forward, I have never asked for anything from "higher-up"; not for myself, nor others.

In Klaus's case, in addition to a scarcity of money and the inability to make decisions about his personal life there was also a fear of falling into the clutches of new and unfamiliar addictive substances. (Years earlier, he had been to "gentlemen's alcohol rehab" a couple of times, but had always recovered and been capable of doing work and creative activity once again.) Apparently, all of it put together was too much for him. In any case, the news that Klaus had departed this life soon spread like wildfire. Apparently he had overdosed on sleeping pills. All of his acquaintances knew, of course, that he took Tazepam, Imovane, and Stilnox; but this is only natural for a person made up solely of nerves.

Nevertheless, everyone was more or less certain that what had happened was not an accident. Someone was even aware of a letter that Klaus was said to have left for the media, but which had "been disposed of," as it apparently contained harsh words about certain politicians of the new age. Klaus's fans scrutinized a couple of his final song lyrics and could make out all kinds of hints and omens in them, but this is unscientific in my opinion.

As an aside: I, who have had to write about my fair share of suicides (this is inevitable for a gossip journalist), am amazed by how ineptly they are carried out. Of course, when the goal is actually to make someone feel sorry for you, when it is a reminder or a cry for attention, then it *has* to fail. But they are often unsuccessful even when the attempter's effort appears to be genuine, and he or she *wants* to relocate to another world. They are still performed very ineptly, because the individual has not taken the care to research what and how beforehand. One must do their homework with suicide! Good gracious—nowadays one can even master the art of bomb-making via the Internet; obtaining information on suicide is certainly easier. Instead, people simply act on an abrupt impulse, totally impromptu, grabbing a scythe from the wall and trying to slit their throats with it. That is simply not how it is done. If people were serious about suicide and made even the slightest effort beforehand, educated themselves and did a dry run, then the percentage of successful attempts would be at 98 percent, not 47, as it is now.

A suicide can be a magnificent thing if work and talent are combined, because even the most trifling of acts takes on a new dimension under a master's hand. You can find people who are talented by birth, of course. Still, such individuals are rarely encountered among the art crowd: they bungle suicide just as they do with every practical task.

Klaus's funeral service was carried out by a creative and captivating eulogizer/undertaker (who was an educated man, possessing a master's degree). Although he belonged to religious circles, he was very tuned in to contemporary culture and global problems, and spoke precisely in the way an educated audience yearns to hear these days—meaning he "did not overdo it" with God, although the eternal dimension was firmly in place. He did not jerk tears from the audience by force, but most people's eyes were still damp by the end. Everyone enjoyed the speech so much that the undertaker was invited back up repeatedly. The grave was already covered and the undertaker sitting in his Volkswagen, which had seen better days, but he had to clamber out again and again. At first he presented a couple of new ideas as an added treat, but then gave the entire speech once again from the beginning. When it ended, everyone was satisfied, clapped strongly one more time (but no longer in rhythm), and headed out. I can't remember any other funerals like that.

I met Jürka, Klaus's companion from The Hearts, at the funeral. I asked whether he was still at his old job, meaning in the entertainment industry or in "show biz." He chuckled and dismissed the question: "Not for years." He said that he was currently working at a small company that manufactures buttons—for shirts, jackets, pants; they even apparently made bra clasps for variation. "So, something totally unrelated to music," he said, grinning.

"But why buttons?" I asked.

"What's wrong with buttons, then?" he asked back.

"Do people buy them?"

"The bulk of production goes to France. But that's more the boss's business. I've been able to feed my family so far."

"Your family?" I asked, raising an eyebrow. "You've got a family? Again? What number is this?"

"The fifth," he said, scratching his jaw. A warmness flooded my heart. Look—a man who doesn't whine or bellyache. He has had children under every regime, and maybe Estonia needs those infants that he feeds with his buttons just as much as it needed those songs, which once helped undermine the Soviet regime.

We walked among the graves of Metsakalmistu Cemetery towards the parking lot. My feet occasionally sunk into the ground; I could feel the springy weight of the moist sand beneath my soles. A lone helicopter flew overhead, and we watched its arc until it disappeared, thwapping, behind the tops of the pines. We drove back to the city in Manglus's new Audi ("a middle-class car with a few characteristics of a luxury car," as he said). He did not hold the wheel between his knees, because we were within the city limits; traffic was much heavier than it used to be, and furthermore, Manglus had gained weight—even his thighs were chunkier, and it would have been impossible for him to repeat the old trick for that reason alone. Tõnis Mägi was singing on the car radio:

*Ilus oled, ilus oled, Isamaa . . .*[26]

"I feel bad for Klaus, that player," Pepe sighed.

Manglus was silent, so that everyone would comprehend how wise he was. "It's not great speed that's dangerous, but great acceleration," he then said allegorically.

"I'm guessing that's from a physics textbook?" Pepe reckoned.

"It's from life's textbook," said Kirill, who was sitting next to him.

I wondered how much money my companions had. Not in their pockets, but in total. Pepe didn't especially care for money, but he had no dependents and had enough for other things. Kirill had been returned two houses in the Kalamaja district. Manglus had a lot of money—he was even richer now than he had been during Soviet times. Word on the street was that he had recently purchased a boutique for his divorced wife as compensation and a photo studio for his daughter as a dowry.

Klaus was in the grave.

The reception was held at a restaurant. There was conflict in the air. Klaus had been extraordinarily famous, and although he had descended into oblivion a little in the meantime, a very large and colorful group came to send him off. The presence of creative intellectuals and freedom fighters was to be expected; however, Klaus had also been cherished by a portion of the former Nomenklatura, who by that time had broken off into all kinds of political parties and businesses. They showed up to the funeral because they also felt that Klaus had been "one of their own." The old and the new, the "formers" (communists) and the "genuines" (supporters of independence) did not get along for the most part; the past was still fresh. The groups already stood separately at the cemetery. The artists and the freedom fighters were on their own, with a number of politicians nearby. Former Komsomol figures and members of the construction *malev* were on their own, as were directors and corporate managers, with politicians (naturally from the other camp) kept to the fringes. It was almost too literal: some were on the one side and others were on the other, with Klaus's open grave like a trench between them. However, these tensions did not stand out very much at the cemetery, because there was plenty of room and the situation demanded that people keep themselves in check. But now, in the restaurant, where everyone was forced to sit down at the same table, the situation quickly became uncomfortable. It turned out that not everyone wanted to be next to everyone else. "Those goddamn commies," said even Mati, who had arrived late, and whom they had wanted to place at the end of the table, where Fatty's adjutants were sitting. "*I'm* certainly not going over by those guys." A few innocent funeral-goers who had already sat down were made to move almost by force, because they had ended up "on the wrong side." The middle section of the table was in danger of emptying out entirely. Some guests even stood behind "one of their own," thus demonstrating their group loyalty, and apparently expected to be served broth and rolls standing-up. In short, they behaved like little schoolboys. The waiters felt uncomfortable but remained silent, because there were many important people there.

When the guests had finally taken their seats after prolonged wrangling and it came time to make toasts in memory of the departed, people even began exchanging barbs across the table. Did one man or another have the right to say those kinds of words about Klaus or not? People do not ordinarily argue at funerals. Luckily, after the third eulogy, the tension lowered and the mood mellowed. Leave it to them to roll up their sleeves and go fight around a corner after a funeral, as if it was a village party!

We went to The Cave after the reception. Manglus was pensively silent. When we had been sitting there for a fair amount of time, he said: "It's not the right way." He said this without any apparent connection to anything, causelessly, but everyone naturally grasped that he was talking about Klaus. Some thought it was inappropriate to talk that way, and that a person's free will to leave this world should be honored.

"If you yourself are so strong, then you *could* have a little sympathy for those who aren't," Maša reasoned while shedding a tear, because she was a good person. Manglus nodded solemnly, but it was an insincere nod; it struck me that there probably wasn't any room for sympathy in his soul.

"Don't you feel sorry for him?" I asked him shortly after, in private.

"I always feel sympathy for the weaker with my heart, but hold towards the stronger with my mind," Manglus remarked without batting an eyelid. "Only the strong survive here in this world."

"Are you strong?" I asked.

"Of course." He gave a compelling, yet patronizing smile. "Who else?"

Yes, who else . . .

The lawyer Karl Maiden was also at our table on that occasion. It was indeed around the time that he started going to The Cave. On the subject of Klaus, he said: "He was the one who did it; he was the one who wanted it—so what are you whining about?" No one responded, because Karl wasn't really in our circle yet, and why argue with a stranger? On top of that, he carried an American Express Gold Card.

A few politicians and party members had trailed us there from the restaurant. Maybe it was out of a sentimental wish to be together with those who had known Klaus more closely; maybe out of an old urge to go take a look at the scandalous "Cave"; or maybe they just wanted to drink more vodka. (The line between artists and party members was no longer as clear as it had been previously—not at all. Some artists had joined political parties because they hoped to gain commissions for their works, to paint someone's portrait, or to erect someone's monument. Or else they wanted to be able to repair their theater's roof, to buy new cellos for their orchestra, or simply hoped for money. On the other hand, there were also a few party members who wrote articles on history or composed poetry.)

"Tell us, you guys—what was Klaus's problem, really?" one

of those party members now asked. There was no clear reply from the crowd; people mentioned a spiritual crisis, a love triangle, and general difficulties.

Lala-Lullu said that Klaus left this life because he was afraid of the competition that was forming, but people shouted her down, saying it would be hard to come up with anything more ignorant than that.

Someone proposed an interesting comparison. Klaus, with his personal dilemmas and heightened sense of honor, was like the man who had to carry a wolf, a rabbit, and a head of cabbage across a river. Klaus needed to ferry over his wife, his lover from the revolution days, and a modern socialite, so that all would be alive and well—all across the very same river (the Pedja, the Lethe) that the pop-singer Jaak Joala was singing about at the time: *Unustuse jõel on kallas kahel pool!*[27]

In response, one of those party members (a "former"; one who had gotten involved in business after the regime change and had become filthy rich) apologized if they found what he was about to say improper, but in his mind, it had to do "only and first and foremost" with money:

"That man you were talking about, that cabbage carrier, or whatever it was—what was he lacking in? Resources, of course. If he'd had more resources, then he would've rented two more boats, and there'd have been no dilemma. Or why rent little boats—he could've rented three nice yachts or speedboats, a captain and a Malaysian servant on each, a bar below deck, where the wolf could've drunk himself into a coma on Tullamore Dew and the goat could get sick on sweet liqueur. The carrot, sorry, the cabbage would've gotten across the river just fine. If a man has money, then he can maintain several families at once; whatever society's rules may be. I've got five families, for example . . ." And he listed off the spots in Estonia where he had them.

Someone asked how the party member knew about Klaus's monetary affairs. The latter replied that during the last few months of his life, Klaus had called him several times in the middle of the night while drunk or high, asking for a loan. No more and no less than two million kroons, with which he would buy the mother of his child a tiny house and the socialite-chick an apartment.

"Did you give it to him?" Tobi asked.

"I didn't."

"Why not?"

"Why should I have?" replied the party member, who was starting to get drunk. "All he ever did was taunt people like me. Always going on about the 'formers'-this, the 'formers'-that. I politely suggested to him—go and ask the ones you made a revolution with. See if your new masters will throw you a scrap of bread or not."

Karl Maiden burst out laughing Homerically. Manglus chuckled, Alja turned hysterical, Maša blurted her most disdainful "You're so *mo-no-chro-maaatic!*" into his face. A dreadful scandal erupted. The party member was driven from the table in shame.

(Just a moment—I'm not entirely sure of that anymore. It's completely possible that Manglus was the one who put forth the comparison with the cabbage, the wolf, and the goat and its connection to money. Yes, that would have been very much his sort of thought process—witty and cynical. And he definitely did so within a smaller group of people, when there were no ladies around. But the party member was driven away from the table that time because he started groping Maša.)

A few months after the funeral, the essayist Maulwurf published an article in a cultural weekly in which he compared Klaus to Hamlet. His starting point was the question: "To be, or not to be?" As we all know, Shakespeare follows these lines with a debate about which would be more noble—to take arms and battle a sea of troubles, or to step out of the game and end one's suffering. The latter may also be interpreted as the "game" in that kind of a form tainting you, in any case. Maulwurf also said that what most distressed and offended Klaus was the prospect of having to compete with third-rate songsters, but not in any artistic manner. He would have had to out-crow them and mimic their buffoonish self-advertising in order to attract the crude interest of an ignorant public. Maulwurf's thoughts did not incite broader interest.

## RUI IN THE ESTONIAN AGE

As far as money was concerned, I myself had nothing to boast about. One morning I went to pick up an honorarium for the first time in quite a while. The amount was several times smaller in comparison with former times, especially taking into account the cost of living. It was also issued in a different place, no longer on Pikk Street. Even so, I again came across Rui on my way back. He still wore his hair long and loose and was still sporting small wire-rimmed glasses, skin-tight frayed jeans, and a satchel. Fat Umbu was still by his side, his inseparable companion. Everything repeated itself as if the intervening time had never even happened.

Rui's greeting once again seemed to express that he had been looking for me for years and that a weight was lifted from his heart upon seeing me. "*There* you are!" he whispered tenderly.

I nodded, attempting to impart that I did not intend to strike up a conversation with him. Yet Rui came to a stop in front of me. Umbu did not catch on to the situation immediately, and stared at me with his mouth agape.

"I've got a foul headache," Rui said. "I'd like to do something to treat it. Give us a little loan! We could, of course, step in somewhere together to celebrate the publication of your immortal translation. That way, you could drink for your own money, too." I mentally weighed what to do. Should I buy my freedom? Rui appeared to read my mind.

"Give me fifty kroons," he repeated insistently. "You've got to give it to me — it's like a sacrifice to the altar."

I remarked that fifty kroons was quite a lot of money, and might twenty-five not be enough to have a few steins at a pub?

"Twenty-*five*?" Rui shouted loudly enough that passersby turned and watched us curiously. Umbu burst out laughing. I felt embarrassment, but that was exactly what Rui was aiming for.

"Twenty-*five*!" he screeched again. "But you can't even get a *half-pint* for that at The Palace!" (The Palace was one of the first elegant and expensive pubs in our city.) Then Rui exhaled and took up his initial posture, becoming chummy and patronizing once again.

"Don't fight it. It was fate that brought us together. A lot's demanded of him who's given a lot." He laughed, showing his long teeth. I had to chuckle. But even this time, he stated the amount of my honorarium almost to the kroon. *That's a guy,* I thought, *who's able to count others' money.* I gave him a fifty-kroon note all the same.

Rui apparently wanted to cheer me up as thanks, and spoke about the new political forces:

"Members of the Independence League have the might of a dozen men. They can appear in any random place as rain, as fog, as rats. But they have to be able to visit the basement of their party headquarters from time to time in order to sit at the oval conference table there. If they haven't done that in a while, then they lose their strength."

When I was left alone again, I unexpectedly felt that I was even a little glad. The Ruis were still out there.

### DIALOGUE BETWEEN A FORMER DISSIDENT AND TWO ARTISTS

Before I continue telling of people's fates, I will use the montage technique one more time. What can you do — the instincts of a former amateur actor and script-adjustor break through! And a drama must have a second act; otherwise, the audience cannot visit the buffet during the intermission. As a complement to the writers' speaking choir presented earlier, I will add a small de-bate — set in an atelier or a pub.

DISSIDENT: *You artistic people sold yourselves off to the commies during the Soviet era. And you got services in return for it, too. And so the things you were doing in the meantime just now — being the torchbearers of freedom or whatever you call yourselves — that was merely a little part of atonement for your grave error. It was cleansing yourselves of the baptizing water of treachery. Even those who did not directly approve of the regime over the preceding half a century must still repent their sins now, because they did not raise their voices high enough against the regime or end up in the Gulag because of it.*
FIRST ARTIST (a more elderly man): *The Gulag? Yes, I under-stand — two uncles of mine and many more relatives died there, too . . . But all the same, isn't that a lot to ask of everyone? Who would*

*have kept the nation alive, then, if we had all been sitting behind barbed wire? Do be sensible, now . . .*

DISSIDENT (pays him no heed): *That's obvious enough—you were all afraid to be sent behind barbed wire, sat here licking the regime's ass . . .*

FIRST ARTIST: *What do you mean?! We weren't singing praises to the regime, you know. We were playing on the borderline the whole time, probing it all the time. It was practically impossible to do anything more.*

SECOND ARTIST (a younger middle-aged man): *That accusation of ass licking only applies to Party members. They enjoyed the benefits and priorities back then and shouldn't escape the nation's just revenge now. They are the ones who should atone for their sins through honest work.*

DISSIDENT: *Here you are mistaken, young man, because you do not understand the truth of the matter. I, as a former student of theology, am familiar with the psyche. You see, members of the Party didn't believe in anything, didn't actually help carry out the slogans that they themselves proclaimed, and lived like maggots in carrion in their colonies—according to the rules enacted there. And they didn't enjoy anyone's respect—or if at all, then only each other's. People would bow before them and curry their favor, but they mocked them behind their backs. Benefits and power—yes, those they had, but nothing more. You, on the other hand, had relatively much in the material sense, and were also loved feverishly by the public. Do understand who you actually were in the Soviet Union for once—the happiest people there could possibly be! Men respected you and women loved you—loved without demanding anything in return. That was the most genuine romantic love there is—you were loved for who you were. Is that not much? Therefore, do not compare yourselves to members of the Party. In reality, the Soviet era was not a paradise for Party members, but for artists.*

FIRST (To the Dissident): *Don't go overboard, now. "People in the arts lived better than members of the Party"—that's unheard of.* (He stands there irritated then begins pacing about the room.) *Unheard of, unheard of . . .*

SECOND: *And right now, most of the former members of the Communist Party have gotten into leading positions again and are*

*enjoying the benefits once more, and this time it's coupled with re-*
*spect; with a different kind of respect, but still with respect—so,*
*how have things gone badly for them, all in all?*

DISSIDENT: *Those two things aren't interconnected. Right now,*
*they are living well thanks to their starting position and their per-*
*sonal qualities, not thanks to the Kremlin.*

FIRST ARTIST: *Screw those commies . . . They don't interest me*
*and I'm not jealous of them . . . But one thing is certain: it's impos-*
*sible to compare the current attitude towards artists with how it*
*used to be.*

SECOND ARTIST (mocking him playfully, but also with the
superciliousness of a younger man): *Are you talking about how*
*women used to crowd around you?*

FIRST ARTIST: *No, that's not what I meant! I mean the idealistic*
*side, the support of our own people. Precisely what you* (points to
the Dissident) *mentioned. How the artist reached the people back*
*then; how he was respected, and how others breathed in the same*
*rhythm as he did. For me, that feeling was more important than*
*the material benefits. No one can take away that feeling, or rather,*
*the memory of that selfless love.*

DISSIDENT (angrily): *So go ahead and live with that memo-*
*ry, what are you lot moaning about! You've had it once, and that's*
*enough—now, scrape by like ordinary folk do!*

SECOND ARTIST: *What a rude guy! Is it their* (gestures towards the older colleague) *fault that the Soviet state was the way*
*it was? Did they set it up? What could they do? Should they have*
*turned down honoraria? That wasn't possible.*

DISSIDENT: *Sing, cash, sing!*

FIRST ARTIST (mumbling in bright misery): *I know that I've*
*been spoiled for good. But all the same—I've been able to feel it! I*
*know that here, we had maybe one of the last places in the world*
*where a white man could experience that kind of a feeling.*

SECOND: *Why has it all turned out this way? How did things*
*start to change? I didn't notice it.*

FIRST: *Who knows for sure! Maybe we became too state-minded.*
*Exactly: the state became our state of mind. We were so caught up*
*in bringing the Estonian state back that our actual state of being*
*slipped from our minds. We became mere citizens, and forfeited our*

*status as artists and critically-thinking intellectuals. Yet an artist cannot be state-minded for long—it will be the death of him, even when it's his own country. He must be in the opposition, living on the periphery or on a knife's edge. For him, intoxication with national progress cannot last longer than the blink of an eye. He must constantly pry, doubt, suspect. Additionally, an artist and an intellectual may only identify with their people for a certain length of time, not forever, or else they will forfeit their intellectual integrity.*

SECOND ARTIST: *Should we not have stood in the vanguards of Estonia's liberation, then?*

FIRST: *Of course we should have. But we missed the right moment when we should have stepped aside and started thinking about art and culture's role in the new society. We transitioned smoothly from the opposition to the position* (laughs) *until it turned out that we weren't needed there any longer. We naively hoped that everything would take shape on its own, because it was our free country. We did not know how to withdraw dignifiedly, indicating that our work was done, and join a monastery—in the figurative sense, of course; the intellectual monastery. We would have been just as poor there in the monastery as we are now, because it is inevitable in a country as small and poor as ours, but we would have retained our dignity and our honor—we would have had it to this very day, and we would have continued to be a shining city on a hill for all, in spite of it all. Instead, we were hoping for who-knows-what. We, the artists of a little hick nation, took it too far and lost it for ourselves.*

SECOND: *So we ourselves are to blame?*

FIRST: *I guess so. You can see it for yourself. People your age don't even take pride in their jobs. Artists don't give a damn whether they're selling donkeys or poetry collections.* (A donkey's hee-haw can sound from backstage if the director so desires.) *The main thing is to make a racket. How could they really expect people to treat them any differently than donkey-traders making a racket on the market square?*

SECOND: *Is there any hope of changing it?*

FIRST: *It could take a generation, in theory. In practice, it's impossible.*

DISSIDENT (has softened up in the meantime, tries to console the artists): *Listen, it's not as if things are all that bad, either . . . We are all Estonian men alike!*

FIRST ARTIST (thoughtfully): *When you look at history, artists have always received subsistence from the rulers and the rich. The Medici, Tretyakov, the Rockefellers . . . The public has never supported serious art.*

SECOND: *Only that our current rulers aren't doing it. The royal court of today doesn't love us at all—they see us more as nuisances. A herd of hicks! Ah, I'd like to live in a time when the powers that be pay the artist and people respect him. I'd even agree to live in the Soviet era if it were like that!*

FIRST: *Begone, Satan!*

DISSIDENT (spits with ire): *You sons of bitches!*

## PROFESSOR OF POLITICAL ANALYSES

Monetary reform took place in June 1992—every person could exchange money in the amount of one hundred and fifty Estonian kroons. Afterward, goods gradually began to appear in shops. Life changed quickly in general. A few more years passed, and Teedu had fully re-profiled himself. His job title was now "Professor of Political Systems." How funny his fears seemed in hindsight, how little basis they had had! You could hear grumbling here or there occasionally—from the newspapers or radio more rarely, and from private conversations or that new thing, the Internet, more frequently; but the witch hunt did not garner a much wider response. Teedu couldn't laugh enough over his trip to Raadi Cemetery back in the day. It seemed so insane, so outright anecdotal now that he was unable to keep it to himself and had told a couple of colleagues—the kinds of people he thought would understand him, naturally. He had told them . . . and regretted it immediately. Not that the colleagues might have passed it on (and if they had, then so what?), but just the same, as a thing of principle. Forget—he needed to forget. The old world had to disappear, to sink to the bottom of the ocean—without a trace.

There had been a time when he was greatly frustrated by the fact that he was not a swift penman. Not that he did not enjoy writing—on the contrary, he delighted in the striking comparisons and other linguistic pearls that popped into his head, and even now, almost twenty years since putting his lovey-dovies down on paper (after which he had given up writing poetry), he would occasionally catch himself wanting to express something in verse. However, this had remained (as the critics would say) within the bounds of sentence and section; lengthier conceptual thinking and—what was particularly important from a Party-history standpoint—its expression in a consciously monotone, reference-laden narrative posed him difficulties. Teedu's articles were mostly in college journals, where there was little likelihood that they would attract anyone's attention later. The sole exception had been that brochure, which he had been afraid would be thrown in his face were he forced to go around collecting re-cyclable paper. But how proud he had been of it at the time! He had Merle purchase twenty-five copies of it (being too timid to do so himself) and gave them to colleagues as gifts. He sent a few copies with dedications to select individuals, including the editorial staff of the magazine *Estonian Communist*. Now, he would have given a great deal to make that brochure nonexis-tent. Still, his reputation in the field was nearly nonexistent in comparison with most of his colleagues, as the more diligent of them could boast heftier publications, some even with hard covers, by the end of the Soviet era. Teedu's name had not been printed on the cover of a single widely-used textbook, nor had it been ingrained into the memories of hundreds of students by way of it. No one would have instantly associated his name with something old and despicable. The more years that passed, the fewer there were who had any close acquaintance with his past. He was able to start from an almost blank slate.

The ability to write came in handy during the new age too, of course; research-based production was in high demand. But what do you know—some kind of a vein had opened up within him, and the articles started coming out much more easily than before. At first, they were about house marks; later on, he was already addressing general social topics, smartly avoiding actual politics. After some time, he was selected to be a member of the Estonian House Mark Society, and was very soon elected as Es-tonia's representative to the global organization. He published several books and promptly became quite respected. After that, he grew closer to a movement that was not nationalist in a fundamentalist sense, but rather more democratic, defending the plurality of opinion and the freedom of speech. Soon, Teedu already dared to state publicly that in addition to the national level, there exists a general humanist level that "we should not forget." This all happened very quickly—over the course of five years. Teedu was just forty-two, and thus a suitor at his best age.

He had met Aaberkukk, his erstwhile competitor for Merle's affections, on the street several times, and they had greeted each other. Teedu felt that Aaberkukk held no hostility towards him, but he resolved to stay on his guard regardless.

There was one event that had a small but definitely catalytic role in Teedu's rapid psychological recovery, which came as a surprise to himself as well. Officially, it had been a summer seminar for archivists and museum workers, which the national umbrella organizations had begun organizing for people in their specialty areas. On the agenda were both seminars for specialist and more general, horizon-broadening lectures, along with swimming and sunbathing. In the evening, there was a bonfire gathering where the participants spoke more freely and exchanged thoughts. By chance, both Teedu and Professor Hasso Miller had been on the list of speakers that time, and on the exact same day. Teedu had been invited to speak about house marks. For some time now he no longer concealed his hobby; on the contrary—he attended events and spoke about it, implying that his involvement in the field back then had been his silent protest against the ruling regime. Miller had recently returned from the US, where he had flown immediately after the regime change in order to lecture about system studies at a university there. He had also quickly defended his doctoral dissertation at the institution, as if to demonstrate that it was no problem at all for the likes of him—not even in the Free World, where those things were treated "seriously"—and that he simply hadn't made the effort, or hadn't wanted to demean himself to the standards of the Soviet system. Miller's lecture preceded Teedu's. No specific topic had been declared—Miller simply had to talk, the silver tongue that he was. Listening to him, Teedu could feel himself getting smarter by the minute once again.

How simply and clearly, but at the same time so eruditely and compellingly Miller spoke! *Why oh why can't I do that?* Teedu asked himself, shaking his head. The audience listened gratefully. Yet when the question-and-answer section came, things turned in an unexpected direction. This was not an ordinary audience, after all — the attendees' professions were all directly connected to memory. And those memories contained quite a number of things that most people were in the process of forgetting. There were also some former freedom fighters working at the archives at that time, who had not gone into politics or made a public career for themselves in some other way. Miller seemed to have been on their minds for quite some time (the same went for a few of the other bohemians who had likewise settled in the archives), and they now tackled him with gusto.

Let it be said that after returning from the US, Miller had worked a brief stint at the Ministry of Foreign Affairs — as a vice-director of policy or something akin to that. Afterward, he held a job with a complicated title, being some kind of specially-authorized individual in a government-associated committee or institute that dealt with sociology, psychology, media, and national defense. People said it was a *propaganda ministry*, which may not go by that name in a democratic country, even though everyone knows that it exists in some form. Miller was allegedly the ideologue for that think tank, and thus stood close to power as he always had, without, however, officially stepping into the spotlight himself even once. *This* is what appeared to ruffle the freedom fighters' and bohemians' feathers the very most.

"You were in power then, and you're in power now, too. Back then, you were a big cheese, and now you're still a big cheese," growled Tarmo Truks, a former dissident and boiler-man who also published short stories.

"Interesting — what kind of power did I have back in the day?" Miller asked with genuine amazement.

"Hah!" Tarmo snapped. "Like we don't know. Although maybe you *didn't* have power officially, but everybody knew you really did."

"You've lost me." Miller looked very much at a loss. "Maybe you are confusing two things: power and empowerment? They *do* share the same root word. That means they're interchange-able, right? Like the boiling temperature and a right angle: both are measured in degrees, although one is one-hundred and the other ninety; but there really isn't much in common between them. Why should I be to blame for being empowered? Or do you not agree that, if you are to approach things with reason, then the best social organization is when smart and skilled peo-ple lead the rest and not vice versa?"

"With *reason* . . .!" Tarmo Truks huffed scornfully. "Nothing here can be resolved by reason. You may be right, according to reason. But according to conscience, you're not. You shouldn't have been allowed to elbow your way up to the top anymore."

"As far as I know, I have never elbowed my way anywhere, if you mean clearing a path for yourself with your elbows and treading over bodies. But all the same, it would be interesting to hear—why should *I* not have been allowed to?"

"How can you not understand? You've already belonged to the elite and sampled the benefits once; you've gotten meat and bananas since you were a kid, and then later on you were treat-ed to the best there was to be had." He was, of course, referring to Miller's parents, who had been old revolutionaries.

Miller snapped back that no one is responsible for their par-ents: "Are you trying to say that at the age of five, I should have demanded to be taken to some especially run-down pre-school? That at home, I should have specially demanded crum-mier food than what others were eating, and that my parents should have switched their apartment for a one-room place in a tenement house? You can't expect that of a five-year-old, can you?! It's illogical."

"Precisely," Tarmo said, not intending to drop the issue. "Guys like you always talk about logic. But this has nothing to do with regular logic. Everyone has the right to get something sometime—that's the only thing that's *valid*, the sole logic there is. That's also why the Bible's greatest consolation for the poor lies in the promise that the first will be the last. But you and others like you have turned it into a joke. You got your hands on your well-being during the last regime; you already got your loot, your bananas and pineapples and dachas. Let the others get some now. Why do you think that only certain people have the right to get things all the time? Are you all made out of some better material, huh? Are we, the rest, not really *people?*" Tarmo had gotten himself fired up.

"Yeah, are you an Estonian man or not?" asked Pelle Angerjas, a pagan rocker who had nodded off during Miller's speech.

"What does that have to do with it?" Miller asked, wrinkling his brow with anger. It appeared that the discussion was being dragged by force into the standard confused sloganeering of creative people, which Miller did not tolerate in the very least.

"If you had any national principles, then you'd voluntarily relinquish your position and give it to me," Angerjas said.

"Oh, shut up, you!" Tarmo growled at him. "We're talking philosophically here."

"There is no guilt on my conscience; my hands are clean," Miller said, yawning already. "Give me one argument for why I should not be involved in what interests me in current society, or, if you insist on believing that is the case, why I should not be at the forefront?"

"Consider Jüri's father. His father died in a prison camp. Because he was killed there—and purely for that reason—you shouldn't have been allowed to become a minister. The cries of his widow and children don't sound into your ear, but their blood falls upon you." Tarmo was on a roll now.

"Firstly, I am not a minister," Miller parried. "Secondly, if you really want to know, then I had Jüri's son—and I assume we *are* speaking about the same Jüri R.—I had his son hired some time ago. He's one of my advisors now. Clever boy. We're going to send him off into the European organizations in a few years. He will be a member of the future Estonian elite, and maybe even the European elite. Yes—former members of the Communist Party are promoting the son of a freedom fighter. By the way, that is *far* from being the only such example. A few individuals have done this almost systematically. *That* is how I understand national reconciliation and national unity to be. I'd rather not talk about it, but you are forcing me to. I just don't understand whether what you are saying is more about the Bible or about bananas. No matter—since it appears to annoy you that I'm situated on a normal economic level . . ."

"Oh, he's being fancy, now . . . shit-u-ated, indeed . . ." Tarmo interrupted with a growl, but Miller did not let it bother him.

". . . Then know that during the Soviet period, I assisted those families that had to directly suffer from the repressions. It was a secret fund established by me and a couple like-minded people, no knowledge of which will ever be shared by anyone."

"And you haven't given *me* anything?" Tarmo exclaimed in astonishment.

"You don't *need* to give to each and every loser. You were a loser back then, and you are a loser right now, too," Miller said, picking up his laptop case from the chair next to him to signal that the lecture was over.

Aaberkukk also attended the event, and once again nodded to Teedu amiably. "That means he's over it," he thought to himself, sighing in relief. Teedu would have even liked to say something to Aaberkukk, but someone approached him at that moment and struck up a conversation.

### ILLIMAR'S LETTER FROM JANUARY 1995

*Honorable Chronicler!*

*(. . .) I spent some time abroad, primarily following Tuglas's*[28] *paths through Paris. As we did not have all that much spending money, we stayed at the home of Guido, who lives in the Saint-Germain district. Perhaps you have heard of Guido—he left in the early eighties. Currently, he is involved in a tourism office and is a freelance model on the side. He also took us sightseeing. We visited the "beehive" (La Rotonde). Yes, here was where they sat and dreamed, and where the whole world was spread out before them. There was a great deal of idealism in the Young Estonia group.*[29] *It passed into me right then—through the chairs we sat upon. They were not the originals, of course, but rather new and plastic—still, some vibrations had been preserved in the space and penetrated the chairs. We also went to other cafés. Sartre is said to have sat at Café de Flore. We peeked over the door—interesting interior decoration. And then*

*that old café where Voltaire went; you know it, of course. Paris is saturated with culture, and its appearance is surprisingly pleasant. I always dreaded finding out that Paris lives off of the brilliance of old times; that it is snobby and empty, like a museum. Of course the living, progressive momentum has presumably diminished from what it once was, but the city is very enjoyable all the same. It is like an extremely ripe strawberry a little before the fruit begins to ferment.*

*We visited Eduard Viiralt's*[30] *grave and placed daisies on the sarcophagus. We were also at Oscar Wilde's grave. I am not a homosexual (unlike Guido), as you know* (how should I have known that?), *but Wilde was a personality of rare dynamism and spirit. Gays are often very spirited, though in their own way.*

I was surprised. My "Learned Friend" had emerged from his Vana-Põgioja shell and started making his way around the world. I wondered what the reason could be. It couldn't be a *woman*, could it? He had not specified whom he meant by "we."

## MANGLUS'S JOBS AND ACCOMPLISHMENTS AT THE BEGINNING OF THE ESTONIAN ERA

I have to go back in time a little. Manglus's fate has been left completely aside; still, it is important—even more so than that of some others.

Just like Mati, Manglus started visiting The Cave less during the transitional period. He would occasionally arrive late at night, as if he had just completed a long day of work. He would stop and stand on or before the doorstep, stepping to the side and inspecting the room through the glass wall. It wasn't unusual for him to not actually come any further. One may infer from this that his goal was not to spend time merrily, but rather to find a necessary person. Sometimes he would sit alone there, ruminating or reading some documents. He was the first person to open a laptop on a table at The Cave. It was said to have cost two thousand dollars—an astronomical amount.

Later, it did turn out that he had been very busy. He kept himself up to date with the winds blowing in the world (maybe that was the root of the rumors that he had acquired all of his

ideas and knowledge of things by leafing through foreign journals) and correctly bargained that they would soon begin blowing in Estonia as well. This was both in the broader sense—in
the fields of politics, money, and power—and more narrowly,
in his own field: how artworks were commissioned, how artists
were compensated, and what would even be considered to be art
from then on. He turned out to be more quick-witted than those
much younger than him, although one would have expected the
latter (not having been spoiled by the old system) to "embrace"
the new era more naturally.

Manglus had begun to establish ties with foreign sister organizations, arts-education institutions, and other hotbeds of
cultural activity long before Estonia formally regained independence. He searched for opportunities to finance new cultural
infrastructure, and did indeed find several sponsors and investors. Every now and again, he would be seen walking around
town with gray-haired gentlemen in elegant suits or scrappy-
looking young foreigners (according to the experts in such matters, that is *precisely* how young foreign millionaires look).

When the Estonian state had already been "locked down,"
Manglus founded an entire new organization—a multimedia
center involved in visual paradigms, narratives, discourses, me-
tempsychosis, self-colonization, psycho-physical counterpoint,
and other fashionable things. In order to establish it, he visited
Brussels (Estonia was not a member of the European Union yet,
but did, however, exist in the so-called Partnership Program)
and talked the money out of officials. As there were very few
people in Estonia who understood these theories, he obviously
became the director of the center, although a public competition was held in the interests of correctness. The center soon
started generating output—Manglus's own held a preeminent
position, which likewise seemed natural. He took this work to
artistic centers in other countries to speak about it, and invited guest speakers from there to visit Estonia. Manglus also took
part in large comprehensive exhibitions, bi- and triennials, as
well as all kinds of congresses abroad. Things continued this
way for three or four years. He employed a number of talented
young people over this period while still, however, making sure
that they were not more talented than him, and that they did

not have too much personal ambition.

Previously, the art world had definite rules that everyone was aware of. Nowadays, one had to grope around in the dark, or ask Manglus, who would share information in a friendly manner, but just a pinch of it. True, others also began to wake up over time, and the brighter ones no longer depended on Manglus. He had a significant lead, however, and the others could not catch up to him. All in all, Manglus emerged from the transitional period even stronger than he had been before. In addition to his clever intuition and his ability to "embrace" the age, his advantage was also due to the fact that he had held a high place in the old hierarchy, and that hierarchy essentially still stood intact. Manglus had previously been the secretary-general of his organization; afterward, his title was "President." He had become the dean of the Art Institute late in the old age; now, there was an "Academy" in its place. During the disorderly period when others did not have a proper overview of things and nothing was checked, he was able to coordinate its affairs and nudge it in a direction favorable to him. But he wouldn't have managed to do this without his personal magnetism and brilliantly calculating intelligence.

My eyes hadn't been fooling me back then—Manglus really had been present at the Song Festival Grounds, back when we headed there from Ott's place and Mati and Klaus had sung *"My fatherland dear ..."* He hadn't been swaying shoulder-to-shoulder with the masses, however, nor had he waved to them from the stage. While we were taking our turns shaking the fat popular leader's hand, Manglus had been a little ways away from us—at "headquarters," so to speak, where he was conversing, preoccupied, with several individuals who would later become a part of the Republic's leadership. In the future, when any politician needed to find something out about culture, he would, for the most part, turn to Manglus.

In connection with this, I have sometimes wondered—had the Soviet regime endured, then what would have become of Manglus? More likely than not, everything would have turned out as it was now. Manglus would still have been a perfect specimen; a Rabelaisian man who eats and drinks a lot, thinks deeply and creates magnificent works of art, earns a boatload of money, loves an entire flock of women, and helps orphans and widows while doing so, along with having a successful career in his field. He would have ultimately accomplished what he wanted, one way or another. True, in the old age he wouldn't have become a dean without joining the Party, not to mention his next step—rising to the post of Minister of Culture. He probably *would* have joined the Party, and no one would have especially blamed him for it. Thus, a ministry seat appeared to be within his reach in either alternative. But after that? People guessed that Manglus would head into the European Union institutions and start directing some kind of a division there. After that, he would become the president of our country—at least that is what a few ladies loyal to him speculated. Manglus would be permitted two presidential terms by law. Afterward, he would head back to Europe again, although he might even go into global politics. This would all happen during the time of independent Estonia, of course. If the Soviet period had continued, then his career would likely have ended with cultural minister (if he were not placed in some semi-figurehead position, such as Deputy Chairman of the Presidium of the Supreme Soviet). When Manglus himself was asked about all of this, he would only chuckle good-naturedly, smile his "winning" smile, and dismiss the idea with a wave—although he did so in a way that implied that things had to happen exactly like that, and that the most unbelievable predictions were destined to come true for him in the most natural of ways.

Years passed. The first session of the reestablished independent Republic's parliament had finished its work, and the second had already been sitting on Toompea for three of its four designated years. The new election campaign was picking up speed. Some had heard that a number of the older freedom fighters were intending to stand aside this time, and people were saying that new faces were needed in politics. Stories about Manglus joining a political party were circulating. I asked if he was thinking about parliament.

"Naturally," he replied, seemingly amazed that someone could ask the question.

"You think you'll get in?" I asked.

"Of course," he replied confidently, as if the matter had already been decided—how could anyone doubt that at *all*! He, the sunshine-boy Manglus, had gotten everything he wanted! Now he was going to drop into politics for a moment and would get it there, too. To specify, he added that he would not formally join the party, but would simply run on its election list.

Then some obstacles arose, however. It seemed that the more tenured politicians (the "old farts") had indeed let Manglus into the game, but then began to hesitate regardless. It rubbed politicians the right way when celebrities were in cahoots with them, as it signaled to the public that the party had a wide base, was powerful and popular. Yet Manglus was not allowed into their inner circle; the core set limits on itself. The "old farts" felt that it was *their* country—*they* had retrieved it from the heavens to the earth, and consequently, governing it was their privilege. It's also possible that the matter was much simpler: that the spots were already full. Nice opportunities could be found in and around politics—opportunities that were to be offered first to those who had been in the party longer and had "gotten their hands dirty." It turned out that talk of the "old farts" clocking out had been premature as well. Only one of them, the oldest "fart" of them all, was discharged. Several of the "he-farts" had remarried—they had small children and demanding wives, and to support their families they needed a decent salary.

The matter ended with Manglus's name being absent from the party's electoral list. I'm certain that it had been there at first, but not ranked high enough to have guaranteed him automatic entry into parliament. Manglus retracted his own name at the last moment, as he believed that if he were to end up not being elected, it would affect his reputation poorly. He wanted to hush up the matter, to strike it from the record, and he was almost successful at doing so. Manglus no longer involved himself with that political party.

The instance should have made Manglus cautious, because it had been the first obstacle on his path. He should have acknowledged that he miscalculated by going at it in a slipshod manner, and that the situation differed from earlier ones. Up until then, everything he had encountered in his life had been relatively tangible and compact, clear and visible. Now, however, the game had been stretched out—there were new associations and parallel power structures that he was not a part of. Had he worked actively towards gaining access to them, then no doubt he would have gotten in and asserted himself there, too. But he hadn't made an effort to do so, because he had taken it for granted that those new coteries would want him for themselves—that a red carpet would be laid out before him, down which they would tread, caps in hands, to greet him. If Manglus had been a little less self-confident and had the patience to wait quietly for a few years, then he probably would have gotten his wishes, and would have sat in parliament in the next elections. And who knows—perhaps he *would* have become the minister of culture. Instead, he slammed the door and made his exit. Why did he miscalculate? Had he simply gotten older and his antennae no longer picked things up? Or had he started drinking too much?

On the surface, he did not appear to be taking it very hard. He did not let his disappointment show to us, nor did he ever talk about his political career again. He immersed himself in his old sphere of activity, accentuating it even more in public and remaining even more "visible." But as for drinking heavily—that much is true.

### THE IDEALISTIC GOSSIP JOURNALIST

Up to now, I have avoided speaking about myself within the bounds of possibility. This has been not out of modesty, but because my life *was* merely one man's life—it was not a *tale of fate*; I did not express the era. Now, however, I can no longer avoid me, because to some extent, I transitioned from being the narrator to a character roughly during the period to be described.

As I already indicated, I worked at a gossip magazine. It began as such. Starting in the mid-eighties, I began sending brief notices to newspapers—at first, they comprised all kinds of conference notifications and other news from my field of activity (concerning Esperantists' camps, for example). When the Republic of Estonia was restored, my income from translating took a sharp dip over the course of four or five years, because relatively little popular literature was published in the language from which I translated. While searching for new opportunities, I sent a few short pieces to the so-called "independent press"—pieces in which I told tales about current celebrities (their names changed) whom I knew during my youth. A former classmate—Marten Uljas, who had become the editor of a gossip magazine—asked whether I might want to publish those pieces with the correct names. I replied that it all depended on who was in question and from what perspective, but that he would have to get the permission of those involved. I didn't want to compromise anyone, although I will gladly play along with an innocent joke. The pieces were never published, but Marten invited me to join the editing staff regardless. I wasn't sure what to think at first, but then I gave it a try, and now I really enjoy it. Currently, I have been working as a gossip journalist for more than a dozen years—I am an old hand at it.

People sometimes believe that a gossip journalist is a superficial, vain individual who is *incapable* of dealing with the enigmas of the age. This is simply not the case—of course he can. What's more—even a gossip journalist is able to fight for the "cause" and be useful. This is precisely what I would like to speak about: it is (if you may) a little of what is called a "personal complex."

Specifically, even I have had my bouts of genius. They happened when I realized what was going on around me. In short: I grasped that the creative intellectuals were starting to lose their positions in society. Until then, their importance had been as natural as the sun rising in the east and setting in the west. It wasn't easy to notice the change at first, because nothing alluded to it. It would be more precise to say that no one gave it any thought; no one analyzed the situation. There were so many new and important things to consider in life. Perhaps if they *had* considered it properly, it would have dawned upon them that from that point forward, the very opposite was true: it sets in the east, not the west, and it isn't the sun, but rather some other celestial body. It seemed like the artists themselves thought about the future less than anyone else. And why *should* they have? They had been accustomed to being the subjects of popular attention for almost fifty years. Mere moments before, they had been living out the highpoint of their careers and experiencing the greatest popularity they had ever known, leading the people like Moses to the Promised Land. After that, the artists took a breather, and when the post-victory-party hangover had passed, most of them returned to their writing desks or ateliers and continued working in basically the same way as they had before. Some even declared contentedly that only *now* could they truly start "practicing," for up until then, they had always been dependent on circumstances outside of the arts. The artist's wings had been clipped first and foremost by the Soviet regime, from which one had to hide his true colors. The artist also had to moonlight in replacement of the free press, which, of course, was nonexistent. Some creative individuals likewise recognized that the popular support of their work had been constricting, since expectations had been ratcheted up to extremely high levels. Several veterans claimed that this had been precisely why they had given up on certain artistic endeavors back in the day, leaving experiments unfinished. The artist had to make a maximal effort and go the sure-fire way (so to speak) all the time, because failure was not a personal affair, but essentially meant letting the nation down. (For example, one poet described how in her dreams, a large man—who other than Kalevipoeg!—appeared in front of her bed and asked: "An' what're ye writing for me?" Then he banged his club three times on the floor demandingly and promised to return.) And the Singing Revolution, the Plenary of Creative Unions, and other key events had undoubtedly been sublime moments—they nevertheless belonged to politics and not to the realm of the artist. Politics were to be handled by the professionals from that point forward, and the artists would be free to follow their "ego"—why shouldn't the results be even more powerful and popular support even greater? And so, gold monuments would be erected to them in fairy-tale Estonia—figuratively, of course.

Where indeed did they get that idea? If they had looked around the world, then they would have seen that things were not like that anywhere. An educated person should have grasped—by drawing upon analogies—that the fame of poets and others in Soviet Estonia was conditioned by specific circumstances, not by the individualism of the nation's psyche. In the very least, a man like Mati Tõusumägi, who held a degree in history, should have understood that. And in their great ecstasy, they evidently believed that the Estonian people were not like ordinary people, but were rather something special. I, however, understood that they were mistaken in this, being idealists and romantics. That nation was not the nation they regarded it to be. Everything we know about Estonian history under the guise of "ideals" has, for the most part, been a means for acquiring some kind of material end, and when the goal has been accomplished, the ideals are no longer all that necessary and quietly recede to the background. Thus, Estonia is an ordinary nation like all others—no better or worse; even if it lacks french fries and ketchup.

That realization was my moment of truth. Everyone was still tooting their horns, because everyone was still buzzing from freedom. But I saw what society was moving towards. I took no malicious joy in this; on the contrary—I intuited something bad, because it would give rise to much tragedy. All in all, I *am* an intellectual and regard intellect as the most important thing in the world. So instead of gloating, I considered what it would be possible to do. For merely in order to gorge on fries and ketchup (more precisely, for the right to *order* those fries in Estonian, not in Russian)—for that, one really might not *have* to make so much of an effort; to sing and stand at the barricades. I grasped that one must employ the appropriate means in every situation. And if it is impossible to change the circumstances, then one must strive to take advantage of them. In doing so, one must abandon one's habitual ways of thinking, and must repress snobbism. If one is capable of doing this, then it is always possible to accomplish something.

I didn't come around to this at first, of course. And if Marten had not offered me a job, then I would never have arrived at my mission. I had been on the editorial staff for three quarters of a year. I completed smaller tasks, just as beginners always do.

I did a couple of brief interviews (one with a lumber business-man, the other with the PR director of the Foreign-Estonia as-sociation, who had founded a personnel-hiring firm in Tallinn) and accompanied the photographer so I could write the picture captions later. The editor-in-chief Mahvalda appeared to be satisfied with me and said I could try my hand at a personality-based story already. With whom? "With some person you know," she said, "that's more foolproof for a beginner." Can it be an artist? "Why not," she reckoned. Artists were still credible.

I had my sights set on a poet. He was a special figure who would occasionally cause scandals, but was generally quite a deep person. It was hard to get him to agree to it—he was per-petually "out of sorts," grumbling, and quarrelsome. That was when the print runs of poetry collections and literature overall were already plummeting. I finally got him to agree to it. During the interview, the poet did not answer my questions, but instead mumbled something about the importance of the spirit, the onerous path of cognition, and the "thing of divine inspiration." In summary, what he said was not especially original and, most importantly, rather indecipherable. I strove to reword it more clearly for the reader. When the story was published, the poet went around town clutching the magazine, showing it to every-one and whining about how awfully he had been treated, how his point had been dumbed down and distorted, and cursed our magazine to the bowels of the earth. Yet half a year later, when I saw him by chance at The Cave, he approached me and awk-wardly admitted that a number of people had "noticed" him since the story was published. He had even been invited to give a poetry recitation, which had not happened in years. He asked the organizers why they had invited *him* specifically. "Well, we saw your picture in the magazine," they said to him with smiles as sweet as honey. When the poet was telling me this, I got the impression that he was ashamed of what had happened, but at the same time surprised and, all in all, quite satisfied.

That was when my grand idea occurred to me. If I had suc-ceeded in blowing wind into that poet's sails so that he was "no-ticed," then why couldn't I do the same for *others* as well? *How did I not come up with that idea straight away?* I asked myself, shaking my head. *And why haven't any of my colleagues come up with it? Why hasn't the slogan "gossip journalists of the world, unite to promote culture" not been heard from any corner? I suppose those things aren't as dear to others as they are to me. No matter,* I decided, *I guess I will have to enter into battle alone.*

I started my preparations. I bought myself a shiny purple blazer to wear at events. It would construct an image that was exclusive to me. I had a handful of colorful neckties tailored for me (scarves, bow ties, and others). I acquired a pair of trendy-looking shoes. I consulted my gay acquaintances on colognes. When that was accomplished, I composed a list of people I would start to promote.

An ordinary citizen might think that a gossip journalist hangs around a place where something interesting is going on, and sees who or what sticks out. That he casts his gaze down upon the crowd of guests and decides whom to take and whom to leave at that very same moment. Like a butterfly catcher, a nature photographer, or a mushroom picker. In fact, this is ordinarily more complicated, and the journalist knows in advance the reason why he is out and about; whom he is looking for. There are many reasons why attention is paid to one individual and not to another, why one makes it into the glossy pages and another does not. Some derive from the editor's general principles, others hinge on the journalist's own preferences. It is almost fifty-fifty, depending on the editorial staff. The journalist has a certain amount of wiggle room in each case, which he utilizes according to his own level of spirituality. It is in this that his nobleness or lowness manifests.

The magazine's general principles proceed from the fact that it is impossible to "cram" the pages full of political people or sexy women alone. Even *we* have to report broadly on society. Many journalists work for the paper, and all have their own interests. Some have specialized in economic figures, others in athletes, a third group keeps tabs on female celebrities, and so forth. The editors select certain topics from their field and propose them at a meeting. These are then discussed and weighed until a decision is made on who will get the front cover that time, who the back cover, and so forth. We generally try to make sure no one is left out. I do have to say, however, that the more time that passes, the more difficult it has been to squeeze in artists. They were once a very hot commodity, but no longer. There has to be some kind of scandal or gossip connected to them, no matter whether it is in a good or a bad sense. Otherwise it's not "attractive," as Editor-in-Chief Mahvalda says (she has changed over the years, unfortunately). My acquaintances from The Cave and other circles (for these new circles no longer necessarily go to The Cave) cannot imagine what battles I have to fight in order to bring ordinary people just a smidgen of their lives through our pages. When I propose one writer or another for the front cover, then I am criticized, and told that "no one *knows* them." I respond of course that, no, they are not known, but that they *have* to be known, because they are interesting—much more interesting than many others. My justifications are not taken into account, for the most part, and some witch, slut, or airhead is put on the front cover. I have had to sit through quite a lot of this criticism. Sometimes I wonder if some journalists got just as much of a pounding from their editors-in-chief during the Soviet era.

Still, I did not despair. I reasoned that if I cannot get there directly, then I can do it *indirectly*. I devised some clever tricks and started to act inconspicuously. For example—I imported my "clients" as smuggled goods. It was hard to do this with text. On top of that, my editor could remove a section of a story at any time. Things were different with photos, and photography *is* what is most important today. Good custom requires that all individuals in a picture be listed in the caption. Ordinarily, the most important person or persons are in the foreground or center, where they are conversing. Next to and behind them are less-familiar, as well as completely unknown characters. Some of them *may* also be creative people. I was naive at first, and strove to honestly select from the collection of photos taken at an event the ones that caught some artistic person in the frame by chance. Soon, I realized that this could not be left to fate. Events had to be staged! I could not do this directly and openly. I would covertly tell an artistic person that interested me to "go and stand with that group for a minute—look, next to that person; we'll take a picture." Thus, what started to unfold was that some bohemian or artist would be in the same photo as businessmen, politicians, female celebrities, or figures of other greater significance. For correctness, they were also mentioned in the caption. No one on the editorial staff was interested in how they had ended up there. What do you know—they just happened to be walking by at that moment and were in the shot! There *are* a lot of people at larger events such as presentations or openings, and even we, the experts on social life, do not know who is acquainted with whom and who is involved with whom down to the last detail.

Initially, I did my staging alone; later, I tried to recruit assistants. At one point, I had two of them—young go-getter boys. I called them "drivers" in my mind, because they drove the "quarry" to the necessary spot, where our photographer Koit and I would attempt to get them in the shot. One of the general principles of a photo editor is that clusters of figures who are interesting and desirable should take shape in the pictures. But that is just the basic level. The next level is to put that kind of harmony somewhat at odds: to have the picture show a group that includes, for example, a religious leader, a union leader, a general, a politician, and then someone from an entirely different opera— say someone from the criminal underworld or a rapper. Or if a promoter of rural life, a bank president, the Father of the Year, an Olympic medal-winner, and . . . a poet are in the conversation circle! That gives a sui generis effect and enriches the coloring.

I did not tell the boys the background of my mission at first, deciding to simply foster an artist's mindset in them. And I did so correctly, because although the boys were talented, I realized after some time that they were not interested in the "colorful additive" to the group featured in the picture (nor the spirit and the ideal), but rather what the additive belonged to—meaning power, money, beauty, and glamour. Neither of them could be of real help for me.

To tell the truth, I myself don't do my work out of a sense of mission alone, either. Art and creativity are worth something as well. I stage interesting compositions. I admit that I tread the boundary at times. I have invited zany figures (I call them "photo models") to events without coordinating it with anyone. Looking at the pictures afterward in the editor's office, everyone emits deep sighs, saying—"Who *was* that?," "How *interesting*," and so forth.

I have also tried my hand at other things apart from staging—the developments of digital technology have not passed me by. I consulted a computer-graphics artist, one of Koit's acquaintances. It turned out that it really isn't difficult to montage someone into a picture. We did it on a couple of occasions. For example, I montaged a semiotician who was not at a party into a photo of a group of people. Luckily, the semiotician did not read our magazine. Yet one must be careful. One time when I had done that trick again, a colleague of mine claimed that the figure in the picture was absent from the depicted event, and that he knew precisely where and with whom that person was at the same time. Things started to get serious. The decision was made to ask the person himself. At first he claimed that, no, he had not been at the party, but to my good fortune, he later admitted he had been so drunk that he could not remember, and that he might have stopped by that party, too. I refrained from montaging after that.

It might sound strange, but it is just as difficult to take someone out of a magazine as it is to squeeze or montage them in. Sometimes you want to remove someone: even when the bosses demand it, sometimes you'd rather not give attention to some disagreeable figure. Removing someone from a photo is difficult—an emptiness is left where they were, unless you take the risk to put someone else in their place. Therefore, you must act preemptively. I have also used my "drivers" as "dispersers," meaning I have had them approach some individual and confidentially/formally inform them: "The president wishes to speak with you, my good sir!" Or something like that. Upon hearing this, the figure is put aflutter in an instant and, adjusting his tie if he is wearing one, rushes off in the direction he is pointed towards. That's the time to snap a photo of the remaining group. Even more extreme cases can happen. I once "accidentally" locked someone in the bathroom who was lukewarm on the question of nationhood, just to keep him out of the magazine columns!

Are my methods moral, and do I have a guilt complex before my editing folk? No, not in the slightest. I am indeed an internal émigré, but one in the service of enlightenment. At first glance, it may seem that my activity has not been all that grand or dignified. Our publication is not for highbrows, but for the general public, after all. But isn't it so that if people get accustomed to grabbing a particular magazine, then it's impossible to break them from that habit? The only possibility is to toss more decent stuff there into the trough, within the bounds of what is possible. How else can you sway people towards the high and lofty?

At times, I feel that I am haunted by the late Klaus's fate — that *that* is precisely what has encouraged me to seriously get going on my mission. I did indeed propose once that he go to the party of "the beautiful and the sexy," but perhaps I was not forceful enough in doing so. He declined, but a polite and delicate person will always decline at the first offer. I was polite and delicate likewise, and did not insist further. Had I been more unyielding, then perhaps I could have saved him. One will not get far with delicacy alone in that field. The more time that passes, the more that people who are somewhat similar to Klaus in terms of type (although no one falls even close to him) have become more receptive to the media's opportunities and offers. Of course, some do dig their heels in against it even now. No — not older folk, as one might suppose. They don't understand what it's all about, for the most part. They can't tell the difference between *Soviet Woman* or *Culture and Life* and, for example, *Society* or *Cosmopolitan*. The cover of our magazine has hosted honorable, elderly married couples and familiar cultural individuals. It's the middle-aged people who are against it: they have their own preconceptions about what is permitted for an intellectual, and what is not. *They* are the fussy ones who regard it as demeaning, or else think the intellectuals are dressed improperly. However, most of them understand it very well. The younger, the better.

This is how I stimulate some future talents, open the gates before them, pave their way. Alas, there are many more whom I would like to help than there are opportunities for doing so. I am incapable of granting everyone's wishes; I am constantly making painful choices. I sometimes feel like a mother who has a large number of children and not enough food or clothes for them all. The happiness is that much greater when you see that one of your actions has been of use, and some talented but timid character has become a powerful and confident leader in his or her field.

I strove to "drive" Mati forward once, too. However, Mati just smiled and said: "You're a great guy by the way, Juku, but you're definitely being stupid right now. Don't come to me about such things anymore. Not that I'm knocking the thing that you're doing, but I have no use for it personally." Of course he had no use for it, because he was so famous. *I* had use for him, not vice versa.

It was not necessary to drive Manglus anywhere. He already grasped what was what.

At first, I thought I would focus solely on furthering the careers of artistic people. Then, however, a grand plan materialized before me. It was part of something bigger. Just as some people can be suddenly struck by some kind of impetus, so did I fall in love with my country at one point. I wanted to help improve it. I thought: why not start promoting young politicians using my method? I hoped to select the right people—honest, talented, and principled—and to guide them, pave their path all the way through parliament, and if necessary, from there on as well. I dreamed about how it would shape into a national undertaking. Something great could arise from our editorial office, we would reorganize Estonia, and so forth. I would have gladly shared my experiences and views. (In dreaming this, I did not rule out the possibility of it being noticed higher up as well, although it was certainly not paramount to me.) Oh, youth; oh, romantic fancies! Nothing grandiose or widespread came from it; to this day, I act alone—*volk-odinochka*,[31] as they say in the criminal underworld.

Overall, things have not gone as smoothly as I envisioned. The artists often do not utilize the boost I have given them correctly. Even *they* appear to be drawn towards the fleshpots. Very serious relapses come up, as psychiatrists would say. And as for the young politicians—to tell the truth, I have not yet been able to boost a single patriotic and ethical figure. As soon as they pick up some steam (whether with or without my help), they start working on something else — their personal career or promoting group interests, but as for statesmanlike thought, they both have it and they do not.

At the same time, I am not embittered by this — not in the slightest. The backfires have toughened me. I know that nothing comes easily. I have tested the limits of opportunity and come to understand what is doable and what is not. There are things that I have never, ever been able to pull off. (For example, to establish a philosophical-literature series in our glossy-paged magazine. Only — why would you need to do that *here*?) Patience — great things come in pigeon steps. And I smooth the way for them, because I *am* an old *zemstvo* worker; an unnoticed slogger of everyday life. No matter how few immediately visible consequences there might be in that job — that's one thing I realized long ago, which nothing has disproved. More than all of those highbrow preachers, those scolders and those rhetoricians do with their behind-the-times talk (so what if it is correct) about cultural importance, culture as a strategic resource of the Estonian nation, open and unopened nationalism, and so on and so forth — I do more in my shiny purple suit coat than that talk does! I am A and a little bit of B too.

For a moment, I had the idea of writing to my Learned Friend about myself and my activities. I wondered whether he would list my mission on his registry of idealistic and romantic phenomena. I secretly hoped he would, of course. Then, however, I refrained. I suppose I was afraid he might not. He, who was a lover of the Crusades, the French Revolution, Judaism, German marches, and the Russian soul — could *I*, with my colorful bow ties and trendy shoes be capable of competing next to them?

## MILLER AT THE PARTY OF THE SEXIES

I have already mentioned the party of the "beautiful and the sexy" — a gathering of our clientele and an annual review. The most recent of these was also attended by Professor Miller. My first thought was, *Et tu, Brute?* Even so, there is nothing to marvel at in and of itself. Miller was a theater fan, blue-blooded, a free-thinker, and went to many parties in general. Naturally, Miller made it known (I heard this from a colleague who interviewed him) that he had come solely out of sociological interest, in order to see the types of people that attend the party, but I was not deceived. I remember how back in the day, a number of writers and artists would visit brothels under the pretext of needing to familiarize themselves with the background for a novel or a painting. And so, now was the time for the Millers to penetrate the background — the rich and fatty background that collects on the floor of the new society like humus.

No matter where Miller went, an enthralled group of forty-year-old ladies would gather around him; women to whom he would make simply-worded comments on the politics of the day, pop philosophy, ecology, and other issues. A few gentlemen who would reverently ask the Professor's opinion were not lacking on this occasion, either. I quietly positioned myself near them and cocked my ears. That man was *truly* good at what he did. The ladies squealed: "*Tell* us, Mr. Miller: when was life better? During the Soviet era or the Estonian one? *You* know *every*thing!" Miller improvised a brief lecture on the spot, which I will present in summary: the question is a pseudo-one, to a great extent. There is no all-encompassing, objective criterion for evaluation. Solely the impressions of an observer are possible. If we take for example the material difficulties, then we inadvertently imagine how awful it would be for us, who are currently living among all kinds of comforts, to manage them. But this is not the right approach, because for the most part, they do not seem all that great for whoever lives among such difficulties perpetually. That person's consciousness is deformed or, to put it more precisely, *adjusted*. The same goes for a person who has been ill for a long time — someone who, subjectively, is not as unhappy as the healthy person standing next to them imagines if he or she mentally steps into the sick person's shoes and is taken aback from the horror of it. The sick person has already formed his or her sick-consciousness, which softens everything. Thus, it is not right to over-glorify a Soviet-era person's sufferings, nor to sympathize with them. We can only be the people we are, here and now, in the specific conditions and singular instance. It is hard for us to say anything about the happiness or unhappiness of others' lives. Miller quoted the cult-poet Alliksaar—"There are no worst or best of times; there is only the moment, in which we are now present," meriting the ladies' amazement, and he continued. Three factors define our evaluation of both the past as a whole and the present day. Firstly: how good a position the evaluator had in the hierarchy of that time or now; meaning whether he was rich or poor, at the upper or lower level of power, and so forth. Secondly, a great deal depends upon one's biological age and health level. Things *were* better in youth, of course! It would be more correct to say that miserable things seemed less miserable then, while on the contrary, good things seem less good at an older age. Coming thirdly is what can be called nature, personality-type, and the preferences that proceed from it. Some enjoy immense freedom, because they want to risk and to act. Life in an open society and a liberal market economy suits them. Others prefer stability and are happier when they do not have to constantly take risks and make decisions. They want to be left in peace. Such people are similarly less demanding. Security is of the utmost importance for them. A strong social society suits them. Happiness is when a personality type and a society type coincide. Everything else, like one's starting position, what their parents desire their career-choice and marriage to be, the society's unemployment level, and so forth all derive from these three things.

Miller smelled good ("Baldini"). He wore a genuine Cartier, and short black arm-hair was visible on the tanned skin next to its gold strap. I seriously considered whether or not I should attend one of his public lectures. He gives them from time to time. Seats at them are said to be in very high demand, almost like at the opening night of an opera. Miller is a very contemporary person.

Sohvi was also at the party. Sohvi is an actress and a house-wife who was the first to strip nude on film during the Soviet era. She said she did so in the name of artistic freedom, to protest the Kremlin's satraps. She became famous across the whole USSR. Sohvi burned out a little in the meantime (she boozed too much), but has now gotten back into shape and is radiant.

Sohvi is one of my idols. She has her own TV show about fifty-year-olds' sex lives. The DVDs of the shows are just about to go on sale, and are predicted to be highly successful.

## ILLIMAR'S LETTER FROM APRIL 1996

*Honorable Chronicler!*
*Our knob factory was shut down. The men were paid their last wages in knobs. Everyone was given several thousand of them. Jass got drawer knobs, Tõiv jewelry-box knobs, Little Kusti got knobs for outhouse hatches, and so forth. You know that oriental parable about eternity, of course. What is eternity? Let us imagine a diamond mountain. Every thousand years, a little bird flies to it and sharpens its beak. When the mountain has been worn down to nothing in that way, then one second of an eternity has passed. I would not be so pessimistic. I would say that when the fingers of Little Kusti and his descendants have worn down those thousands of outhouse-hatch knobs, then one second of an eternity has passed.*

*The factory was the largest employer in these parts. The men drive to Tartu now—there is work there.*

*The store had three kinds of beer, but there were few drinkers because the men are in Tartu and no one else has money.*

*Jõgever joined a political party and is on the municipal council.*

*I sent a few of my written contemplations to media publications, but it appears that they have not been of interest to anyone.*

*I read the Book of Revelations for a change and realized that not everything is ordained to be fulfilled right now—the time will come later. The Book of Revelations clearly testifies that an age of active ideas is to dawn imminently. The time will come when everything will be researched with complete impartiality. Everything that surrounds us. That time will come, it will!*

## KOIT. SNAPSHOT OF THE DAY-TO-DAY LIFE OF A GOSSIP JOURNALIST

A few words also about the photographer Koit, whom we work with and who smuggles creative people into the glossy pages as contraband by my order. I believe that he understands my mission, even though we have never spoken about it outright. Koit also expresses the era, adding his own small, yet idiosyncratic and expressive thread to it.

Koit was no longer young the first time that I came into contact with him in a work setting. The Singing Revolution had caught him at Jesus-age. He came to work for the gossip magazine at the age of thirty-eight, and was now ticking along at fifty-five. Young people were breathing down his neck—even more so than mine, as those able to work a camera suddenly came out in swarms. Koit was an exceptionally good photographer and had loved the field since he was a child. He had apparently attended a photo circle at the Pioneers' House when he was a schoolboy. He got his first job at the Komsomol youth magazine in the seventies. I think I even hazily remember him from some event, where he walked around the room with a light meter. With the cameras of the time, you had to do all the settings by hand, and you would get better at it as you worked.

Koit was a quiet person, but was curious and wanted to get a feel for life. As a result, he had gone on a large number of business trips and traversed half of the Soviet Union. He had been on the Trans-Siberian Railway, with the oil drillers in Surgut, and even on Sakhalin. He was not politically active, but when freedom began to dawn for Estonia, he became excited like many who had previously been self-effacing, decent, and outwardly law-abiding citizens. Koit and those like him had not protested openly up to that point, but when independence came, he rejoiced wholeheartedly and became some of the most self-sacrificing supporters of the new society—due precisely to his decency and loyalty.

Before long, the Balkan War broke out, which was followed by the Kosovo Crisis. Koit confessed to me that he wanted to travel there. It turned out that it had been his dream to become a frontline photographer since he was a child. It was somewhat hard to believe that such a levelheaded person—one who stares at you with benevolent eyes from behind his round glasses and won't speak a single word over the course of half an hour—wanted to go to the battlefield in order to crawl beneath a hail of bullets amid the explosions of artillery; to capture the expressions of the wounded and the dying, the limbs flying through the air, and other surreal things. But it seems that was precisely the case. (By the way, one other good acquaintance of mine — an even more mild-mannered and pleasant man — did not miss a single Eurosport broadcast of boxing matches.)

"Gotta get down to Kosovo," Koit would sometimes mutter completely randomly. Or else the phrase, "When I've taken my trip to Kosovo, then . . ." These remarks made me realize how precious the matter was to him and how it shaped his whole spiritual life. For Koit, the world was divided into pre- and post-Kosovo. Alas, traveling to the Balkans was not easy. There were others who desired it as well, and the foreign-policy situation was messy. Koit continued working at the gossip paper and patiently awaited his hour.

It was probably in 1999. We were supposed to go and visit the artist Peet Lumepart together. The man had been given a state award, and not even our glamour publication could disregard such a thing. Lumepart's glory days had been during the seventies and eighties, when his robust, masculine style was taken by many as a manifestation of Estonia's quest for freedom. Now, his reputation had tarnished a little, just as it had for most figures of that generation, and people younger than thirty-five probably did not care about Lumepart's paintings anymore. I felt I had to do my part to help Lumepart get "visible" once again.

We arrived at his home. The artist lived on the fifth floor of a building at the end of Pärnu Road, which dated back to the first period of Estonian independence. We all knew one another already, but neither of us had been to the artist's apartment before. Koit immediately started looking around with a professional eye to see where to place the subject and what to photograph in general. It was a three-room apartment, and we were alone. One room appeared to be used for storage, while the master was using another for painting. There were several weeks' worth of unwashed dishes in the kitchen, and it reeked a little in there. We took a seat in the living room, which was more or less tidy. I began the interview while Koit wandered around looking pensive, causing Lumepart to occasionally cast questioning glances in my direction.

We took a break after forty minutes, and Koit asked permission to start with the photographing.

"Look, if you could stand here, please," he said, pointing to the broken-lidded toilet in the bathroom.

"What do you mean? In the bathroom?" the artist questioned, visibly unable to believe his ears.

"Yeah, and if you could take your shoes and socks off, if it doesn't bother you, and stand in the toilet bowl. And if you've got nothing against it, you could hold a paintbrush and a palette, you see, like this . . ." Lumepart was one of the few artists who did not use computer technology yet, but instead painted using old-fashioned oil paints.

"Why?" Lumepart asked, probably thinking that Koit had lost his mind. "Does anyone paint in a toilet, huh? Why can't I stand in front of an easel? In the old days, artists were always photographed in front of an easel."

"Yeah, you're right about that—even I've done it that way." Koit stroked his jaw. "But that in-front-of-an-easel composition was forced on us from above and everyone is tired of it. There's no point in doing it like that anymore. Now, it must be done creatively," he explained. "We *have* freedom of creativity now."

"OK, but listen—let's do it where I'm in front of the easel, *you're* taking the picture from the toilet bowl, and Juku photographs the both of us together. I also have a camera. Then you can have your cake and eat it, too." Lumepart highly enjoyed the idea and started to snicker. Koit didn't have a great sense of humor.

"The editor said that if we get an 'attractive' picture from this, then it might even make the front cover," Koit said, attempting to convince Lumepart.

I realized that Koit was a victim of his own profession, and he didn't understand that the laws that applied in his world might not apply in a painter's world at all. The word 'attractive' does not have a magical effect on older people. It did not on Lumepart, in any case.

"Have you no *shame*!" he huffed, starting to give the photographer an earful. "You're not a little boy anymore, you're being *utterly* foolish. How will your colleagues react when they see your name below a picture of me standing in a toilet bowl?"

"Oh, let's not worry about that," Koit said dismissively. He saw a glimmer of hope. "They do much worse *themselves*."

"But what about your famous role models from the photographers' Valhalla? Those war photographers you respect so much, whose pictures you used to have pinned up above your bed—they're there, *too*. What would *they* think of this kind of nonsense?" Lumepart knew about Koit and the Balkans. His criticism was serious, but Koit stayed stubbornly silent. Lumepart was likewise silent, making eye contact with me and sniffing loudly from time to time. Then he went into the bathroom and stood in front of the toilet. He even leaned down and studied the pot, as if hoping to find something in it that might give Koit's intentions an aesthetic legitimacy. Then he returned and declared resolutely:

"No. And overall—you don't need to do anything about me. That goes for the piece, too. Let's stay friends, but . . ."

Koit sighed and said defeatedly: "Fine. We'll do it the ordinary way, then." He photographed the artist dutifully in several kinds of poses, but he seemed dispirited and sighed constantly.

"What are you sighing for?" Lumepart asked, opening a bottle of wine. Our work was almost done there.

"Word's going around that there are going to be layoffs," Koit replied weakly. "No one can be sure of anything. Today you're there, tomorrow . . . That's why I would've needed to make a strong statement. If you'd have stepped into the toilet there, it would have been such a strong statement that I'd be sure to keep my job." Koit was in his second marriage. His children were still small. He would occasionally sigh and say he definitely wouldn't live to see his grandchildren. It would be good if he even just saw his children graduate from college, but no more. "These days, women are having children at forty," he added knowingly.

Lumepart was a grizzly on the outside, but he actually had a very good heart. He naturally started to feel bad for Koit. I could see him grappling with himself. He even made some excuse and went into the storage space in order to think it over. Then he came back, sniffed loudly though his nose again, and said: "Fine, what'll it cost me? No one important will see it.

Let's do it. I don't want anyone to be deprived their scrap of bread because of me."

Koit's expression cleared up in a heartbeat, and he started to chatter, bubbling: "It's not like I've got all that much time left until retirement. Six or seven years, maybe, then the kids'll already be in high school, might be able to manage on their own, some are starting up student companies in school these days, it's not like it was back in our day . . ." He kept spouting off endlessly in the same spirit. Lumepart, looking like a martyr, was already readying himself to step into the toilet, had taken the sock off of one of his feet, and was tugging at the other. At that instant, Koit became rasher, as if he already had the picture recorded in his camera. He said: "Before, you had to worry mainly about equipment; that it might fail you. Now, you've got entirely different worries—you have to break down people's resistance and bother yourself with other such crap; people are as stubborn as *goats* . . ."

Hearing this, Lumepart roared: "No!" And he pulled his sock back on.

"What? Huh? We're not doing it, then?" Koit asked, his expression falling once more.

"No," Lumepart solemnly confirmed.

We sat for fifteen minutes more, until the bottle of wine ran out—Lumepart mainly drank it on his own.

When we were leaving, Koit erupted on the doorstep: "I'll never, *never* get to Kosovo!"

The story about Lumepart was published—not on the cover, however, but in the back.

"Why?" I asked when I met Koit.

"Urmas didn't want to," he replied. Urmas was the deputy editor-in-chief.

Koit never did go to Kosovo, because he developed some kind of a leg problem. It wouldn't go away, and he was limping when we met on the street two years later. One cannot dart around under a hail of bullets with that kind of a leg, of course.

Lumepart, however, drank for several days after that visit of ours—out of immense pity, naturally. And so, no one was happy on the whole.

## ILLIMAR'S LETTER FROM JUNE 1999

*Honorable Chronicler!*
*I went to the foreign Estonians' ESTO festival—the first time in my life. It was held in the United States, in the Midwest. I was very positively surprised. Although things are also great in our homeland and many people who possess enthusiasm, idealism, and romanticism can be found, everything was exponentially great at this festival. I have never seen such an outpouring of spirit anywhere. They have lived for half a century with one idea, with one yearning in their breast, in the name of which they have acted, and now they are seeing it being brought to fruition. We, who live in our homeland—even the most devoted nationalist of us—pay attention to even the tiniest mistake in the new Estonia; they, however, see only the good. We are like parents who note both the good and bad things in our offspring. Yet foreign Estonians are just like grandparents who see their grandchild primarily on Sundays or during school breaks, and so they see their better and sunnier side, and love them without reserve. And if they should also see their faults, then still, as they have already raised some children, they are able to see things in a longer-term perspective; to peer into the future—into a time, when the faults have been corrected and the bad turned into good. Grandchildren will grow up and go to college one day, too. In that sense, foreign Estonians' love for Estonia is indeed a bit too uncritical, but on the other hand, it is more ambitious.*

*In terms of outer similarity, on the level of function or proportion, Foreign Estonia is almost like the father and Home Estonia the mother, because the mother still is the greater body, in which the new develops. Yet things are the reverse in respect to attitude. We here are more like strict fathers who criticize and find faults, saying that our little scion is not developing fast enough and coming into its own. Meanwhile, foreign Estonians love Estonia with a tender motherly love, marveling and coo-cooing it overindulgently.*

*As you can see from my letter, I have implemented an abundance of family paradigms as bases for comparison. Why this is so—perhaps you will hear in the near future.*
*Yours,*
*Learned Friend*

My hunch turned out to be true. Illimar intended to marry—
for the first time in his life. He became a father at the age of forty-
two. I did not dare to ask whether it was motivated by the need
to increase Estonia's population or something more personal.

## TEEDU TÄRN'S OWN MEDAL

It was about two months before Estonian Independence Day
when, one morning, Teedu arrived at work to find waiting for
him, in a mound of newspapers and other correspondence, a
high-quality envelope with "Office of the President of the Republic of Estonia" printed on the upper corner. Teedu froze:
was the President going to arrest him personally? He opened the
envelope, his hands trembling. The formal script on the large
white page informed him that the President was giving him
a medal! Teedu was so relieved that he accidentally sat down
on his attaché case. Yet, he was immediately gripped by a new
sense of panic. Was this really necessary now? It wasn't that the
medal was prestigious and could possibly make anyone jealous.
No, the medal was modest—a fifth-class Order of the White
Star, basically the same that was given to folksingers and local
researchers. (It soon turned out that Teedu was being awarded
for his house-mark activities. This knowledge provided him a
degree of relief.) However, the thing was not the quality of the
medal, but rather the principle—the fact that it was being giv-
en to him at *all*. Attention was being paid to Teedu's person by
way of it; he was being pulled out before the public—look, this
sort of a Teedu exists. But he would have preferred to continue
living his lowly existence. Teedu worried that his past would be
unearthed—a past that he had hoped was reduced to dust, had
vanished. He fell into a depression and lost his appetite. He did
not say anything to Merle at first, merely conferring with himself. He kept quiet about it for almost two weeks. Then, another
white envelope arrived, likewise inscribed "Office of the President of the Republic of Estonia." It contained an invitation to
the formal Independence Day gala at the Estonia Theatre. He
certainly had to fill Merle in on it now, if only for the fact that
the invitation was for two. But in that case, he would also have

to tell Merle the reason for them being invited. Teedu informed his wife about the medal. Merle would not hear another word of her husband's misgivings, hugged him and congratulated him. Teedu was relieved once again, although he inwardly censured his wife for such shortsighted recklessness. Was Merle *really* not afraid that . . . But better to remain silent.

A stressful time began for Merle (she hadn't worked at the Party archive for a long time, by the way—she now worked a city job), as she needed to start thinking about her dress and accessories. It *was* the reception of the president of their Republic, of course! Teedu didn't own a dress suit, nor did he plan to acquire one. It seemed unwise to make such an expense for a one-time occasion. His family's standard of living had not fallen very much compared with what it was during the Soviet era, but that wasn't the main point. In Teedu's opinion, acquiring a suit would be a bad omen. For if you already have a suit, then the opportunities for putting it on will not fail to arise. He would be dragged out before the public more often. Teedu did not want to tempt fate.

Teedu was seated in the last row on the third side-balcony of the Estonia Theatre. Instead of seeing what was going on onstage, he merely saw the faces opposite to him across the auditorium. He almost couldn't even hear anything, because there were journalists and bohemian artists sitting next to him talking amongst themselves, showing off, and making facetious jokes, to Teedu's irritation. Some of them even appeared to be slightly under the influence. *Power is power and rules are rules—they should be respected*, Teedu grumbled to himself, wrinkling his forehead. It was stuffy beneath the high ceiling and Merle appeared to be a little fatigued, although she tried to hide it bravely.

The president's hand-shaking ceremony began once the speeches and the concert were over. It was an hour and forty-five minutes until the upper balcony's turn came. The organizer woman—the protocol chief, slender and short statured, well sculpted like an elegant chess piece—asked them to join the line that wound down the stairs. Teedu waited for the noisy bohemians to go before them. Who knew—maybe one of them would suddenly approach him and ask: "Ooh, isn't that our Party-history teacher? The one who praised Brezhnev so nicely?" When they reached the auditorium that had been rearranged for the hand-shaking ceremony, Teedu handed his invitation to the man who called out the guests' names in a resounding voice, adding who they were. Teedu froze for a second: who would he be introduced as? But he just said, "researcher of house marks." They were some of the last to approach the presidential couple. Merle was beaming. Teedu was afraid of clasping the First Lady's hand too strongly, and therefore barely grazed it. He thought he saw the First Lady smirk lightly.

When they finally reached the banquet hall, the mood of those who had arrived before them was already spirited and the tables of appetizers along the wall almost bare. A waiter with his hair combed back flat against his head offered them a plat-ter of tiny mock clam shells filled with kama[32] cream with stems of grass sticking out of them. It was the First Lady's own recipe.

They were passed by a TV personality who was so famous that Merle went pale. There was no one to talk to; complete strang-ers were buzzing around them. Teedu greeted the dean of the university and Professor Miller, who had a minuscule slit-eyed lady under his arm—a woman from the Orient, judging by her clothing. Teedu's old schoolmate Mati Tõusumägi zipped past them, but he would not have wanted to meet the man for any price. Aaberkukk was standing in the company of two higher-ranking officers at a distance and smiled meaningfully at Tee-du, as if to boost his courage. Still, one of his own kind could be found amongst the crowd. Elmar Sikupere was from the area where their summer home was located. Elmar was stand-ing next to the plaster bust of a celebrated Estonian poetess in the hallway—awkwardly, like how a country person used to feel when ending up in a city. He told them he'd been invited to the reception because he saved a drowning person. He had been awarded a hero's medal for the act; second-class, unfortunately. Elmar had heard someone calling for help in the reservoir and dragged the man out of the water. However, the latter still died. Elmar asserted that the man actually did not die of drowning, but rather from drinking wood alcohol with the other men

that same evening. "I didn't drag a corpse out of the water—
he was still alive and kicking then," Elmar said. However, the
papers that registered the heroic act and the man's death certificate had gotten "mixed up" somewhere, and that was why
he received the second-class medal. "Now that I think about
it, why'd I go and save him?" Elmar reasoned philosophically. "He'd already been marked by Death. If he hadn't reached
for the hooch that night, then he probably woulda been run
over by a tractor the next day." Teedu and Merle pitied Elmar.

Teedu sighed with relief when he was driving back towards
Tartu that night. Nothing awful had happened, and maybe
nothing awful *would* happen anymore, he reckoned. "Yeah—I
definitely could have even gotten a fourth-class medal!" It was as
if Merle could read his thoughts: "Maybe we should have a suit
tailored for you, all the same. You never know—might need it
in the future again." Teedu squeezed his wife's elbow in gratitude and smiled, but shook his head in the dark. A suit truly was
not on his mind. To live—he needed to live. That could be
done without a suit, too.

Nevertheless, things took an unexpected turn, and it seemed
to Teedu as if Merle had foreseen it all. Specifically, a couple of
weeks after the presidential reception, he was contacted by Sten
Karotar, who was an influential person in a certain political party's inner circle in addition to being a well-known public figure.
Karotar had been one of Teedu's students a dozen years earlier,
attending the lectures on Party history that Teedu was still holding at the time. Now, they met by coincidence (if it really was
coincidence) in the old university café. Karotar greeted Teedu
and asked whether he had a little time and if he could take a seat.
Teedu was munching on a buttery pastry and had his mouth
full, so therefore nodded obligingly, trying to repress his anxi-
ety (he became anxious at everything in general), and clenched
the handle of his coffee mug more tightly. Karotar struck up
an ordinary conversation at first. *Like KGB officers*, the thought
popped into Teedu's head. *They would chat before they hit you,
too*. Teedu didn't have any personal experiences in that field,
but he knew recruiters' tactics based on stories he had heard.

He waited patiently for Karotar to explain the actual intention of his approach. It was hardly likely that he had taken a seat to discuss students' level of intellect and the organization of the educational system with Teedu. And soon, the man indeed broached the other subject.

"By the way, I saw you on TV a while back," Karotar remarked. "You were at the presidential reception." Teedu shrugged—ah, well, so what.

"No, no," Karotar reassured, smiling approvingly. "That's great. Even though we have a small country where everyone knows everyone, the president is still the president. Actually, I did want to start from that . . . Look, I understand that you are fully content with your research work right now; you're able to accomplish what you want. I've also heard that the students respect you. But—shouldn't we all consider society more widely from time to time? There *are* so few of us. Given that fact, shouldn't everyone who has the corresponding skills also make their own contribution towards serving society more concretely, on a political level? I don't mean anything permanent, of course. For knowledge is quite obviously your calling. However, one does not rule out the other. At least not—excuse me if I understand this incorrectly—in your field. A surgeon or a violinist, yes—they can lose their qualifications in just a few years. But your field even seems to be contiguous with politics, or is connected to it, at least. That could be a real advantage. What am I doing beating around the bush—in short, we in our party have been talking about you. Would you perhaps want to run for city council?"

Teedu was astounded. What—he . . . ? It was impossible that they didn't know . . . But if truly, by some miracle, they did *not* know, and the truth came out afterward, then *he* would be to blame for not having brought it up at the right moment. It could be regarded as a mortal sin, and he could be made into an enemy. At lightning speed, the decision matured in his head not to delay, but to be immediately honest, right there and then. "But listen, I was in the *Party*—is that really acceptable?" That was the way he asked it, surprising himself with his own courage!

Sten Karotar smiled. "We know about that, naturally. How

could you possibly — no offense — think that we didn't? We know a lot about you. But it's good that you said it yourself, because it shows that your conscience is in the right place. As for that matter, national reconciliation inevitably has to happen in a society as small as that of Estonia. There's no other way to move forward. We cannot brush capable people aside forever because of what they once were. Look around you — you do see how many 'formers' are in leading positions, don't you?" (Tee-du *had* seen this, naturally, but had still thought they all had to have had some kind of personal connection, or had been borne upon some other wings.) "On top of that, every case should be approached individually. There is no such thing as collective guilt. You yourself also realize that we would not turn to you if we had not arrived at the understanding that your previous Communist Party membership is not an obstacle in your case. Aaberkukk thought the same thing. He and I are old brothers-in-arms. By the way, you wouldn't have to join our party. At least not at first." He was silent for a few moments before adding reflectively: "We all have to live on together."

Four months later, Teedu ran for city council. He did not receive very many votes — some received several times more than he did, but there were also those who received fewer. Unexpectedly, even to himself, Teedu became a city councilmember.

During the first sessions, he sat there extremely quietly and would only raise his hand to vote — according to how they had agreed upon in advance at the coalition meeting. When an unexpected situation arose, he would watch to see how Karotar voted before him.

Teedu was appointed to the city's cultural committee.

Another year passed. Karotar asked whether he might join the party. Teedu agreed. And so began his career as a politician. A few months later, prior to the party's next annual regional meeting, Karotar asked if Teedu might agree to make a speech. It was essentially an order. Teedu lost sleep and his appetite again — he did not even enjoy the taste of chocolate candies anymore. All he thought about was how and what to speak about. Ultimately, he decided to shrug everything off so as to liberate himself from his spiritual struggle. If it was time, then it was time.

The room swam before him as he went up to the podium, and his voice trembled when he spoke his first words:

"I am of course a former commie and thus an inferior person and I'm unworthy of blowing my own horn here at all." Teedu had been practicing those words at home for a long time, and they most definitely came from the bottom of his heart. He had believed it to be a suitable introduction, and that the audience would take it as a polite acknowledgement—something akin to an amateur apologizing to professionals. It immediately dawned upon him with horror that he had said something unusual. Everyone appeared to prick up their ears. Karotar's expression displayed apprehension—was that new guy there at the podium plotting to ruin their whole game? Would he crash and burn already in carrying out his first task? Some in the audience glared at Teedu morosely, and there was even hissing and muffled cries of "Out! Get out!" But there were others who were snickering, apparently taking the statement as unusual humor. After a while, Karotar's expression cleared, also. There was relatively strong applause when Teedu finished his speech. Not a bad start for a newcomer! After the meeting, Karotar came up to him and said, smirking: "Well, that was quite an interesting move, all in all. Humanity says a gay farewell to its past. Marx was right about some things."

Teedu repeated his opening sentence at the next (and somewhat more important) meeting six months later. There were more people chuckling than there had been the previous time. True, even now, a few individuals maintained hatchet-faced solemnity, but no one shouted "Out!" Instead, someone called out from the back rows: "Why apologize for nothing!" The applause was also above average on this occasion. Some men even approached Teedu and shook his hand after the meeting. This flooded his heart with relief.

Soon enough, whispers that he had been nicknamed "the former commie and inferior person" in nationalist circles made their way to him, but amazingly, it did not especially interest him. He had read in a cultural weekly about a discussion panel that included freedom fighters, politicians, and social experts, including Miller. The latter had emphasized that there exists a type of person who always stands out more from others, no matter what the social system, because they are more enterprising, capable, and effective. Teedu got the feeling that he also belonged to such a group of people.

Another year passed. The party held its next big meeting, a national congress. Teedu stepped up to the podium and began:

"I am of course a former commie, and thus an inferior person, and I'm unworthy of blowing my own horn at all." He no longer recited this awkwardly or apologetically, but in a dignified, dramatic style, holding pauses. Not like an amateur before pros, but like a pro who actually elevates himself by superficially lowering himself — who hints to all of the other pros how professional he actually is, thus lifting his self-confidence sky-high. And what do you know — well-meaning laughter rustled through the rows, and the audience even started to applaud him already at the beginning of the speech, before he had had the time to say anything else. Overall, only the party's new chairman Karotar was applauded more than he was. This would have consequences!

Elections were around the corner again. Teedu toured the country making appearances every other day; sometimes as much as twice per day. Yet this was not unpleasant for him, nor did it pose any difficulties — his experiences as a college lecturer came in handy. On this day, he had gone to speak at an event held by his hometown's local chapter of the Pensioners' Union. Just as he did everywhere, he acquainted them with the party program, emphasizing the benefits that elderly persons would get if they voted for them. An hour's time passed unremarkably, followed by questions from the crowd, and the event came to a close. When Teedu was gathering his papers and getting ready to leave, he was approached by an older gentleman. *Someone wants a personal audience*, Teedu thought somewhat wearily but sympathetically. It was ordinary for someone to approach him like that after a lecture. It usually wasn't so important what the people said on those occasions; what *was* important was that they came up to him like children. One had to be compassionate with people and hear them out; they had to be encouraged. Teedu was used to it. The man here appeared to be extremely excited, and even waved his arms a little:

"It's me, Kulu. Mr. Kulu—do you remember me? *My heart is restless, for the road calls into the distance.*" Mr. Kulu sang a few measures in the somewhat gravelly voice of an old man.

*Oh my God,* Teedu thought, becoming slightly nervous. Had the former teacher not introduced himself, Teedu would have hardly recognized him. Kulu appeared to have shrunk. It was odd, for although Teedu had grown relatively fast in school and was filed closer to the front of the line than the back in PE class, he had never gotten the impression that Mr. Kulu was shorter than him. But so it was, he thought presently. Bosses and teachers always seem taller than they actually are. People also shrink over the course of their lives. Their legs become larger and hips wider, as if their 'contents' were starting to slip downward like in an old mattress or a bag. Mr. Kulu looked up at Teedu, then seized his hand and shook it.

"I thank you for everything that you are doing for the good of our country and our nation," he said as if giving a military report to someone. "I have always been an Estonian patriot. I am glad that the student, whom I had the highest hopes for back in our day, has become such an outstanding individual. You give us honor! But you still have much to do. What's most important is that you charge forth and you follow your star!" Saying those last words, Kulu came up closer, right under Teedu's nose, cocked his head to the side, stared at him unblinkingly (his squinting, milky eyes apparently saw poorly), and shook Teedu's hand one more time with unexpected force. Then he turned and moved away in a slow, swaggering gait.

*Adios, Mr. Kulu,* Teedu thought melancholically.

Teedu's political party merged with another one in order to perform better in the elections. The outcome was excellent. Even Teedu made it into parliament, the Estonian Riigikogu, seventh-from-last on his party's election list. He wasn't in the lead of those striving for votes nationally, but was also not one of those who get in only due to mandates being redistributed.

The election results were made known before midnight, and then the festivities started. There was a large crowd present, because opinion polls had predicted a good outcome for the party and people knew to ready themselves for celebration. At around one in the morning, Karotar waved Teedu over and asked him whether he might like to join the delegation that was going to go and congratulate their future coalition partners. It was apparently quite clear who would form the new government. Teedu hesitated for a moment, because he knew that both parties also included people who would rather not have seen a coalition. In that other political party they intended to visit, individuals like Teedu were said to have been a thorn in some people's sides during the merger. But should Teedu have to care about it endlessly? *Yes*, he replied to himself.

They were received like honored guests at the restaurant where supporters of the other party had gathered. No one displayed any discomfort. Suddenly, Teedu noticed Mati Tõusumägi. He had not counted on finding him there. As far as he knew, Mati had not run in the elections. He didn't appear to be sticking his nose into politics at all. They greeted each other uncertainly and from a distance, like people who are not sure if they actually know each other. Teedu's first thought was that he would like to talk to Mati. The next moment, however, he became terrified of doing so. He would have had to work up a great deal of courage, but did not think he possessed the strength for doing so that day. As a result, Teedu stayed close to Karotar, listening to what he was speaking about with the other party's chiefs.

When Teedu started heading out from the party an hour later, he spotted Mati in the foyer. Mati appeared to be a little unsteady on his feet already, and was debating what he should do next. He was sitting with his back towards Teedu, and did not see him. Teedu slipped stealthily past the man and ducked behind a corner. When Mati exited, Teedu followed him. Mati stopped every little while and talked to himself in a half-audible voice. For a moment, it appeared as if he intended to plop down on a bench that was occupied by flower sellers in the daytime.

But he walked onward. It was soon clear to Teedu where Mati was headed. To The Cave, of course. Teedu's first thought was to go in after him. He was overcome by an almost irrepressible desire to do so. The feeling was almost as powerful as the one that had driven him to the Song Festival Grounds ten years earlier—to find out how things "really were." This time, he conquered his desire. *Let him go,* Teedu thought. For no amount of money would he have agreed to admit to himself that he also felt a sense of schadenfreude.

### ILLIMAR'S LETTER FROM AUGUST 2000

*Honorable Chronicler!*
(. . .)
   *A pub has now opened where our shop once was. People go there, but there are practically no locals. Instead, it is frequented by romantic ramblers discovering the world, their chests open wide to the winds. The pub belongs to Jõgever. They say a tourist farm and a hiking path will open up next to it very soon. (. . .) Jõgever is said to have discovered health springs in the ground, and intends to set up a spa there. Initiatives like that are undoubtedly derived from grandiose visions. We now have to go to a store that is eight kilometers away. The road there leads through a forest, where one encounters very solitary and romantic spots. There, one can rest one's legs on a fallen log or on a rock and surrender the mind to pondering. There are a lot of strangers in that store, romantic ramblers among them. The product selection is wider than in our old store. Those of our men who aren't employed in Tartu sit on the stairs by the post office in their free time. The post office inspires majestic visions of postboys carrying horns and postal wagons, and causes one to think about the bond between the ages in general.*
   *I am reading* One Thousand and One Nights.

### ILLIMAR'S LETTER FROM OCTOBER 2000

*Honorable Chronicler!*
(. . .)
   *The post office closed down. The men now sit at the bus stop, because you have to sit somewhere. It is very romantic—to sit and*

*watch the lone bus driving away. You wonder where it is going
and whom it is taking with it. Melancholic daydreams that enno-
ble and refine undoubtedly come to mind when doing so. The men
do not sit there for long, of course. First of all, only four buses drive
through here each day, two in the one direction and two in the other. Secondly, there are young rascals who are up to no good there,
and it does not suit for full-grown men to sit with them. The men
are hardened, taciturn, drawn into themselves—genuine Nordic
types with a vast life going on in their heads.*

### DID YOU BELIEVE?

When the Republic of Estonia was restored, Poindexter started
to pose his question in a different form. Instead of asking: "Will
Estonia ever become free?" he now asked: "Did you believe that
the Estonian state would ever become free?" He still would never pose his question to the exact same individual twice. Alas,
Poindexter soon died, the poor man. Rumor had it that he was
the first AIDS victim among the "cavemen." People would only
whisper about the disease during the Soviet era and even at the
beginning of the Estonian era, because it carried a certain stigma.
As Poindexter was no more, I started to ask people whether they
had believed Estonia would be independent again myself, just
for fun. I can permit myself such a question, especially when I
am wearing my purple Boss suit. Then, people find the question is downright erotic. For the most part, people say yes. The
differences lie in how confidently and enthusiastically someone
pronounces their "yes." For the most part, the prettier the woman is, the more genuinely she believed it. Despite being already
at the age at which it becomes difficult to determine women's
ages, a few of those who answer "yes" seem suspiciously young.
And a couple of the young women who have expressed ecstati-
cally how very much they believed in it had not even been *born*
at that time. When I direct their attention to this fact, they are
hurt: can the lack of a material body hold them back from believing? Do I, then, not believe in the astral soul; in karma?
And, in general—how can I be so "flat"?

Actually, there is also a great deal of evasiveness when I pose
my question. Be the social group what it may—I am interested

in the cognitive side of the matter. One must not confuse desire and belief. Most people *desired* freedom, that much is certain—but how could it be believed? Fine, one could have believed that justice would triumph in the long run, as so *"speaks Logos"* (as I discussed before in relation to the Learned Friend). Here, I mean justice in the sense of "the right to exist." But still—*whose* justice? Everyone's own cannot triumph simultaneously; justices compete. Such can certainly be seen from history. How many nations have disappeared? Did justice not apply to them? And why should we leave out the plant and animal kingdoms? Didn't the dinosaurs have the right to survive? Perhaps history's greatest injustice transpired sixty million years ago? No, the dinosaurs did not have *Logos* . . .

Miller believes that people are not lying when they say they believed the Estonian state would come. They believe that they believed. Miller now honors our group with his presence regularly, still doing so in a way as to not leave the impression of wanting to become a permanent member of it.

The topic of belief has been discussed at The Cave several times, too. I remember—sitting at the table were Lumepart, Sõrgats, Vanasaba, Endel, Tobi, Alja, and Maša, among others.

"I don't know whether I believed or not," Lumepart granted.

"Yes, but did you *think* about it?" Tobi inquired. "I really hope you thought about it intensely."

"Well, I certainly did *think* about it on occasion, but it's not as if I thought anything precisely," Lumepart said, and shrugged.

Sõrgats asked how he liked the Estonian state. Lumepart admitted that he did not especially like it, to tell the truth. This came to me as a surprise: Lumepart had a reputation of being a man of conviction, and had refused government commissions during the Soviet era.

"How's that—we *do* have freedom now, don't we?" Sõrgats insisted.

"Well, we *do*," Lumepart said, "but what am I supposed to do with that?"

"What do you mean—you can go and paint what you want, right?"

"You know, I've been able to do that the whole *time*."

"But you still couldn't paint the tricolor flag, could you?" Sõrgats pressed.

"Ah," Lumepart sighed and dismissed the question with a wave. "Why would I want to paint the tricolor? Other color combinations are beautiful, too. You know, back in the day, I would do a painting, it would be bought, and I'd lived modestly for half a year on that. I was able to travel! I saved money and went abroad once every other year for a while. And how, you ask? With some kind of tourist group, as they were. I visited Spain, Greece, Italy—I traveled through all of the places that have something to do with painting. I went to all of the museums there. But now, I can't travel anywhere anymore. No one's buying anything. The museums aren't buying, either. I go help out some old crones that I know on occasion, mowing hay, cutting down trees. I earn myself bread money like that. I still have the strength for it, luckily."

"Do you not have a sense of patriotism, then?" someone asked.

"Well, how don't I? Of course I do—who doesn't? But why does this state not enable me to do anything, then? How long can you call into a forest that doesn't echo back at all?" Lumepart asked solemnly.

## ILLIMAR'S NEW ATTEMPT

Illimar's former (abstract or contemplative) manner of handling life's phenomena had been put on the back burner over the years. He certainly hadn't turned into a social activist, but he no longer mapped out romantic phenomena in time and space as intensively as he did during the Soviet era. This is understandable. You can imagine that if one's everyday environment is exceedingly criminogenic, then he or she does not have an exceptional appetite for watching crime shows. You do not need to read others' lovey-dovies if you yourself have true love. And if your own life is a fairy tale, then you have no use for imagined fairy tales. Life had momentum in liberated Estonia: people's eyes glimmered, and the proximity of the Promised Land was inspiring. Illimar saw his hopes coming to fruition, believing that it would last that way forever. And then he married, on top of it all.

However, an intellectual's primary orientation does not vanish just like that. When the dust had settled and life bobbed back into a more-or-less accustomed form, Illimar found that he had to deal with "normal" things again. For him, "normal" meant the advance of idealism and sublime principles. He began incubating in his mind once again his erstwhile plan to found a center that would research romantic manifestations of life in the broadest sense—the same plan over which Captain Sidorov had once given him an earful.

Setting up the center should have been completely possible now. Although material and prose tended to dominate in life, there was also freedom, so no one could set ideological restrictions on Illimar or threaten him. Illimar wrote to me: *The Center must be completed. It is necessary for Estonia's future. Otherwise, our momentum will diminish and we, as a project of a miraculous nation, will come under doubt.*

One difficult issue was, of course, money. It was not easy to find, as the state was poor and there was not enough to go around for everything. Officials at the Ministry of Culture heard his case, smiled, and promised to help him file the necessary documents—meaning place the center on the business register. No funding was given, however, with the justification that the center was a hobby and, at the very most, belonged to the municipal sphere. No one on the level of national governmental bodies would dare to support the International Center for the Study of Romantic Phenomena if it would have to be done at the expense of pensioners, free school lunches, or AIDS support centers. ("We don't fund UFOs"—that is how one fledgling official put it.) Illimar then decided to turn towards different funding sources. He submitted an application to the recently established Integration Foundation, describing how his center would help to further the integration of Russians and Estonians (among other points, he quoted Merezhkovsky's novel about Peter the Great and the poem "The Scythians" by Alexander Blok). However, those at the Integration Foundation regarded him as a wolf in sheep's clothing; as a raging nationalist. The right foundation he would need could not be found at the Cultural Endowment of Estonia, because the Center would have nothing to do with literature or folk culture. (Someone recommended that Illimar submit an application to the Athletic Fund and associate the project with pole vaulting: a sport where "idealism is to be found" in the athlete's physical arc.) Some interest was shown by private investors (as many of those as Estonia had), but foremost as a work of art. One very wealthy oil-transit businessman replied to Illimar that he would agree to buy the Center when it is finished one day, and to hang it up on his wall.

It seemed impossible to find money in Estonia. Then, one well-known, bow-tied individual recommended (possibly as a joke) that Illimar turn towards the European Union. Estonia had just become a member, and why not take advantage of the fact? The bow-tied man said persuasively and mysteriously while puffing on his pipe: "Hmmm, they've given money for much more fantastical goals, hmmm!"

Illimar spent almost a quarter of a year drafting the application. He tried to do so independently at first, keeping his nose to the grindstone and gritting his teeth, but was still unable to fill out all of the blanks. Finally, he gave in and looked for someone who earned a living with such work. The project's application ended up being seventy pages long. After its submission, Illimar had to answer a host of inquiries in order to dispel suspicions of his undertaking being nationalistic or promoting the nation-state. Illimar emphasized that his focus was on global intellect on a higher level, and that nationality was just a link in a long chain.

Ultimately, he did receive money from the regional support fund, which also issued funding to wooded-meadow cultivators, organic-food producers, and sheep farmers. Specifically, the money came from a sub-fund that was meant for preserving witches' healing methods, magicians' spells, recording the "evil eye" on film, and other phenomena of local cultures.

*Just imagine*, Illimar wrote. *I believed that what I was involved in was a pan-European cause that concerns all of humanity, but now it turns out that it is on the level of woolen socks.*

Yet his spirits were lifted by the fact that money was given for it at all, of course. He walked around town and chose a site for his center. He was confident that things were all wrapped up. At that time, I received the following letter from him.

### ILLIMAR'S LETTER FROM JULY 2004

*Honorable Chronicler!*
*(...) The European Union—can there be anything more magnificent, anything more loftily idealistic than that idea born of a blaze of thought?! Its soaring flight is utterly intoxicating. I do not know how practical the idea is—meaning how far down that road you can go, for it is hard to believe that nations might be capable of relinquishing their national egos that have formed over the course of centuries or even millennia. Yet at least they have signaled that they are aspiring towards those ends, and that is indeed what is important. It signifies an attempt to transcend the bestial germ within us and become an enlightened subject. Once again, we see how intellect attacks dark matter—how a wave of sublime principle lifts man up onto its crest. Estonia must be in the European Union in order to gain entrance to the great feast of romanticism. We have no other choice.*

*The euro as a currency is very romantic—it has my unreserved support. It is once again the fruit of a powerful vision; something that has arisen out of ingenuity, out of a flash of intellect. We must get into that zone. Then, we will be as tough as the Germans or the French— our money will be just as good as their money. The eurozone is beautiful! NATO is beautiful! The fifth article—romanticism squared. How lovely Pria[33] is! Stimulus funds—a garden of wonders!*

Alas, Illimar reveled in this prematurely. The development of information technology crossed it all out. The Internet was to blame. Illimar did not have the patience to wait, and had put the Center's web page up already before there was any center to speak of. He posted his written works on it in addition to program-based public appeals. I doubt that he reviewed all of the texts again before posting them. And so it happened that his article comparing Hitler and Stalin was put forth for the whole world to read. The Russian website gen.ru directed attention towards this almost instantly (which means they had been keeping an eye on Illimar). The article was called a "manifestation of fascism in the Baltics" and an "attempt to rewrite history." This would have meant nothing, because everyone knows that gen.ru is a propaganda tool and that the Russian special services are behind it. However, Illimar's writing was soon discussed in German intellectual circles, and was even summarized on their cultural portal signandsight.com. The reaction was condemning almost without exception, as even Western left-wingers found that Illimar was glorifying Nazism. The world did not understand his expansive and multifarious soul, which could simultaneously have room for a respect for Hitler's inarguable, yet degenerated charisma on the one hand, and a love for Jews on the other. A number of unpleasant, one-sided, and very malicious pieces were published, which brought up (among other topics) the Estonian Waffen-SS and the monument to WWII veterans in Tori; even the Latvian legionnaires' march was mixed into things. The relevant Estonian officials dismissed these, asserting that we have the freedom of opinion, and that the specific piece in no way justifies Hitler's crimes; rather, it analyzes how he managed to deceive so many people. But who would listen to us! Our tiny voice remained feeble. (Miller remarked almost casually that Estonia needs a propaganda ministry.)

The case is truly strange: specifically the Germans, who once allowed themselves to have the wool pulled over their eyes by a man like Hitler—so much so that it really is even ridiculous and pitiful to see in hindsight—are incapable or unwilling to understand now when someone else finds even a smidgen of something attractive in his personality. What is the logic there?

Naturally, the matter found its way to Brussels. The funding designated for Illimar was discontinued (although a small portion of it had probably been paid in the beginning), and it was then announced that the entire project had been declared unacceptable, because "the European Union cannot support the establishment of a center for Nazism."

For Illimar, the only slightly positive aspect of the entire incident was that his "collection" expanded. Yes—even in that situation, my learned friend maintained his intellectual honesty and

loyalty to his main fondness, which was the recording of exceptionally spiritual manifestations. Namely, he added the German
nation's guilt to his list of romantic phenomena. He wrote:

*On the other hand, the Germans are admirable regardless. Is
there a single other nation in history known to have been capable of
guilt* in corpore *and to such a great extent? It is already a metaphys-
ical, almost an ontological showing of remorse. The fact that one
nation is capable of feeling such shame and contrition demonstrates
their greatness of intellect, their spiritual finesse, and the shape of
their system of conscience overall. An indecent people, like an indecent person, is unable to feel shame for a longer period of time. Is
there, for example, a contrition of the Russian people for having an-
nihilated tens of nations in Siberia? Is there contrition of the Turks
for the Armenians and the Kurds? People write nowadays that it
should be time for the Germans to end their contrition; that they
have already served penance enough. However, I believe that for
them, it will never be over for good. In their collective subconscious,
their* arche, *this repentance is merging into tragedy and heroic self-
sacrifice, is completely bafflingly and illogically getting blended with
Siegfried. Perhaps they do not really want to get over this contrition.*

Still, Illimar was disappointed in the European Union from
then on; or, more precisely, in the spirit that wafted through the
corridors of Brussels:

*Stalin's corpse is gradually decomposing in their closet there.
The spurs of his riding boots can be seen through the crack in Stras-
bourg's door. Measuredness, bureaucracy, extreme loyalty, zombie-
like adherence, thunder and flash have been spread over everything.*

For a while, he attempted to set up his center virtually, via
the web page, but only some Palestinians and Somali pirates
(with whom Illimar did not feel himself to be on the same
wavelength) latched onto his initiative.

Poor Illimar! He had been sure that new prospects would
open up in his sphere of interest together with the new era. He
indeed never recovered from that blow.

Six months later, I received one of his most embittered letters.

*Honorable Chronicler!*
(. . .) *Everything is brimming with Harry Potter. He is certainly*

*talked about in the Book of Revelations. Harry Potter is the fifth horseman—the one who will cover the world in darkness. Humanity is most definitely slipping into darkness. The old tribal thing, the age of collective phantoms is returning. The Internet initiated a new manner of community, and social media is leading it forward. Once, long ago in the early ages of humanity, the individual was unable to be alone, because otherwise he would have died. He had to live among his tribe out of necessity. Everything took place in full view of everyone in tribal life; it was impossible to hide anything from anyone else, and this was regarded as normal. As life's material aspect developed, so too did privacy, bit by bit. Free people already had it in antiquity, although to a lesser extent than we generally believe. Privacy became available to wider groups in the late modern period, when goods manufacturing and the construction of small and relatively cheap city apartments increased. Since then and until lately, the tendency has been unidirectional—always moving towards increased privacy. When insularity acquired unprecedented proportions in the meanwhile, it played its own part in the disappearance of faith in God. People no longer felt that they were brothers and sisters—rather, everyone stood separately from one another both physically and spiritually. That era is now coming to an end; individualism is receding, and collectivity is forming in a new dimension. But this is not happening through intellectual substance, on the spiritual level, and likewise not mediated by collective ownership like in a phalanstery, but instead as some kind of a perverse extension of body and mind. Daily life and material things are its sphere of manifestation. All of that which until now had been draped in a veil of decorum (digestion, for example) is gradually becoming public and observable with mutual pleasure. New apartments do not have separate bathrooms, kitchens, or toilets—everything is put together into one immense space. This is regarded as completely normal. Similarly, every person has unlimited opportunities to post his or her entire intimate and digestive lives onto the Internet. While one can be fined for making a puddle or a pile on the street, no one is banned from squatting in the virtual park. And so, everyone is indeed up-to-date with what someone else is eating and how their bowel movements are going. Everything is regressing to that. It has come full-circle. One level is superficially more sophisticated, but this is a mere question of technology—the content is old and the nature of the thing has not changed. Everything is done together again, like in a tribe.*

*A few lines about the WORD. The exchangeability of thought; its severance from the thinker; its alienation onto a stone tablet, parchment, or paper was undoubtedly related to insulation in the more general and philosophical sense, being both one of its causes and its outcome. The intermediate era of written word was simultaneously an era of isolation, or rather one form of its manifestation. Yet, the word itself might not necessarily signify isolation as such. Even today, we can see how that very same word also enables a state of coexistence. The word has been recycled; into a BLABBER cycle. That being said, it is important to understand the kind of conditional degree that the language of the given era has; how metaphoric it is, how circuitously it speaks. The stronger the given aspect is represented, the greater the isolation. In contrary, when the word is one with the person who brings it forth (the speaker or whoever types it into a keyboard) without a feeling of embarrassment or (false) shame, then the word is not isolating in the very least, but rather a primarily uniting force. That kind of a word comes closer to a horse's snort and other vocalizations based on life-communications connected to the body. You can search for parasites in the hides of a thousand-head human herd using a smartphone. The great tendency today is indeed for the word to recede from the conveyable sphere, and move into the direct one-to-one oral sphere. The fact that a word is written externally (as a cell-phone text message, for example) does not mean that it is also that by essence. The word is coming back into the folds of its former, primeval syncretism, where it was accompanied by music, dance, visual art, and theater. In connection, it is impossible not to notice how dance has come to the foreground in the newer era. Not usually as folk dance, which has many sundry functions; nor as social, competitive, or other dance customs; not to mention ballet; but first and foremost as every possible kind of free-form, everyday dance, or even as DANCE as such. Dance communicates and expresses the most general of tendencies, doing so directly. So it was in tribal dances around a fire. Even now, people with traditional lifestyles dance quite often, and can express in dance almost everything that is associated with their everyday lives (including national independence). Of course, they do not dance very complicated things, the point of which might be difficult to convey precisely (Kant's categorical imperative). They do not need to do so, because their lives do not contain such complexities, and the dancers themselves do not think in a complicated manner. Dance communicates feelings, lusts, desires. Dance's wide dispersal in the modern world is no coincidence. Its spread has very obviously happened at the expense of the word (I mean the exact, articulated, and theoretical word); at the expense of the brilliant tool of progress, as Settembrini would say. The dispersal of dance is also accompanied by a neoprimitive psyche. A man writhes and points to his throat (meaning he wants to drink), he quivers and points to his loins—it is clear what he needs, etc. Just like in the prehistoric era. I am not claiming that people were very much more complicated in the intervening centuries. However, the ideal was still the development of spiritual capacity and the refining of the psyche. No longer. In previous centuries, people sang beneath windows and wrote polished love letters; now, you can get by with a lot simpler. Opening up the self is more important than self-enhancement. Dance and social media will meet at a certain point. A merry neotribalism will rule.*

 *Yours,*

*Learned Friend*

### MANGLUS'S STRUGGLES

A true creator who has been struck by setbacks in his personal life will usually find solace in work. Manglus also buried himself in work after his unsuccessful entry into politics, starting to develop his Center even more vigorously. The latter was perfected more and more under his leadership, and amassed fame—people in the cultural world no longer *spoke* of anything other than the Center. Unusual to the Estonian language, people had even begun to capitalize it (which old linguists protested in vain), and it had become almost as important a part of Estonian society as the National Opera and Ballet Theatre or the National Male Choir. Foreign diplomats were taken to the Center and state figures would mention it in their ceremonial speeches when listing off the achievements of the new era of independence (although admittedly, this was customarily at the end of the list).

In February, when the award juries had finished their work yet again, it turned out that Manglus had been given a national prize for his large solo exhibition (he organized one every year)—the most important state recognition that one could receive before an award for lifetime achievement. (The latter is given when said person is assumed to have already accomplished the greater part of his or her main work, which no one believed in Manglus's case.) After that, an art publisher released a lengthy monograph about him. This had only happened to one other Estonian artist prior to his fiftieth birthday, but it had been during the Stalin era and the order had come from higher up.

As I mentioned before, Manglus employed talented people at his Center, and favored them. A few of his protégés were indeed already spreading their wings. Two of his young assistants, Lellep and Helonainen, had become outstanding artists, who were already accumulating their own admirers and followers. One can probably say that both young men even possessed—in one form or another—a spark of original genius. Unfortunately, this became fateful for them. Manglus tolerated and even loved the talented, but reserved genius for himself. He appeared to be afraid that Lellep and Helonainen would grow to become his competitors, and he decided to get rid of them before it was too late. Manglus was able to push Lellep away by falling back on disciplinary rules, as the latter had a romantic drama with his wife Ave (who worked as an assistant at the same Center). Having come to believe rumors that his wife had been unfaithful to him, Lellep had a mental breakdown and jumped out of a sixth-floor window, but survived. And what's more—he promptly ran back up to the sixth floor (the elevator was out of order) and punched his wife in the face. Manglus said he could not accept a man hitting a woman on the Center's premises, and fired Lellep on the spot. At the very moment he said those words (according to folklore), Lellep's legs broke with a loud crack—those very same legs he had just used to climb up the stairs. (But maybe he *didn't* climb them, but rather flew? Who knows, who knows . . .)

Helonainen had no sins to seize upon, and so was sent off quietly, under the pretense of "layoffs." At the same time, Manglus immediately hired someone else for an analogous position, but he knew that Helonainen would not utilize his legal right to apply for it preferentially, because he was a delicate person. Helonainen even gave interviews on the affair to one of our rival publications, but they were unable to whip up a scandal because Helonainen's answers were so restrained and humorous. He left the impression of having a complete understanding of the motives for Manglus's behavior, and even seemed to justify them. Next to the story was a picture of Manglus and Helonainen sitting in a boat on some body of water (allegedly Lake Pühajärv) and fishing.

Having rid himself of possible competitors, the "chief" employed two young go-getter women in their places — Mirva and Tonnensen. The latter was relatively unknown, but seemed quite normal and peaceful. Her girlfriend Mirva, who never removed her sunglasses (which had massive plastic frames and green lenses), was more rowdy, pretentious, and loved more than anything else to talk about self-colonization. She worked at the Center for three quarters of a year, after which she moved abroad, remarking everywhere she went that she had been associated with the Center while simultaneously criticizing it. She ultimately coaxed Tonnensen away, and they moved to London.

This was a completely unprecedented occurrence. Up until then, women had never betrayed Manglus — they remained utterly loyal. Now, however, these two had wanted to lean upon him to rise in prominence, make careers for themselves, and then fly off to who-knows-where. This kind of emancipation of women certainly left a mark on Manglus's egomania. Still, life went on, and even quite satisfyingly. Manglus was able to hide his feelings, and when he was at The Cave or out in public, he left the impression of being a carefree person whose affairs were advancing onward and who was gripping his fate by the horns. Then, however, the scandal broke out.

A gossip journalist nicknamed Mink — a man who was not exceptionally talented and had quite the shady background; you could almost even call him a *filthy* sort of character — had been mercilessly beaten up one night.

The chance passerby who reported the incident to the police wrote in the witness report that Mink had been held by an arm and a leg and swung back and forth until he had gained a

good deal of momentum, and then rammed against the wall of
the Journalists' House. And this had been done several times
in succession (it had even set off the building's alarm system).
Mink was taken to the intensive-care ward. The injuries were
considerable—ruptures, fractures, brain damage. What was
strange was that right from the very beginning, people started
to connect the matter to Manglus. Manglus, nevertheless, had
not even been in Tallinn at the time of the incident, but was on
a trip for hydrotherapy (doing an "enema round," as he said).
To claim that he could have been able to physically participate
in the beating would have seemed outright absurd to us, his
companions. Manglus and Mink were acquaintances, and he
did not hide the fact. On the face of things it would, of course,
have been difficult to connect him (as an aristocrat) to someone
like Mink, because the latter was a lowlife, a journalistic alley
cat, and generally untrustworthy. But here, I would recall an
odd facet of Manglus's personality. He socialized at an exceptionally large amplitude, hanging out with a very broad spec-
trum of characters. There is nothing strange or deplorable about
this in and of itself. When Manglus was just launching on his
starry flight, people believed that such acquaintances were the
first stormy gusts of a person's rich nature; a young man wanting to try out all sorts of options. Yet, these tendencies of his
did not pass with youth, but rather deepened. In his case, this
happened through filters of consciousness and not one-to-one,
as such. Manglus certainly did not enjoy physical filth as a phenomenon in and of itself. By socializing with such people, he
appeared to be saying: I'm so tough that I can even hang out
with this kind of trash; none of it will rub off on me. I can dine
at the presidential palace, then disappear into a den, but be back
at work like a proper bourgeois once again the next morning.

We in the "cavemen" circles were very sympathetic to such
pendular oscillations; but it was indeed a little hard to accept
the fact that Manglus was drawn "downward"—towards the de-
tritus—more than he was "upward." There were periods when
Manglus appeared to be highly enticed by the gutter—his wal-
lowings there were described in lurid colors. It wasn't unheard
of for him to submerge himself in Tallinn's dregs for several

days, mixing with were barefooted squatters from the Kopli ghettos, riffraff poets who would constantly beg for beer money, degenerate former top athletes who were involved in racketeering at the beginning of the new Estonian age, recidivists recently freed from prison, and other outcasts, and taking part in their orgies. He was not afraid of criminals and enjoyed spending time with them. He was able to mimic the behavior and speech of repeat-offender criminals so well that it sometimes made me queasy. I had heard that a true criminal is angered most by someone who is not actually a criminal, but pretends to be one—clothing himself in a stranger's feathers. Manglus loved risk, but was not crazy. Although he was conspicuously well built and had practiced martial arts in his youth, it was obvious that things could have taken a tragic turn for him at times. I was once witness to such an occasion. (Manglus sometimes loved to drag his "cave acquaintances" along to the orgies in order to shock them, enjoying the discomfiture of the artists and bohemians when they ended up in the company of criminals and whores.) As soon as Manglus noticed that the men were starting to eye him suspiciously, he would stealthily give me the sign for "let's get out of here."

When we inquired about his joke-life, he would giggle and answer evasively that "you can get a good thrashing there."

As a result of such contacts, it wasn't uncommon for odd characters to show up in the waiting room of his office in the Center's headquarters; people whose manner and appearance would make the sexy secretary (Manglus always had very sexy and very smart secretaries, and as an admirer of the Bond films, he would call them "Moneypennies") start gasping for air and searching for the security company's alarm button beneath the desk. These kinds of "cellar types" would show up because Manglus had once stuck his elegant business card with reddish-gold lettering into their palm, saying: "Stop by whenever you have time!" (Although he would, of course, be snickering to himself: *Who the hell am I inviting—it's absolutely impossible; isn't it fantastic!*) When it then turned out that the arrival was not mistaken, the secretary would wrinkle her nose but nevertheless dutifully inform Manglus on the internal line that he had a guest. The arrival had usually gone into a cold sweat by that time, as he had expected to find himself in a partially-blackened-out warehouse, a shed, or the backroom of a shop. Instead there was a chic, spacious, white interior that Manglus had furnished according to his own taste, placing a few bizarre and expensive objects in it as well. The guest would already be getting ready to turn tail when the secretary would ask demandingly: "Your name?" And would report "Yoska," "Pobi," or "Shura" into the telephone receiver—whatever it happened to be on that occasion. Manglus would answer simply and plainly: "Yes, I'm expecting him. Please direct him in ... or, no! I'll come out myself." And the secretary would see her adored boss (although *all* of those Moneypennies adored him) reach both hands out towards that criminal, take the man's filthy paw between his noble palms, shake it, and speak warm words to him. After that, Manglus would ask the man to step in back, additionally ordering the secretary from the doorway to serve them coffee and V.S.O.P. cognac.

No matter how long they usually sat for, the arrival's initial nerve would not be restored entirely—even in spite of the warm reception. However, Pobi or Shura would always leave with a particular self-satisfied look upon his face. A few would also try to hit on Moneypenny before going. She would gather up her strength and smile sourly. Usually, she would open up a window after the visitor left in order to air out the room, and would take deep breaths to calm herself down. Soon enough, Manglus—radiating with geniality—would appear from his office, embrace her, and proceed to other ways of touching. Ultimately, the secretary would usually undergo a nervous breakdown and cry.

As I have mentioned earlier, Manglus was not a handsome man—*far* from a "matinée idol" and more like a good, decent average. However, his abnormal lifestyle can in no way be said to reflect his appearance. Quite the opposite—Manglus looked younger and fresher than his years. There wasn't the slightest trace of sagging flesh or a face devastated by early wrinkling, nor a breath that stunk of vodka, decayed teeth, unclipped fingernails, or other signs of letting himself go. And as for his manner of behavior, instead of just going about his job perfunctorily—his only wish being to quickly overcome a hangover by curing like with like and getting back to "den-life" again, as developed boozehounds frequently get in the habit of doing—his colleagues would encounter a clever, dynamic, and businesslike man, who gladly takes problems head-on and is also capable of solving them. It's no wonder, then, that many refused to believe the nasty tales told about him.

And so, he had been seen together with Mink—going or coming somewhere, occasionally also discussing something at the Sparrow Café. Witnesses said that Mink's "trademark," his officer's field bag, had been lying on the ground near the base of the table.

What business were they conducting? I suppose they merely chatted about this and that, Mink doing so seriously and Manglus only making it look as if he were serious. Implications that there might have been something homosexual going on didn't seem credible. Of course, Manglus might have given everything a try, might have tested all possible options, to assert himself more solidly as a prince of life. The fact that he was able to get so many women, and so freely at that, could possibly steer his ideas (being a mobile-spirited person) in the opposite direction. But *Mink*? If it had been some flower-scented ballet dancer or a fop wearing a peacock feather, then maybe. But how could a man like him have a filthy lover like that? It wouldn't have occurred to anyone. And if it *had* turned out to be true, then they would have squeaked. But wouldn't that very aspect have been entertaining to Manglus, as it would have been congruent with the main trend in his world of desires—the greater the contrast, the sweeter it was? Nevertheless, I had gotten the impression that Manglus's "palette" lacked a gay aspect; he did not possess the given passions. He would indeed make jokes in that direction at times (once at an exhibition, for example, in front of a painting depicting Greek boys), but it was casual and just for fun—in order to thicken the ambiguous fog that surrounded his persona. (Sadism was a different story. S&M was indeed something he was into, in my opinion.)

It is also difficult to believe that Mink "set him up with women," as some said. What kinds of women might Mink have been able to bring Manglus that he could not already get himself?

He could even meet those muddy nightingales, those unwashed midday-fairies in his dens to his heart's desire.

One other circumstance seems to be more significant. Word had it that Mink used to be an informer, a snitch, or a "rat." And maybe he was at that time, too. There has been public speculation (although very rarely) in Estonia over whether analogous figures exist in the new regime or not. Simple-minded people have expressed the belief that if you have independence and your own country, then there is no need for secret services and their aids. But how could you get by without the snitches?! Order would slip away. Some have likewise claimed that a person who was an informer in the previous regime cannot be one in the new era. As if you should presuppose that an informer has some ideological worldview, as a consequence of which he or she is solely capable of running snitching errands for a government that represents only a certain political view! How naive! Firstly, snitching does presuppose particular personal qualities, but they involve general ethics and not politics or ideology. Secondly, the very fact that someone used to be a snitch can be used to blackmail them in the new regime, forcing them to become informants again by threatening to make their earlier snitching public. In doing so, the regime might not even reward such persons with trips abroad or privileged phone connections, not to mention paying them a salary—as was the case when the KGB recruited collaborators in earlier times.

Manglus paid these rumors no heed and refused to comment. Although he had never really had the patience to deal with journalists—not even when they were orbiting around him and brownnosing him—he was now surly with them (if not coarse), even though he tried to hide it (he simply did not give them physical access to him). When he talked to us, he would say that journalists needed to be "shown their place," and that the younger ones are much more cheeky than they used to be and do not know "what is what" at all. He would have Moneypenny ream journalists out. ("Do you have any *idea* whom you are *dealing* with?! You could learn a little cultural history before you start calling!") Manglus was confident that the matter would calm down.

And the rumors would probably have faded had the following not happened. Mink was lying in the intensive-care ward, and one of the nurses on night duty claimed that Manglus had asked her to pull the plug on Mink! The story was published on the front page of a gossip paper. Before long, it turned out that the woman was not entirely trustworthy. She had been accused of fraud in an earlier case (of conning money from the elderly), although she had been found not guilty. She started working at the emergency room a couple of months earlier, and before that, she had been unemployed or receiving welfare. Understandably, there was a suspicion that she had *gotten* a job at the hospital with some particular goal, and that she was now surfacing with such a confession, as she hoped to draw attention to herself or . . . was carrying out someone's order. True, she had a diploma as proof of intermediate medical education. However, our investigative journalists soon discovered that no one of that name had ever studied at the former Tartu School of Medicine. Consequently, the diploma had been forged. The journalists also uncovered that Manglus and that nurse (she was, by the way, a highly attractive thirty-four-year-old redhead) had been seen together . . . at the Värska Sanatorium.

Manglus himself refused to comment on the matter and didn't make any effort to take the given woman to court for defamation, claiming that he didn't want to get his hands dirty. Even at that stage, the Mink-saga would soon have fizzled out into nothingness, overshadowed by newer and more interesting events, because there was no evidence against Manglus. But then, the woman herself disappeared! And not only did she disappear, but in a way that her long limbs were sticking out of a dumpster in the Tiskre subdivision one morning. They said the street cleaner who discovered her nearly fainted. Now the case became very serious for Manglus, because he was unable to submit a convincing alibi for the night on which the nurse had supposedly disappeared. Tens of females indeed surfaced to offer Manglus an alibi of having been at their place at the time. It was a moving sight, but Manglus didn't accept their help. Two semi-secret societies claimed that Manglus had been attending their meetings and taken part in all kinds of rituals, but neither of those societies were especially respected, so Manglus denied his connection to them.

If anyone had asked me whether I believed Manglus might have been capable of doing anything to someone like Mink if he had threatened his career, then I would have replied with a heavy heart that—yes, I do. Manglus would have pulverized him. Both him and the nurse.

Mink regained consciousness, but it became evident that his mind was no longer in any kind of shape—the bangs against the wall of the Journalists' Building really had been quite powerful. He was no longer able to read or write, and wasn't fit to be a witness in the opinion of the court doctors.

There was intense speculation in the media as to what Mink would have had to say. Someone claimed that he had been in possession of lists of former KGB collaborators. And that he had intended to publish them in his paper just then. Yet this allegation was crap, because where would Mink have gotten those lists? Even if he *himself* had been a snitch, that wouldn't necessarily mean that he knew others. The documents in question had been transported to Moscow by then.

But it turned out that a few of those lists *were* still available, albeit in an indirect form. The Lithuanians had been more foresighted than the Estonians, and had managed to make copies of their own analogous documents in time. They were not published in full, in the interests of national reconciliation, although comments were indeed made in one institute's publications. The names of non-Lithuanians and foreigners were also present in the Lithuanians' papers, and Manglus's was among them. It didn't take long for that information to reach Estonia. Journalists swooped down on the materials, catching a whiff of blood. They were ultimately disappointed, however, because Manglus was barely mentioned, and was praised as both an artist and a person (!) at that. It couldn't be read between the lines that there was a direct connection between him and the special services. Once again, it appeared that the case would be left at that. But not long afterward, a new public scandal erupted. This offered nothing special to those who were thirsty for Manglus's blood; but still, the case itself was extremely juicy—almost like a soap opera.

The matter concerned a woman with whom Manglus had been involved at one time. We remembered her well. Maige had studied theater in Moscow. She was a sunny girl, small, slim and blond, lovely and intelligent (she gave off the impression of being twenty-seven at the age of forty, when we had last seen her). At that time, Maige had been married to a Russian-Jewish dissident a good deal older than her, whom she had meet in Moscow circles. Maige cooked him meals, corrected his manuscripts that spoke about life in the labor camps and were published under a pseudonym in the West (they have also recently been published in Estonian), slept with him, and raised their child. Maige took care of the dissident when he started to become feeble (each year spent in a prison camp counts as two for most people), saying she did so out of a sense of mission. People snickered, but were also a little jealous. Maige seemed out-of-bounds as a girlfriend. Manglus, of course, felt that he had to attempt to ensnare Maige; he was allured by such difficult tasks. Maige was Manglus's lover for several years. The dissident was already very ill at that time, and soon exited this world. Maige's relationship with Manglus ended a year after her husband's funeral. The girl had apparently come to realize that she was just one trophy in a professional hunter's collection, and that it would not shape into anything lasting. Maige had her own Jewish ancestors, and departed Estonia in the early eighties. She first went to Israel, then to Germany, ultimately making it to America, where she worked at a radio station for a few years before going on to be active in the film world—where she apparently found success. Now, that very same Maige Dolukhanov had written an open letter to the Estonian media, in which she said she had been a KGB informer for a long time, and that she had already been recruited in Moscow.

"I had to speak about this at last in order to find peace of mind before I go to stand before the Almighty"—such is how she ended the letter.

People didn't believe her at first. Some thought that Maige's "confession" had been borne of a playful post-menopausal craving, or a lust for revenge. *But revenge against whom?* some asked with a shrug. It couldn't be against Manglus, could it? Some said that Maige "had a few screws loose."

Talk of Manglus's KGB past picked up new momentum; several articles were published. Nevertheless, it seemed to me that the authors themselves did not take their accusations seriously, either; rather, they were taking advantage of a chance to raise hell and take jabs at a celebrity. Manglus and Maige had concealed their relationship—only a few lone individuals from the "cavemen" knew about it, even. Oh, all the stuff that was getting dredged up now! We were able to read, for example, that they would walk down opposite sides of the street from each other, or that "one followed slightly behind." When they went to a concert at the National Opera House, they sat in separate places—sometimes one was in the auditorium and the other on a balcony. They stood casually behind each other in line for refreshments at intermission in order to exchange a few words in a whisper, but did not risk sitting at the same table. Afterward, they would arrive at Manglus's atelier in separate taxis (Maige's always stopping a hundred meters away). Countless other similar claims were also made—what important details!

Those were good days for the media in general. The public was interested in a story's psychological and philosophical aspects. Had the girl been the dissident's partner solely in order to keep an eye on him and report about it to state organs, or did she truly love the dissident and care for him selflessly? Is it possible to truly love someone without wanting anything in return or to otherwise benefit from it? What is the breadth of the human soul, and what can fit into it? Is it possible that Maige reported nothing about her own husband, and "compensated" for it with rich data on the man's acquaintances? Progressing logically: if she loved Manglus genuinely, then is it possible that she was simultaneously using the man as a springboard to reach the inner ring of the "cavemen" to collect information there? Does one rule out the other? Some even dared to speculate that KGB girls could still love genuinely, too; that their work and feelings were disconnected, like with male gynecologists.

(We are hardly likely to ever find out. I could look *dyadya* Valdur up and ask him, but I'm not sure whether he would say or not. Not that he *shouldn't*, but he would not say it on principle— that is his little revenge against the whole world. And how would

I find *dyadya* Valdur anyway? He last worked at the civil-defense headquarters. It was one of those places—a sinecure, where a portion of KGB officers bummed around after they retired. So, it was during the Soviet era; a couple of decades ago.)

I myself wrote a piece on the topic as well. The title was: "Emotional Life—the New and Old Currency." But Mahvalda changed it, thinking I might confuse people in the banking sphere by putting it that way. Instead, she replaced it with: "The Sexy Snitch's Feverish Love." I didn't protest—it *was* more hard-hitting.

Many caricatures of Manglus were published. He was labeled as the "Face of the Week," "The Loser," and other such names in newspaper columns. The press had already turned against him by that time, using a condescending and even derisive tone when writing about him. The puny, inept wordsmiths allowed themselves to have a merry time at his expense. Scores of details from his private life were hauled out into the daylight. I heard hints from colleagues at other publications that someone somewhere was telling editors to keep the case steadily "on the flame." They even called the affair a "precedent-setting case." Miller said it wasn't all really directed against Manglus personally. There was simply a need to teach some prominent person associated with the arts a lesson, and Manglus happened to pop up at the right moment. Why was this necessary? Miller also had a cynical theory about that. The higher-ups allegedly didn't want people to respect artists too much or to see them as one of their own, as it had been during the Singing Revolution. The artists' place in the nation's heart had to be taken over by the political forces designated for such a position—by the so-called "professionals"; the "clean-past" parties. This couldn't be done directly, as that would be noticed; rather, it was to be indirect—via the showmen, media stars, and pundits. Artists, on the other hand, were to be ghettoized in order to be portrayed as illusionists, cheap/buyable craftsmen, or clowns. They had to be given a negative branding for this to happen, and the Manglus affair was ideally suited for it. Let the people see that a cesspool lies behind their respectable appearances—that instead of dignity and idealism, there is only unprincipled hedonism. (If this kind of "master plan" did actually exist, then its architects were indeed behind the times, and all their efforts were for naught.)

What effect did these events have upon Manglus's reputation? Until then, he had been seen as a highly outstanding individual, moral and progressive. We, the "cavemen," knew better, but we didn't go around yelling it everywhere. In our closed circle, we were even able to appreciate his new escapades—they were certainly piquant. But how many *Feinschmeckers* do we really have here in Estonia? For the greater part of society, Manglus's ties to any kind of Mink were simply deplorable, and his reputation took a nosedive. He had undoubtedly had enemies before as well, because he had managed to offend quite a lot of people with his cold arrogance. And now, those persons lifted their heads.

As the Center was on the state budget, Manglus stepped down from its directorship when it was announced that he was a suspect in the case. His contract would have ended a year later, anyway.

Manglus was threatened with a lawsuit. This seemed impossible to us, and Manglus himself laughed about it—there had to be some way for him to get out of it. Doubtless he already thought he knew whom to call and what to do. And he most certainly made those calls and did those things. However, the lawsuit came regardless. What of it—Manglus went to court with a smile on his face. He was defended by the lawyer Karl Maiden—the same who had started going to The Cave just before Klaus's funeral. This was not the first time that Karl had taken part in such proceedings. His cases often became very famous afterward, and were even talked about abroad. As this involved a renowned individual, interest in the proceedings was above average; especially since shady circumstances were sprinkled into the mix. Some observers were indifferent to Manglus but not to the lawsuit itself, hoping for some sort of more general revelation to come out of it, and that a lesson would be taught to all of "them"—meaning the artists, who were demanding all kinds of special rights. Others in turn (and on the contrary) wished a harsh sentence upon Manglus because he had sullied the artistic community's good name, even though creative intellects were to be "left alone." A third group of people were generally displeased because they didn't want old affairs to be dug up, since "we *already* tend to overdo it with memory, anyway." And then there were also a number of lawyers who—being in the field—were not intrigued by the moral aspect of the story, but rather just its legal aspect.

To my dismay, the court hearing was open to the public and the courthouse was brimming with people. A few attendees were almost lightheartedly cheerful, as if they were convinced that there would be a quick end to the whole absurd affair. Others were solemn and distraught, while a third group feigned a blasé attitude. To my astonishment, Manglus, who would usually dress selectively and expensively (yet in an inconspicuous manner), was dressed up as an artist for the hearing, clothed as if for some kind of carnival. He wore a black velvet jacket; a reddish-gold scarf; tight dark-green pants, on the knees and seat of which were sewn brown leather patches (there were matching ones on his jacket elbows); shoes with upturned toes; and a "Rembrandt beret." (Where had he gotten ahold of them? Had he walked through a theater wardrobe before the hearing—together with some actress perhaps?) It was a poor choice—he should have dressed modestly or even penitently. On top of all of that, a curved pipe hung from the corner of Manglus's mouth; it was not lit, of course, but he did pretend to "puff" at it, complete with the corresponding thumb movements. He stuck the pipe into his breast pocket for the duration of the hearing.

He appeared to be enjoying his situation and answered the judge's questions succinctly and wittily, so at points it was hard for us to suppress our laughter. The prosecutor was a younger woman, severely gorgeous. Manglus was condescendingly amiable towards her, occasionally flirtatious, occasionally patronizing, nodding at the woman's accusations, correcting her grammar on a couple of occasions—in short, behaving like an internship advisor with his college student and not like a defendant.

The prosecutor spoke about Mink—a little orphan boy,

whose development was the fault of the Soviet regime. At the same time, she depicted Manglus as a heartless careerist who had been part of the *Nomenklatura* during the Soviet era, and who had also snuck his way into it in the Estonian era. She said he was a wolf in sheep's clothing who had no sympathy for those ideals for which the artistic community called the people to the barricades. It was absolutely crazy to listen to: they wanted to make a degenerate (who was now half-insane) into a national hero in court with the media's assistance, but wanted to paint a very unflattering picture of an artist.

Karl naturally shot down all of the prosecutor's accusations. However, she had a couple of trumps up her sleeve. For example, she proved that Manglus had probably been aware that Maige was an informer. Still, that point was irrelevant. Ultimately, everything still focused on Manglus's alibi for the night the nurse was stuffed into a dumpster. I will not rest upon the details. In short: Manglus had submitted his own version, but the prosecutor presented a witness who refuted the alibi. Manglus then sighed theatrically and said that he had underestimated the investigatory authorities, and that it seemed they had proven that they were able to hand difficult (!) tasks as well. And he presented his new alibi, which was confirmed by two witnesses. Why did he not state the correct alibi immediately? He simply *willed* it to be so. He was *above them*. Why had he not at least informed his lawyer about his plans? Because he was above *him*, too. In summary, it meant that he had knowingly issued a false statement and deceived the investigative authorities.

Lively discussion bubbled in the hallways during the break.

"Those journalists should be kept in check. You can't just let any old newshound douse you in slime!"

"But it can't be like that, either—everyone blowing the horns right away! We have a state based on the rule of law! Isn't everyone *equal* before that law, then?"

"Of course they are. But think about it—what'd we make our own country for, huh? While before, any commie or KGB skunk could pulverize you thanks to his connections, now, every scum journalist can do the very same—ahh, what's the world coming to?!"

"Regardless, you can't justify things arbitrarily. Goddamn it—are we in Europe or aren't we?"

"Of course we are, but our journalists appear to believe that they only have *freedom*, and have forgotten about responsibility. What Jannsen and Juhan Peegel[34] taught, that a journalist must be a small step ahead of the people—they haven't gotten that through their skulls yet."

"I admit that it's the dark side of our young democracy. But we shouldn't throw the baby out with the bathwater—a censor would be even worse."

"What should we do, then?"

"Every person has the right to reply to an article that defames him and restore his good name!"

"Heh heh heh, darlings—it appears you're not familiar with the laws of mass communication. When a negative shrapnel of information has been set in flight, then it's practically impossible to refute it. You can't restore a good name in full—some part of the slime will always be left on you."

And they carried on and on in the same spirit.

We were certain that Manglus would be found not guilty; in the worst case, he would be given a monetary fine. Manglus himself seemed to hold the greatest confidence in this, for when the judge began to read out the ruling, he seemed remarkably uninterested. Instead of listening with a submissive look on his face, his eyes were searching out someone in the audience, whom he waved to. When the judges sounded the verdict, "four months, one month of which will be actual shock incarceration, the remaining being conditional with a one-year probationary period," the meaning behind them apparently did not sink in, because he snickered condescendingly.

After the ruling was made known, Manglus's enemies almost openly rubbed their palms together in delight; his friends and others who were displeased with the outcome were downcast, shrugging their shoulders and whispering among themselves, still unable to accept the fact.

"They handed it to our sweet Mangs," I heard someone say on the courthouse stairs when I was leaving. And I could not understand whether it was said just as a statement of fact, or as gloating, or actually in sympathy.

That same night at The Cave, we naturally discussed what had transpired. Pekka was also there. We asked his opinion.

"Say that it's crap," someone demanded of him frankly. "Such a thing shouldn't be allowed to happen in the Free World."

Pekka was evasive and said he wasn't up to speed on the details.

"The details aren't what's *important*. We're talking in *principle*!"

"Yeah, and what is that principle about?" Pekka asked curiously.

"But he's done *so much*. We're talking about a lifetime accomplishment of several men here. We're not dealing with any kind of ordinary figure, you know," Endel huffed indignantly.

"I don't know exactly how the law functions in your state," Pekka said cautiously, "but the fact that he is an important and respected person doesn't mean all that much. At least not with us, it doesn't."

"So, in your mind, he should go to jail? Is that what you're saying?" Maša rebuked him.

"He's a *wizard*, a *wizard*," whispered little Anks aka Angelina, who had drunk more than her fill.

Pekka changed the subject.

They appealed the ruling, of course. As a result, the month of actual imprisonment was replaced by a conditional sentence. The prosecutor did not intend to argue against the new ruling—she was rumored to have said in private that it was enough to teach him an initial (?) lesson. Karl celebrated jubilantly in The Cave the night that the second ruling was announced, and bought us an abundance of rounds. Manglus was nowhere to be seen. He had Karl inform everyone that he would appear in our company only after a month's time, because the shock incarceration had actually been intended to punish our social group, which would have been forced to get by without him for a month. The joke was the kind Manglus would make, alright, and I was cheered, believing that nothing could break him.

Understandably, the media wanted interviews from Manglus before and after the ruling was changed, and he was invited to speak on several television programs. He went and behaved very arrogantly. His words were not addressed towards his opponents in the lawsuit or the organs of justice, which the press might have even enjoyed, but towards the *journalists*. And yet, now would have been the time for Manglus to put on a more benevolent face, being the last chance to restore his good name just a little. What was happening no longer seemed logical to me. Of course, Manglus did not hold the majority of journalists in high opinion. However, he *had* always felt an extreme, almost lustful joy in being extremely polite to people he inwardly despised. And before the Mink saga, he had been outwardly polite to journalists, too. Now, it seemed as if maintaining constant self-control had become tedious for him; the mask had become the bearer's burden. Manglus relaxed, like someone who wants to be done with everyone. At the same time, of course, it could also have been the case that he simply did not assess the situation correctly; that his antennae did not pick up signals in the new social context as sharply as they had before. Perhaps he felt that he could be above the media, too; could ensnare it. I remember, for example, how a journalist asked him on one program:

"How do you *feel* after such a decline?"

Manglus chuckled and said, "Don't you worry. I'll rise again soon. Oh, yes I will."

"Really?" the journalist asked, expressing disbelief.

"With your own help, by the way," Manglus added, pointing to his conversation partner. And he snickered again. He was so confident in himself—he believed that he could wrap everyone around his finger and make them dance to the tune of his pipe. At that, he was mistaken. For these were new journalists, and they really knew nothing about Manglus—not about his work nor about his legacy, not to mention his membership in such a plethora of inner circles. To them, he was simply a man of the former era whose path into politics had gone sour, and who had not gotten caught in the pincers of a state based on the rule of law.

It is dreadful to think about it in hindsight.

The media hung him out to dry.

When Manglus organized his next big exhibition, it was only mentioned in the cultural weekly. Previously, his exhibitions had always been printed in a very visible place in all publications. True, one tabloid published a cover story about him at the time, but the piece glaringly overlooked the exhibition — the main emphasis was on Mink and Maige.

After a while, he was no longer written about at all. If he was ever mentioned, his name blipped by like some negatively-connoted refrain; a handy and worn-out example of the fact that everyone is treated equally under the law — pompous officials just as well as prestigious intellectuals. In the public eye, Manglus's name started to stand for the corruption of intellectuals, for downfall, for spiritual lowness. The "newbies" found this fitting, but it was also to the liking of the "formers." Such individuals seemed to be saying: "Those artists turned their noses up too high. Their role in the bringing about the Republic was not so great at all. There were also other people involved, whose contributions were even more important."

The "precedent-setting case" had justified itself.

Although Manglus resigned from the Center's directorship and was no longer a member of its advising body either, his name was so strongly attached to the institution that all of the Center's sponsors who did not want to swim against the political current promptly fell away. The Center didn't receive even half of the state funding it had before, either (this was, of course, partially a circumstance of the overall economic decline, which was just beginning at that time). The Center started to quickly wane, and two non-profit organizations were formed in its place after three quarters of a year.

Even so, Manglus still tried to put on a good face, at least whenever he came into contact with us. True, such times became ever more infrequent. He didn't want to reminisce about his lawsuit at all, and was silent about the Center. Occasionally, it appeared as if he intended to turn an entirely new page in life. "My work is done. The school of thought has been set up. Everything here around us is ready," he stated, gesturing vaguely around him. "Now I *myself* can live, can travel, can feel joy." Actually, he drank very heavily. That was already visible from far away.

Half a year later, the two of us were sitting outside the café upstairs from The Cave, at street level. I was overcome by discomfort and sympathy. Manglus's face was puffy and he was out of shape overall—his once athletic body now looked stumpy. He spoke with difficulty, fumbling for words, and tended to lose his breath. A familiar-looking middle-aged lady passed a few meters away from us and, demonstrating the politeness of a cultural person, greeted us first. She was an expert in women's studies. She was wearing long dark pants.

"Do you know her?" Manglus asked. "Wearing long pants— hmm. She's sewn them herself."

"So what?"

"Just saying . . . although . . . there's always something awful about homemade pants. That's been my idiosyncrasy. From an early age already.

I didn't say anything, because people can display very bizarre idiosyncrasies. Manglus continued: "I remember how Lembe and I met for the first time—you do know her name is Lembe, right?—back then, she was already wearing homemade pants." I still couldn't come up with anything to say, and Manglus started to snicker. "I know what I'm talking about. I took them off of her *myself* and checked out the stitching. It was in the Soviet era." He paused pensively. "And she has the same kind of pants right now. There are certain people who can never, not during any regime, manage to buy themselves a decent pair of pants, but bungle things up sewing them for themselves instead." He rocked closer to me: "Make sure that you, Juku, never start sewing pants for yourself. It doesn't suit you." And he laughed devilishly. Manglus was not gay, but he enjoyed perversity. And I was glad all the same that he was able to be above the situation. That was the last time I saw Manglus act cheekily. Mae, his final lover, arrived moments later—a schizo, but an honest person; a programmer who walked around barefoot. I wanted to entertain Mae and told her about the conversation we had been having. But instead of cheering up, Mae almost went into a hysteria, grabbing Manglus by the chest and shrieking: "What's with you and those pants? How can a person like you dip so low?" (I immediately regretted having spoken, but truly—I had the best of intentions.)

"What pants? You shouldn't shake a dying man," Manglus said. His eyes were strangely transparent. A week later, he no longer exited his home.

Why did Manglus drink himself to death? Apparently, he didn't want to become a legendary geezer from a past era, who sits and growls in a corner of The Cave. He would be viewed with awe at first, but the more time that passed, the more he would be joked about, because the traces of his fame had been written into snow that melted so long ago that it is not even possible for today's people, even if they have the very best of intentions, to reach the springs of his past glory. Manglus allegedly said that the best time to drink champagne is when you've eaten shit your whole life. That idea is not original, of course, and he had probably heard the vulgar saying from some "character" in the Kopli ghettos. But what do I know of that. I'm just a vole. Voles do not drink champagne—although they would like to.

Manglus's funeral was well attended, even very much so, although I had expected more, to tell the truth—something outright exceptional. The service went by peacefully, perhaps in part because the nationalists and the "genuines" were not in attendance, and not all that much friction could happen with the "formers." People shook hands and expressed mutual sympathy. The audience was upstanding, especially for the funeral of a person who had been in the arts. Although I had been aware that Manglus's "kingdom" did not solely comprise the art world, it surprised me that this other "kingdom" figured so broadly even now. Incredibly bizarre figures showed up at the cemetery. Maybe it didn't reflect the actual extent of the amplitude of Manglus's social circle (for example, the Kopli ghettos were weakly represented, in my opinion), but regardless—some of the funeral-goers resembled mafiosi, others Freemasons, a third group transsexuals. One bouquet was wound in a tricolor ribbon with something written in Arabic letters on it. Two bouquets had Russian-language dedications. Burly men with skulls on their sleeves and collars briefly took up guard positions next to the coffin. Due to my job, I should have found out who they were, but I felt it wiser to delay doing so for a little while. Business circles were remarkably well represented. I wasn't surprised to notice several former authorities who had been in high positions—people who were called "nationalist communists." Incidentally, there was also a relatively large group of people who were unfamiliar to me, who lacked even the slightest glamour. They kept to themselves, and a few of them were crying. I found out from talking to colleagues that they were officials who had once worked under Manglus and remembered him as a legendarily good boss.

Needless to say, there was an abundance of artists and other "cavemen." It is better that I do not speak about the women—there were so many of them. From the frail, middle-aged, and mostly poorly dressed old maids, with whom Manglus had studied at art school way back when, to the spring-chicken babes with eyes bloodshot from crying, who were apparently his last students from the academy. A range of veiled widows in refined mourning dresses and visibly wealthy, red-cheeked businesswomen were nestled between them. Each and every one had been Manglus's lover. Yet, interestingly enough, none of them quarreled with one another because of it; no one aspired for any kind of exclusive title or throne in retrospect.

Manglus's casket was closed; he would not have *wanted* to show himself to us, either.

Nevertheless, one small scandal unfolded. The crowd had already parted to both sides and the pastor was getting ready to give the order to carry the coffin out when Mink appeared in the chapel. He marched straight over to the coffin, and his arrival was so unexpected that no one thought to block his way. Then Mink suddenly raised his leg and pretended as if he intended to urinate on the coffin like a dog. He sniggered malevolently in the process. Cries rang out, and Mink was torn away from the casket by his shirt.

Rui was also present at the funeral, wearing a peculiar cape and

smelling of mid-range cologne—he expressed his sympathy to
Manglus's widows and girlfriends in hushed tones. During the
speeches, he broke away from the crowd and strolled between
the graves with a deeply ponderous expression on his face, his
arms folded behind his back, staring up into the sky.

Just as with Klaus's funeral, a lone helicopter flew overhead
when we were starting to leave the cemetery—everyone craned
their necks involuntarily and followed it with their eyes until it
disappeared, thwapping, behind the crowns of the pine trees.

The reception was held in a restaurant that was already renowned during the Soviet era, and which had become very
classy once again in the hands of new owners a few years earlier.
Everything there went routinely. The attendants took their seats
without elbowing one another, although some camps naturally
formed. Still, no barbed comments were exchanged across the
table as they had been at Klaus's funeral. Civilization had progressed meanwhile.

Afterward, our clique went to The Cave in order to feel a little more at ease. All in all, Manglus had been one of the most
outstanding members of our congregation even in spite of his
title of "world prince," and although we never stated it explicitly, we felt that we did not want to surrender the memory of him
to anyone else. We drank moderately, reminisced about funny
and heartfelt escapades that the departed had been embroiled
in (we were not short on these in Manglus's case); some even
shed a few tears. Mati gave a brief but moving speech. In reality, it was not customary to give speeches in The Cave (chamber
conversation and jesting was practiced there instead), but Mati
could grant himself the privilege. He said that Manglus had
been a good artist and one of the few truly original personalities
of our age.

Mirva showed up at The Cave late that evening—her hair in
a purple bob, her cheeks sagging, and green sunglasses perched
on her nose. She claimed to have arrived directly from abroad; I
cannot remember anymore whether it was from the Yessentuki
Creative House or from Baltimore, where she had participated
in an international project. She hadn't even heard of Manglus's
fate. When she was told the reason for people having gathered

together that day, she took a deep swig of Vana Tallinn and lit up a cigarette. "Ohh," she then sighed reflectively. "This little life of ours sure has sped up. You look away for a second, go away for a short while, and your former BF's already in the *graveyard*."

The lawyer Karl also arrived at midnight and alleged that all of those bouquets and what-have-you with ribbons in Arabic and Russian had been ordered by Manglus himself. Karl had apparently helped him draft his will. Why did Manglus do that? Just for a laugh. Karl ruined a few people's moods with this announcement, but, oppositely, a flame of fascination sparked in the eyes of some of the younger persons: what a tough old geezer! His own death was right before his eyes, but he was *still* orchestrating! However, Karl doused their enthrallment by clarifying that Manglus had already drawn up his will two years earlier, before there was even the slightest hint of the Mink debacle. He did it just for fun, as a way to pass the time, when the two of them happened to be drinking together.

"But Mink? *That* surely couldn't have been in the will," someone argued, thinking of the dimwit's leg-lifting.

"Yeah," Karl agreed. "That wasn't from Manglus anymore—that was life itself."

When I think back to what happened, one metaphor or image always comes to mind: a tug-of-war. Death or Destruction is on one side and Manglus is on the other side. Between them is a river: the Lethe, the Pedja—whatever. Strung across the water is a rope, which is the person's life. Each party holds on to their end of the rope and strives to tug as much length for themselves as they can. Manglus is stronger. Death is still young—he has no right to Manglus yet; his time has not yet come. He does gain a little strength with every year, and with it more length in rope, but so far, the greater portion is proudly in the hands of his opponent.

Because of this, Manglus toys with Death like a cat with a mouse: provoking it, giving in a little, then a little more—pretending that his strength is coming to an end. So there is only just a little bit of rope left in his hands, looking as if it will slip into the water in just a second, but . . . then he tugs again with all his might, and after a couple of pulls, he is once again holding a long length of the rope! What can really happen? He is so strong, cunning, and vigilant that he always hits just the right moment and yanks the rope back to his side.

But one time, things go differently. He has again allowed a long length of the rope out of his hands, so that there is only a tiny span left in his palm. For ultimately, the feeling *is* very arousing—playing with life like that. Ordinarily, he is extremely watchful at that very instant and can sense precisely the split second at which he cannot give in any more. But this time, he is not paying attention, or is too self-confident, and all of a sudden ... whoops! ... the rope vanishes from his palm and slips into the water. He cannot get ahold of the end anymore. *How can it be? That's impossible! That's not right!* he would like to shout to someone. This is not possible, of course—the others are yelling and astounded as well. One simply does not *die* so young, for naught. But even so, that is precisely how it went.

I am not certain whether this is the right interpretation, however. Death is actually *very* much a departure. I sometimes felt as if Manglus was sneering at us a little—at those who were left behind.

A tiny part of an era had come to an end with Manglus.

### RUI'S TRANSFORMATION

I was coming from a funeral again. An absolutely amazing video artist whose professional name was "Pelmeni" had died unexpectedly. He had been a relatively young man—just fifty-two. Pelmeni had frequented The Cave for a while and belonged to our social group. Lately, he had been seen there rarely; people said that he was working hard, that he had gotten a second wind in the creative sense. No one knew for sure what caused Pelmeni's death. Some claimed that it was AIDS, others poverty. We bid farewell to him at the Pärnamäe Crematory. I did not stay for the reception because a love-affair piece needed touching-up. I took the train to the Balti Jaam station and was walking down Nunne Street towards the editorial office. Suddenly, I glimpsed a figure at a distance that seemed simultaneously both familiar and not. As the distance between us dwindled, I became sure that, yes, it was Rui . . . to a certain extent. All that was left of the old Rui were his small, round, wire-framed glasses and his long hair, which was now washed and pulled back into a ponytail with a claw clip. In place of his frayed, skin-tight jeans and satchel were a light sky-blue sweater and soft, white, fustian pants. Rui held a small case—something between an attaché and an old-fashioned midwife's handbag. I assumed out of habit that he would ask for a loan of five euros for a little "hair of the dog," and that he would say, "a lot's demanded of him who's given a lot." Instead, Rui greeted me with a dignity that was probably supposed to resemble a nobleman, although it came off more like a butler.

"How's that?!" I asked.

"Ah," he said, and shrugged. "Enough of life's hardships. I want to get to the land of milk and honey, too."

"What are you up to, then?" I asked, interested.

"I enrolled in a private college and am studying law," he informed me. "I can work as a paralegal next year already, although I'd still like to aspire towards prosecutor. My goal is to specialize in big and especially profitable criminal cases. I'd also enjoy sexual crimes and espionage stories."

The latest winning Eurovision song abruptly started playing from somewhere. I thought that there must be some car window open nearby, but no—Rui tapped his smartphone; it was his ring tone.

"I was wondering—where were you headed?" Rui asked. I named a random location.

"I've got a little time before my lecture. I'll come and walk you there. Haven't had a chance to talk in a long time," Rui said, keeping me in his clutches.

He spoke about all kinds of things on the way, such as how he didn't want to let himself be seen together with bohemians, as it was "bad advertising." He stated that "whoever has property also has responsibility," and that "Estonia must be a trustworthy partner for its allies." I got the impression that he had started reading newspapers. He further said that he was planning to lease a car. He had apparently also acquired his first stocks. Finally, he shared instructions on how to take out a payday loan.

"You're really getting *married*?" I asked.

"Sure, why shouldn't I?" Rui responded, not seeing the irony of the situation. "Can't a feeling of fatherhood pulse in my loins, then—huh? Can't my body call out for children?"

I was breaking off in the direction of the office and preparing to say goodbye. Something seemed to be weighing on Rui's heart, however—that was the actual reason that he had come to accompany me.

"Listen, you seem to have your leg in the media world—or what am I talking about—you're in it up to your *neck*," he said, laughing at his play on words. "Might it be possible to arrange a little photo series of me? Rich people read your publication. If they see *me* there, then I'll be able to get to the top more quickly."

I replied that he would have to go to some reception or opening in that case.

"My thoughts exactly," Rui said, nodding. "You'll throw together some invitation for me."

I nodded so as to not argue.

"By the way," he said, looking around as if afraid that someone might overhear us. "I can tell *you*—we're old friends. Look, I haven't made a final decision just yet. Being a lawyer in sexual cases is really something, but it's still in Estonia. And Estonia is small—oh, how small. I want to see the world, want to come to know all of those God-blessed places that you otherwise only see on TV. How long can I look away, holding my finger in my mouth? Who can keep me here by force? The Republic of Estonia isn't able to chain me down. And so, I've been thinking about one thing in connection with that. What if I try to get into diplomatic school? Tell me honestly—would I measure up, in your opinion?" I replied with a fair amount of vagueness, which he interpreted in the direction pleasing to him, and continued: "I'd like to end my days as the Estonian cultural attaché somewhere in the South Sea Islands, surrounded by grass-skirted chicks. That'd be just the ticket, wouldn't it?" And he burst out laughing triumphantly without waiting for an answer. "But that photo series," he added, growing serious again, "we'll get working on that."

Left to myself, I thought: *Oh, Rui—you, too . . .* That was a sign of the end of an era, *too*. When even the Ruis are starting to seek a cozy little nook in life, starting to build a nest, to craft together a career for themselves, to consider pension funds, then society has most definitely changed. The race of insolent thrift-store shoppers, witty twaddlers, shruggers/gesticulators, and others living for the moment is dying out. Genuine bohemians no longer exist. Today's bohemian is one who checks to make sure he is still being photographed when he is "acting the bohemian." In order to get onto a TV discussion panel, into the seat designated for a bohemian, he bickers unflaggingly with other bohemians, using entirely non-bohemian measures, stoking intrigue in the good old Communist Party spirit. All this to be able to make a "bohemianish" scene on TV, and thanks to that, to grab some doe-eyed chick's behind out in public somewhere as the "celebrity bohemian."

Soon, it will indeed be the case that the only people who shrug things off are gays who dare to come out of the closet. But even most of *them* will look around thrice to make sure they are still being photographed.

### TEEDU'S STARDUST

Once more, Estonian Independence Day was just around the corner. "What number is this already?" Teedu wondered. Most people would likely have been unable to say right off the bat how long the new independence period had lasted. It had been a fair amount of time—that much was for sure—but they couldn't seem to recall any bigger anniversary.

Routine events and customary rituals accompanied the celebration, receptions were held, and medals handed out. This year was supposed to be Teedu's turn. He did not really have a proper medal yet; one fitting of a statesman. Big Jaan, their party leader (Karotar had gone off into business) had hinted that the old fighters would be given theirs first, and only then would they go out to the "newbies." This was in order not to upset public opinion or bruise the nation's sense of justice. And as for Teedu—he *had* still been an instructor of Party history, even though it was very long ago; it almost felt like it was in a former life or on a different planet, and so Teedu would occasionally feel quite truthfully that it hadn't been *him*, but a different person. None of his fellow party members had mentioned the fact. For some time now, Teedu no longer began his speeches with the sentence that had become famous nearly a decade before, either. (One of the dailies had even published a caricature back then, in which a bubble came from the speaker's mouth reading: "I am of course a former commie and thus an inferior person and am unworthy of blowing my horn.") The line "didn't work" anymore; the new generations did not understand it. For them, it wasn't a joke, nor was it irony (not to mention taking it word-for-word). What commie? Why inferior? The world was full of Socialists, even a few commies among them — *they* seemed to be doing pretty well! The Commissioner for Gender Equality, a young woman, had commented in the media in his favor. Yet Teedu still found that it was better to remain in the background.

By now, the old fighters had all received their medals and the next lot's turn was at hand. This also included Teedu. And so it went. Teedu read the list of recipients in the newspaper with pleasure. Although the party headquarters had informed him long before that the matter was decided, he was unsure about it up until the last minute. The medal ceremony was held at the Kadriorg Palace. The decoration was not special in and of itself—a Second-Class Order of the National Coat of Arms—but it was a solid award regardless; there was no reason to be ashamed of it in any way. The first-class medal was given to foreigners and certain select individuals. *Things actually went very well, even*, Teedu mused. It goes without saying that he attended the presidential Independence Day gala. All of the members of the Riigikogu were invited. It had generally been rare for Teedu *not* to attend in recent times. He could still remember how the last president, a formerly high-level figure from the Soviet era, had walked around with his wife after the handshaking ceremony, and how many people had loved him more than the *new* president, who was a foreign-born Estonian. This memory boosted Teedu's spirits and gave him added confidence when he and Merle were strolling through the throng of people, exchanging greetings, and clinking glasses.

With every nod, Teedu wondered whether this or that person he was greeting belonged to the old or the new age. There seemed to be an almost equal number of them. Thus, everything had run its course naturally. Society was stable, just like during the Ming dynasty. No kinds of interruptions, new movers and shakers, or clean pages. This filled his heart with peace.

A couple more years passed. Teedu gave interviews. There were a lot of journalists—from TV, radio, dailies, and the online media. He sat comfortably in an armchair, his pensive gaze focused on the back wall of the studio beyond the camera lens. The timbre of his voice was exemplary, his posture was thoughtfully optimistic, as is fitting for a more elderly statesman. When speaking about actors, people sometimes say they really have reached the point, at which they've "drunk a face for themselves." Teedu was not an actor, nor had he drunk. It was just that he had suddenly gained greater relief at the age of fifty-six. Now, the hour to look back upon his road to victory had come.

Teedu spoke:

"The existence of the land and nation of Estonia had been brought to the brink of catastrophe. Plans for phosphorite mining threatened to lay waste to the soil. The demographic situation had turned very tense due to forced immigration. A bilingual context was taking shape and gradually reducing Estonian to a 'kitchen-language' status. Under these conditions, the patriotically minded elite was left with no choice but to bolster the hidden resistance and wait for the right moment to restore independence. Contributing towards these ends were city and country folk as well as creative intellectuals, whose endeavors were coordinated by a more free-minded and nationally-thinking wing of people that had previously participated in state governance. While the enthusiasm and sublime principles that ignited the masses came from the intellectuals and the freedom fighters, others who possessed practical experience in state governance knew how to properly channel these emotions in order to arrive at the optimal outcome." He remembered this all quite honestly, from personal experience!

The interviewer, the channel's news anchor (naturally their leading man), was wearing a suit instead of his usual jean jacket for the occasion, and had abandoned his customary conversational style (being on the offense), nodding pensively at Teedu's every sentence. The young print journalists next to the camera seized the words from Teedu's lips and scribbled them into their notebooks.

*Is this really what a "time to shine" is like?* Teedu wondered while driving towards the Viimsi suburb after the interview. In his mind's eye, he could already see himself as the chairman of his party faction. But why not run for the position of parliamentary deputy-chairman? He would probably not be able to rise much further. Yet even these thoughts were bright, and so he started to hum:

*And the wind and the storms and a starflight by night, my heart is restless and the road calls me into the distance.*

"What kinda song is *that*?" Madeline asked from the passenger seat, perplexed.

## ILLIMAR'S LETTER FROM OCTOBER 2007

*Honorable Chronicler!*
*(. . .) Foreign Estonians are starting to blend in with local ones. They have become more sober minded and practical than they used to be. Their eyes burn less. Nevertheless, one cannot make this claim about all of them equally. A certain geographic ranking holds sway in terms of eye glint. The closer to home one comes from, the less his lamps glow. The eyes of Estonians from Sweden and Finland do not burn anymore at all. The foreign Estonians from the remaining European countries are situated in the middle of the ranking. The North American ones, however, burn at almost their former brightness. Zeal and idealism have still been preserved over there, especially among older persons. The middle-aged and younger generations take the Estonian cause more prosaically there as well, without any exceptional emotion. However, the flame of Estonianism burns most brightly in the most far-off places, such as in Australia or Argentina. Sublime principles are most noticeable in the Estonian Houses there. I indeed have my ear to the ground now*

*to see whether it might perhaps be possible to move to some such*
*country. I want to live amid idealism. I would like to end my liv-*
*ing days in a place where one might be able to read Anna Haava*
*and Karl Eduard Sööt to hundred-year-olds in the local Estonian*
*House. I want time to stand still.*

(. . .)

My golden pen pal! He was so very thirsty for romanticism,
yearning for his idealism-tub, but still had to realize that this
did not really exist in practical life, nor *could* it. The trumpets
cannot blast forever, you know. He did not go to any of these
far places, of course, for where was he to get the money to do
so? On top of that, he now had a child and a wife.

### MATI BURNS BRIDGES

My story is starting to reach its decisive stage.

In Mati's case, I must first go back several years' time—to
when he went to visit Fatty for Klaus's cause. It's possible that
the negative experience he had there influenced what follows.
In any case, he took part in a debate program on TV a few
months later. Mati had ranted and raved about politicians earlier, too, but it had been kept to hallways or the pub table. Now,
he voiced extremely sharp criticism of the government's culture
policy and, more generally, the trough into which Estonian development had slipped since the restoration of independence.
He remarked that this direction served to split society, not unite
it. As it was a cultural program that was broadcast at a little-
viewed hour of the night, Mati's statements would not have
gained great attention had other media outlets not amplified his
words. Some pundits hinted between the lines that Mati had
been at the studio in a heightened state of mind, which was a
euphemism—for what, was obvious. But after everything, the
whole matter descended into oblivion. Mati kept editing his
magazine and was rumored to be writing his third novel.

But then, about a year later, someone somewhere apparently
found that Mati should be "utilized" better. It was a well-known
fact that he was not interested in a career as an active politician.

The matter indeed involved the Central Estonian Anti-Espionage Administration. One of the top director's terms there was coming to a close, and candidates for his successor were being considered. Mati's own candidacy could seem random, but only at first. The country was small and still young at the time; there were far from enough trained people for every job available. The position required someone who was honest and patriotic through and through, in addition to being intelligent and having a broad outlook. Mati gave his informal yes. It is possible that he decided this in order to have a change, out of intellectual interest, and—as the popular new expression went—in order to take on new challenges; but certainly also due to his civil-mindedness. However, something unforeseeable happened. Some documents (where indeed could they have come from, and who could vouch for their authenticity?) that registered the KGB's attempt to recruit Mati as an informer at one time were leaked to the public. The KGB officer's report had put these words into Mati's mouth: "There's no point in you guys recruiting me because I'm the kind of man who will blurt out all of your secrets to the first person I come across when I get a drop of booze in me." Such a thing was news to *me* as well. No, not that the KGB had wanted to recruit him, because Mati himself had talked about it. Nor was there anything exceptional in the excuse for his refusal, because dozens of others had used a similar line of reasoning in their day. (Didn't I *myself* also use it? No, that wasn't with the KGB, but when the actor S. had a dreadful wish to confess his complexes to me; I did not want to listen, and said that I might blab about it—which, alas, was exactly what S. was hoping for!) The surprise was that Mati had *also* employed such an excuse—that he had not told the recruiters to "piss off" right then and there without greater ado. For some reason, we had believed that Mati, having a strong backbone, would not start devising excuses. (A few young politicians popped up demanding outright that Mati and his kind should have told the "kay-gees" off in plain Estonian!) I do not know, of course, what kind of an expression Mati wore while saying it to them. He might also have done it in a way so that the "kay-gees" realized Mati was ridiculing them, and in summary, it *would* have had almost the same effect as telling them off. Alas — paper does not reflect this. However, that was not the main thing. Although the reason why Mati spoke that way should have been clear to all, especially given the fact that he was keeping alcohol firmly in check during that time, his opponents now took advantage of the document. Can a person who "admits his weakness so readily" be entrusted with a job that would require him to handle secrets? And, of course, they referenced that aforementioned TV program, in which Mati had spoken in a "heightened state of mind." A piece titled "Alcoholic for Anti-Espionage Director?" was published in one daily. Friends told Mati with a heavy heart that the matter would unfortunately have to be called off.

The media reacted in several ways. People on one side formed the opinion (some with glee, some with regret) that Mati had "played himself out"—that he had been a splinter in the rulers' eyes for a long time already (the unoriginal expression "he's past his prime" was used), and now he was "making it easier" for them to get rid of him. This was certainly a malicious overstatement, because Mati was generally regarded with sympathy even in the progressive circles of power — there was no kind of collective vilification. While other of his former companions had gradually receded from the public eye, there were a fair number left. Yet the main thing was — who *was* Mati then, all in all, that he needed to be "removed"? From where? From what? He held no important position or power. No — some journalist was attempting to either portray him as a dragon slayer or to demonize him.

One well-intentioned journalist speculated that the matter would be forgotten and Mati would be able to continue his career (once again — what career?) after a while. Others reckoned that he probably wouldn't be allowed to do so regardless, because he had become "unpredictable." They claimed that he could be offered sinecures for the rest of his life, but would no longer be permitted to go before the public; or if he was, then it would be in his retirement years. He could spin tales of his memories then, and if he were drunk, then people would just say that he was soft in the head from age. A third group believed, however, that he no longer (?) *wanted* to go into politics. The granule of truth in all that might have been that since Mati had not felt drawn to the profession of politics during its heyday (following the restoration of independence), then why would it have appealed to him now? A reliable political machine had stepped into the place of daring decisions, self-sacrificing efforts, and noble flurries of activity. Different-suited figures from before were busying themselves on the topmost floors of power—they were more systematic and rigidly-formed, more restrained, stress-tolerant, and routine-loving. They would have expelled Mati as a foreign body after a while, anyway. Until that time, he would have been a lion on their coat of arms; a living symbol who attested their own connection to the sacred cause and the continuity of the main agenda. Mati could have been someone who had to be tolerated, but was not one of "them." Personally, I think that Mati was bored by it all. He mocked the "newbies" (calling them "drones"). Still, as long as he aligned with the political views of the "oldies," he should have also tolerated the "newbies," because the "oldies" were bound to the "newbies" by way of party unions. This apparently got on Mati's nerves.

Mati's work contract ended after a couple of years and he did not apply for the position again, saying it was due to a lack of motivation. He appeared to be becoming ever more critical, and started behaving challengingly. For example, he had been seen together with a couple of "formers" in a city pub. On the one hand, this was his way of scorning the "newbies" (check it out—for him, even old troglodytes are more human and sympathetic than stingy, boilerplate party members); on the other hand, there is no doubt that Mati indeed had things to speak about with those "formers"—no matter whether he was debating with them or simply reviling them (the latter happened frequently and they tolerated it quite patiently, for some reason). They possessed the same epochal background and the code derived from it. Mati was at least able to bicker with the "formers"; the "newbies" slipped out of his grip. These meetings also had another consequence. A couple of "formers" made him a proposal: "Our companies have a little money left over, and we'd like to hand out an art award, too." Mati started laughing at first: should that award be given in the name of the workers and the kolkhoz women? However, they explained to him that they (the "formers") would not stick their nose into things— they would merely provide the money, while the selection and everything else would be left to the artistic persons themselves. They would simply like to help when things were hard for the country. Back at The Cave, Mati shook his head in amazement: "I would never have believed that you can talk about art with some commie industry-boss, too." The old *Nomenklatura* suddenly appeared more culture-loving than the new. (More specifically, Taavi Rõhejõgi had worked on the Planning Committee and Jaan Väle on the Supply Committee during the Soviet era. I didn't know either of them personally, but had heard that both had been stingy, fish-eyed *Nomenklatura*-brothers during the stagnation period. Now, one was involved in shipping and the other in construction—both were exceptionally important figures and immensely rich.)

Nevertheless, this new friendship did not last for long, and Mati got into a tremendous fight with the "formers" before long (the award was indeed still issued). In one interview, he remarked that "not everyone who should be done away with *has* been yet."

Back then, I wondered what Agnes might think of Mati's vociferations. Agnes was rarely seen with Mati at The Cave at that time. Her expression was very solemn in general. It was also the first time that Mati's old companions began to feel worried about him. His writing did not appear to be progressing. We felt that some kind of a job should be arranged for him. And so, Mati was offered the opportunity to start heading the editing of our most important daily's cultural section. The editor himself was a younger man, but was one of the "newbies" who got along well with the "oldies" and maintained a mental bond with them. Soon enough, Mati was nicely ensconced and able to busy himself on the cultural scene uninterrupted. At first, it indeed seemed that he was satisfied and avidly involved in his work. Unfortunately, this momentum did not last for long. Mati apparently didn't completely understand what a news daily was. Here, I authorize myself to criticize him a little bit, too, because I am quite familiar with the press as a result of my life experiences. In short: when art and sublime principles are already esteemed in society, then almost anyone who has taste and conscience can manage such a position. It is difficult when the conditions are otherwise—like how they had turned out to be now. People's minds were caught up by completely different things, but Mati still wanted to talk about art and lofty principles. Even so, art, for example, really no longer *existed* in the traditional sense. Meaning—it did a little, of course, but was found somewhere on the margins; new forms of it that were reported in newspapers on pages titled "The Scoop" and "Media" had nudged their way to the foreground. If I may repeat myself: one must always take advantage of the opportunities the era offers; one shouldn't necessarily attempt to stubbornly sail against the wind, nor to march away, offended. Adaptation is the only option. People can be educated, and even sublime principles can be promoted by way of "The Scoop" and "Media," or in their shadow. But not head-on and openly, because no one will pay any attention to you then. Thus, that sort of newspaper job shouldn't be entrusted to just anyone (following the principle: "the main thing is that he or she be an intellectual"). As sad as it may be, old favors do not count for anything here—figures of old cannot make do, for the most part. (That said, I am still reminded of the beginning of World War II, when after the first brilliant attacks by the German tanks, the old French cavalry marshals were forced to retire. They couldn't understand the direction in which warfare was moving.) The dailies and other mass media are now the true strongholds from the standpoint of spreading culture. "Marshal" Mati did not grasp this.

He had some momentum in his first attempts, but it was all in an old-fashioned style. He then saw that he was facing a wall, shrugged, and said that it was all just "hopping around in vain"—the nation was degenerated, the politicians were dimwits, and so on. Even so, his opportunities could have been several times more promising than mine in my purple suit. Mati could have done anything and everything if he had cared to. But I suppose he was not that kind of person anymore. Besides, he didn't enjoy sitting in meetings twice a day at fixed times.

His nature balked at it. On top of that, the second meeting started at three o'clock. Sitting with others and having a lunch-time beer became especially pleasant at that very hour. I was sometimes witness to his internal struggle to leave his beer and go to the meeting. It sometimes happened that he *didn't*. He was scolded then, and probably given formal warnings too. However, this did not sound the alarm bells yet. He worked that way for many long years and, all in all, did his job quite well.

Mati was awarded an important decoration on the next anniversary of Estonian independence. This did not appear to sit well with him, because at the presidential gala, he wore the honorary pin that accompanied his decoration on his suit lapel (he would not hear a single word about a tailcoat, as Agnes told us), even though according to etiquette, he should wear the medal itself on formal occasions. When a TV reporter asked him during the festivities what feelings he had and how the high-level decoration would affect his future activities (it happened to be a very young reporter), then Mati gave a light shrug for the camera and said tragically that all he had left to sacrifice was his own heart's blood. The reporter kid was visibly taken aback by such a reply; Mati, however, seemed to be very fond of that expression (which apparently popped into his head at the same moment he answered), because he repeated it instead of answering the reporter's next question. He likewise attempted to take the microphone out of the reporter's hand and start singing something into it. The reporter finally realized that Mati was in a rowdy state, and left him alone. No one understood what Mati had meant by "giving his heart's blood," but many people saw or heard about the broadcast.

The matter was discussed at The Cave, also. Miller said that the ones who have given their heart's blood should be thanked, but not idolized. For they performed as they saw fit, and received spiritual satisfaction from it as well. However, not everyone has to or even should have their blood spilled. *Should Tuglas have refused to say a few warm words about the Soviet regime (which he did do insincerely) instead of allowing the NKVD*[35] *to slam his fingers in a desk drawer?* Miller asked rhetorically.

Tuglas could have been allowed to *say* whatever he wanted—
what is important is what he *wrote* otherwise. So, to be cruel,
one could say that whoever truly has nothing other than their
heart's blood to sacrifice can go ahead and sacrifice it. However, whoever has something better might *not* sacrifice it. Miller
also said that a dissident is truly happy. If he or she had been
born into an open society, then the person could not have been
a dissident—just like how we never know how many potential
sculptors live in the desert, or how many Napoleons' talents are
wasted during a long period of peace. Some of our recent dissidents would be no one at all right now, because they could
not even be bothered to finish school in their day; but presently, they have become important figures. These days, individuals with dissident tendencies have nothing better to do than to
fight against global warming or for minorities' rights, which is
not quite as glorious, all the same.

"Goddamn communist!" Mati hollered, and tried to throw
a punch at Miller. Miller had practiced martial arts, however,
and ducked to the side.

Miller is a cynical opportunist; he entertains himself at the
expense of the creative intelligentsia. But his words were not
false.

Something was off between Mati and Agnes—we gradually
started to pick up on that. Mati didn't bother to go home in
the evenings anymore, but instead sat in The Cave and ranted. Over time, he had acquired the habit of speaking about his
wife by first name in any group of people, as if everyone should
have known who she was. And so, he explained to random people at midnight that "Agnes says" one thing one time and another thing some other time, and that "Agnes's patience is at its
limits." We felt sorry, although we were unable to decide which
one of the two we felt *more* sorry for.

Agnes was, in my mind, an honest woman of above-average
intelligence, was exceptionally capable, and her heart was in the
right place in terms of nationalism. Yet in the end, even that
kind of a woman will want to get everything out of life she believes she is entitled to. If it appears to her that her relationship

is going sideway and doesn't seem to be heading for a happy ending, and if she has (to use common Soviet-era wisdom) a dozen years maximum left to tick as a woman, then spirit and fatherland will probably be put on the back burner. A yearning to be buried in the same grave with the right person develops powerfully during a certain period of life (ordinarily happening earlier for women than for men). The person begins to look around to see where this gravemate can be found, and begins to worry whether or not something might still "happen" with them. A woman will then start to do what she has almost forgotten about in the meantime: going out socially on her own, timidly at first—like a kitten that finds itself in new surroundings—but soon more self-confidently.

Agnes had not yielded to life, which shows that she had a strong character, and I am all the more sorry for Mati for having gambled away that kind of a woman. Agnes went to study at Stanford for a year, and afterward was sent to work in Brussels, where a joint initiative between the International Court of Justice, the United Nations, and the European Union had resulted in the formation of a committee tasked with developing a new system for explaining the principles of a state based on the rule of law to nations with a traditional way of living, i.e. "nature peoples." Agnes's ethnographic experiences and the fact that she had grown up in a totalitarian society were a great plus for her, and she was appointed the vice-chairwoman of the committee. The Belgian capital became her permanent place of residence. This effectively meant that their marriage was over. Mati did not follow Agnes. He would have considered it demeaning to live on his wife's wallet, and he wouldn't have been able to find a job there. And Agnes apparently didn't invite him very insistently, either.

And so, Mati divorced his smart and beautiful wife. When he was three-sheets-to-the-wind at The Cave, he would curse her, saying, "Agnes is a slut—her grandmother was already a slut." He had never met Agnes's grandmother, of course.

After that, Mati started spending even more time at The Cave. He also started to get hammered even more quickly, tending to mumble and behave unpredictably. He could, for example, give someone a dressing-down for no reason at all, but then become ebulliently affectionate, or vice versa.

Back in the day, he would always sigh, wishing that the busier period of his life would pass by so that he might have time to read again and educate himself in general. Now, he had as much time on his hands as he could ever want and could have read just as well as written, but one got the impression that he didn't especially care to do either. One time, I noticed from a distance that he took something out of his portfolio, put his glasses on, and began studying it. When I stepped closer to him, I saw that it was our magazine. Mati stowed it away when he saw me. On the one hand, I was flattered that Mati also read our publication, but on the other, I have to admit that I would have been even happier if he had been reading something a little more highbrow. Although, I suppose he no longer cared to discuss or focus on serious problems. Whenever anyone, mostly a newcomer to our social group (his older acquaintances did not make the effort anymore), tried to talk to him about philosophy, for example, then he would make the compelling argument that he had studied Latin and read a religious philosopher (probably Anselm of Canterbury) of the High Middle Ages in the original language. When the conversation leaned towards global politics, he would play his "trump" of having personally taken part in political life and "overthrown the government," which we, the rest of us, have *not* done, and would end by saying "beat that." When there were females in our company, it was hard to understand whether he wanted to hit on them or offend them, because he jumbled both together. Although he himself claimed that sex no longer interested him, and complained that women were no longer attracted by intellect, he probably continued to believe out of inertia that women were clinging to him as they had before, and that the privilege and the obligation to fertilize the "flock of Estonian women" fell upon *his* shoulders.

He sat alone in The Cave ever more frequently. This was not because anyone avoided him in particular (those kinds of people also existed, but they numbered few). His friends were leaving his side more in the figurative sense. People generally went to The Cave less often than before. This was partly because the years had taken their toll—a few had left this world for good, others had health problems (one year in "Cave life" tended to count for two). Most just wanted a lifestyle change, however. People had switched their goals and their preferences. Some were in a happy marriage—or, at least, their latest one—or were otherwise living soberly and decently; some were involved in business; some were participating either directly or indirectly in politics, and it was no longer suitable for them to be hanging around a pub. There were also some who had continued with their former activities, and hadn't changed their lifestyle—but even *they* had more responsibilities as the years passed, and thus less time left for The Cave. Frequenting The Cave was no longer common for younger artists—they socialized elsewhere and otherwise. For the most part, they regarded the Cave crowd as being a bit off their rockers. And so Mati *had* no social groups to choose from, and didn't reject from his table certain people with whom he would not have sat together for any price ten years earlier. He would idle there with a couple of sozzled artifacts, mumbling, none of them listening to one another, each doing their own thing.

There were also brighter moments, of course—such as isolated days in late October, pure and shining. On one such occasion, Mati spoke to us about how he had been stalked by a recurring dream for quite a while:

"Some people approach me from out of nowhere. A huge number of men, women, children, geezers, crones of all ages . . . It happens on some bleak field. I guess it is an early morning in fall, because it's like I am seeing everything through a fog. The grass is cold and damp, the people's faces are all the color of clay, their expressions are uniformly mournful and solemn. They are defeated and wretched, miserable farmers, factory workers, and provincial people in want. They stop and stand with silent reverence at first, but then ask: 'Are we not *people*?' And they fall silent again, not wanting a response, because the answer really lies in their question. Why do they ask *me* that, and what do I have to tell them? I'm overcome with heavy grief every time."

Maša recommended that he go see the psychiatrist Dr. Muld, who was said to have helped many intellectuals at difficult moments.

"Wait," Mati said, "I haven't told you the end yet . . . When that crowd of people there on the pasture comes even closer, then I see that they *aren't* people, but rather a herd of cattle that has ambled over to the roadside to inspect the random passerby. When I wake up after that, my grief is even deeper. *What is that herd to blame for?* I ask myself. *Or what am I to blame for?*"

Pepe said that, in that case, Mati should turn to a veterinarian.

## TIME, YOU OLD WHORE

It is interesting to wonder sometimes "What would have happened if . . ." Fine—Manglus would have become the Minister of Culture and the Deputy Chairman of the Presidium of the Supreme Soviet, or even *the* Chairman, sticking certificates of honor into people's palms, just like fat old Müürisepp[36] had done for Mati's great-uncle. But what would have become of *me* had a revolution not happened in society? I suppose I would have carried on translating from that obscure language (why am I hiding it anymore—it was Old Persian) as well as from more common languages. To this very day, I have not given up my translating work. No, this is not because I fear that the Estonian era might disappear, leading to the return of the old regime. I simply enjoy keeping myself in intellectual shape; I am waging a war against the general clichéing of society with my Old Persian.

What causes a person to feel that he is no longer young? I suppose it starts when he is greeted on the street by a suspiciously large number of elderly people he does not recognize. The older gentlemen chuckle at you as if you are one of them, squat old maids look you mischievously in the eye, as if they have some kind of a right over you. A person then wonders who the devil they might be and where he has met them, until he recalls—yes . . . And if he happens to face a mirror in a slightly absentminded state, the first thought entering his mind is that one of those quarter- or half-geezers he encountered on the street has crept into the mirror. Only one element of this baffles him: if *he* is alien to his own self, then how do those geezers and old maids recognize him? The reactions are asymmetrical.

It's a strange feeling, like being in a weightless existence—if by "weight" you mean "memory." I feel like I'm a man without a past. No one remembers what I did before. It's impossible to find the slightest trace of me as a once translator of Old Persian—or, at least, it's not easy. I typed my name into Google: all of my activity as a gossip journalist is on the Internet down to the last title, but in connection with Old Persian—not a single link. There was no Google back when I translated from Old Persian. Nor did it exist when Communist Party history was taught in colleges; thus, no one knows who Teedu Tärn used to be. Or who Mati Tõusumägi was. Those who now come into contact with the latter for the first time are left with the impression that he is some kind of older-middle-aged prole writer. Who has *always* been that way.

Orwell had a ministry in which the employees constantly rewrote old newspapers so that the articles published in them might correspond to the new facts. As a result, the present seemed to grow more logically and harmoniously out of the past. This thought is a fine image and absolutely sound in its own time; but yes, truly—that ministry would only be necessary in a totalitarian society that had few publications and one main narrative. Everything really should be constantly rewritten in such a place, because if it were not done (and this was not done completely in the Soviet Union, for example), then alternative narratives or at least memories of them would also persevere in spite of it all. A quarter of a century had passed since the Molotov-Ribbentrop Pact, but young Mati Tõusumägi had received an overview of it that was antithetical to the official version. This was partly by way of oral tradition, but he also secretly saw microfilms of old newspapers and read banned books that were stored in a restricted archive. This was the system's mistake and inconsistency. There shouldn't have *been* any sort of restricted archive. Even Teedu was able to learn about the actual Molotov-Ribbentrop Pact, although he had been trained to accept the official version.

Things are different now. An Office of the Ministry of Truth would be unnecessary. Why make the effort of rewriting earlier articles when no one is interested in them *anyway*? In the Google Age, the old newspapers have fallen into oblivion as surely as the epigraphs on stones in the desert sands of Egypt. Now, only the present and the future are of importance. This kind of a situation is grotesque, because despite it being possible to familiarize oneself with the past more broadly and thoroughly than ever before, very few have a hunger for it (supply and the market-economy also apply in this field). Such a defense *is* the most trustworthy one. Voluntary slavery is always the surest kind.

I can partly understand this avoidance of the past. Memory and history bind and oppress — such as when people want to change themselves, to remake themselves or become someone different; not bit-by-bit, through "ethical Protestant work," but rather by taking a leap, wishing upon a golden fish, or following a whim. In such a case, the person's earlier hypostatic existence can be a stone in their shoe, because there will always be someone who will shout out of place: "But we *know* and *recognize* him from an earlier time, and for a long time he was completely different; how can he be like *that* all of a sudden, now! Something doesn't seem to fit here." In short, the observer will put the person's new "I" in doubt by crying out that the emperor wears no clothes. But if no one remembers you from before — or no one *wants* to remember, because non-remembering is an unwritten law and forms part of the code of good behavior — then no one will expose you; and in this case, you may go ahead — change on, becoming ever, incessantly new. You will not be slapped with any sanction for doing so. Everyone is allowed to take on whatever persona he or she wants; everyone is free to create a "profile" for themselves. And isn't the renewal and renaming of oneself one of people's favorite activities these days? (A person was freed spatially by moving from village to city; now, they are also freed temporally — he or she is able to start with a clean slate in both cases.)

Time is dangerous for a man like me, who still perceives the past. Not specifically, but on the whole. You get nowhere; every teensiest thing can be seen from ten different angles, and there are really only exceptions and paradoxes to be found. Always "looking at it from the one side, then from the other." For example, I am sometimes haunted by the thought, *I wasn't by any chance a snitch during the Soviet time, was I?* Straight off, I say with certainty that I was *not*, but then I am overcome with doubt—maybe I actually *was?* You cannot read about it anywhere (due to the fact that the documents were allegedly destroyed, that is). True—I did not go to meet the "kay-gees" one-on-one under a bush or in a hotel room, did not turn anyone in, and did not sign any collaboration contracts. Nor did I receive any benefits in exchange for my possible services. But even so, we would sometimes banter with those figures at The Cave. Who knows what they plucked out of our discussions for themselves there? Perhaps they saw me as partially one of their own? For it's true that I got a telephone in my apartment relatively quickly, all the same—I was only on a waiting list for four years (some were on it for ten). Maybe the "organs" gave it a prod? No, I am generally certain that I was not a snitch. But there are a number of others who are, on the other hand, certain of something else. Of having been a freedom fighter, for example. But *I* know that he was no kind of freedom fighter. For where did he fight, then? In what events did he take part, what kinds of manifestos did he sign? There is nothing. But, you see, now he talks and writes about how he was a freedom fighter, smiles dignifiedly and makes allusions to the "underground resistance," so you don't know whether to laugh or cry. That's what it comes down to—my certainty against his. How are you to act, then? Perhaps the thing is that I am making a judgment about him and others (and not myself) on the basis of *actions*—or, rather, on the basis of what *showed*; whereas he is judging according to how he thought and what he felt in his heart. He has created some kind of a self-portrait. Yet, once again—how many hooligans are right by their conscience but scoundrels by their deeds? Am I then a scoundrel by my own mind, though I was an honest man according to my deeds? No, I was also honest in my heart . . . well, almost. For why do I have these kinds of thoughts, anyway—wondering if I was possibly a snitch?

If a person is 100 percent normal and sure of himself, then he could not come up with even a shadow of such doubt.

I have wondered about my acquaintances—might one person or another from my childhood and youth have been a snitch? (I no longer wonder about who is a snitch now, in the time of the Estonian Republic, because that would truly drive me to the bottle.) I know that many are troubled by those questions nowadays. At an after-party following a performance, Junglane—a short, somewhat chubby man with stubby arms and legs, fat cheeks, a beard, and glinting eyes, like a giant elf— sat down next to me. He looked as if he wanted to talk. And what do you know—he soon started to confess:

"All of the time, I have the feeling that I was a snitch in a former life. You get what I mean by 'former life' . . . I certainly didn't snitch directly, but I guess I still snitched in some round- about fashion all the same." The elf fell silent and peered at me out of the corner of his eye to see how I reacted—whether I would regard him as an idiot or not, and whether it was worth continuing.

I said: "I know that feeling well, Ervin—it's rather familiar." The elf coughed in gladness to hear this and continued his confes- sion, which lasted for a good half an hour. Finally, he put his hand on my elbow (it did not extend any farther), and confessed:

"I guess I even spilled the beans a little about *you*, old boy. Where it was, you'd better not ask; I can't tell you for sure, any- way. And what I said about you—that I know even less." He paused before finishing: "But all the same—I really apologize for it deeply!" And he hopped off the chair.

Occasionally, I would like everything to be settled already. I would like to visit the cemetery to see "where I'll be put." I would like all of my acquaintances to stop by there. But not sorrowfully—rather, more like how good friends are invited over to a backyard to see some new bush or a finished outdoor fireplace. ("Here—this is my grave; it's just lovely, isn't it? Got it *really* cheap for that money, right? No, it wasn't on sale . . .") And afterward to the gazebo for tea. Or like going to a roof- raising party. Precisely—a grave *is* a person's roof-raising party, just flip-flopped, upside down. We need cemetery reform. In Estonia, politicians talk about administrative reform, educational reform, and many other reforms — some even talk about a reform in thinking; but there is not one word about cemetery reform in a single political party's program (I browsed through all of them, keeping an eye out for it). But there *could* be. The problem is more widespread, of course. Estonians are perpetually complaining that there is little social cohesion. That's how it goes — people no longer feel a connection with the previous generations. Everyone is separate here in this world. In that sense, quite a number of things could be accomplished with scant resources. For example: every ten years, all of those who have died in the meantime could be somehow collectively remembered — on the national level and in a "higher" sense. First of all, special people — death census-takers — could go from house to house and record who has died in one apartment or another over the decade. (This could naturally also be done on the Internet, but human contact would be better.) Their names could be read out loudly on a Sunday morning, while bells were ringing, for the sake of variety. Not necessarily in a church. I really like how they recite the names of the victims of a terror attack in America.

### ILLIMAR'S LETTER FROM SEPTEMBER 2008

(. . .) *The weather is rainy. We put a new boiler in my father-in-law's apartment, in the ceiling between the bathroom and the kitchen. The sink basin is bluish. Mardi's business did not work out — you remember, I told you that's what would happen. (Why should he have told me that?) Leelo has not stopped by our place for two months. I wonder — does she see herself as proud? Maaritsa's illness was apparently caused by overdoing it with nettle soup. Our institution bought its workers lunch for the end of the year. It is a great tradition. I have not written to you about that yet, have I? It was quite a decent undertaking — everyone was able to choose between soup or an appetizer, then the main course, and finally dessert for some, coffee with a glass of brandy for others. Pleasant. I tried to read Sophocles that evening. Boring.*

*Please correct me if I might be mistaken.*

## ILLIMAR'S LETTER FROM JANUARY 2009

*Honorable Chronicler!*

(. . .)

*I visited Paris again. Ten years have passed since the last time. We decided to take a vacation. There was quite a good breakfast at the hotel in the mornings. To tell the truth, I had prepared for the very worst, because as I had heard, the French do not eat properly in the morning, but instead only snack on long loaves of bread. Minna and I even thought about bringing some things along with us (ham, for example — Kessu the Pig was bled and smoked in time for St. Michael's Day at their place in the country). But luckily, the French have progressed with the times, and the selection was tip-top. You see — the European Union really has been of use: the French have started eating properly. Say what you may, but if there is no egg dish (scrambled eggs or simply beaten) and fried sausage at a hotel each morning, then in my opinion, a trip abroad does not have the right taste to it — no matter how important those Louvres or pyramids may be. (. . .) For the cuts on your leg* (I had gotten some cuts on my leg as a result of a great deal of dancing, and had complained to Illimar about it), *I recommend warmed propolis — it is definitely sold as a tincture at the pharmacy (it is alcohol-based, and thus relatively painful), but above all, I would recommend some ointment that has propolis in it. My colleague from Vana-Põgioja, who also works as a folk healer, helped me when I twisted my ankle one time and my shoe would not fit on my foot. His mother's homemade propolis ointment with lamb- and plum-fat worked wonders. I rubbed a thick layer onto the top of my foot and wrapped it tightly in gauze. The swelling disappeared in a single day! I bought myself an ointment like that for reserve a couple of months ago from a shop by the stairs leading to the Tartu market fish hall. It is called "wound ointment" and contains propolis and beeswax. A blue label, round white bottle. Fifty grams cost forty kroons. Made by the Tartu County Mölleste Herbal Farm. I give you this information just in case, because maybe they operate in Tallinn as well.*

*Just in case, please do forgive me.*

I read that letter several times over. Something was wrong. A pain entered my heart. That lofty intellect appeared to be doomed. I wanted to help Illimar. I decided to invite him to the "beautiful and the sexy" party. The first attempt to socialize him had indeed foundered a dozen years ago. But why not try again? Times had changed. I hoped that the party would stimulate Illimar, would direct his thoughts back to noble things. Even apart from that, from purely professional considerations, a person who knows Latin, Greek, and Hebrew and looks like Count Tolstoy *is* a rarity. Why should there only be witches, sluts, gamblers, and bankruptcy-masters in gossip papers and at their parties? I decided to give Illimar a "boost."

I did not have to wait long for the opportunity. Our parties have become more frequent. They used to take place once a year; then, the decision was made to have them twice — in early spring and fall. Now, they have become even more recurrent: parties are held at all times of the year. And proposals have been sounding to make them monthly, because demand is ever increasing as we gain more and more beautiful and sexy people. I go to almost every one of those parties. The novelty has diminished, but work is work. I asked Illimar whether he would come. He wanted to know first of all whether food would be provided as well. Hearing that it would, he agreed. "Hopefully you will come with your wife?" I asked him out of formality. No, he and his wife were separated. Minna left. Or rather, *he* left. He was living in a one-room apartment outside of the city (in Maardu).

The day of the party arrived. When I got there, my colleague Julia from a competing publication (we always invite them, too, and they us likewise) was already on the scene, lounging majestically on a leather couch in the foyer like a mafia godmother allowing her hand to be kissed; or like a beloved teacher thronged reverentially by former students. Esteemed ladies of the arts as well as a few sublime-principle men were orbiting around her, flattering her selflessly, telling their stories in honey-sweet tones, smiling and begging for attention — all so that Julia, a former author of children's plays, might mention them in her publication.

Illimar soon arrived looking like a Russian peasant, wearing a red shirt and ankle-high boots, constantly stroking his full beard. He did not inspect his surroundings like he had once done when visiting The Cave, but instead walked around wearing a haughty and focused expression, his hands clasped behind his back. He clapped loudly and even yelled something softly after the opening speeches and the popular artists' performances, but did not make any acquaintances. When the guests were invited to the banquet room, he devoured the food in a masculine fashion (he stood in line for the grilled salmon at least twice). Afterward, I saw him giving orders to a waiter passing through the room carrying bottles: "You, there—mightn't you ...?" I requested that he join first one group, then another, so that Koit might be able to photograph him with some influential social group (I did not tell Illimar about this). I wasn't able to do anything more for him—I was working. Illimar left as soon as he had filled his belly, not showing an interest in anything else. A few nymphs later told me that they had regarded him as a "decoration."

I happened to be standing on the balcony when Illimar was in the foyer, treading towards the door with heavy footsteps. I saw that he was walking with his left arm and his right leg forward, and vice versa, not like before.

I also noticed Teedu Tärn at the party, which surprised me a little. Although politicians now attend such events more frequently, unlike in the early years of the Republic—their secretaries mooch tickets off of me or the editor-in-chief—I had not encountered Teedu earlier. To me, it had seemed that he was not suitable for such events by *format*. It did not have to do with dignity so much as pure old-fashionedness. I had deemed Teedu to be too unglamorous to strut around a party of "the beautiful and the sexy." But there he was now, and not alone, but with a young sprite, whom I had seen him with for the last six months. I had last encountered them during my morning run, while they were slogging their way up the Toompea hill. Teedu was walking half a pace ahead, as if implying that they had a working relationship and there was "nothing here" at all. The sprite was wearing a black pantsuit with a white blouse, which

is like a uniform for the government crowd. The sprite's coun-
tenance was serious, impenetrable. That's also characteristic of
the government crowd—the immense burden of responsibility
that rests upon their shoulders seems to leave no room for smiling or taking pleasure in the little things. I heard through my
Toompea-ears that the sprite was Teedu's adviser, named Madeline Kirss. I also found out that she was the daughter of Teedu's
wife Merle's best girlfriend from her college days. Her mother's
name was Urve; I remember her well. (Urve had the face of Gre-
ta Garbo, but her body, as they say, "didn't catch up"—her legs
were a little . . . well, village men call them "piano legs." Therefore, I immediately looked at Madeline to see whether or not
she had her mother's legs. Sometimes there is a beautiful mother and a manly man, but the daughter is not pretty, because
womanly beauty is still womanly beauty. But no—Madeleine's
legs were straight and graceful, so I understood right away that
she had gotten her legs from her father.)

Now, at the party of "the beautiful and the sexy," I remarked
that miss Madeline's look no longer resembled a negatively
charged magnet that repels objects, but was more like melted
butter. And she did not walk half a step behind Teedu, but rather remained by his side. They took their steps and turned to the
left and the right together like soldiers at a parade, with the one
difference that their hands were interlaced. And when anyone
asked something to either one of them (mainly Teedu), they
both answered—almost in unison. One could see right away
that the girl had taken care of her boss, because Teedu's hair
was secured in a ponytail with a hair clamp and he was wearing a shiny jacket (almost like mine). Maybe she had made a
bit too much of an effort, for the jacket seemed to be a little
"much" on Teedu—he looked like a round, foil-winged beetle.
But yes, they were shaping into a couple, or had already shaped
into one; that much was clear. I mused—oh, the ways of fate!
Merle, the pert-breasted beauty, the head of her class, went for
the somewhat bad-breathed (mentally) Teedu, but he ultimately left her for the daughter of her own best friend. And it was
Merle *herself* who had asked Teedu to employ Urve's daughter
as his secretary.

Back in the day, people would say that someone "is living with their housekeeper." Occasionally, one would marry that housekeeper, but it wasn't seen in a good light. One way or another, that kind of a relationship lowered a man in his circles. Nowadays, it's not a problem — many members of parliament marry their housekeepers. And so, there has been an influx of egalitarianism in life. When men start courting such women, then they *do* start wearing their hair in ponytails and weaving rubber bands that usually hold stacks of money into their gray hair. (I suppose the rubber bands *are* taken from stacks of money, because the stacks have to be unbound, seeing how much they spend on their housekeepers.) They acquire the most state-of-the-art smartphone, ascend stairs quickly — tap-tap-tap — and move very nimbly in general, tremble emotionally from time to time, and use a copious amount of young slang.

I saw Agnes for the first time in over two years at that party. One might have guessed that she was ten years younger. This was probably due to the relief she felt at having dissolved her tethers, as well as a sense of guiltlessness (for taking that step had undoubtedly required a great exertion of willpower from Agnes) and the whirlwind of starting a new life, in addition to cosmetic surgery. She was in the company of an older gentleman, whom no one in our crowd knew; consequently, he must have been a foreigner.

Rui was also at the party of the beautiful and the sexy, not to mention Miller.

Teedu and Madeline were mentioned at the editorial office the next day. At first, we thought that we would limit it to a "buzz," but then the deputy-editor Tommi said Madeline could possibly be a rising political star, and it would be sager in the long run to do a cover story on her. Hearing that, Jaanus, our man who thinks for himself, asked how this could be so — Teedu *was* a former commie, wasn't he? He implied that he wouldn't do the piece, even though it would have been right up his alley, since he normally handled the politicians. "Then someone else will do it," Tommi remarked with a shrug. A couple of days later (I don't believe it was only because of Teedu — some kind of chemistry between Jaanus and Tommi was off; in reality, gossip journalism did not sit right with Jaanus from the very beginning—he was more interested in higher arts), the editor-in-chief let him go at Tommi's suggestion (people now say that some kind of chemistry is developing between *them*). Tommi himself had indeed belonged to the National Independence Party once, but that was not the issue.

Illimar—or, rather, "we"—did not luck out. Not one of the photos that he was in was published. The deputy editor obviously had some plan of his own for whom he wanted to publish that time.

## OLIVIA

I really cannot say the exact reason why, but I got the urge one day to go to The Cave. I had not been there for several years, to tell the truth. "The truth" means that I went there occasionally, of course—that is natural for a gossip journalist. But it was a different kind of "going"—for work, mostly in order to meet with someone at a predetermined time and for a predetermined aim. Not like in the old days, when going to The Cave meant everything and nothing, because you never knew exactly what might happen there. On those occasions, the point was indeed to *go* to The Cave and to *be* there. I would now do interviews from time to time there, because The Cave was normally quiet, especially during the daytime. And when the interview was done, then the interviewee and I left together; I felt no impulse at all to stay behind alone in order to "look around a little while longer." Sometimes, I would also go to The Cave in the daytime for a speedy lunch.

On this day, however, I had gotten the desire to specifically *go* to The Cave. I suppose it had been quietly smoldering within me for a long time; but now, it swelled into an intense nostalgia. I hadn't seen many of my former companions in quite a while. Luckily, there were a lot of people at The Cave, meaning half of the tables were full. I glimpsed a number of familiar faces. Sitting in a corner booth was a larger group that included the naughtily smiling architect nicknamed "Tie Model" and

the more elderly avant-garde artist Paplev, who had been sober
for five years, but then said that it had been enough to prove his
character, and continued drinking as he had before. (Paplev became emotional very easily, crying the profuse, saltless tears of
an intoxicated person.) The drunkard-poet Jaan B. Kask and one
other poet, who was likewise famed for his self-destructive passion for drinking, were here socializing with them. Then there
were the inseparable companions Kirill and Pepe, the female
cellist Malle, Alja, Maša, and a couple other ageless bluestock-
ings. I sat with them and ordered a vodka and juice—I had not
drunk my "usual" in *years*, but did so now out of old habit. I
was flooded with a warm feeling for a moment. I asked one former companion then another about what had become of them
in the meanwhile. The others did not appear to comprehend
my question. What "meanwhile"? In what while? I deduced
from their responses that they had not noticed my several-year
absence from The Cave. This perturbed me slightly on the one
hand, but on the other, I felt a strange sense of relief. I listened
to their conversation. They gossiped unrestrainedly, vehemently.
I found out that the artist Svante was apparently a construction worker in Finland now. He used to paint bright and very
elegant works depicting microfauna. The Estonian market had
been crazy about him for a while—all the wealthier people who
bothered to buy art had already hung one of his glossy parame-
cia or shiny amoebas in their parlor or bedroom. His penetra-
tion into foreign markets had been unsuccessful, however. But
Svante earned a good living in Finland, because he was talented
with his hands. The legendary poet and dandy Aarne Õrnloo,
who had a rosebud mouth and a lecherously sticky look, like
rock candy, had married a radiant widow who had inherited a
cement factory from her early-departed husband. (So people
said: the poet Õrnloo has married a cement factory.) In spite
of this, Õrnloo was said to be going to the Ministry of Culture
to demand that, as a poet, he be exempted from paying rent
on his apartment. The many-talented and multifaceted characters Kirill and Pepe both taught at children's art schools—one
in Nõmme, the other in Viimsi. It was hard for me to imagine
this: they, the game players and sunshine boys, going to give

lessons to children according to the rules! But so it was.

"We're goin' into slavery each and every mornin'," Pepe said, and nodded. "We aren't as free as *some* are." And he pointed to Maša.

"I'd really like for someone to take *me* into slavery, too," Maša said with suppressed rage. "And for someone to pay my social tax for me. I have to keep track of how to survive at *all*. Damn it—I'm becoming totally *mo-no-chro-maaatic* like this!" Kirill and Pepe looked at each other and laughed, but their laughter was not cheerful.

The conversation turned to the stage director Ain, who had left the theater some time ago and joined a political party. There, he had risen at first to the post of adviser to a minister, and a spot in parliament was within each. Recently, however, he had been caught driving with a 0.2 blood alcohol level. This had aroused unwanted attention before the elections, and his fellow party members temporarily worked him onto television, where he hosted a game show. I had seen Ain on-screen. He was a little too ostentatious, in my opinion.

"He *is* a vain person, in reality," Sõrgats agreed.

"But he's drunk himself to pieces," Malle reckoned. "And they heap makeup onto him! My god, imagine what he might be like without the makeup!"

"Yeah, *just* like an old man," Sõrgats agreed. "But he tries to smile so sweetly."

"That's sex appeal," Tie Model explained. "Masculine sex appeal."

Kirill soon rose from the table: "I have to go now."

"Are you going to prepare your lesson plans?" Tie Model jeered. He was living relatively well in the new era, because he had rich clients who ordered blueprints of small castles from him.

The fifty-year-old graphic artist Tiina left at six thirty, having to attend a comic opera so as to, as she said, "learn something from it."

When I stepped outside for a moment to make a call (there was poor service in the cellar) and returned, the table had been joined by an older female writer, whom I knew only superficially;

the others probably didn't know her at all. I couldn't recall having seen her in The Cave often in the old days, either. But here
she was now, a glass of wine before her. You can generally tell
from far away when a person wants to spill their soul. If at all
possible (meaning if one is not on a tight schedule and is not so
down in the dumps themselves to be unable to bear the other's
moaning), then one should hear the person out—that has been
my principle. The female writer had a lean, intelligent face, a
broad forehead and well-groomed gray hair, and an abundance
of inexpensive but tastefully selected rings, leaving the impression of being a proper yet impoverished intellectual. Here is her
story, because if it does not express the era, then I truly do not
know what does.

Olivia Ariste's maturation as a writer had been untradition-
al, since she had not made her debut—or at least not been
published—during her youth, but rather only at a ripe age. Before that, she had been a copy editor at an agricultural magazine. Her arrival on the literary scene coincided with the transition period, when the laws, customs, and habits of the old age
were not completely valid anymore, but the new ones were not
yet in place.

"They used to gild you head-to-toe," she blurted out. "I
came too late and no one gilded me. I have never had massive
print runs and I have never earned enough from my stories and
novels to live off of them. I still live where I used to before—in
a two-room apartment in a nine-story block in the back part of
the Mustamäe district; I still go to work by trolley and have to
struggle to make ends meet. My standard of living has not improved, and I have not gotten anything for my work." I knew
what she meant by that. In the old days one could, for example,
receive an apartment through a creative union. It took time,
but the line moved forward nevertheless. Olivia had been in
this line and had already gotten quite close to the front. Had
she made her debut five years earlier, she would have been accepted into the Writer's Union five years earlier, too, and would
have received her perks; at least the first portion of them. The
things it can do to a person to be exacting with oneself! There
was nothing left to hand out anymore by the time she managed

to become a "formidable" writer—everything was already running as it always does in a market economy. On her current
salary, it would have been very difficult for Olivia to purchase
an apartment closer to downtown, which had been her life's
dream. She would have had to save for several decades in order
to do so. "I hate public transport," she said vehemently. "I walk
for eight kilometers when the weather is even close to nice."

"Why don't you drive?" I asked, but immediately realized
the pointlessness of the question. "Or bike?"

"If I were younger, then I certainly would. But an old hag
pedaling on slippery streets—I dunno . . ."

Olivia's present standard of living was classic in some senses,
since most writers and artists around the world had always lived
the very same. She undoubtedly understood this fact, being an
educated woman. "I worked during the Soviet era and I work
now, too. I haven't had the fortune of being a freelancer; of
thinking only about my creative work. It's easier for me, in that
sense—I'm accustomed to it. It's harder for the ones who have
lived off of honoraria up until now to adapt and start earning their
daily bread with some other job. For me, writing has always
been done 'by lamplight,' after a day's work. No matter—it
can be done that way, too," Olivia said. Still, she was apparently
more troubled by another matter.

"And I've missed out on the respect, too. Back then, I had
not become entirely respectable yet, as there were many more
respectable people around; and now, I think I *could* become respectable"—she was not bluffing; I repeat: she had become relatively "formidable"—"but there isn't really *anyone* who is anymore."

Olivia was right. The feelings people had for writers during
the occupation can never be experienced by their younger colleagues of the present day—no matter how much more interesting their lives may be. Seen this way, there was a kind of a
balance; but Olivia felt that she was too old to utilize the advantages of the new era.

"I'm no longer fit for wandering around the world as a back-
packer," she admitted. True—even *I* was unable to envision an
older woman walking along mountain passes and valleys very

well, what with her osteoporosis and other hidden ailments. This also in the figurative sense.

Olivia was anguished by the fact that she had been unable to taste love and respect, and yet, a memory of its possibility endured within her. It had been relatively easier for others who had no inkling of the possibility.

I could have consoled her, saying that even if she was younger right now, nothing would come of any new breakthrough, because she would not be let anywhere near the new hierarchies and systems of perk distribution. Younger colleagues would still see her as a remnant of the old age. They would put her in the same boat with those who had raked in state awards and funding during that distant era; with those who were translated into the languages of "brotherly peoples" by way of Moscow, and whose works even spread in the West by way of "progressive" publishers. The ones who had their fair share of perks just as well as honor and love. (The fact that the receivers of these had been obliged to forego a part of their freedom seemed ever more abstract in hindsight.) The youth do not inspect every single résumé; they don't wonder with each specific person whether or not he or she had been an exception who had been skipped in line back in their day. Young people would believe that Olivia had also been a member of the main group; that *she* had already gotten her hands on the loot. Now it was the *younger* artists' turn — they are simply demanding what is coming to them by biological right. They wish to validate themselves in every way, to exploit their market share, to personally decide and appoint who will receive the awards, who will be in fashion, who is a classic. Olivia would not be given a chance anymore. Thus, she was right to be angry at fate. Falling between two ages is awful!

I went to the bar to order. While the barman served the person in front of me, I overheard a toothless old man — it was the former lead dancer at the National Ballet nicknamed "Understand" — speaking at a side table with a young pup, who was wearing a red scarf and had a very polished and artistic appearance overall.

"The system was worse back in the day, but it seemed like the people were better, *understand?*" the old man said.

"How's that possible? Aren't they interconnected? What else is a system if not communication carried out by *people*?" the young pup argued. "In our lecture on semiotics ..." And he spoke about what he had heard in class.

"Look, I can't say exactly," said the old man, who had allowed the young pup's speech to breeze past his ears. "That system—it was a fine sort of thing. It brought out different qualities in people. It was rather nasty, that system—it was repelling. That's why there were relatively fewer people who were turned bad by it than were turned good, because people simply drew back from the system, they didn't get near it, you know? And that's why it *felt* like there were a real lot of good ones. I suppose they probably weren't really good through and through, but that's how it seemed. Right now, the *system* is good. But everyone gets really close to it, or the system itself comes close, so there aren't any boundaries and everything is one and the same. Now, you can see everything. But a person isn't *just* good. It brings out all of that tiny bit of good, too, of course, that system does; but it brings out the bad as well, which people have many times more of. No one tries to hide it, either—everyone just lets their bad sides show as if it were nothing. As if they think that when it's *our* turn, then the bad that shows through it can't really be all *that* bad; that your own bad is better than a stranger's bad. *Understand?*"

## MATI

I realized that there was something wrong with Mati again when I saw an interview in the paper he worked for with a legendary cultural figure, on the occasion of his seventy-fifth birthday (the cultural figure had concurrently received a prestigious award of thanks for lifetime achievement). People always look to see who the interviewer is on such occasions. Ordinarily it's a very important journalist speaking to the celebrated figure, as is proper (just like at the pub in a Tammsaare novel—speaking landowner to landowner). Naturally, Mati would have been the most right man for the job. The cultural figure was one of those first-Republic men; a member of the Church who had been Mati's mentor in his Tartu days. They shared a common background, mindset, and cultural code. As such, when I began reading the story, I did not even check to see who the author was. However, the interview seemed somehow light—everything was in order, but it was all fairly predictable and common knowledge, so soon enough, I looked down to the end of the piece. It *wasn't* Mati, but instead some quite unknown journalist! This put my heart to rest on the one hand, because it would have been saddening if Mati had written such a bad piece, but on the other hand, it worried me that *he* had not been sent to do the interview.

I looked into the matter by way of my sources and found out that Mati *was* supposed to write the story at first, but he had been so sauced every single day before the interview that he wasn't fit to be let near the maestro, and that the unknown journalist had apparently been his last-minute replacement. And in general—wasn't I aware "how things are with Mati," then?

A couple of days later, I clicked through the list of the publication's editorial staff online. Mati's name was written there, although no longer as a department director. Apparently the rumors were true, for when I started to think about it, I realized that Mati had indeed written very little lately, and even *those* stories had been brief and bland—more like announcements. And so, he had been left out for good now. Yet since he was a former celebrity all the same, he was not simply dismissed, because it would have drawn undesired attention to the paper. He was kept on the payroll, possibly for some kind of a minimum salary, but was basically being allowed to vegetate.

Miller asked whether one of us should tell Mati that he should not practice such a lifestyle anymore, because it could end badly for him.

Maša attacked Miller: "You, in all your great wisdom, probably never feel sympathy for *anyone*, do you?"

"Regardless," Miller replied diplomatically (with ladies, he always behaved in a way that emphasized his knightly qualities), "I feel sympathy for kittens and cripples. But I honestly do not understand how a person who is otherwise smart can be so romantic with certain things."

Mati's friends did not leave him in trouble for good this time, either. His next subsequent soft landing was arranged. Absurdly, the Central Estonian Espionage Administration came into play again. Mati could not be trusted with true spying, naturally—neither counterintelligence nor active espionage. Even if you were to leave out the media uproar that would have been let loose in that case, Mati was truly not in a suitable condition for it anymore. He required a position where he would not *need to do* any substantial work, although he *could* nevertheless do a little if he wanted to and it interested him. The post of Director of the Estonian Anti-Espionage Museum turned out to be that kind of a job. It is doubtful whether such a museum existed at all, because classified espionage ordinarily does not *have* museums (they only have monuments in the most extreme cases). Perhaps that museum was founded specially for Mati, but what's more likely is that it was completely fictitious.

There was nothing more that Mati's friends could do for him. A couple of people in the education system and at publishing houses saw to it that a small excerpt from Mati's first book, *The Springs of Life*, was perpetually printed in school readers, and that children knew his name. Even *that* was better than nothing.

It was painful for me, "Serenus Zeitblom," to watch all of this.

### ILLIMAR'S LETTER FROM AUGUST 2009

*Honorable Chronicler!*
(...)
*I attended a church seminar in Tartu. It was what it was, but it wasn't especially much—I did not get a spiritual high. During the break, there was a small table set up with coffee and cookies. Butter cookies are good because they are tasty and simultaneously filling. One provost's wife served her little homemade meat pastries that were just begging to be eaten! Afterward, I went to the Tartu Bus Station and bought a ticket (I asked to be on the next bus, being certain that as there were only twenty-three minutes left until five o'clock, then that would be when the next one was leaving). While waiting, I purchased a meat pastry and a forty-gram glass*

*of Vana Tallinn from the snack bar. The pastry could not contend with that of the provost's wife, of course, but I had gotten hungry in the meantime. I wanted to board the bus then, but it turned out that it was not the right bus; or, more precisely—I did not have the right ticket. When I had asked for a ticket from the counter earlier, it did not even cross my mind that one bus might depart before mine. I should have run straight from the ticket stand onto the bus. It was my own fault, although they could have said something. Now, I had to buy a new ticket and 120 EEK went up in smoke once again; otherwise, I could have gotten one more meat pastry and another forty grams of Vana.*

*I have been stocking up on honey and garlic over the days. I chop garlic up in the blender and mix it half-and-half with honey in a jar. One teaspoon with every meal does the trick.*

*I recommend that you go mushroom picking, too. I know of a place—you can find it if you drive out from Aegviidu. Marinated milk-caps are very good, delicate, and slightly sour.*

*Otherwise, my heart is at peace. That which needed to be done was done.*

*I apologize if I have already written about all of this.*
*Now one more dark beer, and then bright dreams.*


## TEEDU

Teedu and Merle were separated. He naturally left the apartment to his ex-wife; he took the cabin. Teedu lived in a hotel during sessions of parliament, spending some nights at Madeline's place in Viimsi. Her parents worked as dentists in Sweden (which was good, because Teedu would have felt uncomfortable around a "mother- and father-in-law" of his own age), so Teedu could have moved in with Madeline for good, but he preferred to stay at a hotel together with other members of the Riigikogu who were from out of town. This way, he was able to converse with the latter and be "near business" in general. Such a lifestyle similarly troubled his conscience less than a new, perpetual cohabitation would have; not to mention actual marriage. Teedu's soul was undoubtedly troubled. His children were already grown-up, of course: one was studying in England and the other in Norway. That was not the problem. However, Teedu imagined that it would be easier for Merle to hear that he was living in a hotel room and not in a Merivälja villa. Merle certainly looked very good for her age—an entire page about her had even been published in a gossip magazine recently; but still.

Otherwise, life felt beautiful.

Alas, Teedu was not destined to taste that for long. Madeline pestered him for as long as it took to help her down the path that led to Brussels. The girl went there and networked independently. She soon successfully took part in a competition for recruiting European Union officials, and was indeed swallowed up in Brussels. They continued to be a couple in the public eye, but what kind of a relationship is it when the young woman only visits Estonia once every two months? Madeline did not come back more frequently. She had allowed Teedu, whose graying hair was bound behind his neck with a hair clip, to lay with her so that she could get to the EU capital and start tinkering with justice-system reform. She was a consultant at an office where her direct superior was also an Estonian—Agnes Tõusumägi.

It happened that about a year after Madeline's move to Brussels, I was required to interview Teedu. It had come to be his turn once again, for how many of those true politicians—the heavyweights—are there in our little society, really? We went to their parliamentary café on Toompea. Teedu looked older—now, one could confidently guess that he was sixty-four instead of fifty-eight. However, he was clean and proper, dressed in a suit, his hair no longer in a ponytail, but rather trimmed short. His facial features had become craggy because his jowls were sagging, but on the whole, there was a sense of liberation in his appearance. I realized what it was—he was no longer pressured by the need to keep himself in shape next to a beautiful girl.

"Coffee or tea?" I asked, as I had been the one who invited him.

"Coffee," he answered. "Although . . . I shouldn't, really. My heart is pounding and my blood pressure is up. But it's that kind of a habit, you see. You remember—in the old days, it was always the case that poorer people drank tea and richer ones coffee? I haven't gotten over that." He smiled guiltily.

I remembered how a server at The Cave had asked the same question of Mati a few days earlier.

"Coffee ... no! ... tea!" Mati had said, almost angrily. "Green, please!"

Maybe he had health problems as well. Although it seemed to me from the way he had changed his order halfway that he had some vague desire to establish solidarity with dissidence: he wanted to be in opposition to the main agenda. Apparently in his own personal ledger, tea stood closer to the giving of heart's blood than coffee.

When Teedu and I had chatted for three quarters of an hour and the story material had been collected (Koit and his camera had already left earlier, as usual), Teedu pointed to my voice recorder: "Turn your gadget off now, please." I did so. "This is in private, you understand—off the record," he spoke, feigning a blasé attitude. "I'll tell you with complete honesty: it was hard for me to talk to Madeline. We often did not understand each other, even though both of us very much wanted to; at least *I* did. We only understood work in the same way, but how long can you talk about work? And I *need* to talk; I belong to that period of time when people *mainly* talked. Things are different now, people are ..."—he searched for the right word— "people are touch-sensitive."

"So, that means you are voice-sensitive—that's *also* very innovative," I said, trying to joke.

"That's the real reason why I sent her to Brussels," Teedu continued, popping a chocolate candy into his mouth.

"*You* sent her?"

"I'm a man of honor, you know. She was wasting herself on me. Some buy a Lexus when that happens. I didn't give her a fish, but rather a hook. But don't put all of that in the article," he warned me once more. Then he expressed an interest in whether I still hang around the art circles. He had come up with the idea to reprint those poems that had once been included in a self-published journal—naturally with a corresponding footnote. Would it be a rational act, in my opinion?

"Of course, why not," I replied. Afterward, I thought—how strange: at one time, he would have given anything to erase any trace of those poems; now, however, he wanted to make them public at any cost.

Teedu's verses were indeed published in a literary magazine. According to his wishes, it was accompanied by the editor's note: "First printed in so-and-so." One might guess that for Teedu, the note *was* the most important thing. He hardly wanted to gain fame and fortune as a poet—in spite of the fact that he had lost Madeline and that in such occasions, older gentlemen sometimes turn sentimental. The local elections were right around the corner.

Mati, however, managed to marry once more. It was not a marriage, to be precise, but a coupling. The woman was one of his admirers who was nearly ten years his junior, but still from the same generation as we were. Among other talents, the nymph could list all the poetry classics of the sixties and the seventies from memory. The coupling had a positive effect on Mati at first. Once, when he was decently buzzed but not yet aggressive, he told us:

"You're all thinking—why am I with Terje? But I've got nothing to talk about with those younger ones. They're such idiots!" Tobi interrupted him to say that they are not idiots, but just "different." Mati nodded and then explained in great detail "how idiotic the youth still are."

Soon afterward, Mati received the highest state honors of Latvia and Lithuania, as well as a service medal of the Republic of Finland. The Cultural Endowment of Estonia gave him an award for lifetime accomplishment. He was made an honorary citizen of Tallinn. Both *The Springs of Life* and *The Assistant Teacher of the Sign of Aldebaran* were translated into Polish, Bulgarian, Slovak, Finnish, and Latvian; the first novel was also published in French and German.

Sometimes, rarely, he would sing alone at The Cave.

I turned my computer on and opened my inbox. Spam again. Half the world appeared to want to enlarge my penis, and the other half deemed me dumb enough to believe that somewhere, some computer is organizing lotteries, is blindly drawing names, and I have become the lucky winner of millions of euros. But there was a letter from Illimar, too! (For the last couple of years, even *we* had abandoned the traditional postal service and transitioned to the electronic one.)

## ILLIMAR'S LETTER FROM APRIL 2010

*Honorable Chronicler!*

(. . .)

*I deeply apologize, just in case. If you should jar pickles, then pay heed to the following. They should be on the floor in the kitchen for the first day or two—they will start fermenting in a fairly warm spot until there's a smidge of foam along the rim of the jar. Place some kind of a bowl under the jar, naturally.*

*Every housewife has her own recipe, but my favorite is to chop two cloves of garlic in addition to the classics (i.e. blackcurrant leaves, horseradish, dill blossoms/seeds, boiled and chilled + strained salt water, to which I also add a teeny bit of sugar) for my 3 liters. I blend that entire green mush. The pickles I cram densely side-by-side. I fill the jar like so: firstly, at the very bottom, putting one layer of green, then one layer of pickles (side-by-side and sticking up—that way you can fit more), then green, then pickles again, etc. Finally, I pour salt water over it. But I suppose you can experiment for yourself.*

*This year, I certainly cannot be bothered to fool around with it, because there's no decent cellar here in my Maardu apartment, and it's annoying to have those little jars cluttering up your fridge.*

*I am going to go eat my fill, have a 0.5-liter lager bought from the budget store, and then rest.*

*P.S. Mashed potatoes are also good. Have you considered drying apples? It does not take all that much time, and they are good for snacking on their own in winter, or else to boil into a fruit jelly.*

## THE BIG PARTY

A grand event was on its way—the twentieth anniversary of independence. Quite a number of things were planned for it in addition to the annual rituals. For example, prosperous oil-transit companies and other corporations joined forces to organize a grandiose reception. It was not planned as an alternative or a balance to the presidential gala, but unlike the latter, to which

all kinds of other well-to-do people were invited, the businessmen's reception was meant for all of those who had made a significant contribution to the restoration of independence. Invitations were received by freedom fighters, nationally-minded
communists, enterprising foreign Estonians, intellectuals, artists, and others. The event looked as if it would set a paradigm.
Calls for full national reconciliation had recently started to
sound in the press and in the general public. A final line should
be drawn under the past! It had happened long ago in words,
but in reality, people would occasionally talk behind one another's backs and differentiate between who was "genuine" and
who was "former." The reception was supposed to shape into
a "reconciliation party." Therefore, the decision was made at
the very last minute (people whispered that it was under pressure from the ruling party) among the board members of the
non-profit organization established for the event (which was
symbolically named "The Salt of the Earth") to also invite another camp of people—those whose contribution to the restoration of independence had been smaller, or who had even been
against it at the time, because they had been blind to the truth.
They were certainly not invited in equal numbers or indiscrim-
inately, but they were invited nonetheless (wisecrackers started
calling the invitations that were sent to them "B-invites").

A parade traversing Tallinn to the Song Festival Grounds was
planned for before the reception. However, since quite a large
number of people with canes, crutches, and all sorts of other
bodily supports arrived from both camps (all in all, a quarter of a
century had passed since the days of their glory acts), and on top
of that the weather was cold, buses were ordered and people were
requested to board them. (While this was happening, someone
made the gallows joke: "now it's off to deportation.") The guests
sat at the Song Festival Grounds and sang a little, then went to
cemeteries and placed flowers on graves. Before long, the buses
zoomed back to the city center, and the party could begin.

I was in attendance as a journalist, as usual (although this
time without my purple jacket). I walked and looked around,
sniffed and listened here and there, striving first of all to get a
feel of the general atmosphere. I realized that time had truly

done its work and not all of the "genuines" were around anymore: Aaberkukk, for example, was absent, apparently living
in a nursing home. All of a sudden, I saw that Mati and Teedu
were conversing in a corner! It had such an unusual effect upon
me that I decided to slip into their company.

"Those were the times," Teedu was saying for already the nth
time. "Oh, my brother—those were the times!" He was overcome by a spiritual blaze. *And the wind and the storms and a
starflight by night* treaded heavily on his tongue, but he did not
lose his self-control, fully understanding that the song was unsuitable for that setting.

Mati was already loosened up and mumbling cheerfully:
"Yeeah, yeeah . . ." From time to time, he would slap his thigh
and shake his head: "We sure *did* have some fun!" Then, however, he stared warily at Teedu, appeared to recognize him, and
then exclaimed hoarsely:

"Wait, what times? What times're you *talking* about!? There
*were* no times!"

"How's that, there weren't times?" Teedu asked, startled.
"There were *some* kinds of times."

"Well, what times were *those*?" Mati angrily demanded.

"You remember how we made those journals back in the
day?" Teedu asked, picking up steam. "We copied them on a
typewriter, tapping away the whole night through, your own sister Anu was in on it . . ." He fell silent mid-sentence. When his
poems had been published in a literary magazine a few months
earlier, then for a moment, while reading them, Teedu got the
feeling that he himself had actually put the periodicals together.
Alas, he couldn't check whether he had or not, because he had
stealthily stuck his sole copy of it into a public trash can thirty
years earlier. He went to the National Library the following day
and browsed the journals collected there. But no matter how
much he searched, he couldn't find his name among the list of
compilers. *Strange*, Teedu Tärn rumbled, but did not allow his
mood to dip. Even if it was not physically and literally, then in
the wider sense and figuratively, he *had* nevertheless compiled
journals—so very many of them—in his soul. And was that
not the main point? Still, when he thought back to it now, then

he realized that he and Mati in all likelihood did not make any journals together—neither physically nor spiritually. But Mati was already mumbling away merrily:

"Yeeah—those journals; they were *fierce* little things, weren't they. Wait—were you kicked out of college the same year as me because of them? Or did they still keep you registered until the next fall?"

Teedu found himself in a predicament. Had he truly been kicked out? Wait, wait ... But a new picture had already materialized in his memory—there was no shortage of them on that day.

"Do you still remember how we defied them that time at the Party meeting?" he asked Mati excitedly. "We said that such and such is the law, but the *partorg*—it was still old Tammemets then—just kept going on about how for a communist, the highest law is his very *own* communist's conscience. He gave us a dressing-down. And we were almost written up for it, on top of that. Do you remember?" But Teedu seemed to be hit by the realization that he and the half-dissident Mati Tõusumägi probably could not have *been* present at the same Party meeting. But Mati had not even been listening to him, and carried on in his own line of thought:

"But do you remember how you and I beat up the Russians?" he giggled. "The Kolpakov Boys?"

Teedu pretended to be straining his memory with all his might, but then answered cautiously:

"I'm sorry, but we probably didn't beat those Russians up together. If you mean a physical beating, of course, because in the mental plane, I sure ..."

Mati leered at him for a while again, then stated decisively:

"Well yeah—you're such a shit guy that you and me *definitely* didn't beat 'em up." His eyes turned towards me. A slight tremor passed through my body. On occasion, when he was drinking vodka, Mati had started to think of me as an underground figure in retrospect. This time was no different.

"But look—Juku and I gave 'em such a beating that the *ryssas'* teeth were flying left and right!"

I remarked amiably that he was indeed mistaken—I could

not have beaten up the Russians with him because I did not know how to fight then, nor do I now. I said this genuinely, almost apologetically.

Mati eyed me attentively: "Yeah, you're right; you weren't there, my mistake, sorry." He fell silent. "But who was it, then?" he asked thoughtfully. "There *was* someone, I remember that clearly." He looked around searchingly, as if endeavoring to catch sight in the thousand-member crowd of the one with whom he had once beat up the Kolpakov Boys.

I had to leave them shortly in order to stage a photo, in which a young poet—a rising star with the pseudonym Ao Staardom—was standing next to the legendary Forest Brother Elmar Rehv. When I arrived back at the table, Mati and Teedu were still in the past.

"Ah, hm, what in the hell—that's *definitely* not how it was, now," Mati was saying.

"It *was*, it *was*," Teedu asserted heatedly. "That's *exactly* how that thing was."

"Was it, huh?"

"I'm *telling* you it was!"

Mati took a sip from his wine glass, wiped his mouth, and said:

"Goddamn—we really could've gone at it tougher than that!"

"Yeah, we could have; but we were going at it anyway," Teedu agreed.

"You're actually a really great guy," Mati said after a while. Teedu smiled happily.

The rapper Cuius Pots walked past the table and whispered conspiratorially that the afterparty would be at The Cave.

## THAT SAME PALACE, THAT SAME PARTY

The mirrored hall, foyers, and corridors were teeming with people, all holding glasses, their expressions joyous and their conversation lively. Many were already acquainted with one another, and the time breezed past. *Clink!* and *hello, hello, clink!* and *hello, hello!*—for several consecutive hours. It was impossible to talk to everyone you wanted to. Time was also taken up giving interviews to the print journalists—and every last paper had a representative there—and there were also three video cameras and several photographers on the scene, demanding group pictures. And so it happened that two old acquaintances, Jüri and Jaan, met only in the coatroom when they were leaving. One was a poet, the other an actor; both had taken an active role in the events of a quarter century ago.

"Let's go sit somewhere for a little while longer," Jaan proposed. Jüri gladly agreed.

The men stepped into their old haunt and ordered brandy. The drinks seemed a bit expensive to the pensioners, but for a celebratory occasion—why not. Sitting at the table next to them was a cheerful gang of younger people, who were connected to others like them at the other end of the world through their electronic devices.

"Those whippersnappers sure are going at it these days," Jaan remarked, chuckling.

"Hold on—it's better if you talk into my right ear, my other one doesn't hear too well," Jüri excused himself.

Jaan repeated what he had said. "And what's most important—the young folks've gone into politics, too," he added.

"Precisely. They don't have any experience yet, but they're learning," Jüri said, nodding.

"Yes, they're learning. For who else will lead the Estonian cause onward!" Jaan said with a chuckle.

The waiter brought them glasses, the men congratulated each other, and clinked them.

"And *we* actually saw it with our own eyes!" Jüri said, wiping his mouth.

"Yes," Jaan said, doing the same. "It's a new era now. Just think about all the possibilities."

"It really is fantastic how things have progressed," Jüri agreed.

"And it's only getting better," Jaan asserted.

"Although some things *could* be better," Jüri reasoned.

"Some things could *always* be better," Jaan chuckled, and both smiled tenderly.

As they had already discussed history and political struggles quite enough that day, the men's conversation tilted towards everyday matters, including their common acquaintances. Jüri had heard about some, Jaan about others. The former had heard that the painter Homusk had flown abroad for good. He lived in a small town in Normandy and was said to be painting flowers and portraits—of the pharmacist, the hairdresser, the zoning official, and other members of the local upper strata. He had to complete one painting a day in order to survive. "Well, *we* don't have to do as much here," Jaan said. "We've got the Cultural Endowment—that supports us." He spoke in turn about the musical interpreter Anderson, who was now playing in a city orchestra in Finland. He had told his parents that on paydays, he always thought—It's sure good that I don't have to earn a living in Estonia!

"Ah, those kind of guys can get lost!" Jüri said, gesturing with irritation. "We wouldn't have won our freedom or restored independence with men like that; we'd still be living in a Russian state."

"Precisely," Jaan said, and told Jüri about how his fellow actor Olof, who used to be a favorite among the ladies, was now "making it as a mechanic" at a former fishing kolkhoz.

"Well, he's a Saaremaa boy, after all," Jüri remarked. "Of course I remember him—he had hands of gold. One time, our car broke down on a road trip. He took the transmission out and fixed it right there." And Jüri spoke about a colleague of his own—the writer Ohak, who was said to be a grade school teacher now. "He doesn't write all that much anymore, and his pension ain't gonna be enough on its own!"

"Yes, that's how it is," the other sighed. "Life is hard."

"How are you doing yourself?"

"Oh, my pen's still scratching away."

"How much do they pay for a poetry collection these days? What did you get for your last one?"

"I don't know; hasn't been transferred yet," the other answered evasively. "But I get other collaborative commissions, too."

"Who's commissioning them?"

"Oh, all kinds of people; even a few advertising agencies."

"You earn much with that?

"A pretty penny."

"What've you advertised?"

"That, well . . . hmm . . . ah, it's slipped my mind! But I have; yes, I have."

"Listen, you seem to be better off than I am right now—maybe you can treat me to this next one? I don't even have my debit card on me right now, forgot it in the pocket of my other jacket."

His companion opened and closed his mouth for a moment—was it really necessary to brag?—but then gestured gallantly towards the server.

"What are you up to yourself?"

"Oh, I'm invited to make appearances on occasion; it's an old actor's thing. But it's not as if I earn anything with that. My audience is poor."

The server brought new glasses. The men sat for another hour or so, and then Jüri glanced at his watch: "Listen, it's after midnight already. Time sure flies! My doctor says I shouldn't stay up late. I have high blood pressure."

"Yes," the other concurred, "and I have a long road ahead of me."

"Oh? Where are you living, then? You used to live in the Writer's House, didn't you?"

"We sold that apartment off a long time ago. Moved to Mustamäe. I got a nice little sum out of it—put it into a short-term savings account and get a little extra pension that way. And where are you now?"

"I moved out of Mustamäe, actually. I live out in Kolga now. The air is better. My knees are worn through. Doctor Maripuu said that sea air is supposed to be good for legs like these."

"That's *really* far away."

"How often do I really come to the city, though? And rent and heating are a lot cheaper out there. But I'm not going back there tonight, naturally. I'll spend the night at my grandson's place."

The men walked a short ways together. They began to run out of things to talk about.

"Look me up sometime."

"Yes, we'll get together. For as long as there are still men like us."

They shook hands and bid each other farewell. They nodded without really looking directly at the other and went their separate ways, as if fleeing. When he had walked ten meters, Jaan turned and called back to Jüri:

"But everything's *great!*"

"Yeah, yeah—everything's great!" Jüri called back.

When there were twenty meters between them, Jüri added:

"Exactly what we wanted!"

"Didn't we want it, then?" Jaan's reply sounded.

"That's what I'm *saying!*" Jüri shouted.

"I thought that maybe you didn't like something!" Jaan's voice sounded from the distance after a while.

"No, I like it all!" came the reply.

They were no longer in sight of each other when the breeze brought Jaan's final words from around the corner:

"We haven't lived for naught!"

"Of course not—where are you getting that?!" Jüri answered, but Jaan was no longer in earshot.

A cute young couple sitting on a bench at a distance had been observing them for some time. "What're they shouting about?" the young girl asked, puzzled.

"Ah, I guess they're remembering their youth," her young man reckoned expertly. "They're expressing their former ideals. They're clearly old Bolsheviks."

## ILLIMAR ROBINSON'S LAST LETTER, FROM MARCH 2010

*Honorable Chronicler!*

(. . .)

*I'm frying croquettes at the moment. Homemade ones do not have that "factory taste" which is, for me, unacceptable; when you go and buy croquettes made of chicken, or some sort of beef or what-have-you—to me, they always have the exact same "chemistry" to them. I know exactly what is in them and how much of it. I hope to one day progress so far as to also start grinding my own meat. I have already visited shops to acquaint myself with the meat-grinder displays, and I'm in correspondence with the world's experts in the field. Many countries have centers for meat grinding. They should have some kind of an umbrella organization. It could be established in Tartu. I am submitting a respective application to the Cultural Endowment.*

*You wrote that you are "going at it." Please detail what you mean by the word "going." Is it more like moving away from yourself (in the vectoral sense), or is it the nudging of objects horizontally with an outstretched hand?*

*Nato is very romantic. It's like the musketeers. One for all and all for one. We are living in a great age! Whoever came up with that Nato certainly had to be a real genius and must have really loved romanticism. Estonia must get into Nato—then, even we will be able to walk along the walls of our castle like important men. And the halberd-holding guards will salute our men at the door, and the handmaidens will rush up to meet them and serve them java on a platter.*

*I understood that I have offended you, with your sense for delicacy! But I am a simple degenerated village schoolteacher. Oh ye, sentenced to death—remember that it is more genuine to grill liver with garlic than with onion.*

Poor Illimar—he had already forgotten that Estonia had been a member of NATO for some time already. I asked him in my letter: "Tell me, Illimar—did you believe that Estonia would become free?" But he no longer replied. He was last working as an operator at a memory institute; I have been meaning to inquire there about him for a while, but something always comes up.

## TALLINN *AL MARE*

I was left with an hour and a half of free time in the afternoon, and decided to walk around town instead of lounging in the editorial office. On my stroll, however, I got the idea of taking a peek into The Cave. I go there three to four times a year now—primarily on business, when some kind of a show is going on there.

The place is apparently having a harder time making ends meet. As a result, the people leasing The Cave switch out frequently, and most of them redesign the rooms—for they have both money and ambition in the beginning. I remember that they put in new urinals in the men's room during the first renovations fifteen years ago—sparkling clean, the most luxurious items in the entire pub. The woman who was the proprietor then was walking around on opening night making bullfighter gestures and shouting "*Olé!*" at every table. She was attempting to be in the spirit of the new age, thinking that people who worked at an artists' pub also have to be artistic. Even that is now long in the past. The next proprietor installed a black light in the toilet so that no one could find their veins there. There are also video cameras installed in it, apparently; I haven't asked.

It usually takes me a little while to orient myself in The Cave after every renovation. A toilet was moved into the space where there had been a phone booth in the very beginning; now, there is a coatroom there, with some hooks and cupboards. There was a tea bar, then a chess nook in place of the old toilet for some time. The bathroom was brought back to its old location for a while, but the telephone booth wasn't restored, because everyone already had cell phones. A hooded glass booth for smokers was set up in its place.

About five years ago, an annex adjoining The Cave was built at street level, which people started to call the "street cave." It's a relatively compact café enclosed behind a glass wall. Chairs and tables are placed directly on the sidewalk when the weather is nice. There are relatively many visitors to the "street cave," because they don't need to climb any stairs and can dart off quickly when necessary. On this day, I decided to sit there at first, thinking that maybe I *wouldn't* actually descend into The Cave, seeing as how the cellar is dim and there still isn't much in the way of ventilation. I ordered my usual whiskey. I have gradually started to drink on a regular basis. Alcoholism kills more slowly than stress.

The doorman looked bored as he sat on a chair next to the door. If he only knew how exciting a life his predecessors had had a quarter of a century ago! More often than not, they were required to fend off the people wishing to enter. Just six or seven years ago, an audience would step into The Cave on occasion to stare around the space, seeing whether or not some celebrity might be sitting there. But they usually weren't, and the audience was forced to stare at one another instead. Life's pulse is beating elsewhere, the celebrities are going elsewhere; no one knows this better than I do, for I make my *living* from celebrities' lives. In truth, celebrities do change places. And if I am to be quite specific, then these are not the exact same celebrities either, because they *themselves* are switching out ever faster. All in all, there are more of them than ever before. Dwelling on this, I am sometimes reminded of the lines from the ESSR anthem: *Now wave, grain, and beat out, hammer!* I feel as if that grain really is waving and the hammer is beating out—in all kinds of old factory buildings, creative centers, secretive bunkers, and elsewhere, where artists who are just about to become famous do their work.

Sipping my whiskey, my thoughts drifted towards those who used to come here and are growing ever distant from me. To me, all of them—the majority, who are fading away in nursing homes or quietly extinguishing otherwise, as well as the few who are still plodding on with all their might, whether out of inertia or actual artistic inspiration—resemble the characters of Greek tragedies. They are tragic, in the sense that is dealt with in aesthetics textbooks. The heroes themselves are not to blame for their demise, or for what happens to them at all. They are guided by forces and carried by currents that are greater than them, and which they are incapable of controlling. They do not even *sense* them for the most part—they are playthings in the hands of fate. It could very well be that if they were to sense those currents, then they would change their behavior to avoid their current demise. But they would no longer be heroes then, but rather insignificant figures like me. My kind will survive everything; we are not doomed. I am a gossip journalist from a small, educated, mixed-blood nation, who in his free time translates texts from Old Persian that no one reads.

I stared out at the square extending before me. The city in early spring, pigeons and tourists, seagulls and a few skateboarders.

Suddenly, I saw a familiar figure. Jeans, a beige sweater, a satchel over his shoulder. It was Pekka! He was not alone, of course—he was explaining something to a small troop around him. Tourists, obviously. Such a familiar sight. It reminded me of the sea. You stand on the shore and ponder that those waves were splashing the very same way here thousands of years ago, even before the first civilizations formed, and will continue to splash even after us. Pekka was visiting Estonia to show Finnish tourists the Song Festival Grounds and the Open Air Museum in Rocca al Mare back when we were still living in an "empire of evil," and also visits now that we are civilized, and perhaps will continue visiting even when all of Estonia has turned into a museum where everything is just one big "al Mare" and the tourists ask when the Arabs left.

I had heard that Pekka was now involved in cultural tourism, taking Finns to Estonia's ancient castles and monastery ruins, to its village folk dances, to its smoke saunas, its symphony orchestra concerts and its galleries. And why not—who else if not he, who has been in such close contact with the local culture and the figures in it for the last couple of decades? *Is he stopping here by chance right now, or has he put The Cave on his itinerary?* I wondered. *Is he serving it up to experts interested in "cultural archaeology"—in the Stonehenge of Soviet-era intellectual life?*

Pekka had not seen me yet, so I had some time to observe him. He had only aged a little in appearance and still looked good. (Perhaps they really *are* stuffed full of vitamins? We should do a story about that in our magazine . . .) Ah, and now Pekka was approaching the bored doorman in front of The Cave. I cocked my ears. I wasn't sure, of course—maybe he and Heiki had some kind of a deal, and the doorman was a part of his show; just like an idyllic shepherd passing a hiking group in the Alps seemingly by chance, the sheep wearing little bells around their necks, as Thomas Mann described.

"It's true that artists and writers used to go here back in the day, isn't it?" Pekka asks the doorman.

"Yeah, I think I heard somethin' like that," the latter replies, scratching his balls through his pants pocket. "Yeah, all kinds of 'em. Poets and actors and film guys and . . ."

"And they were the *only* ones who came here?"

"Yeah, and not all of 'em even fit."

"Unbelievable! Fantastic!" the tourists murmur in fascination, nudging one another. "Artists went here!"

"Do you miss them?" one lady asks the doorman.

"Ah, well—whether I *miss* 'em, I dunno. It's interesting now, too. There are young people, but on the other hand, y'know, this place was sort of special back then."

"And those artists had money to drink with, then?" Pekka inquires, developing an informative conversation.

"Yeah, they had money like we got mud. I guess the state paid them a salary," the doorman Heiki says, nodding.

"Does it not anymore, then?" that same lively-spirited lady asks. I imagine she's a left-wing Finn.

"No, the state doesn't pay anything now. But the political parties were supposed to. A few artists are on their payrolls; I believe I'm able to confirm that." (Where had he heard such an expression—"I believe I'm able to confirm . . ."? Heiki the doorman's face seemed somehow familiar. Could it be the very same Heiki Bern . . . ? It seemed like it was. He was out in the boonies at first, played quite big roles, then came to the capital and played smaller ones here. But all the same, he was an actor here for a good twenty seasons. He was laid off five years after the Republic came. He was involved in real estate in the meantime. Then came the economic depression. So now, he had ended up as a doorman. Well, even that position has its creative moments. I wondered whether he was "in character" right now or not, and if he was, then was it his bosses' orders, or voluntarily, to "spice things up"?)

"But what are they paid for—do they have any sort of power, or something?" the lady asks. The doorman is at a loss for an answer. He's not *that* clever. And if he were, then it would be wiser to stay silent. A doorman has his own professional ethics.

"OK, everyone—we will now go down and have a look," Pekka says, and glances at the clock on the nearby church steeple. "I can't give you my word that any artist is sitting down there right now, of course; it's still early." (As if it were like observing birds or animals in the wild—take your binoculars out and step up into the viewing tower. Grab your traps and your microscopes, because the Artist might be coming. He will appear from behind a bush or a thicket or climb out of a manhole. Do a taxonomical analysis. Let him drink from your glass, then pluck it out of his hands and take a DNA sample.) Pekka notices me at this moment. He looks directly at me: I understand what he is thinking. He is weighing whether or not he could show me to the group; whether I could play an artist for the tourists. Being a sensitive person, he naturally comprehends that I would not be enthralled by the prospect. Yet it could also be that he doesn't deem me a sufficiently suitable example. For although the lines between writer and journalist are not as clear as they used to be, I—as a gossip journalist—am nevertheless not enough of a purebred "former"; I do not whine or beg, but have adapted and am able to get bearably by in the material sense (I am si-tu-ated!). Pekka waves to me and walks downstairs with the group trailing him.

I think about Pekka. I don't want to be unjust towards him, because I like him. Even more so since the changes have affected *him* as well. In the old days, everyone wanted to sit near him and converse. He was never alone. He had a positive and pure aura, wasn't angry or vain, and was neither as ironic nor as romantically ready to strike as the majority of us were. As a result, he had a good effect on us. He was a natural person—an envoy from the natural world, where people lived a natural life. Not that he is dreaded or warded off by anyone *now*; quite the opposite. When he joins a group, everyone greets him cheerfully with a Finnish "*hei-hei*." But, for the most part, no one has the time to converse with him for as long as they used to. Everyone is very optimistic and energetic and running somewhere. All you really hear is:

"I'm going to take down the exhibition and lug the paintings to a new place. The van just freed up . . ."

"I have a meeting with a customer . . ."

"I might be able to do a little fresco in this one place . . ."

"I need to write a column by this evening . . ."

"I have a business lunch . . ."

"The producer wanted to change one scene . . ."

"I've got an installation ..."

And so on and so forth.

You hear the Finnish goodbye, "*moi-moi*," more and more. Everyone chuckles a little at that "*moi*"—they never use it in private, and maybe the *Finns* don't even use it anymore; but everyone says it to Pekka like that and chuckles, because that's exactly how it was one time. Saying "*moi*" to him is like a kind of ritual, carrying out a custom that will bring good fortune. They have a soft spot for him and probably even love him in their own way. They love him ... then leave him with their "*moi*."

I suspect that Pekka would like to converse with someone more in depth on occasion. Just like many good Finns, he would enjoy long and pleasant talks about work. But in these parts, no one has the time for that anymore. Everyone discusses something with a fire burning in their eyes; everyone wants to do everything in a new way, but to get money for it in the old way—*now wave, grain, and beat out, hammer!*

For a long time already, Pekka has not been the only one of his kind, either. Dozens of new Pekkas who are much more pekkaish than Pekka himself have arrived in Estonia. There are heaps of foreigners of every language—some of them rich and condescending, most of them poor and unknown but harboring great hopes. Nevertheless, Pekka is still special; at least for those middle-aged and older persons who still have their wits about them. To them, it feels like Pekka survived the intermediate period together with them and is *one* of them.

After fifteen minutes, the clutch of cultural tourists is back above ground. I hear through the open door that Pekka is sending them to an art exhibition with a guide to accompany the visit—a critic, who happened to be below. Then he walks up to me.

"Well, and what are *you* doing hanging around here? Let's go and sit downstairs a little while instead; we'll talk and drink a beer. Ah, I see that you're drinking whiskey already. So early—it isn't even three o'clock yet! A gentleman doesn't drink hard alcohol before five. But let's go down, anyway. Take your drink with you."

"Why go down there?"

"I don't know; it somehow seems more romantic to me like that. You would always be there in the old days. Everything up here is somehow so commonplace." He gestures around us. Walking down the stairs, I read the posters glued to the wall. There's a plethora of them—one A4-sized paper glued onto the next, plastering the entire wall. They invite you to poetry readings, film screenings, exhibition openings, dance shows, "happenings," performances, interdisciplinary functions, public debates, art-salon evenings, discos, and other events. *Now wave, grain . . .*

The bar is now located where the nook used to be, where back in the day the belle dragged Mati so she could kiss the celebrity in the dark.

The room is relatively empty, but a few people are nevertheless visible in the dim light. Karl the lawyer is there with his "retinue." I try to avoid him noticing me. I don't tolerate him all that well. He's a perfectly sensible man if you speak to him one-on-one and soberly, but as soon as there's a third person with you, he starts to show off. And when he gets even drunker, he berates me in everyone's earshot, calling me a "used-up hygiene products' journalist" and a "shit sniffer." But when there's no one else around, he hints that he would like to be in our magazine. (He does not beg, but rather hints that he would buy his way in.) Pekka and I overhear that he has a court case tomorrow, and if he wins he'll get two million, or maybe even two-and-a-half. We chuckle at this. It is good to sit in the company of a person with whom you share common memories. We do not need to say or prove anything to each other. For an instant, it seems like everything has not gone so very terribly after all, and that things are as they should be. I take my new little book of poetry out of my bag and show it to him—a collection of minimalist texts. I published it just recently—naturally all at my own expense. Out of spiritual necessity. One young and talented artist made a few vignettes for it. I like them, being an old-fashioned person. I suppose it benefits the artist as well. His honorarium will be a series of his own photos in our magazine.

Half an hour later, Pekka looks at the clock and says he has to accompany his group to one more art exhibition. Meanwhile, a woman descends the stairs, makes herself comfortable, and starts talking to the barman. It's a waitress on her day off. She certainly was not here yet in my day—she is too young for that—but knows another waitress who used to work at The Cave and is now retired. I have seen them conversing in a city bar on a couple of occasions. And so, she remembers the lost continent from the memory of memories. She became very excited when I asked her about it. That means that there are still some with whom the old age sits quite well.

When Pekka returns, I find out that Mati Tõusumägi is in the café upstairs. Apparently he hasn't been coming to the city lately, which is news to me. They say he drinks at home or with strangers in some third-rate bar.

"How's he . . .?" I ask.

Pekka makes an indistinct gesture. I realize that Mati is inadequate.

We get up to leave after forty-five minutes. I cannot stay any longer. Sohvi has a reception and I promised to stop by her dressing room. Sohvi is at her peak right now.

"It's time for me, too," Pekka says, and nods. "How long can they really stand looking at those twelve pictures there in the salon?"

Picking up my bag, I think to myself that I will not come here voluntarily for three months.

We ascend the stairs and peek into the "street cave." I see with horror how things are, and sigh.

"You go ahead and take off," I tell Pekka. "I'll stay here and make sure nothing awful happens, just in case."

Pekka nods with a look of understanding and worry, and walks briskly away, his satchel thumping against his side. I step up to Mati's table.

"Is this *really* that famous writer of yours!?" I hear from over my shoulder. Karl has come up behind me.

## EPILOGUE

I must add that while penning the last chapter, word came that Mati is no more. It wasn't unexpected; his health declined gradually, but went quickly downhill towards the end. Mati himself described it as the lights being turned off in a house. First of all in the cellar and the attic, where people generally go more rarely, then in the bedrooms and the kitchen, until finally only one little light remains glowing above the front steps. And even *that* only turns on when someone crosses the radius of its sensor—meaning when someone speaks to Mati. He himself *was* that house, that sensor. To put it plainly, Mati drank himself to death. He couldn't be bothered to live anymore. Too young? Barely fifty-eight. Surprisingly, he wasn't at all unhappy. This was confirmed by everyone who had come into contact with him over the last couple of months, when it was clear he was dying. Many said that he radiated "the other side"—almost like the peaceful bliss of a holy man—and seemed hypnotically concentrated. Mati told me that so much had happened in his life, and there had been so much beauty, that everything that might still be coming would no longer offer anything to a man like him, because it would not even come close to what had been before. "I don't want another life," he said simply. I guess he meant it.

The sun was shining—that very same sun, very same sea, very same city.

That's where Mati Tõusumägi was buried.

The funeral was very moving—a lovely funeral, as older people would say. How much patriotism there was! It seemed like everything that remained of it poured into the cemetery all at once. And so, it seemed to me like I was taking part in a Night Song Festival, or a pocket edition of the Singing Revolution. I was present in another dimension for a moment. Or at a theme party.

What a collection of people! The Chief himself appeared—together with a briefcase carried by his aide, a handsome young man, pale and as straight as a match. (I am going to try to get a picture of them in our magazine; I gave Koit the corresponding orders. It wouldn't be for the cover, because we generally don't report on funerals. But they'll make the inside covers—a double-page spread.) The head of the armed forces was in attendance, as was the second-in-command of the Estonian Defense League (the first-in-command was training at West Point at the time), a leading religious figure, several deans, important representatives of civil society, as well as friends and brothers-in-arms. Many of the latter had been away from Estonia for many years. Time goes by so quickly. Almost all of them had pudgier cheeks, and a few had also grown beards, so I did not even recognize them at first. I was aware that one was a bungee jumper, another helped starving Africans, a third was running an oil business in South America, a fourth had fought in Chechnya. I had never really understood the itch that continued to drive Che Guevara onwards after Cuba. But now, seeing those men, I started to get it.

There were many beautiful women in attendance. Both those who had known Mati and been in love with him, as well as their daughters, who were also very beautiful, but in a new, different way. A fair amount of those mothers, by the way, were also maintained in the modern fashion (botox, implants, artificial buttocks, and other such touch-ups). Some, however, looked exactly how beautiful women had during the seventies and the early eighties, and the abundance of that fading yet magnificent beauty increased the impression of being at a theme party. Standing next to the daughters (but also next to some of the more vivacious mothers) were their fiancés (some of them politicians, while others were businessmen or otherwise successful).

There was no room for me in the chapel. At first, the funeral organizers had seriously considered the idea of erecting a giant screen outside—just like during the World Cup. One computer company had even agreed to take care of the "technical side," but the organizers apparently thought that it would be "too progressive."

There were others who did not fit inside, either. We conversed politely outside. Many stood in reverent observation, shifting their weight onto one leg, their hands folded in front of them at the waist, their head cocked in the direction of the chapel. The thought of whether we were six meters away from the chapel or closer popped into my mind. I could hear the voice of an actor starting to read the classic Gustav Suits poem "The Church Bell": "*Heng niikui taiva poole püvväs . . .*"[37] After that, a tenor began to sing with such passion and feeling that even I—a purple-jacket-wearing gossip journalist who, on that occasion, was indeed wearing black, but who does not spend his free time believing in God—had thought for a fraction of a second that maybe, just maybe, Mati would soon meet his Maker.

I took my place near the grave site in a timely manner and also shifted my weight onto one leg. The coffin was borne by eight men, because it was very big. I have probably forgotten to mention that Mati was the size of a giant—a massive mountain of a man, just as his father, old Arnold Tõusumägi, had been.

One more elderly blond woman walked alone behind the coffin—I believe it was Mati's sister Anu. I cannot say if his brother was there or not; I had never seen him, nor would I have recognized him. Someone nudged me, saying—Look, those two there (a younger middle-aged woman and a man) are Mati's children. Agnes was unable to come from Brussels; she had an important session.

Since the dearly departed had been so popular, an agreement was made in regard to the number of speeches, so that the event would not drag on into infinity. Even so, ever more new and unregistered speakers stepped up, and it *is* improper to tug a person back from the edge of a grave when he or she wants to say a few last words to the deceased. The pastor was the same that had been at Klaus's funeral. And although he had honed his skills even further in the meantime, having an even more powerful impact than in Klaus's case, in the interest of saving time, people did not begin calling him back on this occasion, although some did try. One moron, for example, shouted "Encore!" although it was probably more out of a desire to flaunt that he had gone to see the ballet in Paris. Security men dragged him away. (Yes, that funeral even had security!) Yet the pastor was not offended by it in the very least, being absorbed in the proceedings and giving a very dignified impression (he had recently finished his doctoral dissertation on Bultmann's demythologization).

I would have come to the funeral anyway, because Mati was one of my oldest acquaintances. However, since I happened to be there, I concurrently performed my everyday journalistic work. It was a working funeral for me, so to speak—unfortunately not the first that year. I believed that I could pay Mati my last respects in the very best way by doing just that. I also drove a talented young poet right up next to the Prime Minister so that Koit could photograph them together, although the poet did not want to go—he tried to duck out of it, the empty-headed animal, so I almost had to lead him there by force.

I stood in the parking lot in front of the cemetery gates and stared into the sky. It was empty and cloudless. Mati had once wished for his ashes to be sprinkled across Estonia. However, he had abandoned the idea because he couldn't be certain that one of our country's two helicopters would be in working order at the time.

All of a sudden, I heard a thwapping sound growing louder, and the aircraft appeared over the tops of the pine trees. It was still flying, then.

I was waiting for Koit, who was supposed to drive me to the city. I didn't go to the funeral reception because lately the crowds at such events have been so big. Everyone has made amends with one another; everyone feels that "it was their deceased, too," and that they have the right and the obligation to fall into communion with the departed. Among others at the reception, one will also encounter many poor artists (and "cavemen") who simply want a full belly and to drink a bit of vodka. Each and every person will be buzzing around each and every other person, and you really cannot converse with anyone. On top of that, I had other things to do that evening. (Sohvi and I are doing our next interview for her autobiography—it's going to be a real hit!) I eyed the funeral-goers ducking into their cars, feeling freed from the tension and wearing expressions of relief, as people usually do after a service.

My mind wandered to Mati's words about why he did not want a second life. On the one hand, I too am happy to have been witness to such an interesting era. In just *ten years* from now, no one will be able to imagine that such a life had existed at all. The "cavemen" have gone down in history, and even I might someday go to the grave with that blissful knowledge. I have lived in a time machine—I know that. I have been chosen.

On the other hand, I wonder—why did so much have to happen in the lives of one generation? It would have been possible to bear only if not thought about. I would like to lose my mind and my memory. And I know what would make that happen. I don't know why I don't take the opportunity. I should go. Dear Sohvi is waiting. My steamy Sohvi.

I have my wits about me.

I have my wits about me, yet.


2009–2011

# ENDNOTES

1 A main character in the classic literary pentalogy *Truth and Justice* by Anton Hansen Tammsaare.

2 Communist Party of the Soviet Union.

3 The Forest Brothers were a partisan group that waged guerilla warfare in support of the first Republic of Estonia during the invasions and occupations beginning in 1940. Latvia and Lithuania had similar movements.

4 Revered Estonian theologian, philosopher, and poet (1909–1985).

5 Konstantin Päts, the first State Elder and president of the Republic of Estonia. Päts leaned towards autocracy late in his leadership of independent Estonia, before being imprisoned and then deported at the beginning of the first Soviet occupation.

6 Under-the-counter alcohol purchasable from taxi drivers, mainly during the Soviet era.

7 Ado Grenzstein (1849–1916) played a part in the Estonian National Awakening; however, his views and contribution have been subject to controversy, as he was a supporter of Russianization.

8 Historical marks of property, resembling glyphs or runes.

9 An administrative Soviet subdivision typically two steps below the national level.

10 The 8th Estonian Rifle Corps was a Soviet Army unit formed in 1942, and was composed of mobilized ethnic Estonians.

11 A *malev* is a traditional organized grouping of Estonian youth that gathers to socialize and conduct various paid or volunteer activities.

12 A historical cultural region in South Central Estonia.

13 The historical cultural region of the Seto people, situated south of Lake Peipus in the present-day territories of Estonia and Russia.

14 Colloquial name for the Finnish Helsinki daily *Helsingin Sanomat*.

15 Kalevipoeg (the main character in the Estonian national epic) directly translates to "Son of Kalev."

16 The setting of A. H. Tammsaare's *Truth and Justice* pentalogy.

17 "What a monstrosity!" (Russian)

18 Vorkuta in northern Siberia was the site of one of the more notorious camps in the Gulag system.

19 The Selkup are a people inhabiting northern Siberia, who speak a Samoyedic language of the Uralic family.

20 Baikal-Amur Mainline.

21 The St. George's Night Uprising, which began on the given night in 1343 and lasted until 1345, was an attempt by the indigenous Estonian population to overthrow the Danish and German rulers who had conquered Estonia during the Livonian Crusade.

22 A small snack consumed with vodka, lit. "something to bite after" (Russian).

23 Vanemuine is the god of song in national-romanticist Estonian mythology. The phrase "Lend me your zither, Vanemuine!" is found in the first lines of the Estonian national epic *Kalevipoeg* by Friedrich Reinhold Kreutzwald.

24 A simple traditional Estonian folk dance.

25 A Russian horse-drawn machine gun cart.

26 "You're beautiful, you're beautiful, Fatherland . . ."

27 "The river of dreams has a bank on both sides!"

28 Friedebert Tuglas (1886–1971) — Estonian writer and co-founder of the Estonian Writer's Union.

29 Young Estonia (*Noor-Eesti*) was a neo-romantic literary group co-founded by F. Tuglas in the early twentieth century.

30 Eduard Wiiralt (1898–1954) — Estonian graphic artist.

31 "Lone wolf" (Russian).

32 Kama is a traditional Estonian food made from fermented milk and ground grains.

33 "*Põllumajanduse registrite ja informatsiooni amet* (Estonian Agricultural Registers and Information Board): an Estonian government agency established to handle the distribution of EU agricultural aid.

34 Johann Voldemar Jannsen (1819–1890) and Juhan Peegel (1919–2007) were two "founding fathers" of journalism in Estonia.

35 The People's Commissariat for Internal Affairs, a Soviet organ directly responsible for the Gulag and the predecessor to the KGB.

36 Aleksei Müürisepp (1902–1970) was a Soviet official, also holding the posts of Chairman of the ESSR Supreme Soviet Presidium and Deputy Chairman of the USSR Presidium of the Supreme Soviet.

37 "Towards heaven my poor soul seems to soar . . ." (South Estonian).